SCAND
Short

SCANDINAVIAN
Short Stories

SENATE

Scandinavian Short Stories

Stories selected from
*The Masterpiece Library of Short Stories, Volume XIX,
Scandinavian and Dutch,* issued by
Allied Newspapers Ltd., in association with
The Educational Book Company Ltd, London.

This edition published in 1995 by Senate, an imprint of
Studio Editions Ltd, Princess House, 50 Eastcastle Street,
London W1N 7AP, England

ISBN 1 85958 132 3

Printed and bound in Guernsey by
The Guernsey Press Co. Ltd.

Contents

CONTENTS

SWEDISH   FREDRIKA BREMER
                                      1801–1865

HOPES

I HAD a peculiar method of wandering without very much pain along the stormy path of life, although, in a physical as well as in a moral sense, I wandered almost barefoot—I *hoped*, hoped from day to day ; in the morning my hopes rested on evening, in the evening on the morning ; in the autumn upon the spring, in spring upon the autumn ; from this year to the next, and thus amid mere hopes, I had passed through nearly thirty years of my life, without, of all my privations, painfully perceiving the want of anything but whole boots. Nevertheless, I consoled myself easily for this out of doors in the open air, but in a drawing-room it always gave me an uneasy manner to have to turn the heels, as being the part least torn, to the front. Much more oppressive was it to me, truly, that I could in the abodes of misery only console with kind words.

I comforted myself, like a thousand others, by a hopeful glance upon the rolling wheel of fortune, and with the philosophical remark, "When the time comes, comes the counsel."

As a poor assistant to a country clergyman with a narrow income and meagre table, morally becoming mouldy in the company of the scolding housekeeper, of the willingly fuddled clergyman, of a foolish young gentleman and the daughters of the house, who, with high shoulders and turned-in toes, went from morning to night paying visits, I felt a peculiarly strange emotion of tenderness and joy as one of my acquaintance informed me by writing, that my uncle, the Merchant P—— in Stockholm, to me personally unknown, now lay dying, and in a paroxysm of kindred affection had inquired after his good-for-nothing nephew.

With a flat, meagre little bundle, and a million of rich hopes, the grateful nephew now allowed himself to be shaken uphill and down-hill, upon an uncommonly uncomfortable and stiff-necked peasant cart, and arrived, head-over-heels, in the capital.

In the inn where I alighted, I ordered for myself a little—only a very little breakfast—a trifle—a bit of bread-and-butter—a few eggs.

The landlord and a fat gentleman walked up and down the

saloon and chatted. " Nay, that I must say," said the fat gentleman, " this Merchant P——, who died the day before yesterday,
he was a fine fellow."

" Yes, yes," thought I ; " aha, aha, a fine fellow, who had heaps
of money ! Hear you, my friend " (to the waiter), " could not you
get me a bit of venison, or some other solid dish ? Hear you, a cup
of bouillon would not be amiss. Look after it, but quick ! "

" Yes," said mine host now, " it is strong ! Six thousand
pounds ! Nobody in the whole world could have dreamed of
it—six thousand ! "

" Six thousand ! " repeated I, in my exultant soul, " six thousand ! Hear you, waiter ! Make haste, give me here six thou——;
no, give me here a glass of wine, I mean " ; and from head to heart
there sang in me, amid the trumpet-beat of every pulse, in alternat-
ing echoes, " Six thousand ! Six thousand ! "

" Yes," continued the fat gentleman, " and would you believe
that in the mass of debts there are £180 for cutlets, and £1000 for
champagne. And now all his creditors stand there prettily, and
open their mouths ; all the things in the house are hardly worth
two farthings ; and out of the house they find, as the only indemni-
fication—a calash ! "

" Aha, that is something quite different ! Hear you, youth,
waiter ! Eh, come you here ! take that meat, and the bouillon,
and the wine away again ; and hear you, observe well, that I have
not eaten a morsel of all this. How could I, indeed ; I, that ever
since I opened my eyes this morning have done nothing else but eat ?
(a horrible untruth !), and it just now occurs to me that it would
therefore be unnecessary to pay money for such a superfluous
feast."

" But you have actually ordered it," replied the waiter, in a state
of excitement.

" My friend," I replied, and seized myself behind the ear, a place
whence people, who are in embarrassment, are accustomed in some
sort of way to obtain the necessary help—" my friend, it was a
mistake for which I must not be punished ; for it was not my fault
that a rich heir, for whom I ordered the breakfast, is all at once
become poor—yes, poorer than many a poor devil, because he has
lost more than the half of his present means upon the future. If he,
under these circumstances, as you may well imagine, cannot pay for
a dear breakfast, yet it does not prevent my paying for the eggs
which I have devoured, and giving you over and above something
handsome for your trouble, as business compels me to move off from
here immediately."

By my excellent logic, and the " something handsome," I removed from my throat, with a bleeding heart and a watering
mouth, that dear breakfast, and wandered forth into the city, with

my little bundle under my arm, to seek for a cheap room, while I considered where I was to get the money for it.

In consequence of the violent coming in contact of hope and reality I had a little headache. But when I saw upon my ramble a gentleman, ornamented with ribbons and stars, alight from a magnificent carriage, who had a pale-yellow complexion, a deeply-wrinkled brow, and above his eyebrows an intelligible trace of ill-humour ; when I saw a young count, with whom I had become acquainted in the University of Upsala, walking along as if he were about to fall on his nose from age and weariness of life, I held up my head, inhaled the air, which accidentally (unfortunately) at this place was filled with the smell of smoked sausage, and extolled poverty and a pure heart.

I found at length, in a remote street, a little room, which was more suited to my gloomy prospects than to the bright hopes which I cherished two hours before.

I had obtained permission to spend the winter in Stockholm and had thought of spending it in ways quite different from what now was to be expected. But what was to be done ? To let the courage sink was the worst of all ; to lay the hands in the lap and look up to heaven, not much better. " The sun breaks forth when one least expects it," thought I, as heavy autumn clouds descended upon the city. I determined to use all the means I could to obtain for myself a decent subsistence, with a somewhat pleasanter prospect for the future, than was opened to me under the miserable protection of Pastor G., and, in the meantime, to earn my daily bread by copying—a sorrowful expedient in a sorrowful condition.

Thus I passed my days amid fruitless endeavours to find ears which might not be deaf, amid the heart-wearing occupation of writing out fairly the empty productions of empty heads, with my dinners becoming more and more scanty, and with ascending hopes, until that evening against whose date I afterwards made a cross in my calendar.

My host had just left me with the friendly admonition to pay the first quarter's rent on the following day, if I did not prefer (the politeness is French) to march forth again with bag and baggage on a voyage of discovery through the streets of the city.

It was just eight o'clock, on an indescribably cold November evening, when I was revived with this affectionate salutation on my return from a visit to a sick person, for whom I, perhaps really somewhat inconsiderately, had emptied my purse.

I snuffed my sleepy, thin candle with my fingers, and glanced around the little dark chamber, for the further use of which I must soon see myself compelled to gold-making.

" Diogenes dwelt worse," sighed I, with a submissive mind, as I drew a lame table from the window where the wind and rain

were not contented to stop outside.   At that moment my eye fell
upon a brilliantly blazing fire in a kitchen, which lay, Tantalus-like,
directly opposite to my modest room, where the fireplace was as
dark as possible.

"Cooks, men and women, have the happiest lot of all serving
mortals!" thought I, as, with a secret desire to play that fire-
tending game, I contemplated the well-fed dame, amid iron pots
and stewpans, standing there like an empress in the glory of the
firelight, and with the fire-tongs sceptre rummaging about majestically in the glowing realm.

A story higher, I had, through a window, which was concealed
by no envious curtain, the view into a brightly lighted room, where
a numerous family were assembled round a tea-table covered with
cups and bread baskets.

I was stiff in my whole body, from cold and damp. How empty
it was in that part which may be called the magazine, I do not say ;
but, ah, good Heavens ! thought I, if, however, that pretty girl,
who over there takes a cup of tea-nectar and rich splendid rusks
to that fat gentleman who, from satiety, can hardly raise himself
from the sofa, would but reach out her lovely hand a little further,
and could—she would with a thousand kisses—in vain !—ah, the
satiated gentleman takes his cup ; he steeps and steeps his rusk with
such eternal slowness—it might be wine. Now the charming girl
caresses him.   I am curious whether it is the dear papa himself or
the uncle, or, perhaps—— Ah, the enviable mortal ! But no, it
is quite impossible ; he is at least forty years older than she. See,
that indeed must be his wife—an elderly lady, who sits near him on
the sofa, and who offers rusks to the young lady. The old lady
seems very dignified ; but to whom does she go now ? I cannot
see the person.   An ear and a piece of a shoulder are all that peep
forth near the window.   I cannot exactly take it amiss that the
respectable person turns his back to me ; but that he keeps the
young lady a quarter of an hour standing before him, lets her curtsy
and offer her good things, does thoroughly provoke me.   It must be
a lady—a man could not be so unpolite towards this angelic being.
But—or—now she takes the cup ; and now, oh, woe ! a great
man's hand grasps into the rusk-basket—the savage ! and how he
helps himself—the churl ! I should like to know whether it is her
brother—he was perhaps hungry, poor fellow ! Now come in, one
after the other, two lovely children, who are like the sister.   I
wonder now, whether the good man with one ear has left anything
remaining.   That most charming of girls, how she caresses the
little ones, and kisses them, and gives to them all the rusks and the
cakes that have escaped the fingers of Monsieur Gobble.   Now she
has had herself, the sweet child ! of the whole entertainment, no
more than me—the smell.

What a movement suddenly takes place in the room ! The old gentleman heaves himself up from the sofa ; the person with one ear starts forward, and in so doing gives the young lady a blow (the dromedary !) which makes her knock against the tea-table, whereby the poor lady, who was just about springing up from the sofa, is pushed down again ; the children hop about and clap their hands ; the door flies open ; a young officer enters—the young girl throws herself into his arms. So, indeed ! Aha, now we have it ! I put to my shutters so violently that they cracked, and seated myself on a chair, quite wet through with rain, and with my knees trembling.

What had I to do at the window ? That is what one gets when one is inquisitive.

Eight days ago, this family had removed from the country into the handsome house opposite to me ; and it had never yet occurred to me to ask who they were, or whence they came. What need was there for me to-night to make myself acquainted with their domestic concerns in an illicit manner ? How could it interest me ? I was in an ill-humour ; perhaps, too, I felt some little heartache. But for all that, true to my resolution, not to give myself up to anxious thoughts when they could do no good, I seized the pen with stiff fingers, and, in order to dissipate my vexation, wished to attempt a description of domestic happiness of a happiness which I had never enjoyed. For the rest, I philosophised whilst I blew upon my stiffened hands. " Am I the first who, in the hot hour of fancy, has sought for a warmth which the stern world of reality has denied him ? Twenty-five shillings for a measure of firewood. Yes, *prosit*, thou art not likely to get it before December ! I write !

" Happy, threefold happy, the family, in whose narrow, contracted circle no heart bleeds solitarily, or solitarily rejoices ! No look, no smile, remains unanswered ; and where the friends say daily, not with words but with deeds, to each other, ' Thy cares, thy joys, thy happiness, are mine also ! '

" Lovely is the peaceful, the quiet home, which closes itself protectingly around the weary pilgrim through life—which, around its friendly blazing hearth, assembles for repose the old man leaning on his staff, the strong man, the affectionate wife, and happy children, who, shouting and exulting, hop about in their earthly heaven, and closing a day spent in the pastimes of innocence, repeat a thanksgiving prayer with smiling lips, and drop asleep on the bosom of their parents, whilst the gentle voice of the mother tells them, in whispered cradle-tones, how around their couch—

> The little angels in a ring,
> Stand round about to keep
> A watchful guard upon the bed
> Where little children sleep."

Here I was obliged to leave off, because I felt something resembling a drop of rain come forth from my eye, and therefore could not any longer see clearly.

"How many," thought I, as my reflections, against my will, took a melancholy turn—"how many are there who must, to their sorrow, do without this highest happiness of earthly life—domestic happiness!"

For one moment I contemplated myself in the only whole glass which I had in my room—that *of truth*—and then wrote again with gloomy feeling : "Unhappy, indeed, may the forlorn one be called, who, in the anxious and cool moments of life (which, indeed, come so often), is pressed to no faithful heart, whose sigh nobody returns, whose quiet grief nobody alleviates with a 'I understand thee, I suffer with thee!'

"He is cast down, nobody raises him up ; he weeps, nobody sees it, nobody will see it ; he goes, nobody follows him ; he comes, nobody goes to meet him ; he rests, nobody watches over him. He is lonely. Oh, how unfortunate he is! Why dies he not? Ah, who would weep for him? How cold is a grave which no warm tears of love moisten!

"He is lonesome in the winter night ; for him the earth has no flowers, and dark burn the lights of heaven. Why wanders he, the lonesome one ; why waits he ; why flies he not, the shadow, to the land of shades? Ah, he still hopes, he is a mendicant who begs for joy, who yet waits in the eleventh hour, that a merciful hand may give him an alms.

"One only little blossom of earth will he gather, bear it upon his heart, in order henceforth not so lonesomely, not so entirely lonesome, to wander down to rest."

It was my own condition which I described. I deplored myself.

Early deprived of my parents, without brothers and sisters, friends, and relations, I stood in the world so solitary and forlorn that, but for an inward confidence in heaven, and a naturally happy temper, I should often enough have wished to leave this contemptuous world. Till now, however, I had almost constantly hoped from the future, and this more from an instinctive feeling that this might be the best, than to subdue by philosophy every too vivid wish for an agreeable present time, because it was altogether so opposed to possibility. For some time, however, alas! it had been otherwise with me ; I felt, and especially this evening, more than ever an inexpressible desire to have somebody to love—to have some one about me who would cleave to me—who would be a friend to me—in short, to have (for me the highest felicity on earth) a wife—a beloved, devoted wife! Oh, she would comfort me, she would cheer me! Her affection, even in the poorest hut, would make of me a king. That the love-fire of my heart would not ensure the faithful being at my side from being frozen was soon made clearly sensible to me by an involuntary shudder. More dejected than ever, I rose up and walked a few times about my room (that is to say, two steps right forward, and then a turn back again). The sense of my condition followed me like the shadow on the wall, and for the first time in my life I felt myself cast down, and threw a gloomy look on my dark future. I had no patron, therefore could not reckon upon promotion for a long time ; consequently, also, not upon my own bread—on a friend—a wife, I mean.

" But what in all the world," said I yet once more seriously to myself, " what helps beating one's brains ? " Yet once more I tried to get rid of all anxious thoughts. " If, however, a Christian soul could only come to me this evening ! Let it be whoever it would— friend or foe—it would be better than this solitude. Yes, even if an inhabitant of the world of spirits opened the door, he would be welcome to me ! What was that ? Three blows on the door ! I will not, however, believe it—again three ! " I went and opened ; there was nobody there ; only the wind went howling up and down the stairs. I hastily shut the door again, thrust my hands into my pockets, and went up and down for a while, humming aloud. Some moments afterwards I fancied I heard a sigh. I was silent, and listened. Again there was very evidently a sigh—and yet once again, so deep and so mournful, that I exclaimed with secret terror, " Who is there ? " No answer.

For a moment I stood still, and considered what this really could mean, when a horrible noise, as if cats were sent with yells lumbering down the whole flight of stairs, ended with a mighty blow against my door, and put an end to my indecision. I took up the candle, and a stick, and went out. At the moment when I opened the door my light was blown out. A gigantic white figure glimmered opposite to me, and I felt myself suddenly embraced by two strong arms. I cried for help, and struggled so actively to get loose that both myself and my adversary fell to the ground, but so that I lay uppermost. Like an arrow I sprang again upright, and was about to fetch a light, when I stumbled over something—Heaven knows what it was (I firmly believe that somebody held me fast by the feet), by which I fell a second time, struck my head on the corner of the table, and lost my consciousness, while a suspicious noise, which had great resemblance to laughter, rung in my ears.

When I again opened my eyes, they met a dazzling blaze of light. I closed them again, and listened to a confused noise around me— opened them again a very little, and endeavoured to distinguish the objects which surrounded me, which appeared to me so enigmatical and strange that I almost feared my mind had wandered. I lay upon a sofa, and—no, I really did not deceive myself—that charming girl, who on this evening had so incessantly floated before my thoughts, stood actually beside me, and with a heavenly expression of sympathy bathed my head with vinegar. A young man whose countenance seemed known to me held my hand between his. I perceived also the fat gentleman, another thin one, the lady, the children, and in distant twilight I saw the shimmer of the paradise of the tea-table ; in short, I found myself by an incomprehensible whim of fate amidst the family which an hour before I had contemplated with such lively sympathy.

When I again had returned to full consciousness, the young man embraced me several times with military vehemence.

" Do you then no longer know me ? " cried he indignantly, as he saw me petrified body and soul. " Have you then forgotten August D——, whose life a short time since you saved at the peril of your own ? whom you so handsomely fished up, with danger to yourself, from having for ever to remain in the uninteresting company of fishes ? See here, my father, my mother, my sister, Wilhelmina ! "

I pressed his hand ; and now the parents embraced me. With a stout blow of the fist upon the table, August's father exclaimed, " And because you have saved my son's life, and because you are such a downright honest and good fellow, and have suffered hunger yourself—that you might give others to eat—you shall really have the parsonage at H—— Yes, you shall become clergyman, I say !—I have *jus patronatum*, you understand ! "

For a good while I was not at all in a condition to comprehend, to think, or to speak ; and before all had been cleared up by a thousand explanations, I could understand nothing clearly excepting that Wilhelmina was not—that Wilhelmina was August's sister.

He had returned this evening from a journey of service, during which, in the preceding summer, chance had given to me the good fortune to rescue him from a danger, into which youthful heat and excess of spirit had thrown him. I had not seen him again since this occurrence ; earlier, I had made a passing acquaintance with him, had drunk brotherhood with him at the university, and after that had forgotten my dear brother.

He had now related this occurrence to his family, with the easily kindled-up enthusiasm of youth, together with what he knew of me beside, and what he did not know. The father, who had a living in his gift, and who (as I afterwards found) had made from his window some compassionate remarks upon my meagre dinner-table, determined, assailed by the prayers of his son, to raise me from the lap of poverty to the summit of good fortune. August would in his rapture announce to me my good luck instantly, and in order, at the same time, to gratify his passion for merry jokes, made himself known upon my stairs in a way which occasioned me a severe, although not dangerous, contusion on the temple, and the unexpected removal across the street, out of the deepest darkness into the

brightest light. The good youth besought a thousand times forgiveness for his thoughtlessness ; a thousand times I assured him
that it was not worth the trouble to speak of such a trifling blow.
And, in fact, the living was a balsam which would have made a
greater wound than this imperceptible also.

Astonished, and somewhat embarrassed, I now perceived that the
ear and the shoulder, whose possessor had seized so horribly upon
the contents of the rusk basket, and over whom I had poured out my
gall, belonged to nobody else than to August's father, and my
patron. The fat gentleman who sat upon the sofa was Wilhelmina's uncle.

The kindness and gaiety of my new friends made me soon feel at
home and happy. The old people treated me like a child of the
house, the young ones as a brother, and the two little ones seemed to
anticipate a gingerbread-friend in me.

After I had received two cups of tea from Wilhelmina's pretty
hand, from which I almost feared taking, in my abstraction of mind,
more rusks than my excellent patron, I rose up to take my leave.
They insisted absolutely upon my passing the night there ; but I
abode by my determination of spending the first happy night in my
old habitation, amid thanksgiving to the lofty Ruler of my fate.

They all embraced me afresh ; and I now also embraced all
rightly, from the bottom of my heart, Wilhelmina also, although not
without having gracious permission first. " I might as well have
left that alone," thought I afterwards, " if it is to be the first and
last time ! " August accompanied me back.

My host stood in my room amid the overturned chairs and tables,
with a countenance which alternated between rain and sunshine ;
on one side his mouth drew itself with a reluctant smile up to his ear,
on the other it crept for vexation down to his double chin ; the eyes
followed the same direction, and the whole had a look of a combat,
till the tone in which August indicated to him that he should leave
us alone, changed all into the most friendly, grinning mien, the proprietor of which vanished from the door with the most submissive
bows.

August was in despair about my table, my chair, my bed, and so
on. It was with difficulty that I withheld him from cudgelling the
host who would take money for such a hole. I was obliged to
satisfy him with the most holy assurances that, on the following day,
I would remove without delay. " But tell him," prayed August,
" before you pay him, that he is a villain, a usurer, a cheat, a—or if
you like, I will——"

" No, no ; heaven defend us ! " interrupted I, " be quiet, and let
me only manage."

After my young friend had left me, I passed several happy hours
in thinking on the change in my fate, and inwardly thanking God

for it. My thoughts then rambled to the parsonage ; and heaven knows what fat oxen and cows, what pleasure grounds, with flowers, fruits, and vegetables, I saw in spirit surrounding my new paradise, where my Eve walked by my side, and supported on my arm ; and especially what an innumerable crowd of happy and edified people I saw streaming from the church when I had preached. I baptized, I confirmed, I comforted my beloved community in the zeal and warmth of my heart—and forgot only the funerals.

Every poor clergyman who has received a living, every mortal, especially any one to whom unexpectedly a long-cherished wish has been accomplished, will easily picture to himself my state.

Later in the night it sunk at last like a veil before my eyes, and my thoughts fell by degrees into a bewilderment which exhibited on every hand strange images. I preached with a loud voice in my church, and the congregation slept. After the service, the people came out of the church like oxen and cows, and bellowed against me when I would have admonished them. I wished to embrace my wife, but could not separate her from a great turnip, which increased every moment, and at last grew over both our heads. I endeavoured to climb up a ladder to heaven, whose stars beckoned kindly and brightly to me ; but potatoes, grass, vetches, and peas entangled my feet unmercifully, and hindered every step. At last I saw myself in the midst of my possessions walking upon my head, and whilst in my sleepy soul I greatly wondered how this was possible, I slept soundly in the remembrance of my dream. Yet then, however, I must unconsciously have continued the chain of my pastoral thoughts, for I woke in the morning with the sound of my own voice loudly exclaiming, " Amen."

That the occurrences of the former evening were actual truth, and no dream, I could only convince myself with difficulty, till August paid me a visit, and invited me to dine with his parents.

The living Wilhelmina, the dinner, the new chain of hopes for the future which beamed from the bright sun of the present, all surprised me anew with a joy which one can feel very well, but never can describe.

Out of the depths of a thankful heart, I saluted the new life which opened to me, with the firm determination that, let happen what might, yet always *to do the right, and to hope for the best.*

Two years after this, I sat on an autumn evening in my beloved parsonage by the fire. Near to me sat my dear little wife, my sweet Wilhelmina, and spun. I was just about to read to her a sermon which I intended to preach on the next Sunday, and from which I promised myself much edification, as well for her as for the assembled congregation. While I was turning over the leaves, a loose paper fell out. It was the paper upon which, on that evening two years before, in a very different situation, I had written down my cheerful and my sad thoughts. I showed it to my wife. She read, smiled with a tear in her eye, and with a roguish countenance which, as I fancy, is peculiar to her, took the pen and wrote on the other side of the paper :

" The author can now, thank God, strike out a description which would stand in perfect contrast to that which he once, in a dark hour, sketched of an unfortunate person, as he himself was then.

" Now he is no more lonely, no more deserted. His quiet sighs are answered, his secret griefs shared, by a wife tenderly devoted to him. He goes, her heart follows him ; he comes back, she meets him with smiles ; his tears flow not unobserved, they are dried by her hand, and his smiles beam again in hers ; for him she gathers flowers, to wreathe around his brow, to strew in his path. He has his own fireside, friends devoted to him, and counts as his relations all those who have none of their own. He loves, he is beloved ; he can make people feel happy, he is himself happy."

Truly had my Wilhelmina described the present ; and, animated by feelings which are gay and delicious as the beams of the spring sun, I will now, as hitherto, let my little troop of light hopes bound out into the future.

I hope, too, that my sermon for the next Sunday may not be without benefit to my hearers ; and even if the obdurate should sleep, I hope that neither this nor any other of the greater or the less unpleasantness which can happen to me may go to my heart and disturb my rest. I know my Wilhelmina, and believe also that I know myself sufficiently, to hope with certainty that I may always make her happy. The sweet angel has given me hope that we may soon be able to add a little creature to our little happy family ; I hope, in the future, to be yet multiplied. For my children I have all kinds of hopes *in petto*. If I have a son, I hope that he will be my successor ; if I have a daughter, then—if August would wait—but I fancy that he is just about to be married.

I hope in time to find a publisher for my sermons. I hope to live yet a hundred years with my wife.

We—that is to say, my Wilhelmina and I—hope, during this time, to be able to dry a great many tears, and to shed as few ourselves as our lot, as children of the earth, may permit.

We hope not to survive each other.

Lastly, we hope always to be able to hope ; and when the hour comes that the hopes of the green earth vanish before the clear light of eternal certainty, then we hope that the All-good Father may pass a mild sentence upon His grateful and, in humility, hoping children.

LOVE AND BREAD

WHEN young Gustaf Falk, the assistant councillor, made his ceremonial proposal for Louise's hand to her father, the old gentleman's first question was : " How much are you earning ? "

" Not more than a hundred knonor[1] a month. But Louise——"

" Never mind the rest," interrupted Falk's prospective father-in-law ; " you don't earn enough."

" Oh, but Louise and I love each other so dearly ! We are so sure of one another."

" Very likely. However, let me ask you : is twelve hundred a year the sum total of your resources ? "

" We first became acquainted at Lidingo."

" Do you make anything beside your Government salary ? " persisted Louise's parent.

" Well, yes, I think we shall have sufficient. And then, you see, our mutual affection——"

" Yes, exactly ; but let's have a few figures."

" Oh," said the enthusiastic suitor, " I can get enough by doing extra work ! "

" What sort of work ? And how much ? "

" I can give lessons in French, and also translate. And then I can get some proof-reading."

" How much translation ? " queried the elder, pencil in hand.

" I can't say exactly, but at present I am translating a French book at the rate of ten kronor per folio."

" How many folios are there altogether ? "

" About a couple of dozen, I should say."

" Very well. Put this at two hundred and fifty kronor. Now, how much else ? "

" Oh, I don't know. It's a little uncertain."

" What, you are not certain, and you intend to marry ? You seem to have queer notions of marriage, young man ! Do you realise that there will be children, and that you will have to feed and clothe them, and bring them up ? "

[1] A krone is worth about 1s. 1½d.

" But," objected Falk, " the children may not come so very soon. And we love each other so dearly, that——"

" That the arrival of children may be prophesied quite safely." Then, relenting, Louise's father went on :

" I suppose you are both set on marrying, and I don't doubt but what you are really fond of each other. So it seems as though I should have to give my consent after all. Only make good use of the time that you are engaged to Louise by trying to increase your income."

Young Falk flushed with joy at this sanction, and demonstratively kissed the old man's hand. Heavens, how happy he was—and his Louise, too ! How proud they felt the first time they went out walking together arm in arm, and how everybody noticed the radiant happiness of the engaged couple !

In the evenings he came to see her, bringing with him the proof-sheets he had undertaken to correct. This made a good impression on papa, and earned the industrious young man a kiss from his betrothed. But one evening they went to the theatre for a change, and drove home in a cab, the cost of that evening's entertainment amounting to ten kronor. Then, on a few other evenings, instead of giving the lessons, he called at the young lady's house to take her for a little walk.

As the day set for the wedding drew near, they had to think about making the necessary purchases to furnish their flat. They bought two handsome beds of real walnut, with substantial spring mattresses and soft eiderdown quilts. Louise must have a blue quilt, as her hair was blond. They, of course, also paid a visit to the house-furnishers', where they selected a lamp with a red shade, a pretty porcelain statuette of Venus, a complete table service with knives, forks, and fine glassware. In picking out the kitchen utensils they were benefited by mamma's advice and aid. It was a busy time for the assistant councillor—rushing about to find a house, looking after the workmen, seeing that all the furniture was got together, writing out cheques, and what not.

Meanwhile it was perfectly natural that Gustaf could earn nothing extra. But when they were once married he would easily make it up. They intended to be most economical—only a couple of rooms to start with. Anyhow, you could furnish a small apartment better than a large one. So they took a first-floor apartment at six hundred kronor, consisting of two rooms, kitchen, and larder. At first Louise said she would prefer three rooms on the top landing. But what did it matter, after all, so long as they sincerely loved each other ?

At last the rooms were furnished. The sleeping chamber was like a small sanctuary, the beds standing side by side like chariots taking their course along life's journey. The blue quilts, the snowy sheets,

and the pillow-spreads embroidered with the young people's initials
amorously intertwined, all had a bright and cheerful appearance.
There was a tall, elegant screen for the use of Louise, whose piano—
costing twelve hundred kronor—stood in the other chamber, which
served as sitting-room, dining-room, and study, in one. Here, too,
stood a large walnut writing-desk and dining-table, with chairs to
match ; a large gilt-framed mirror, a sofa, and a bookcase added to
the general air of comfort and coziness.

The marriage ceremony took place on a Saturday night, and late
on Sunday morning the happy young couple were still asleep.
Gustaf rose first.   Although the bright light of day was peering in
through the shutters, he did not open them, but lit the red-shaded
lamp, which threw a mysterious rosy glow over the porcelain Venus.
The pretty young wife lay there languid and content ; she had slept
well, and had not been awakened—as it was Sunday—by the rumb-
ling of early market waggons.   Now the church bells were ringing
joyfully, as if to celebrate the creation of man and woman.

Louise turned over, while Gustaf retired behind the screen to put
on a few things. He went out into the kitchen to order lunch. How
dazzlingly the new copper and tin utensils gleamed and glistened !
And all was his own—his and hers.   He told the cook to go to the
neighbouring restaurant, and request that the lunch be sent in.   The
proprietor knew about it ; he had received full instructions the day
before.   All he needed now was a reminder that the moment had
come.

The bridegroom thereupon returns to the bedchamber and taps
softly : " May I come in ? "

A little scream is heard.   Then : " No, dearest ; just wait a
minute ! "

Gustaf lays the table himself.   By the time the lunch arrives from
the restaurant, the new plates and cutlery and glasses are set out on
the fresh, white linen cloth.   The bridal bouquet lies beside Louise's
place.   As she enters the room in her embroidered morning wrapper,
she is greeted by the sunbeams.   She still feels a little tired, so he
makes her take an arm-chair, and wheels it to the table.   A drop or
two of liqueur enlivens her ; a mouthful of caviare stimulates her
appetite.   Fancy what mamma would say if she saw her daughter
drinking spirits !   But that's the advantage of being married, you
know ; then you can do whatever you please.

The young husband waits most attentively upon his fair bride.
What a pleasure, too !   Of course he has had good luncheons before,
in his bachelor days ; but what comfort or satisfaction had he ever
derived from them ?   None.   Thus he reflects while consuming a
plate of oysters and a glass of beer.   What numskulls they are,
those bachelors, not to marry !   And how selfish !   Why, there
ought to be a tax on them, as on dogs.   Louise is not quite so severe,

urging gently and sweetly that perhaps the poor fellows who elect
the single state are subjects of pity. No doubt, if they could afford
to marry they would—she thinks. Gustaf feels a slight pang at his
heart. Surely happiness is not to be measured by money. No, no ;
but, but—— Well, never mind, there will soon be lots of work, and
then everything will run smoothly. For the present there is this
delicious roast partridge with cranberry sauce to be considered, and
the Burgundy. These luxuries, together with some fine artichokes,
cause the young wife a moment's alarm, and she timidly asks Gustaf
if they can afford living on such a scale. But Gustaf pours more
wine into the glass of his little Louise, reassuring her and softening
those groundless fears. " One day is not every day," he says ;
" and people ought to enjoy life when they can. Ah, how beautiful
life is ! "

At six o'clock an elegant carriage, with two horses, pulls up before
the door, and the bridal pair take a drive. Louise is charmed as
they roll along through the park, reclining there so comfortably,
while they meet acquaintances on foot, who bow to them in obvious
astonishment and envy. The assistant councillor has made a good
match, they must think ; he has chosen a girl with money. And
they, poor souls, have to walk. How much pleasanter to ride, without effort, leaning against these soft cushions ! It is symbolical of
agreeable married life.

The first month was one of unceasing enjoyment—balls, parties,
dinners, suppers, theatres. Still, the time they spent at home was
really the best of all ! It was a delightful sensation to carry Louise
off home, from her parents, at night, when they would do as they
pleased under their own roof. Arriving at the flat, they would
make a little supper, and then they would sit comfortably, chatting
until a late hour. Gustaf was all for economy—the theory of it,
that is to say. One day the young bride and housekeeper tried
smoked salmon with boiled potatoes. How she relished it, too !
But Gustaf demurred, and when smoked salmon day came round
again he invested in a brace of partridges. These he bought at the
market for a krone, exulting over the splendid bargain, of which
Louise did not approve. She had once bought a pair for less money.
Besides, to eat game was extravagant. However, it would not do
to disagree with her husband about such a trifling matter.

After a couple of months more Louise Falk became strangely in-
disposed. Had she caught cold ? Or had she perchance been
poisoned by the metal kitchen utensils ? The doctor who was called
in merely laughed, and said it was all right—a queer diagnosis, to
be sure, when the young lady was seriously ailing. Perhaps there
was arsenic in the wall-paper. Falk took some to a chemist, bidding
him make a careful analysis. The chemist's report stated the wall-
paper to be quite free from any harmful substance.

His wife's sickness not abating, Gustaf began to investigate on his own account, his studies in a medical book resulting in a certainty as to her ailment. She took warm foot-baths, and in a month's time her state was declared entirely promising. This was sudden— sooner than they had expected ; yet how lovely to be papa and mamma ! Of course the child would be a boy—no doubt of that ; and one must think of a name to give him. Meanwhile, though, Louise took her husband aside, and reminded him that since their marriage he had earned nothing to supplement his salary, which had proved far from sufficient. Well, it was true they had lived rather high, but now a change should be made, and everything would be satisfactory !

Next day the assistant councillor went to see his good friend the barrister, with a request that he endorse a promissory note. This would allow him to borrow the money that would be needed to meet certain unavoidable forthcoming expenses—as Falk made clear to his friend. " Yes," agreed the man of law, " marrying and raising a family is an expensive business. I have never been able to afford it."

Falk felt too much ashamed to press his request, and when he returned home, empty-handed, was greeted with the news that two strangers had been to the house, and had asked for him. They must be lieutenants in the army, thought Gustaf, friends belonging to the garrison of Fort Vaxholm. No, he was told, they could not have been lieutenants ; they were much older-looking men. Ah, then they were two fellows he used to know in Upsala ; they had probably heard of his marriage, and had come to look him up. Only the servant said they were not from Upsala, but were Stockholmers, and carried sticks. Mysterious—very ; but no doubt they would come back.

Then the young husband went marketing again. He bought strawberries—at a bargain, of course.

" Just fancy," he triumphantly exclaimed to his housewife, " a pint of these large strawberries for a krone and a half, at this time of year ! "

" Oh, but, Gustaf, dear, we can't afford that sort of thing ! "

" Never mind, darling ; I have arranged for some extra work."

" But what about our debts ? "

" Debts ? Why, I'm going to make a big loan, and pay them all off at once that way."

" Ah," objected Louise, " but won't this simply mean a new debt ? "

" No matter if it does. It will be a respite, you know. But why discuss such unpleasant things ? What capital strawberries, eh, dear ? And don't you think a glass of sherry would go well now after the strawberries ? "

Upon which the servant was sent out for a bottle of sherry—the best, naturally.

When Falk's wife awoke from her afternoon nap on the sofa that day, she apologetically reverted to the subject of debt. She hoped he would not be angry at what she had to say. Angry? No, of course not. What was it? Did she want some money for the house? Louise explained:

"The grocer has not been paid, the butcher has threatened us, and the livery-stable man also insists on having his bill settled."

"Is that all?" replied the assistant councillor. "They shall be paid at once—to-morrow—every farthing. But let's think of something else. How would you like to go out for a little drive to the park? You'd rather not take a carriage? All right, then, there's the tramway; that will take us to the park."

So they went to the park, and they had dinner in a private room at the Alhambra Restaurant. It was great fun, too, because the people in the general dining-room thought they were a frisky young pair of lovers. This idea amused Gustaf, though Louise seemed a trifle depressed, especially when she saw the bill. They could have had a good deal at home for that amount.

The months go by, and now arises the need for actual preparation —a cradle, infant's clothing, and so forth.

Falk has no easy time raising the money. The livery-stable man and the grocer refuse further credit, for they, too, have families to feed. What shocking materialism!

At length the eventful day arrives. Gustaf must secure a nurse, and even while holding his new-born daughter in his arms is called out to pacify his creditors. The fresh responsibilities weigh heavily upon him; he almost breaks down under the strain. He succeeds, it is true, in getting some translation to do, but how can he perform the work when at every touch and turn he is obliged to run errands? In this frame of mind he appeals to his father-in-law for help. The old gentleman receives him coldly:

"I will help you this once, but not again. I have little enough myself, and you are not my only child."

Delicacies must be provided for the mother, chicken and expensive wine. And the nurse has to be paid.

Fortunately, Falk's wife is soon on her feet again. She is like a girl once more, with a slender figure. Her pallor is quite becoming. Louise's father talks seriously to his son-in-law, however:

"Now, no more children, if you please, unless you want to be ruined."

For a brief space the junior Falk family continued to live on love and increasing debts. But one day bankruptcy knocked at the door. The seizure of the household effects was threatened. Then the old man came and took away Louise and her child, and as they rode off in a cab he made the bitter reflection that he had lent his girl to a young man, who had given her back after a year, dishonoured.

Louise would willingly have stayed with Gustaf, but there was nothing more to subsist upon.   He remained behind, looking on while the bailiffs—those men with the sticks—denuded the flat of everything, furniture, bedding, crockery, cutlery, kitchen utensils, until it was stripped bare.

Now began real life for Gustaf.   He managed to get a position as proof-reader on a newspaper which was published in the morning, so that he had to work at his desk for several hours each night.   As he had not actually been declared a bankrupt, he was allowed to keep his place in the Government service, although he could hope for no more promotion.   His father-in-law made the concession of letting him see his wife and child on Sundays, but he was never permitted to be alone with them.   When he left, in the evening, to go to the newspaper office, they would accompany him to the gate, and he would depart in utter humiliation of soul.   It might take him perhaps twenty years to pay off all his obligations.   And then—yes, what then ?   Could he then support his wife and child ?   No, probably not.   If, in the meantime, his father-in-law should die, they would be left without a home.   So he must be thankful even to the hard-hearted old man who had so cruelly separated them.

Ah, yes, human life itself is indeed hard and cruel !   The beasts of the field find maintenance easily enough, while of all created beings man alone must toil and spin.   It is a shame, yes, it is a crying shame, that in this life everybody is not provided with gratuitous partridges and strawberries.

A ROYAL SALUTE

How long and hard the waiting was!

For half an hour he had walked the floor of the hall. At every turn he had stopped at her bedroom door and listened. Not a sound! Again he would take up his monotonous pace, would again stop at the small, mysterious arras door and again listen, listen, breathless, with fear in his eyes. Never a sound! It was becoming unendurable.

He went to the window and looked out. It was a clear, sunny spring morning. The river rushed by; the water sparkled and glittered. Here and there the sunshine played on a belated cake of floating ice, which drifted slowly out from under the bridge. Seagulls circled around it and dived shrieking for fish.

Painters and other working men were preparing the ships for their first spring sailing; they were making everything new and shining. A number of tramps had come out from their winter refuges in cellars and garrets to earn a little money by working in the harbour. Even bad whisky is not to be had for nothing!

The young husband opened the window and drew a deep breath. Oh, how good it felt to inhale the bracing air! The drawn look left his face and his pulse beat more quietly.

From the far-away barracks on the other side of the river the bugle sounded. Its tones came clear and distinct through the pure, thin spring air. Then the sounds were lost in the noise of the street, and the man closed the window.

He went to the dining-room and inspected the table carefully. His good friend, the doctor, deserved a good luncheon after everything was over.

"You are sure it is from the oldest bottle?" he inquired of the maid, indicating the decanter, whose contents shone in the sun. "From the one on the right-hand side?"

"Yes, sir."

"Go and order some good, strong coffee. Tell the cook to be sure to have it strong. Dr. Wetterling must have some good coffee."

"Yes, sir."

35

He arranged things here and there on the table, taking the decanter and holding it up to the light. The thought struck him that this was the wine his wife liked best. She always enjoyed it with him at dinner. He remembered their standing jokes about this wine; how he had toasted her as " Lady Tipsy," and how his wife had answered him, shaking a threatening finger : " Yes, this old, fiery wine has brought forth many a little difference of opinions, but the end has always been a laugh and a kiss."

And now the doctor and he would drink together, after she——
Two big round tears rolled down his bearded cheeks.

" Curse it ! Why should I feel like this ? " he murmured, and again went into the anteroom to take up his walking and waiting.

Again the same fear, the same painful certainty assailed him that in there a desperate struggle was going on, and that in some way, while it did not touch him directly, it was all for his sake.

It was his adored wife who had to suffer this. With insistent force the thought possessed him that love was a responsibility as well as a joy. For her it meant now life or death.

" Life ! Oh, my God, if she should lose her life ! "

How fervently he loved his Astri ! From the very first moment he had met her in Lysekil, where the swift days of his courtship had passed, how beautiful, how eternally beautiful it had been ! When they were married, during the days of their honeymoon—could anything be better, could any love reach higher than this ? he had thought. Yet now, as he waited before her door, he told himself that something greater, mightier, holier, had come into his life. He felt as if the sensitive strings of his heart had been cut. And yet this waiting, this consuming longing for her ! If he could only kiss her hand—the hand of the woman who now meant more to him than his own life, more than all else in the world !

" You must have patience," the doctor had said.

Patience ! But how could he be patient, with so much at stake ? To know how terribly she was suffering, how she fought death to give life, and outside he stood, a useless creature, unable to shield her from the curse of fate !

" In sorrow thou shalt bring forth children ! " Slowly he repeated the words. How often he had read them when he was a boy at school. Then they had meant nothing to him ; and now, what an eternity of meaning the words held—his wife's martyrdom, her maternal love, her joy bought by her agony. And even when God uttered the curse He held the man responsible for the woman.

Absorbed in his thoughts he paced back and forth. Suddenly a heartrending cry, another one, a despairing groan—then silence.

Numb with fright, pale as death, a pitiful, helpless figure, he staggered to the door and listened.

Sight and feeling seemed to have left him; but the faintest sounds burst on his ears like peals of thunder. He heard the low, swift orders of his friend, the muffled sound of feet, the voice of the nurse in quiet question—and through it all the painful moaning of his wife.

"My poor Astri! My poor, sweet love," he whispered.

In a paroxysm of grief he flung himself on a divan and moaned.

"Save her, my God, save her! I will believe in Thee if Thou art merciful!"

. . . .

A deep sigh, as of one suddenly freed from an intolerable burden, and then a feeble cry came to his ears.

"It is over," he cried, leaping up. "We have a child! My Astri and I—we have a child!"

Then came the reaction. The excitement had been too great. The change from boundless fear and uncertainty to intoxicating joy was too much for him. He sank down in a chair and wept like a child, smothering his sobs so that the patient should not hear him.

Then his heart filled with unspeakable bliss. The overstrained nerves gave way; he felt numb, as if he had been drugged. His brain seemed to stand still.

The door opened and the doctor entered.

He rose quickly. "How is she?"

"All right; she only needs rest, much rest."

"Is it a boy or a girl?—quick, tell me."

The doctor in his shirt sleeves, perspiring from his work, smiled at his friend's impatience and hesitated a moment. At last he said:

"It is a boy; how could it be otherwise?"

"Really? Is it really?"

He peered over the physician's shoulders toward the bedroom.

"May I go in now? Only a minute, please?" he asked like a pleading child.

"Yes, but only for one look," the doctor joked.

He opened the door and stood on the threshold. There in the broad white bed, exhausted and pale, lay his young wife, and beside her a little form wrapped in soft blankets.

Motionless, he stared at his wife. He could not utter a word, but the great tears that rolled down his cheeks told of his emotion.

She opened her eyes, which in the dim light seemed even darker and bigger than before, but with an abundance of bliss and tenderness. With feeble hand she motioned to the slumbering little one, her face expressing supreme happiness.

"Goran."

"Astri."

He opened wide his arms, as if to enfold wife and child. Then he fell on his knees at the bedside, kissed her hand in adoration, as if the young mother were a queen, and rested his head on the edge of the bed as if in prayer.

" Goran," she repeated softly, pressing her hand feebly against his cheek ; then she lay still, her fingers resting on his brown curls.

" Are you sleepy, my child ? " he asked.

There was no answer. He looked up. She was asleep.

Carefully and tenderly he kissed her hand and laid it gently on the blue silk coverlet. For a long time he looked at her. Her sleep seemed to be quiet. Only the corners of the mouth moved nervously. He touched the little one with his lips and stole out, slowly, softly, as he had come in.

Dr. Wetterling met him at the door. " Well, is everything all right ? " he asked.

" She is asleep."

" Good ; then I can go now. All she needs is sleep and—no excitement. And now tell me what you think of your boy. Isn't he a fine youngster ? "

" Yes, he looks like his mother."

" That's what fathers say always ; they're astonishingly modest."

" Don't talk nonsense ! " said Bergh as he led the way to the lunch table. " Let's have a bite to eat ; we deserve it," he went on.

" Why, you had nothing to do but to wait."

" That was enough. I never went through such an ordeal in my life."

" Well, you know there must always be a first time."

They seated themselves. With his watch on the table Dr. Wetterling started to eat, hastily and silently, while his host poured the wine. The physician replied briefly to his questions regarding the condition of the young mother. No, she was not exactly exhausted —but care must be taken. Would it be necessary to send her to some watering-place ? Oh, no, one of the little islands near Stockholm would do just as well. Good ; then the husband might remain near Astri.

Dr. Wetterling took up his watch, rose and held out his hand.

" Good-bye, and thank you," said Bergh.

" In case anything should happen send for me at once," the doctor admonished as he left.

Bergh walked to the window and smoked silently for a time. It was just noon. The spring sun shone warm through the glass, and the pure air restored his shattered nerves. Ships were passing to and fro on the river.

Suddenly there came a flash from the castle on the island, a thick white cloud of smoke and a loud report, that set the windows shaking.

Bergh started. His first thought was of his wife.

Again the window-panes rattled. They were firing the royal salute.

He threw aside his cigar, and hurried to the bedroom.

The patient was awake and moved restlessly about. The nurse tried to calm her, but at every report of the guns she started up with a violent effort.

" Something must be done," cried the nurse. " If we can't keep her quiet——"

" Astri, Astri, for God's sake, calm yourself."

He took her in his arms and kissed her.

" My child," she cried. " I want my child ! "

" Send for a doctor—Dr. Wetterling—quick ; send both girls," Bergh commanded in a panic of fear. He left the room, pale and helpless, feeling rather than seeing the flashes from the heavy guns, and shuddering at the loud reports that followed. He drew the curtains, placed pillows and cushions in the windows, but without result. He shook his fists in helpless rage and cursed the brutal noise.

When he returned to the room he found it in confusion. The child cried unheeded, while the nurse struggled by main force to keep the sick woman in her bed. The man ran to and fro, distraught, uttering unintelligible cries.

" Stop, don't lose your head," the nurse commanded curtly. He turned to the bed, and seized his wife's hands. His touch seemed to quiet her ; she moaned faintly. Then she slowly opened her eyes.

" Don't cry, my Goran," she said, as she saw the tears rolling down his cheeks. " It will soon be over."

Then her mind wandered again. She asked to be propped up with pillows ; she would suffocate there, she cried. Her husband kissed her on the forehead, and she turned on him angrily. He did not love her any more, he was brutal, he had come there to torment her. He had stolen her child. He was a brute, a devil ! For a time she became still, and Bergh held her quietly in his arms. Suddenly she flung out her hands with a sharp cry. Her body stiffened a moment, and then fell back limply. Outside a gun boomed sullenly. It was the royal salute. To Bergh's ears it was indeed a royal salute—to the queen who had given her life to give a new life to the fatherland.

GUSTAF AF GEIJERSTAM

SWEDISH

B. 1858

THE SECRET OF THE WOOD

IT was a long way to the Reed Marsh. First one had to follow a narrow path through the heart of the wood, a path that wound in and out of tall pine trees, and now and again led over bare rocky slopes. Just where these rocky slopes ended the Peat Bog began.

The small hillocks were crowned with dwarf fir trees, and when the bog-myrtle bloomed, the air was filled with an aromatic scent that attracted insects to the spot.

It was quite a long way over the Bog too ; for even when one had crossed it, and ascended the hill (from the top of this hill one could see the lake lying as calm and clear as a mirror between its fir-clad shores), one had not yet reached the end of one's journey.

For the cottage stood on the farther shore of the lake. If one wished to reach it on foot, there was still a long way to go.

Otherwise, if one just stood on the shore and shouted loud enough, after a short interval there would appear on the opposite side a little bent old man with a red pointed cap on his head, who would walk cautiously down the stony slope to the water's edge, where he would get into a ramshackle old punt and start off to fetch the waiting visitor.

It would be difficult to understand why this little lake was called the Reed Marsh, for there was no marsh visible anywhere, nothing at all but the cheery waters of the little lake, that looked so bright and pleasant after the long walk through the shadowy wood.

There were no reeds to be seen either, at first. The only reeds there were were hidden away in a creek, and in this bed of reeds every springtime some ducks would build their nests, and, as soon as the young ones were hatched, swim about in undisputed possession of the calm waters. Jacob, the old boatman, says that he could never shoot with a gun. " When I was young," he said, " I tried all I could, but never managed it, and now I am too old to learn, so it can't be helped." Jacob has rowed many travellers over the lake, and this is nothing to wonder at seeing that he has lived so long in the cottage by the Reed Marsh that no one knows just when he moved into it, not even he himself.

Jacob and his wife were a strange couple.   Martina had seen both the Lady of the Woods and the Water-sprite ; she knew, too, what it meant when the Will-o'-the-wisp flickered over the peat-moss, and all the sounds of the woods were understood by her.

Jacob had been a charcoal-burner in his youth, and had been able to earn enough to keep himself.   Martina had gathered berries, sold chip-baskets, and helped in the houses down in the village at Christmas or Easter time.   She was known far and wide, for she always gave full measure, her berries were always fresh and newly-gathered, and there was no fear of finding unripe ones at the bottom of the basket.

There had been three sons in the little cottage by the Reed Marsh, but they had all gone out as workmen in the villages where there was a chance of earning more money, and where the whispering of the wood could not be heard.

Martina and Jacob used to sit and talk about these sons in the long winter evenings when they were alone.   But as the years passed, it became still ever quieter round the old couple, and as the quiet and the solitude made themselves more and more felt, Martina and Jacob drew closer to one another, and forgot the outside world, and felt no wonder at being forgotten in their turn.   The wood sang its song to them, and the little they asked of life was granted to them, up to the day on which Jacob found himself unable to leave his bed.

" You will have to see to things for a bit, Martina," he said, " and when I am up and about again you can take a rest."

They had to do without many things while Jacob was ill.   There was no one to bring home game from the wood, or fish from the lake. The worst of all for Martina was providing fodder for the cow.   She worked away with the sickle, and carried home as much as she could manage.   But very often she had to sit down and rest, and then she would have a good cry, alone in the wood, for she never allowed the tears to come when she was at home.

Then one winter, while Jacob was still confined to his bed, the greatest misfortune of all came to them.   Their one and only cow died for lack of food, and after this happened there was no alternative for poor old Martina but to go to the village and beg.   It was terribly hard for her, she who had never asked for charity from any one before.

She walked along quickly, carrying a milk-can in one hand and a beggar's wallet on her back, and there was a worried expression on her wrinkled old face.   She never lingered anywhere, for was not Jacob lying at home alone and helpless.

Things went on in this way for two years, but Jacob did not get better. Neither did he get worse. At last it got so that it made no difference to him whether it was summer or winter, sunshine or rain. It was just one long day of misery that never seemed to end.

"If I could only die," Jacob used to say, "it would be easier for you."

And Martina would say with tears in her eyes, "What would become of me if you died?"

In her heart of hearts she knew very well that things could never be worse than they were, but she could not say so to poor Jacob while he lay there helpless. . . .

Then there came a day in summer when Martina was trudging along on her way home from the village. She had not much to carry, as people were tired of giving, and the wallet on her back was very light, and so was the milk-can she carried. The sun was shining brilliantly when she came to the Peat Bog. A little farther on she stopped to look at the whortleberries ; there were so many of them, though they were not ripe yet. How quiet and lonely it was just there. Martina let her wallet slip off her back, stood the milk-can on the ground, and sat down. She was so tired, tired of everything. If only the Lady of the Woods would come now and give her something ! Or the One, whose name she hardly dared even whisper to herself, He who was always at hand when any one was in real distress ! Why didn't He come now ?

And how was it that she saw nothing, she who used to see so much ? Why was the wood silent ? And why was there no one to go back with her to the cottage and see how things were, and help an old woman to carry a load that was too heavy for her unaided strength ?

But the wood remained silent round about Martina, and she began to feel frightened. For the first time in her whole life she was afraid of being alone in the wood. It was as if the trees were closing in on her, and, trembling all over, she rose from her seat on the ground, hung the wallet over her shoulders and took hold of the milk-can. For a moment she stood there trembling, listening to the deep silence that sounded to her like one long, heavy sigh. Then she went on her way, and never stopped until she reached the spot by the lake where the old punt lay, into which she stepped without loss of time, and began to row across to the opposite side. She was afraid to look behind her, because it seemed to her that there were hands stretched out ready to seize her if she did. The roots of the trees, the moss-covered stones, the old rotten trees, and the tree-stumps all seemed to be alive, but they all kept silent, and their silence filled the air. She heard the ducks quacking, but she would not turn her head to look at them, only rowed on rapidly, never stopping till she reached the shore, where she left the punt and hurried up to the cottage.

Jacob lay in his bed, he had lain there for two years now. When Martina came in he did not open his eyes, and, still trembling from her fright in the wood, she gathered an armful of sticks from the floor, and lighted a fire in the stove. The firelight did not reach as far as the corner where Jacob's bed was, and from where she sat, Martina could not see whether he was asleep or awake.

" Is that you, Martina ? " sounded suddenly from the corner behind the window. " You *have* been a long time."

" I was tired and rested awhile in the wood," answered the wife. " How have you been to-day ? "

" Just the same as other days," Jacob answered. His voice was so clear and so gentle that Martina got up and went over to him.

" I think I must have slept a little," went on the old man, " and I have been thinking."

" What about ? " asked Martina. How strange it was !—she felt as if the wood had followed her right into the cottage, and brought fear with it.

Jacob moved his head, and the light fell on his face. It was thin and colourless, but the old eyes were shining.

" I would like to see the sun once more before I die," he said. " I have always loved the sunshine, and the calm lake and the wood by it. Do you think you could manage to carry me so far, if I helped a little ? "

Martina sat down on the side of the bed.

" What do you want to go out there for ? " she said. Jacob looked at her with eyes that had grown wonderfully clear and bright all of a sudden.

" I want to die," he said. " And you must help me. It cannot be very difficult to die. I can't go on living any longer. And when I am gone there will be no need for you to go to the village and beg for food for me."

It seemed to Martina, once again, as if the fear she had felt in the wood had followed her into the cottage. She understood the sick man's wish—long before he spoke of it she knew—it was as if she had heard it all before.

" You must help me into the punt," said the old man, " and push it away from the shore. Then you must come up here again and not see any more."

Jacob's eyes sought his wife's with an expression in them like to that in the eyes of a child when it begs for the realisation of its dearest wish. And as she sat there, Martina felt that it was meant to be, it was this that had caused her to feel afraid in the wood.

" When do you want to go ? " she said, and her old eyes were full of tears.

" The sun is shining now," said Jacob. And his voice was like that of an impatient child that will not wait.

" I have lain here for two years and thought of nothing else," continued Jacob.

Then Martina went over to the window, and sat down and tried to think. She had not read much, and she did not know much either. She sat quite still for some time, and Jacob never said a word to disturb her in her thinking. At last she got up from her seat, and, looking out, saw that the sun was still shining. And then, without another word, she lifted the old man from his bed, carried him outside, and seated him on the doorstep. He had grown so thin and fragile that he was no weight to carry. And Jacob sat there and looked at the sunshine, and the wood, and the lake, and everything that had once been his. " Help me farther now, if you can," he said at last.

Then Martina took him up in her arms and carried him down to the punt, but when she had placed him in it her head drooped, and she stood there dumbly, holding Jacob's hand.

" Now push out the punt," said the old man in a low voice, " and when you have done so, go back to the cottage, don't stay here. Take down the Bible and read it. God certainly understands all about this ; He knows how things have been with us."

Then Martina gave his hand a farewell pressure, and, after pushing the punt out from the shore, stood watching until it had got into deep water, after which she returned alone to the cottage. There she sat down and began to read, not the Bible, but Thomas à Kempis. She had never possessed other books than these two, and one was the same as the other to her. When she had read as much as she wanted to, she replaced the book carefully on the shelf. Then she went out, and saw that the punt was empty, and, sitting down on the shore, Martina thought over many things, and finally she repeated the Lord's Prayer while she gazed out over the calm waters of the lake.

Back once more in her cottage, the old woman hung clean sheets in front of the windows, and strewed the path down to the lake with spruce twigs. And then she went to bed, and for the first time in her life slept alone in the cottage by the Reed Marsh.

·   ·   ·   ·   ·   ·   ·

When Martina went down to the village afterwards to get some one to help find Jacob's body, and arrange about the funeral, she just related the facts as they were, exactly as she knew them.

But no one believed she was telling the truth, until some of them, returning with her to the cottage, saw the clean sheets at the windows and the fir-strewn path, and were convinced of the truth of her story.

And when Jacob's body had been found and laid ready for burial on the bed on which, during his lifetime, he had spent so many weary years, there were quite a lot of mourners present. And every one understood that that which had happened should be kept secret, for it was the secret of the wood, and Martina had not really known what she was doing when she helped Jacob to his death.

SELMA LAGERLÖF   SWEDISH
B. 1858

THE OUTLAWS

A PEASANT had killed a monk and fled to the woods. He became
an outlaw, upon whose head a price was set. In the forest he met
another fugitive, a young fisherman from one of the outermost
islands, who had been accused of the theft of a herring net. The
two became companions, cut themselves a home in a cave, laid
their nets together, cooked their food, made their arrows, and held
watch one for the other. The peasant could never leave the forest.
But the fisherman, whose crime was less serious, would now and then
take upon his back the game they had killed, and would creep down
to the more isolated houses on the outskirts of the village. In
return for milk, butter, arrow-heads, and clothing he would sell his
game, the black mountain cock, the moor hen with her shining
feathers, the toothsome doe, and the long-eared hare.

The cave which was their home cut down deep into a mountain-
side. The entrance was guarded by wide slabs of stone and ragged
thorn-bushes. High up on the hillside there stood a giant pine, and
the chimney of the fireplace nestled among its coiled roots. Thus
the smoke could draw up through the heavy hanging branches and
fade unseen into the air. To reach their cave the men had to wade
through the stream that sprang out from the hill slope. No pursuer
thought of seeking their trail in this merry brooklet. At first they
were hunted as wild animals are. The peasants of the district
gathered to pursue them as if for a baiting of wolf or bear. The
bowmen surrounded the wood while the spear carriers entered
and left no thicket or ravine unsearched. The two outlaws
cowered in their gloomy cave, panting in terror and listening
breathlessly as the hunt passed on with noise and shouting over
the mountain ranges.

    •   •   •   •   •   •   •

Tord was the name of the fisherman. He was but sixteen years
old, but was strong and brave. He had now lived for a whole year
in the wood.

The peasant's name was Berg, and they had called him " The
Giant." He was handsome and well-built, the tallest and strongest
man in the entire county. He was broad-shouldered and yet

slender. His hands were delicate in shape, as if they had never known hard work, his hair was brown, his face soft-coloured. When he had lived for some time in the forest his look of strength was awe-inspiring. His eyes grew piercing under bushy brows wrinkled by great muscles over the forehead. His lips were more firmly set than before, his face more haggard, with deepened hollows at the temples, and his strongly marked cheekbones stood out plainly. All the softer curves of his body disappeared, but the muscles grew strong as steel. His hair turned grey rapidly.

Tord had never seen any one so magnificent and so mighty before. In his imagination, his companion towered high as the forest, strong as the raging surf. He served him humbly, as he would have served a master, he revered him as he would have revered a god. It seemed quite natural that Tord should carry the hunting spear, that he should drag the game home, draw the water, and build the fire. Berg the Giant accepted all these services, but scarce threw the boy a friendly word. He looked upon him with contempt, as a common thief.

The outlaws did not live by pillage, but supported themselves by hunting and fishing. Had not Berg killed a holy man, the peasants would soon have tired of the pursuit and left them to themselves in the mountains. But they feared disaster for the villages if he who had laid hands upon a servant of God should go unpunished. When Tord took his game down into the valley they would offer him money and a pardon for himself if he would lead them to the cave of the Giant, that they might catch the latter in his sleep. But the boy refused, and if they followed him he would lead them astray until they gave up the pursuit.

Once Berg asked him whether the peasants had ever tried to persuade him to betrayal. When he learned what reward they had promised, he said scornfully that Tord was a fool not to accept such offers. Tord looked at him with something in his eyes that Berg the Giant had never seen before. No beautiful woman whom he had loved in the days of his youth had ever looked at him like that ; not even in the eyes of his own children, or of his wife, had he seen such affection. " You are my God, the ruler I have chosen of my own free will." This was what the eyes said. "You may scorn me, or beat me, if you will, but I shall still remain faithful."

After this Berg gave more heed to the boy and saw that he was brave in action but shy in speech. Death seemed to have no terrors for him. He would deliberately choose for his path the fresh-formed ice on the mountain pools, the treacherous surface of the morass in springtime. He seemed to delight in danger. It gave him some compensation for the wild ocean storms he could no longer go out to meet. He would tremble in the night darkness of the wood, however, and even by day the gloom of a thicket or a deeper shadow could frighten him. When Berg asked him about this he was silent in embarrassment.

Tord did not sleep in the bed by the hearth at the back of the cave, but every night when Berg was asleep the boy would creep to the entrance and lie there on one of the broad stones. Berg discovered this, and although he guessed the reason he asked the boy about it. Tord would not answer. To avoid further questions he slept in the bed for two nights, then returned to his post at the door.

One night, when a snow-storm raged in the tree-tops, piling up drifts even in the heart of the thickets, the flakes swirled into the cave of the outlaws. Tord, lying by the entrance, awoke in the morning to find himself wrapped in a blanket of melting snow. A day or two later he fell ill. Sharp pains pierced his lungs when he tried to draw breath. He endured the pain as long as his strength would stand it, but one evening, when he stooped to blow up the fire, he fell down and could not rise again. Berg came to his side and told him to lie in the warm bed. Tord groaned in agony, but could not move. Berg put his arm under the boy's body and carried him to the bed. He had a feeling while doing it as if he were touching a clammy snake ; he had a taste in his mouth as if he had eaten unclean horseflesh, so repulsive was it to him to touch the person of this common thief. Berg covered the sick boy with his own warm bear-skin rug and gave him water. This was all he could do, but the illness was not dangerous, and Tord recovered quickly. But now that Berg had had to do his companion's work for a few days, and had had to care for him, they seemed to have come nearer to one another. Tord dared to speak to Berg sometimes, as they sat together by the fire cutting their arrows.

" You come of good people, Berg," Tord said one evening. " Your relatives are the richest peasants in the valley. The men of your name have served kings and fought in their castles."

" They have more often fought with the rebels and done damage to the king's property," answered Berg.

" Your forefather had great banquets at Christmas time. And you held banquets too, when you were at home in your house. Hundreds of men and women could find place on the benches in your great hall, the hall that was built in the days before St. Olaf came here to Viken for christening. Great silver urns were there, and mighty horns, filled with mead, went the rounds of your table."

Berg looked at the boy again. " Were there no banquets in your home ? " he asked.

Tord laughed : " Out there on the rocks where father and mother live ? Father plunders the wrecks and mother is a witch. When the weather is stormy she rides out to meet the ships on a seal's back, and those who are washed overboard from the wrecks belong to her."

" What does she do with them ? " asked Berg.

" Oh, a witch always needs corpses. She makes salves of them, or perhaps she eats them. On moonlit nights she sits out in the wildest surf and looks for the eyes and fingers of drowned children."

" That is horrible ! " said Berg.

The boy answered with calm confidence, " It would be for others, but not for a witch. She can't help it."

This was an altogether new manner of looking at life for Berg. " Then thieves have to steal, as witches have to make magic ? " he questioned sharply.

" I suppose so," answered the boy. " Every one has to do the thing he was born for." But a smile of shy cunning curled his lips, as he added, " There are thieves who have never stolen."

" What do you mean by that ? " spoke Berg.

The boy still smiled his mysterious smile and seemed happy to have given his companion a riddle. " There are birds that do not fly ; and there are thieves who have not stolen," he said.

Berg feigned stupidity, in order to trick the other's meaning : " How can any one be called a thief who has never stolen ? " he said.

The boy's lips closed tight as if to hold back the words. " But if one has a father who steals—— " he threw out after a short pause. " A man may inherit house and money, but the name thief is given only to him who earns it."

Tord laughed gently. " But when one has a mother—and that mother comes and cries, and begs one to take upon one's self the father's crime—and then one can laugh at the hangman and run away into the woods. A man may be outlawed for the sake of a fish net he has never seen."

Berg beat his fist upon the stone table, in great anger. Here this strong, beautiful boy had thrown away his whole life for another. Neither love, nor riches, nor the respect of his fellow-men could ever be his again. The sordid care for food and clothing was all that remained to him in life. And this fool had let him, Berg, despise an innocent man. He scolded sternly, but Tord was not frightened any more than a sick child is frightened at the scolding of his anxious mother.

. . . .

High up on one of the broad wooded hills there lay a black swampy lake. It was square in shape, and its banks were as straight, and their corners as sharp as if it had been the work of human hands. On three sides steep walls of rock rose up, with hardy mountain pines clinging to the stones, their roots as thick as a man's arm. At the surface of the lake, where the few strips of grass had been washed away, these naked roots twisted and coiled, rising out of the water like myriad snakes that had tried to escape from the waves but had been turned to stone in their struggle.

At the entrance to the lake there was a forest of rushes as high as a man's head, through which the sunlight fell as green upon the water as it falls on the moss in the true forest.   There were little clearings among the reeds, little round ponds where the water-lilies slumbered.   The tall rushes looked down with gentle gravity upon these sensitive beauties, who closed their white leaves and their yellow hearts so quickly in their leather outer dress as soon as the sun withdrew his rays.

One sunny day the outlaws came to one of these little ponds to fish.   They waded through the reeds to two high stones, and sat there throwing out their bait for the big green, gleaming pike that slumbered just below the surface of the water.   These men, whose life was now passed entirely among the mountains and the woods, had come to be as completely under the control of the powers of nature as were the plants or the animals.   When the sun shone they were open-hearted and merry, at evening they became silent, and the night, which seemed to them so all-powerful, robbed them of their strength.   And now the green light that fell through the weeds and drew out from the water stripes of gold, brown, and black-green, smoothed them into a sort of magic mood.   They were completely shut out from the outer world.   The reeds swayed gently in the soft wind, the rushes murmured, and the long, ribbon-like leaves struck them lightly in the face.   They sat on the grey stones in their grey leather garments, and the shaded tones of the leather melted into the shades of the stones.   Each saw his comrade sitting opposite him as quietly as a stone statue.

The green light pierced through their eyes into their brains like a mild intoxication.   They saw visions among the reeds, visions which they would not tell even to each other.   There was not much fishing done.   The day was given up to dreams and visions.

A sound of oars came from among the reeds, and they started up out of their dreaming.   In a few moments a heavy boat, hewn out of a tree trunk, came into sight, set in motion by oars not much broader than walking sticks.   The oars were in the hands of a young girl who had been gathering water-lilies.   She had long, dark brown braids of hair, and great dark eyes, but she was strangely pale, with a pallor that was not grey, but softly pink tinted.   Her cheeks were no deeper in colour than the rest of her face ; her lips were scarce redder.   She wore a bodice of white linen and a leather belt with a golden clasp.   Her skirt was of blue with a broad red hem. She rowed past close by the outlaws without seeing them.   They sat absolutely quiet, less from fear of discovery than from the desire to look at her undisturbed.   When she had gone, the stone statues became men again and smiled :

" She was as white as the water-lilies," said one.   " And her eyes were as dark as the water back there under the roots of the pines."

They were both so merry that they felt like laughing, like really laughing as they had never laughed in this swamp before, a laugh that would echo back from the wall of rock and loosen the roots of the pines.

. . . .

While a child, Tord had once seen a drowned man. He had found the corpse on the beach in broad daylight, and it had not frightened him, but at night his dreams were terrifying. He had seemed to be looking out over an ocean, every wave of which threw a dead body at his feet. He saw the rocks and islands covered with corpses of the drowned, the drowned that were dead and belonged to the sea, but that could move, and speak, and threaten him with their white stiffened fingers.

And so it was again. The girl whom he had seen in the reeds appeared to him in his dreams. He met her again down at the bottom of the swamp lake, where the light was greener even than in the reeds, and there he had time enough to see that she was beautiful. He dreamed that he sat on one of the great pine roots in the midst of the lake while the tree rocked up and down, now under, now over the surface of the water. Then he saw her on one of the smaller islands. She stood under the red mountain ash and laughed at him. In his very last dream it had gone so far that she had kissed him. But then it was morning, and he heard Berg rising, but he kept his eyes stubbornly closed that he might continue to dream. When he did awake he was dazed and giddy from what he had seen during the night. He thought much more about the girl than he had done the day before. Toward evening it occurred to him to ask Berg if he knew her name.

Berg looked at him sharply. " It is better for you to know it at once," he said. " It was Unn. We are related to each other."

And then Tord knew that it was this pale maiden who was the cause of Berg's wild hunted life in forest and mountain. He tried to search his memory for what he had heard about her.

Unn was the daughter of a free peasant. Her mother was dead, and she ruled in her father's household. This was to her taste, for she was independent by nature, and had no inclination to give herself to any husband. Unn and Berg were cousins, and the rumour had long gone about that Berg liked better to sit with Unn and her maids than to work at home in his own house. One Christmas, when the great banquet was to be given in Berg's hall, his wife had invited a monk from Draksmark, who, she hoped, would show Berg how wrong it was that he should neglect her for another. Berg and others besides him hated this monk because of his appearance. He was very stout and absolutely white. The ring of hair around his bald head, the brows above his moist eyes, the colour of his skin, of

his hands, and of his garments, were all white. Many found him
very repulsive to look at.

But the monk was fearless, and as he believed that his words
would have greater weight if many heard them, he rose at the table
before all the guests, and said :

" Men call the cuckoo the vilest of birds because he brings up his
young in the nest of others. But here sits a man who takes no care
for his house and his children, and who seeks his pleasure with a
strange woman. Him I will call the vilest of men."

Unn rose in her place.

" Berg, this is said to you and to me," she cried. " Never have I
been so shamed, but my father is not here to protect me."

She turned to go, but Berg hurried after her. " Stay where you
are," she said. " I do not wish to see you again."

He stopped her in the corridor, and asked her what he should do
that she might stay with him. Her eyes glowed as she answered that
he himself should know best what he must do. Then Berg went
into the hall again and slew the monk.

Berg and Tord thought on awhile with the same thoughts, then
Berg said, " You should have seen her when the white monk fell.
My wife drew the children about her and cursed Unn. She turned
the faces of the children toward her, that they might always remember the woman for whose sake their father had become a murderer. But Unn stood there so quiet and so beautiful that the men
who saw her trembled. She thanked me for the deed, and prayed
me to flee to the woods at once. She told me never to become a
robber, and to use my knife only in some cause equally just."

" Your deed had ennobled her," said Tord.

And again Berg found himself astonished at the same thing that
had before now surprised him in the boy. Tord was a heathen, or
worse than a heathen ; he never condemned that which was wrong.
He seemed to know no sense of responsibility. What had to come,
came. He knew of God, of Christ, and the Saints, but he knew them
only by name, as one knows the names of the gods of other nations.
The ghosts of the Scheeren Islands were his gods. His mother,
learned in magic, had taught him to believe in the spirits of the dead.
And then it was that Berg undertook a task which was as foolish as
if he had woven a rope for his own neck. He opened the eyes of this
ignorant boy to the power of God, the Lord of all justice, the avenger
of wrong who condemned sinners to the pangs of hell everlasting.
And he taught him to love Christ and His Mother, and all the saintly
men and women who sit before the throne of God praying that His
anger may be turned away from sinners. He taught him all that
mankind has learned to do to soften the wrath of God. He told him
of the long trains of pilgrims journeying to the holy places ; he told
him of those who scourged themselves in their remorse ; and he told

him of the pious monks who flee the joys of this world.

The longer he spoke the paler grew the boy and the keener his attention as his eyes widened at the visions. Berg would have stopped, but the torrent of his own thoughts carried him away. Night sank down upon them, the black forest night, where the scream of the owl shrills ghostly through the stillness. God came so near to them that the brightness of His throne dimmed the stars, and the angels of vengeance descended upon the mountain heights. And below them the flames of the underworld fluttered up to the outer curve of the earth and licked greedily at this last refuge of a race crushed by sin and woe.

.   .   .   .

Autumn came, and with it came storm. Tord went out alone into the woods to tend the traps and snares, while Berg remained at home to mend his clothes. The boy's path led him up a wooded height along which the falling leaves danced in circles in the gust. Again and again the feeling came to him that some one was walking behind him. He turned several times, then went on again when he had seen that it was only the wind and the leaves. He threatened the rustling circles with his fist, and kept on his way. But he had not silenced the sounds of his vision. At first it was the little dancing feet of elfin children ; then it was the hissing of a great snake moving up behind him. Beside the snake there came a wolf, a tall, grey creature, waiting for the moment when the adder should strike at his feet to spring upon his back. Tord hastened his steps, but the visions hastened with him. When they seemed but two steps behind him, ready for the spring, he turned. There was nothing there, as he had known all the time. He sat down upon a stone to rest.

Then he went on again, while the forest beneath him waved like a sea in storm, although it was still and calm on the path around him. But he heard something he had never heard before. The wood was full of voices. Now it was like a whispering, now a gentle plaint, now a loud threat, or a roaring curse. It laughed, and it moaned. It was as the voice of hundreds. This unknown something that threatened and excited, that whistled and hissed, a something that seemed to be, and yet was not, almost drove him mad. He shivered in deadly terror, as he had shivered before, the day that he lay on the floor of his cave, and heard his pursuers rage over him through the forest. He seemed to hear again the crashing of the branches, the heavy footsteps of the men, the clanking of their arms, and their wild, blood-thirsty shouts.

It was not alone the storm that roared about him. There was something else in it, something yet more terrible ; there were voices he could not understand, sounds as of a strange speech.

Then suddenly he knew who was speaking to him in the storm.

It was God, the Great Avenger, the Lord of all Justice. God pursued him because of his comrade. God demanded that he should give up the murderer of the monk to vengeance.

Tord began to speak aloud amid the storm. He told God what he wanted to do, but that he could not do it. He had wanted to speak to the Giant and to beg him make his peace with God. But he could not find the words; embarrassment tied his tongue. "When I learned that the world is ruled by a God of Justice," he cried, "I knew that he was a lost man. I have wept through the night for my friend. I know that God will find him no matter where he may hide. But I could not speak to him; I could not find the words because of my love for him. Do not ask that I shall speak to him. Do not ask that the ocean shall rise to the height of the mountains."

He was silent again, and the deep voice of the storm, which he knew for God's voice, was silent also. Then was a sudden pause in the wind, a burst of sunshine, a sound as of oars, and the gentle rustling of stiff reeds. These soft tones brought up the memory of Unn.

Then the storm began again, and he heard steps behind him, and a breathless panting. He did not dare to turn this time, for he knew that it was the white monk. He came from the banquet in Berg's great hall, covered with blood, and with an open axe-cut in his forehead. And he whispered: "Betray him. Give him up, that you may save his soul."

Tord began to run. All this terror grew and grew in him, and he tried to flee from it. But as he ran he heard behind him the deep, mighty voice, which he knew was the voice of God. It was God Himself pursuing him, demanding that he should give up the murderer. Berg's crime seemed more horrible to him than ever it had seemed before. A weaponless man had been murdered, a servant of God cut down by the steel. And the murderer still dared to live. He dared to enjoy the light of the sun and the fruits of the earth. Tord halted, clinched his fists, and shrieked a threat. Then, like a madman, he ran from the forest, the realm of terror, down into the valley.

. . . . . .

When Tord entered the cave the outlaw sat upon the bench of stone, sewing. The fire gave but a pale light, and the work did not seem to progress satisfactorily. The boy's heart swelled in pity. This superb Giant seemed all at once so poor and so unhappy.

"What is the matter?" asked Berg. "Are you ill? Have you been afraid?"

Then for the first time Tord spoke of his fear. "It was so strange in the forest. I heard the voices of spirits and I saw ghosts. I saw white monks."

" Boy ! "

" They sang to me all the way up the slope to the hilltop. I ran
from them, but they ran after me, singing. Can I not lay the spirits ?
What have I to do with them ? There are others to whom their
appearance is more necessary."

" Are you crazy to-night, Tord ? "

Tord spoke without knowing what words he was using. His shy-
ness had left him all at once, speech seemed to flow from his lips.
" They were white monks, as pale as corpses. And their clothes are
spotted with blood. They draw their hoods down over their fore-
heads, but I can see the wound shining there. The great, yawning,
red wound, from the axe."

" Tord," said the giant, pale and deeply grave, " the Saints alone
know why you see wounds of axe-thrusts. I slew the monk with a
knife."

Tord stood before Berg trembling and wringing his hands. " They
demand you of me. They would compel me to betray you."

" Who ? The monks ? "

" Yes, yes, the monks. They show me visions. They show me
Unn. They show me the open, sunny ocean. They show me the
camps of the fishermen, where there is dancing and merriment. I
close my eyes, and yet I can see it all. ' Leave me,' I say to them.
' My friend has committed a murder, but he is not bad. Leave me
alone, and I will talk to him, that he may repent and atone. He will
see the wrong he has done, and he will make a pilgrimage to the
Holy Grave.' "

" And what do the monks answer ? " asked Berg. " They do not
want to pardon me. They want to torture me and to burn me at
the stake."

" ' Shall I betray my best friend ? ' I ask them. He is all that I
have in the world. He saved me from the bear when its claws were
already at my throat. We have suffered hunger and cold together.
He covered me with his own garments while I was ill. I have
brought him wood and water, I have watched over his sleep, and
led his enemies off the trail. Why should they think me a man
who betrays his friend ? My friend will go to the priest himself, and
will confess to him, and then together we will seek absolution ? "

Berg listened gravely, his keen eyes searching in Tord's face.
" Go to the priest yourself, and tell him the truth. You must go
back again among mankind."

" What does it help if I go alone ? The spirits of the dead follow
me because of your sin. Do you not see how I tremble before you ?
You have lifted your hand against God Himself. What crime is like
unto yours ? Why did you tell me about the just God ? It is you
yourself who compel me to betray you. Spare me this sin. Go to
the priest yourself." He sank down on his knees before Berg.

The murderer laid his hand on his head and looked at him.   He measured his sin by the terror of his comrade, and it grew and grew to monstrous size.   He saw himself in conflict with the Will that rules the world.   Remorse entered his heart.

" Woe unto me that I did what I did," he said.   " And is not this miserable life, this life we lead here in terror, and in deprivation, is it not atonement enough ?   Have I not lost home and fortune ? Have I not lost friends, and all the joys that make the life of a man ? What more ? "

As he heard him speak thus, Tord sprang up in wild terror. " You can repent ! " he cried.   " My words move your heart ? Oh, come with me, come at once.   Come, let us go while yet there is time."

Berg the Giant sprang up also.   " You—did it— ? "

" Yes, yes, yes.   I have betrayed you.   But come quickly. Come now, now that you can repent.   We must escape.   We will escape."

The murderer stooped to the ground where the battle-axe of his fathers lay at his feet.   " Son of a thief," he hissed.   " I trusted you—I loved you."

But when Tord saw him stoop for the axe, he knew that it was his own life that was in peril now.   He tore his own axe from his girdle, and thrust at Berg before the latter could rise.   The Giant fell headlong to the floor, the blood spurting out over the cave. Between the tangled masses of hair Tord saw the great, yawning, red wound of an axe-thrust.

Then the peasants stormed into the cave.   They praised his deed and told him that he should receive full pardon.

Tord looked down at his hands, as if he saw there the fetters that had drawn him on to kill the man he loved.   Like the chains of the Fenrir wolf, they were woven out of empty air.   They were woven out of the green light amid the reeds, out of the play of shadows in the woods, out of the song of the storm, out of the rustling of the leaves, out of the magic vision of dreams.   And he said aloud : " God is great."

He crouched beside the body, spoke amid his tears to the dead, and begged him to awake.   The villagers made a litter of their spears, on which to carry the body of the free peasant to his home. The dead man aroused awe in their souls, they softened their voices in his presence.   When they raised him on to the bier, Tord stood up, shook the hair from his eyes, and spoke in a voice that trembled :

" Tell Unn, for whose sake Berg the Giant became a murderer, that Tord the fisherman, whose father plunders wrecks, and whose mother is a witch—tell her that Tord slew Berg because Berg had taught him that justice is the corner-stone of the world."

A DETHRONED KING

Selma Lagerlöf

I

THE uneven suburb street, slippery from the autumn rain, echoed with voices. Doors stood open, windows were filled, heads were bent together with significant nods. " He has run away." This was what the women whispered, what the sparrows twittered, what the wooden shoes pattered. " He has run away. The old shoe-maker has run away. The owner of the little house, the husband of the young wife, the father of the pretty child, has run away. Who can understand it ? "

There is an old song :

> Beside the hearth a husband old,
> Far from his side the young wife cold ;
> The lovers roam the forest deep,
> While children for their mother weep.

The song is old and often sung ; many know it.

But this was a new song. The old husband was the fugitive. On his work-table lay his farewell message. A letter had lain beside it, which the young wife had read, but no one else had seen.

The young wife was in the kitchen idle. A neighbour passed to and fro, arranging the table, laying out coffee-cups, making every-thing ready, and dropping a tear betimes, which she would wipe away with the towel in her hand.

The wise women of the suburb sat ranged stiffly about the walls. They knew what was suitable in a house of mourning, and they cherished the sorrow in stony silence. They had made themselves free for the day to stand by the forsaken wife in her grief. Their work-roughened hands lay quiet in their laps, their weather-worn skin fell into deep furrows as thin lips closed tight over tooth-less jaws.

Among these bronze statues sat the blonde housewife with her sweet dove's face. She did not weep, but she sat trembling, so frightened that she seemed about to die of fear. She clenched her teeth hard, that none might hear their chattering. She started in terror at a step, a knock at the door, or the voice of any one addressing her.

She had her husband's letter in her pocket, and thought of sentence after sentence in it. One read : " I can no longer endure to see you two together." And again : " I know now that you intend to run away with Erikson." And still again : " I do not want you to do that, for the evil talk would make you unhappy. I will go away so that you can be free and marry again in honour. Erikson is a good workman ; he will provide well for you." And still further : " They can say of me what they will. I am happy so long as they cannot say evil of you, for you could not endure it."

She could not understand it. She had never thought of deceiving him. She had liked to chat with the young journeyman, but how could that harm her husband ? Love is a disease, but it is not fatal. She could have endured it patiently all her life. How could her husband have guessed her most secret thoughts ?

The thought of him tortured her. He must have watched her with torn soul. He had wept because of his years, maddened at the strength and courage of the younger man. He had trembled at every whispered word, at every smile, at every handshake. His burning jealousy, his growing madness had made an entire love tragedy of something that had no form or life.

She thought of how old he was, as he went away that night. His back was bent, his hands shook, the torture of many nights had wrecked him. He had gone away to escape this life of wearing doubt.

And she remembered other sentences of the letter. " I will not expose you to shame. I have always been too old for you." And then another : " You will be respected and honoured. Keep your own counsel, and all the shame will fall on me."

The woman shook with growing terror. Was it then possible to deceive others—to deceive even God ? Why should she sit here, receiving the pity accorded to a sorrowing mother, honoured like a bride on her wedding day ? Why was she not the homeless, the friendless and despised one ? Could God be thus deceived ?

Above the big desk hung a little bookshelf, and on it was a great book with brass clasps. The book contained the story of a man and a woman who had lied to God and to man. " How is it that ye have agreed together to tempt the Spirit of the Lord ? Behold, the feet of them which have buried thy husband are at the door, and shall carry thee out."

Thus she sat, staring at the book, listening for the feet of the young man. She started at every sound. She was ready to stand up and confess, ready to fall down and die.

The coffee was ready. The women moved gravely, with noiseless steps, around the table. But the housewife took no heed of their actions. She was beside herself with terror.

One of the women began to talk. She knew what was suitable

in a house of mourning and that the time for breaking the long silence had now come. But the housewife started up as if stung by a whiplash. What would the woman say? " Anna Wik, wife of Matthias Wik, confess! You have lied to God and to us long enough. We are your judges, we will pronounce your sentence and we will tear you to pieces."

But no, the women began to talk of men, and all spoke in their turn. It was no praise of men they sang. Every evil ever done by men was dragged to the light of day, as soothing balm for the forsaken wife. Wrong following injury—strange creatures, these men!

The wife of the fugitive felt the sting of this talk. She attempted to defend the incorrigibles. " My husband is good," she said.

The women started up in anger. " He has run away. He is no better than the others. An old man like that has no right to forsake wife and child. Do you really believe him to be better than the others ? "

The woman trembled. She felt as if she were being dragged through a hedge of thorns. She turned red and tried to speak, but she could not. Why did God let such things be ?

What if she should take out the letter and read it aloud ? Then this stream of venom would be turned on her. Deadly terror clutched her heart. She half wished some daring hand would draw the letter from her pocket in spite of her ; she herself was not capable of doing it. The sound of a hammer came in from the workroom. Could no one hear the note of victory in the blows ? All day long this hammering had angered her, but no one else understood it. All-knowing God, hast Thou no servant who can read the heart ? She was ready for her sentence, if only she herself need not confess. She listened for the feet of the young men, ready to fall dead at the sound.

II

Several years later a certain divorced wife married a shoemaker who had been a journeyman to her husband. She had not desired it, but had been drawn into it, as the fish on the line is drawn into the boat of the angler. She had sent away the journeyman and had tried to live alone. She had wished to show her husband that she was innocent. But where was this husband, so indifferent to her fidelity ? She suffered poverty, her child was in rags. How long did he think she could wait ?

Erikson was successful. He had a shop in the town, rented an apartment and bought velvet furniture for the parlour. All stood ready, waiting for her. At last she came, when poverty had broken her courage.

At first she could not shake off her terror. But nothing happened, and each day saw her happier and more secure. She enjoyed the respect of all about her, while she knew that she did not deserve it. It kept her conscience awake and made her a good wife.

After several years her first husband returned to his house in the suburb. It was his property, and he settled down there and began work anew. But no customers came and decent people would have nothing to do with him. He was despised, while his wife grew in honour and position. And yet he had done right and she wrong.

The man kept his secret, but it was nigh to choking him. He felt himself sinking into sin because every one thought him a bad man. He took up with whatever companions he could find, and began to drink.

When he had sunk thus far, the Salvation Army came to town. A large hall was hired and meetings were held. From the very first evening all the scum of the streets met there to play their pranks. After a week Matthias Wik decided to join the fun.

There was jostling in the street and crowding at the door ; pushing from strong elbows, words from sharp tongues ; there were street urchins and soldiers, servant girls and charwomen ; peaceful police and noisy ruffians. The Salvation Army was new and very modern. Before its attraction the dance-halls emptied, the wine-shops languished.

The hall was low-roofed, the benches were rough, the floor splintered, the ceiling hung damp in spots and the lamps smelled rancid.

The platform was empty, for the performance had not yet begun. There were whistling and laughing and breaking of benches. The *War Cry* flew from group to group like a kite ; the audience was enjoying itself.

Then a side door opened and cold air streamed into the hall. Sudden attentive expectation succeeded the noise. At last they appeared, three young girls with tambourines and dark blue bonnets almost covering their faces. They fell on their knees as soon as they had climbed to the platform. One of them began to pray aloud, with raised head and closed eyes. Her voice cut like a knife. The silence was intense during the prayer. The street ruffians were not yet ready for their fun ; they were waiting for the confessions and the singing.

The young girls " laboured " vigorously. They sang and prayed, and sang and preached. Smilingly they told of their happiness. Before them sat an audience of ruffians, who now began to stand on the benches and fill the hall with their noise. Through the heavy noisome air the girls on the platform could see hideous faces rise and fall. How brave was this little army, how proud its consciousness of having God on its side ! It was of little avail to mock and jeer at these girls in the great hats, they would remain the victors over all the work-hardened hands, the cruel faces and the cursing lips.

" Sing with us," they cried. " Sing with us, it is good to sing." They intoned a well-known melody, accompanying themselves on their tambourines and repeating the first verse several times. Some of those nearest the platform joined in. But an obscene street rhyme sounded from the door, words fought against words, whistling against the music. The girls' strong, well-trained voices combated the quavering boys' tones and the men's growling basses. But the stamping and shouting in the doorway drowned their words, and their singing succumbed like a wounded warrior. The uproar was hideous. The girls fell on their knees and lay as if helpless, with closed eyes and bodies swaying in silent agony.

Slowly the noise died away, and at once the captain began to speak. " O Lord, Thou wilt make all these Thine own. We thank Thee, O Lord, that Thou wilt take them all into Thine army. We thank Thee, O Lord, that we may lead them to Thee."

The crowd hissed and howled in anger, as if protesting against their surrender. They seemed to have forgotten that they had come of their own free will. But the girl continued to speak, and her sharp, clear voice pierced the noise and conquered it.

She ordered one of her comrades to step forward and tell her story. The girl came forward with a smile, and fearlessly, in the face of all this scorn and laughter, she told the story of her sin and her conversion. Where had this former kitchen-maid learned thus to brave scorn and jeers ? Some of those who had come to scoff grew pale. Whence had these girls their power and their courage ? Something Higher was behind them.

Matthias Wik stood by the door, in the very thickest of the crowd. He looked drink-sodden, but he was sober this evening. As he stood there, he thought again and again : " If I could but speak ; if I could but speak ! "

This was the strangest place and the strangest company he had ever seen. A voice seemed to be saying to him, " This is the reed into which you may whisper ; these are the waves that will carry your voice afar."

Suddenly the singing crowd started, for they seemed to hear the roar of a lion. A strong and terrible voice spoke terrible words. The voice mocked at God. " Why should men serve God ? God deserted His servants, He had deserted even His own Son. God helps no one."

The voice grew stronger and louder every minute. No one of those present had ever heard such anger bursting from a crushed and broken heart. The hearers bowed their heads, like travellers in the desert when the storm-wind blows.

The mighty words thundered against God's throne like blows of a giant hammer. They thundered against Him who had tortured Job ; who had allowed the martyrs to suffer ; who had allowed His followers to burn at the stake. When would He cease giving the victory to Evil ?

Some had tried to laugh at first. They had thought it a joke, but they saw now that it was bitter earnest. Several rose to go to the platform. They sought refuge with the Salvation Army, shelter from him who would draw down God's wrath on their heads.

In sharp, penetrating tones, the voice questioned them and asked what reward they awaited from their service of God. They need not be too sure of heaven—God was miserly with His heaven.

There was a man who had done more good than was necessary to win eternal salvation. He had made greater sacrifice than God demands. But he fell into sin later, and life is long. He had squandered his salvation here in this world, and would go the way of the damned.

The voice roared like one of the terrible northern storms before which the ships flee into the harbours. While the blasphemer spoke women hurried, trembling, to the platform. They seized and kissed the hands of the Salvation Army soldiers. One conversion followed another ; the soldiers could scarce receive all who thronged. Boys and old men praised God on their knees.

The speaker went on. His words intoxicated him. He said repeatedly to himself : " I speak, I speak—at last I speak ! I tell them my secret—and yet I do not tell it." And for the first time since his great sacrifice he felt free from sorrow.

III

It was a Sunday afternoon in summer. The town lay like a wilderness of stone, like a moon-illumined landscape, silent and deserted. On the roads leading out to the forest pedestrians carrying baskets mingled with cyclists, schoolboys with knapsacks, and dancing children. The rearing horses of a brake flung out their hoofs over the groups of wandering families. A daring apprentice climbed on the hub of the wheel, and daintily gloved hands thrust him back amid shouts and laughter.

In the forest the nightingales sang, the oaks mourned with their black trunks, while the beeches reared high temples, story on story of glancing green. The troop of wanderers seated themselves in the grass around their baskets, shining beetles crawled about them, chattering crickets helped to make joyous their Sunday outing.

Suddenly the crickets vanished in the grass and the nightingale sang louder, as the sound of tambourines approached. The Salvation Army marched in under the beeches, starting the people up from their lazy comfort. The dancing floor and the croquet ground were forsaken, the swings and the *carrousel* emptied themselves of their gay visitors. The crowd pushed toward the camp of the Salvation Army, the benches were soon filled, and every little hummock held a group of listeners.

The Army had now grown strong and mighty. The blue bonnet framed many a pretty face, and many a strong pair of shoulders wore the red coat. The cobbler Matthias Wik, the mighty blasphemer, now stood as ensign on the platform steps, while the red flag drooped gently over his gray head. The soldiers of the Army had not forgotten the old man to whom they owed their first victory. They sought him out in his solitude, they were not afraid to talk to him, they swept his floor and mended his clothes. And they let him speak in their meetings.

And he was happy now that his long silence was broken. He stood no longer solitary, an enemy of God. Fresh, surging power pulsed through him, he was happy when he could find an outlet for it, happy when the hall resounded to the roar of his leonine voice.

He spoke always of himself, told each time his own story. He painted the fate of the misunderstood, he spoke of sacrifices to the blood, sacrifices left unrewarded and unknown. He disguised his story, he told his secret and yet did not tell it. He became a poet, he won power to move the heart. For his sake many a hearer gathered before the platform. The rich, fantastic pictures drawn by his sick brain held them spellbound, listening enthralled to the words of heart-moving lamentation in which his grief found vent.

Where had he learned the power to bring proud men to their knees at his feet? He trembled when he began to speak. But then calmness came over him, and wave after wave of grief-heavy words rose from the untouched depths of his great sorrow.

His speeches were never printed. They were like the cry of the hunter, like the blast of a horn, awakening, exciting, startling and encouraging—something that could not be caught, that could not be reproduced. They were like quivering lightning and rolling thunder and set all hearts quaking in gloomy terror. The last drop of the cataract may be counted, or the whirling play of surf-loam painted, more easily than the mocking, whirling, swelling, mighty stream of these speeches could be caught and held.

While Matthias Wik spoke, that Sunday in the forest, his divorced wife sat among the audience. She had wandered out to the woods in the morning on her husband's arm, matronly and respectable. Her daughter and the apprentice carried the picnic baskets, and the servant followed with the youngest child. All were cheery, contented and happy. Anna's conscience slumbered like a satisfied child. When, not long ago, she had seen her first husband stagger, half drunk, past her window, she had felt an ugly sting at her heart. Then she heard that he had become the idol of the Salvation Army.

This had quieted her, and now she was come to hear him.   And she understood him.   It was not Uriah he spoke of, it was himself.   He writhed under the thought of his own sacrifice ; he tore pieces from his own heart and threw them to the crowd.   And the depths of this unceasing sorrow yawned before her like an open grave.

IV

Anna Erikson was a frequent attendant at the meetings now, listening often to her husband.   It was always of himself that he spoke, and though he disguised his story she understood it.   Now he was Abraham ; now Job ; now Jeremiah, whom the people cast into a well ; now Elisha, mocked at by the children on the high road.

His grief appeared bottomless to her, borrowing every shade of meaning, masking itself in every guise.   She did not understand that the man was healing himself through his words ; that his soul danced and laughed for joy of the poet's power within him.

She had taken her daughter to the meetings.   The girl had not wished to go.   She was dutiful, virtuous, severe ; no spark of youth fired her blood, she had been born old.   She had grown up ashamed of her father.   She held herself straight and unbending, as one who would say : " Look on me, the daughter of the despised man !   Is there one spot on my robe ? "

Her mother was proud of her, but she sighed sometimes and thought : " If my daughter's hands were less white, their caresses might be warmer."

The girl entered the meeting-hall with a mocking smile.   She hated everything theatrical.   When her father stepped to the platform she turned to go, but Anna Erikson's hand clasped hers firmly as a vice.   The girl sat still, and the stream of words began to pour over her.   But more than the words was what spoke to her through her mother's hand.

This hand cried out aloud in pain and writhed in agony.   Then again it lay still and dead, then pressed and pressed her own in feverish wildness.   Her mother's face betrayed nothing ; the hand alone struggled and suffered.

The old speaker described the martyrdom of silence.

Anna Erikson's hand lay in that of her daughter.   The hand said : " This man is himself a martyr to his silence ; he has been falsely accused ; with a single word he might free himself."

The girl accompanied her mother home.   They walked in silence, the younger woman's face hard as stone.   She was trying to call back all that her memory held of those days.   Her mother looked at her anxiously.   What could she know ?

The next day Anna Erikson invited her old friends to drink a cup of coffee with her.   They were the same women who had sat with her that day of her loneliness in the suburb. One new friend was there, Maria Anderson, Captain of the Salvation Army.

The conversation turned on simple things ; the women sat chatting and laughing, gentle and care-free. Anna Erikson could not understand why she had ever feared them or thought they would condemn her.

When she had given each her second cup of coffee, and they sat contented and happy behind the plates piled high with cake, she began to speak. Her words were solemn, but her voice was steady.

" One is careless when one is young. A girl who marries without thinking carefully of what she is about to do can bring great unhappiness to herself. Who could have had a harder fate than I ? "

They all understood this, for they had all mourned with her.

" When one is young, one has little wisdom. One is silent from shame when it were better to have spoken. She who does not speak at the right moment may repent it all her life."

They all believed this to be true.

She had heard Matthias Wik speak yesterday, as often before, she said. She must talk to them of him now, she could not endure the pain she felt when she thought of what he had suffered for her sake. And yet she felt that it had not been wise of him, old as he was, to marry such a young girl as she had been then.

" In my youth I did not dare tell you. He left me from pity, for he thought I loved Erikson. He left me a letter telling me this."

She read them the letter, a tear rolling down her cheek.

" His jealousy had deceived him. There was nothing between Erikson and myself then ; we did not marry until four years later. But I must tell you this now—Wik is too good to be misunderstood any longer. He left his wife and child, not from wickedness, but because he loved them. I wish every one to know this. Captain Anderson will, perhaps, read this letter aloud in the Army meeting. I wish that Wik shall be restored to respect and honour. I know I have kept silence long, but one does not want to betray oneself for a drunkard. Now it is different."

The women sat as if dazed. Anna Erikson's voice trembled a little as she added, smiling weakly :

" I suppose now you will not want to visit me ? "

" Oh, yes, of course—you were so young, Mrs. Erikson. It was not your fault ; it was his fault in letting himself be deceived."

She smiled to herself. Were these the sharp beaks that were to tear her flesh ? The truth was not dangerous nor was a lie dangerous. The feet of the young men were not without her door.

Did she know that on that very morning her eldest daughter had left her home to go to her father's house ?

V

The sacrifice Matthias Wik had made for the sake of his wife's honour became known. He was admired, although some laughed at him. His letter was read aloud at the Army meeting. Several in the audience wept in pity ; people pressed his hand in the street. His daughter came to live with him.

The next few evenings he was silent at the meetings. He felt no impulse to speak. Then he was asked to speak again.

He mounted the platform, folded his hands, and began. When he had spoken a few words he halted in confusion. He scarce knew his own voice again. Where was its leonine strength. Where was the roaring of the northern storm, the mighty, welling outpour of words ? He could not understand it.

He staggered back. " I cannot speak," he murmured. " God has taken from me the power."

He sat down on his bench and rested his head on his hands. He concentrated all his will power on thinking out a subject on which he should speak. Had that ever been necessary before ? His thoughts whirled in confusion.

Perhaps if he stood up again, in his accustomed place, and began with his accustomed prayer, he might find the words again. He attempted it. His face was ashen grey, sweat stood out on his brow as the eyes of the crowd were turned on him.

Not a word came to his lips. He sank down on his seat, weeping and moaning in pain. His gift had been taken from him.

Deadly fear gripped him. It was a fight for his very life. He tried to hold fast what had already fled beyond recall. He wanted his sorrow back again, that he might be able to speak once more.

As if drunk, he staggered again to the platform, stammering senseless words. He tried to remember what he had heard others say, what he himself had said before. He stared eagerly around for the attention, the trembling, the breathless awe ; but it was no longer there. His greatest happiness had been taken from him.

He fled back into his darkness. He cursed his fate, cursed because he had converted his wife and daughter through his words. He had possessed a priceless treasure and had lost it. His grief was heart-rending, but it is not on such grief that genius feeds.

He was a painter without hands, a singer who had lost his voice. He had spoken only of his sorrow ; of what could he speak now ?

He prayed : " O God, if to be honoured is to be dumb, and to be despised is to have the power of speech, then let me be despised again ! If happiness is silent and sorrow alone has words, then give me back my sorrow ! "

But he had lost his crown. He was more miserable than the lowest, for he had fallen from the heights. He was a dethroned king.

OLD AGNETA

Selma Lagerlöf

An old woman, who was small and thin, and whose face, though colourless and faded, was neither hard nor wrinkled, went lightly up a mountain path. She wore a long cloak and a frilled cap, and carried a prayer-book, and there was a sprig of lavender in her folded neckerchief.

She lived in a cottage far up on the mountain-side, where the trees left off growing. It stood right on the edge of a broad glacier, that carried its ice-stream down from the snow-clad mountain tops above, to the depths of the valley below. And there the old woman lived quite alone, for all those who had belonged to her were dead.

It was Sunday, and she had been to church. But somehow, instead of feeling the happier for her pilgrimage, she felt sad. The minister had preached about death and the souls of the damned, and it had made a great impression on her. For she had suddenly recalled having heard in her childhood how numbers of lost souls wandered in the everlasting cold of the heights above her dwelling. She remembered story after story about these wanderers on the glaciers, indefatigable shadows, hunted by the icy mountain winds. A great dread of the mountain seized her, and it seemed to her that her cottage lay terribly high up. Fancy, if those invisible ones on the heights descended the glacier! And she was quite alone up there! As she thought of her loneliness, which caused her much sorrow and preyed upon her mind unceasingly, old Agneta became more melancholy still. It was hard to be so far away from everybody.

Then she began to talk to herself. It had become a habit with her up there in the solitude of the mountains. " Old Agneta," she said " you sit up there in your cottage and spin and spin. You have to toil and moil every hour of the day so as not to die of hunger. But is there any one who is the happier for your being alive ? *Is* there any one, old Agneta ? It might be so, if you had one of your own people still living ; and if you lived farther down, nearer the village, you might be of use to some one ! You are too poor to keep a dog or a cat, but you could give a night's lodging to a beggar now and then. You shouldn't live so far from the high road. Why, if you could just once give a drink of water to a thirsty tramp, you would feel that you were of some use in the world, old Agneta ! "

And sighing, she thought to herself that not even the peasant women, who gave her flax to spin, would grieve if she were to die. Certainly, she had tried to do her work well and conscientiously, but probably there were many others who could do it still better !

And here she began to cry, for the thought had come into her mind that perhaps the minister, who had seen her sitting in her place in church for so many years, didn't really care whether she were there or not !

" I am like a dead person," she said ; " nobody cares whether I live or die ! I am already frozen with the cold and the loneliness— at least, my heart is ! If only some one needed me ! I tell you," she went on, raising her hand toward heaven, " unless you find me some one to whom I can be of use, I shall just lay me down and die ! "

At that moment, a tall, grave-faced monk came along the path towards her. Seeing that she was unhappy, he turned and walked with her, and she told him what was troubling her. She said that if God did not send her something to live for, she would become as one of those unhappy wanderers on the glacier.

" God can certainly do that," said the monk.

" Don't you see that God is powerless up here ? " exclaimed old Agneta ; " there is nothing here save cold, empty solitude ! "

They climbed higher and still higher to where the moss covered the rocky slopes, and mountain plants with hairy leaves grew along the side of the path. And then the monk caught sight of Agneta's cottage, under the glacier.

" Oh ! " said he, " is that where you live ? Then, you are not lonely, for you have company enough. Just look ! "

And speaking thus, he formed a circle with two of his fingers, and holding it in front of the old woman's left eye, bade her look through it at the mountain. But old Agneta only shuddered and closed her eyes. " If there *is* anything to be seen up there," she said, " I would rather not see it. Things are quite bad enough as it is up here ! "

" Well, good-bye, then," said the monk. " I do not think you will have a second opportunity of seeing such a sight ! "

Moved by curiosity at these words, the old woman opened her eyes, and gazed through the circle at the snow-covered mountain. To begin with, she saw nothing out of the ordinary, then she could distinguish something white moving on the snow. And then she saw that what she had taken for mist, and fog, and light-blue shadows, were in reality hosts of lost souls !

Little old Agneta stood there shaking like a leaf. This was just what she had heard told as a child. The dead, who died unshriven, wandered up there in the everlasting cold, suffering untold agonies! Looking again, she perceived that most of them were wrapped in something long and white, but that all were barefooted and bareheaded. There were countless numbers of them, and more and more kept coming while she looked. Some walked with a proud and haughty step, and others so lightly that they appeared to be dancing over the ice-fields; but old Agneta noticed that the feet of every one of them were cut and bleeding from contact with jagged pieces of ice.

She saw, too, how they ceaselessly pressed close one to another as if to get some warmth, but almost immediately resumed their solitary way, scared by the chill of death that came from their bodies. One might have thought the cold that reigned on the mountain emanated from them, and that it was they who kept the snow unmelted, and made the mists so chilly!

And then old Agneta noticed that all were not moving, but that some of the lost ones were standing still, as if frozen into rigidity, and that they appeared to have been standing in this way for years, as only the upper part of their bodies was visible above the snow and ice in which they were well-nigh buried.

The longer she looked, the calmer did the little old woman become. Her fears left her, and instead of feeling afraid as before, now she felt heartily sorry for all these tormented souls, whose pain never ceased, and who had no resting-place for their poor, bleeding feet. And how they shook and shivered with the cold too, the terrible, biting, piercing, intolerable cold!

There were many young ones among them, but there was no youth in their faces, which were blue with cold. They appeared to be playing, but all their joy was dead. They shivered unceasingly, and walked as if they were old men and women, instead of girls and boys, while their feet seemed to seek out the sharpest ice-fragments to tread upon.

Then the monk took his hand away, and old Agneta saw nothing but the bare, empty, snow-covered waste. A few heavy blocks of ice lay scattered about, but they contained no frozen spirits of the dead, and the blue gleam on the glacier did not come from bodies embedded in the ice. The wind was chasing some snowflakes. Nevertheless, she was certain that what she had seen through the circle was real, and she said to the monk:

"Is it permitted to do something for those unhappy ones?"

He answered: "When did God deny to Love the right to do good, or to Compassion the right to comfort?"

With these words he left her, and old Agneta went quickly in to her cottage, and sat herself down to think.

She spent the whole evening trying to think of some way to help the unhappy wanderers on the glacier. She didn't have time to remember that she was lonely.

The following morning she went down to the village. She was smiling to herself, and the burden of her old age seemed to have grown lighter ; and as she walked along, she talked to herself.

" The dead do not care about red cheeks and a light step," she said ; " they only ask for a little warmth, but the young ones do not think of that !   Where would the souls of the departed find a refuge from the boundless cold of Death, if the old ones here on earth did not throw open their hearts to them ? "

She bought a big bundle of candles at the general shop in the village, and ordered a cartload of firewood from a peasant, but in order to pay for all this, she had to take back double as much flax as usual to spin.

Towards evening, when she was back in her cottage, she repeated many prayers, and endeavoured to keep up her courage by singing hymns, but in spite of this, it sank lower and lower.   However, this did not prevent her from doing what she had set her heart on doing. She made up her bed in the inner room of the cottage ; in the fire-place in the outer one she placed a great armful of wood and set it alight.   She put two lighted candles in the window, and opened the outer door as wide as it would go.   Then old Agneta retired to bed.

She lay in the dark, listening.

Yes, those were certainly footsteps !

Some one seemed to be sliding down the glacier, some one who moaned and crept with halting steps around the cottage, not daring to enter.

This was more than old Agneta could bear.   She jumped out of bed, rushed into the outer room, banged the door to, and locked it. It was really too much, flesh and blood could not stand it !

She heard the sound of heavy sighing outside the cottage, and of uneven steps, as of one whose feet were sore and bleeding.   They seemed to be going farther and farther away towards the glacier. She heard the sound of sobbing too, but soon all was quiet again. And then old Agneta was terribly distressed.

" What a coward you are, you old duffer," she said, apostrophis-ing herself as was her wont.   " The fire will go out, and the candles that cost such a lot too.   Is everything to be wasted just because you are a miserable coward ? "

She left her bed once again, and, with her body shaking, and her teeth chattering with fear, went into the outer room and opened wide the cottage door.   Then she lay down again and waited.

She was not afraid now.   She was only fearful that she might have frightened the wanderers away, and that they would not attempt to come back.

And then she began to call them in the dark, just as she used to call when she was out with her flock of sheep as a girl.

" My little white lambs in the mountains, come down from the heights ; come, little lambs, come, come, come ! "

Then it was as if a mighty wind rushed down from the mountain-top, right into the cottage.

The old woman heard no footsteps, nor any sighing, only the shriek of the wind as it entered her dwelling. But she thought she heard some one whispering, " Hush, hush, do not frighten them ! "

She felt, without seeing it, that the outer room was packed to overflowing, and that the walls were well-nigh giving way under the pressure. And then old Agneta became happy and contented, and, folding her hands, she fell asleep.

When the morning came, she thought it was all a dream, for everything was as usual in the outer room. The fire had burned itself out, the candles likewise. There was not even so much as a drop of tallow left in the candlesticks.

.   .   .   .

As long as she lived, old Agneta continued to care for the dead in this way. She worked hard at her spinning all through the day, in order to be able to have a fire burning in the outer room every night.

And she was happy, for she knew that some one needed her.

There came a Sunday when she was not in her usual place in church. Some men from the village went up to her cottage to see if anything was the matter. They found her already dead, so they took the corpse with them back to the village for burial.

Very few people followed old Agneta to the grave on the following Sunday. And those who *were* there did not look at all sorrowful. But suddenly, just as the coffin was about to be lowered, a tall, grave-faced monk appeared in the cemetery, and, standing still, he pointed to the snow-clad mountain above. And they who stood by the grave saw the whole mountain bathed in a rose-coloured radiance and right across it they saw a procession of tiny yellow flames, like those of burning candles, winding along. And there were as many of these tiny yellow flames as there had been candles bought by the dead woman for the unhappy wanderers on the glacier.

Then the people said, " Praise be to God ! For she, who had none to mourn her down here, succeeded in finding friends up there in the great solitude of the mountains ! "

HATTO, THE HERMIT

Selma Lagerlöf

HATTO, the hermit, stood in the desert and prayed to God. The storm was on, and his long hair and beard blew about him as wind-whipped grass blows about an old ruin. But he did not brush back the hair from his eyes, nor did he fasten his long beard to his girdle, for his arms were raised in prayer. Since sunrise he had held his gaunt, hairy arms outstretched toward heaven, as untiring as a tree stretching out its boughs, and thus he would remain until evening. It was a great thing for which he was praying.

He was a man who had suffered much from the wickedness and dishonesty of the world. He himself had persecuted and tortured others, and persecution and torture had been his portion, more than he could endure. Therefore he had gone forth into the wilderness, had digged himself a cave on the river bank, and had become a holy man whose prayers found hearing at the throne of God.

Hatto, the hermit, stood on the river bank before his cave and prayed the great prayer of his life. He prayed God to send down the Day of Judgment upon this wicked world. He cried to the angels of the trumpets, who are to herald the end of the reign of sin. He prayed for the waves of the sea of blood, in which all injustice should be overwhelmed. He prayed for a pestilence that should fill the churchyard with rotting heaps of corpses.

Round about him was the wilderness, barren and desolate. But a little farther up the bank stood an old willow with shortened trunk, which swelled out at the top to a round hump, like a queer head, and from it new, freshly-green twigs were sprouting. Every autumn the peasants from the unwooded flatlands robbed the willow of her fresh new shoots. But every year the tree put forth new ones, and on stormy days the slender, flexible twigs whipped about the old willow as hair and beard whipped about Hatto, the hermit.

It was just on this day that a pair of water thrushes, who usually built their nest on the trunk of the old willow between the new twigs, had decided to begin their work. But the wild whipping of the twigs disturbed the birds. They flew up with their bits of dried grass and root fibres and had to turn away with nothing accomplished. Then it was that they caught sight of old Hatto.

No one now living can picture to himself how moss-grown and dried-up, how gnarled and black and generally unlike a human being such an old desert hermit can become. His skin clung so close to forehead and cheekbones that his head looked like a skull, and only a tiny gleam down in the depths of his eyeballs showed that there was still life in him. The dried-up muscles gave no curve to the body ; the outstretched naked arm was merely a couple of narrow bones, covered with hard, wrinkled, bark-like skin. He wore an old, black cloak, clinging close to his body. He was tanned brown by the sun and black with dirt. His hair and beard alone were of a lighter shade, for rain and sunshine had faded them to the grey-green hue of the under side of willow leaves.

The birds, flying about uneasily and seeking a place for their nest, took Hatto, the hermit, to be another old willow, cut off by axe and saw in its heavenward striving. They flew about him many times, flew away and returned again, took note of the guide-posts on the way to him, calculated his position in regard to protection from storm and birds of prey, found it rather unfavourable, but decided to build there on account of the close vicinity of the stream and the reeds, their chief source of supply. One of the birds shot down suddenly and laid a bit of grass in the hermit's outstretched hand.

The storm had abated a little, so that the straw was not blown from his hand at once, but the hermit did not pause in his prayer. " Come soon, Lord, come to destroy this world of sin, that mankind may not still more increase its load of guilt. Release those still unborn from the burden of life ! For the living there is no salvation."

The storm roared out again, and the bit of grass fluttered out of the hermit's great, bony hand. But the birds came again and endeavoured to erect the corner-stone of their new home between his fingers. Suddenly a dirty, clumsy thumb laid itself over the grass spears and held them in firm position, while four fingers arched over the palm, making a peaceful niche where a nest would be safe. The hermit continued his untiring supplications, and before his eyes danced fever visions of the Day of Judgment. The earth trembled, the skies shot fire. He saw black clouds of hurrying birds beneath the glowing firmament ; herds of fleeing animals spread over the earth. But while his soul was filled with these visions of fever, his eyes began to watch the flight of the tiny birds that came and went with lightning dashes, laying new straws in the nest with little chirps of pleasure.

The old man did not move. He had made a vow to stand the entire day with outstretched arms, in order to force God to hear him. As his body grew weaker the visions in his brain took on more vivid form and colour. He heard the walls of the cities falling and the

crash of tumbling houses. Crowds of people fled in screaming terror
before him, and behind them came the Angels of Vengeance and of
Destruction, tall figures in silver harness with stern, beautiful faces,
riding on night-black horses and swinging scourges of braided white
lightning.

The little thrushes built and built busily all the day, and their
work progressed finely. There was no lack of material in this
wilderness of rolling ground with stiff grass and brush, and on the
river bank, with its reeds and rushes. They could not take time for
dinner or supper. They flew back and forth, glowing with interest
and pleasure, and when dusk came they had reached the peak of
their roof.

But before evening fell the hermit's eyes had come to rest on their
labour more and more. He watched them in their flight ; he scolded
them when they were clumsy ; he grieved when the wind spoiled
their efforts, and he became almost angry when they stopped a
moment to rest. Then the sun sank and the birds sought their
accustomed resting-place among the reeds—safe from all harm, for
no enemy could approach without a warning splash of the water or a
quivering of the reeds.

When morning broke the thrushes thought at first that the events
of the preceding day had been but a beautiful dream.

They found their guide-posts and flew straight to their nest ; but
the nest had disappeared. They peered out over the moors and flew
high up to gain a wider view. But there was no sign of nest or tree.
Finally they sat down on a stone by the water and thought the
matter over. They wagged their tails and turned their heads to
right and left. Where were nest and tree ?

But scarcely had the sun raised itself a hand's breadth over the
belt of woods beyond the stream when their tree suddenly came
wandering up and stood itself upon the self-same place it had occu-
pied the day before. It was as black and as gnarled as before, and it
carried their nest on the tip of something that was probably a thin,
upright bough.

The birds began to build again, without attempting to ponder
further over the many miracles of nature.

Hatto, the hermit, who chased the little children from his cave and
told them that it were better for them if they had never seen the light
of day ; he who waded out deep into the mud of the river to hurl
curses after the flagged boats filled with gay young people rowing
past ; he from whose evil glance the shepherds carefully guarded their
flocks ; he did not return to his place on the river bank because of
thought for the little birds. But he knew that not only every letter
in the Holy Book has its own mystical meaning, but that everything that God allows to happen in the natural world has its signifi-
cance also. And he had discovered what it might mean, this sign

of the birds building in his hand : God had willed that he should
stand with outstretched arm until the birds had raised their young
—could he do this, then would his prayer be heard.

But on this day the visions of the Last Judgment came to him less
and less. Instead, his glance followed the motions of the birds with
greater attention. He saw the rapid completion of the nest. The
tiny builders flew around it and examined it carefully. They
brought a few rags of moss from the real willow and plastered them
on the outside as a finishing decoration. They brought the softest
young grass, and the female bird pulled the down from her breast to
furnish the inside.

The peasants of the neighbourhood, who feared the evil power
which the prayers of the hermit might have with God, were used to
bring him bread and milk to soften his anger. They came now and
found him standing motionless, the bird's nest in his hand.

" See how the holy man loves the little creatures," they said, and
feared him no longer. They raised the milk can to his lips, and fed
him with the bread. When he had eaten and drunk he drove them
away with curses, but they smiled at his anger.

His body had long since become the servant of his will. He had
taught it obedience by hunger and scourge, by days of kneelings and
sleepless nights. Now his muscles of steel held his arms outstretched
days and weeks, and, while the mother bird sat on her eggs and did
not leave the nest, he would not go to his cave, even to sleep at night.
He learned how to sleep standing, with outstretched arms.

He grew accustomed to the two uneasy little eyes that peered
down at him over the edge of the nest. He watched for rain and
hail and protected the nest as well as he could.

One day the little mother left her place. Both thrushes sat on the
edge of the nest, their tails moving rapidly, holding great consulta-
tion and looking very happy, although the whole nest seemed filled
with a frightened squeaking. After a little they set out upon an
energetic gnat-hunt. One gnat after another fell before them and
was brought home to that which squeaked and peeped up there in
his hand. And the peeping grew more intense whenever the food
was brought in. It disturbed the holy man at his prayers. Gently,
very gently, his arm sank down on joints that had almost lost the
power of motion, until his deep-set, glowing eyes peered into the
nest.

Never had he seen anything so ugly and so miserable—naked little
bodies, with a few scattered down-tufts, no eyes, no strength to fly,
nothing but six great open beaks.

He could not understand it himself, but he liked them just as they
were. He had not thought to make an exception of the old birds in
his prayers for the great Doom, but when he now implored God
to release the world through utter destruction, he made a silent

exception in favour of these six little helpless creatures.

When the peasant women brought him food he no longer rewarded them with curses.   As he was necessary for the little ones up there in his hand, he was glad that the people did not let him starve.

Soon six little round heads peered all day over the edge of the nest.   Old Hatto's arm sank to the level of his eyes more and more frequently.   He saw the feathers grow out of the red skin ; he saw the eyes open and the little bodies round out.   The fortunate inheritors of all the beauty with which nature endows the feathered denizens of the air came early into their heritage.

And meanwhile the prayers for the great destruction came more and more slowly from Hatto's lips.   He believed he had God's promise that it should come as soon as the little birds were able to fly.   And now he stood there, seeking an escape from God.   For he could not sacrifice these six little ones, whom he had watched and cared for.

It had been different before, when he had had nothing of his own to care for.   Love of the small and the helpless—that love which every little child must teach to the dangerous grown man—this love came over him and made him hesitate.

Sometimes he wished that he could throw the entire nest into the stream, for he still believed that those alone are to be envied who die without having known care or sin.   Was it not his duty to save these little ones from beasts of prey, from cold and hunger and all the many ills of life ?   But as he was pondering on this a hawk swooped down on the nest to kill the little ones.   Hatto caught the robber in his left hand, whirled him around his head and threw him far out into the stream.

Then came the day when the little ones were ready to fly.   One of the old birds sat inside the nest, trying to push the young ones out on to the edge, while the other flew about and showed them how easy it was if they would only try.   But as the young ones would not overcome their fear, both old birds flew out before them, showing off all their prettiest arts and tricks.   They turned and twisted in the air, they shot up straight as does the lark, or they hung motionless on rapidly fluttering wings.

But the little ones would not move, and then Hatto decided to interfere in the matter himself.   He gave them a careful push with one finger, and thus ended the dispute.   They tumble out, trembling and uncertain, hitting at the air as bats do ; they sink down, but rise up again, they find the proper motion and use it at once to regain the nest.   The old birds come back to them in happy pride, and Hatto chuckles.

It was he who had brought the matter to such a happy conclusion. And now he pondered most seriously the question as to whether a loophole of escape could be found for God.

Perhaps, when one comes to think of it, perhaps God holds this earth like a bird's nest in His right hand, and perhaps He loves those within it—all the helpless children of earth. Perhaps He is merciful to them whom He had vowed to destroy, just as the hermit was merciful to the little birds. Of course, the hermit's birds were much better than God's human beings, but he could still understand that God might have pity for them in His heart.

Next day the nest was empty, and the bitterness of loneliness came over the hermit. His arm sank slowly down at his side, and it seemed to him that all nature held its breath to hear the roar of the trumpets announcing the Last Judgment. But in the same moment all the birds returned and settled down on his head and shoulders, for they had no fear of him. And a light shot through the tortured brain of the old hermit. He had lowered his arm every day to look at the birds !

And then, as he stood there, the six young birds flying about him, he nodded, smiling, to some one whom he could not see.

" Thou art free," he said, " Thou art free. I did not keep my vow, therefore Thou need'st not keep Thine."

And it seemed to him that the hills ceased from trembling and that the river sank quietly into its bed to rest.

VERNER VON HEIDENSTAM

SWEDISH

B. 1859

THE LION'S CAGE

NUM EDDAULA was head of the Brotherhood of The Truthtellers. The brethren, who were either merchants or learned interpreters of the most ancient writings, lived apart in their homes, but once every year, at the first new moon after the Feast of Beiram, they assembled by night in a distant mountain gorge, clothed in white garments and carrying torches.

One night, when Num Eddaula was returning from one of these annual assemblies, he said to the servant who carried his torch :

" We have just taken the oath of our Brotherhood to speak the truth in every case except one, namely, the one in which it is a question of our own good deeds. For these we are to keep secret, even at the cost of a lie, and we are to make it our aim to die forgotten. What reflects the calm grandeur of Eternity more beautifully than Oblivion ?

" There is no more beautiful spot on the whole Earth than a forgotten grave ! There the grass whispers differently from other places. The twittering of the birds has a different note in it. Hearken to me, my friend ! The Sultan is so enraged with The Truthtellers, because of their outspokenness, that he has sworn to exterminate them with the sword, unless I pay the penalty with my head ; and I am easily recognised by the star-shaped birthmark near my eye. I myself will carry mine own head to the Sultan. But a good deed is one no longer when it is commended. Were the Brethren to suspect my intention, they would bind me hand and foot and hide me, and defend me to the uttermost.

" Therefore shalt thou follow me secretly, and when I have suffered, thou shalt bury my body in some unknown spot ; after which thou shalt noise it abroad that I was overpowered and taken, when I was trying to escape."

As soon as it was light the servant threw down the torch, and they descended to the flowery field by the Castle of Timurtasch, where the Sultan's pleasure camp was situated.

Num Eddaula was bewildered at the sight of all the splendour.

78

He listened eagerly to the words of a slave who told him that the Swedish king lived in the castle, half prisoner and half guest of honour, surrounded by his little band of warriors.

"Let us go to him," he said to his servant, "for I am weak, and the sight of a hero will endow me with strength. And my tired old eyes will gladly close for ever when they have seen him."

They went through the garden, where the summer sun shone through the leaves of fig and mulberry trees. When they reached the castle steps they met some Turks who had been to look at the king, and among these they saw the Sultan himself disguised as a janissary.

Num Eddaula squeezed himself close against the wall and pulled his hair over the birthmark near his eye, but he felt on his wrist the breath from the mouth which that very same evening would pronounce his death sentence! A hero, he *must* see a hero, or his courage would begin to waver.

A door was opened. He took a few hasty steps forward and bent down, and gazing through a hole in a screen he beheld the King. . . . The spacious chamber, the carpets of which had often been trod by the feet of the Sultan's dancing-girls, was so lavishly decorated with many-coloured arabesques that Num Eddaula thought he was looking into a bower, where enchanted spiders had spun their golden webs between flowers and creeping vines.

Against the farthest wall a narrow camp bedstead was placed, and on it lay the King. Without soldiers and without power, he was nevertheless still the absolute Ruler over a distant kingdom, yet he did not even possess sufficient money to pay for the gifts that were indispensable would one have an interview with the Sultan.

He could not humble himself in the presence of the foreign ambassadors, and present himself before the Sultan as a defeated and destitute fugitive. He blushed at appearing to his lackeys and grooms as a disarmed prisoner, obliged to submit to the will of another, however often and however eagerly it was repeated that, whatever happened, it was always in accordance with his gracious commands.

It was because of this that he had retired to his bed, although it was not health he lacked, but money; and had remained there month after month, refusing even to put his foot to the ground, and having himself carried to a couch in a sheet, when the bed had to be remade. His two physicians-in-ordinary, Skraggenstjerna and Neuman, noticed with alarm that his limbs were growing stiff and paralysed like a fakir's, who, in order to glorify his Maker, remains seated on a rubbish-heap in the same position for a lengthened period of time!

In vain they begged him to leave his bed at least once every twenty-four hours, and walk a few steps on the carpet!

To Num Eddaula it seemed that he beheld one of the holy men who, seated beneath some shady oak tree or on the sunny side of some remote " turba," received respectful greetings from the passers-by.

Between his fits of coughing, Professor Eneman, who suffered from weak lungs, had just finished an account of his travels.   Out of two bottles he had brought with him, he extracted some young crocodiles, and while they were being burned alive on a heap of glowing coals placed on a brass tray before the bed, he showed how they threw out green and black venom.

The King rested his arm on the pillows and looked down on the writhing reptiles.   " I wonder if one could kill a full-grown crocodile with a sword," he said ; " one can do anything, if only one has the will."

Chancellor von Müllern, whose clothes were very shabby, and who had just begun to act as head-cook, there being no one else, passed his hand over the faded skirts of his coat with a simper.

" Can one also, if one only have the will, make curd-cake without eggs or cream ? " he asked.

" One can get that which is required . . . if necessary, with the sword," answered the King.

Grothusen sniffed and drummed with his fingers on his gold-laced hat ; then, addressing himself to Müllern, he said in a low voice : " If the worst comes, one can get the needful by paying 40 per cent."

" Of what do they speak that they appear so light-hearted," asked Num Eddaula of a lackey who stood near, but the man looked confused and answered at random : " They are talking about one of the most beautiful passages in the Gospels,"—saying which he slipped on the polished floor and knocked aside the screen, disclosing as he did so the presence of Num Eddaula to the King, who, as soon as he caught sight of the venerable old man, beckoned to him to come nearer, and ordered Grothusen to act as Master of Ceremonies.

" Thou art of a surety a wise man," said the King.   " Wouldst thou have the courage to stand where the bullets whistle through the air ? "

Num Eddaula's head drooped, and he stroked the white beard which reached to his waist reflectively.

" I belong to the Truthtellers' Brotherhood," he replied, " and may not credit myself with any virtues, but answer me this, thou who art a hero !

" If thy earliest teachers had said to thee, ' Thou shalt not kill, not even the cruellest and most loathsome of reptiles ! ' . . .   If the great ones who surround thee, and all the people were to say to thee every morning, ' Thou shalt not kill, for to take life is a sin. Remain in they kingdom and watch over the harvests, although by so doing thou reapest no applause.'—Hast thou the courage to do this? Hast thou the courage to humble thyself in adversity and confess thyself beaten, and to forgive thine enemies? "

The King's brow contracted, and he frowned. " But ought not a good soldier rather to resist to the end? " he asked.

" Thou who hatest lies and who wouldst never let others make thee out to be more perfect than thou wast," said Num Eddaula in reply, " lofty and noble is thy brow, and large thine eyes ; but there are ugly lines around thy tightly-closed lips. They appear to be smiling, but it is not so. It is something very different ! They tempt God. They say that *thy* will is His. Thou broughtest thy people together and they were beaten in the fight. When God has vanquished a people, He rolls a heavy piece of rock over the grave, and ordains silence. He wishes to see once again yellow fields and playing children. But thou continuest the strife alone—and against Him.

" All witnesses to the truth, all they who endure, and all those who are humble in adversity and proud in misfortune, all these came forth to see thee, but now they have turned away from thee.

" Maybe there have been many great men and kings born of thy people, but was ever one of these more fitted to be a soldier of light than thou wast from the very beginning ? But thou fearedst oblivion. A star should have been lighted and remained burning on thy grave for a thousand years ! But misfortune overtook thee, for God desired the overthrow of thyself and they people.

" And now complete thy work as a hero ! Put aside vain applause as thou hast put aside wine and women ! Do it humbly or proudly, which thou canst ! Go forth and seat thyself with those who are vanquished and destitute. Thou hast command over they features ; have command also over thyself. Thou art capable of better things than those thou hast accomplished, and God never forgives a hero for acting thus.

" Never did He lift up in His right hand a brighter jewel than thou, and never did He in His wrath cast a work of His creation into such depths of darkness . . . and for this cause do I love thee—for I am but a mortal man. No man have I loved as I love thee. But be on thy guard ; there are others who love thee and who are more dangerous than the worst enemies and slanderers."

" And which are these ? "

" The fools ! They have noticed the lines round thy mouth and have interpreted their meaning in their own fashion.

" The fools do not turn away from thee. They cling tightly to thy garments. They need a ' fool-hero,' an arch-fool, crowned with laurel wreaths, and they will elect thee with shouts of joy.

" The fools will not care about thy character—they like not human beings ! They resemble the little monkeys in the palm grove at Hidjas, squatting on the stone gods and eating dates in the sunshine ; as soon as they hear a human being's footstep, they begin to jump from branch to branch, screaming shrilly while they give chase.

" O King, thou fearest not death ! God will stretch out His hand and give it thee one day in pity, when He remembers how thy boyish hand wielded the sword of the Cherubims. His vengeance will strike deeper still. He will give thee to the fools."

" Thou goest far in thine outspokenness."

" I would only probe the depths of thy courage, seeing that thou art a hero. Hast thou the courage to die forgotten ? "

The King's brow contracted still more as he sought for an answer. He sat crosswise on the bed with the coverlet wrapped tightly round his legs and feet.

Num Eddaula crossed his hands on his breast and bowed himself.

" There remaineth therefore much for which thou lackest courage," he said.

Grothusen smote the brass tray with his bat.

" Thou who art a Truth-teller . . . who can say whether thou dost not glory in thy humility ? Who can say that to die remembered does not demand courage too ? "

Num Eddaula closed his eyes and his thin fingers clutched the empty air around him as if in agony.

" There spokest thou the truth, O noble one," he replied. " Fame is impure slander, impure honour ! It is a false glitter, which causes the proud man to appear humble and the humble man to appear proud. King, who read thy last thought before sleep came to thee ? Who saw thee alone and in darkness, when sleep forsook thee ? Who will one day be able to place his hand on thy bier and say, ' Such a man was he ! ' Only the fools will dare to say, ' Ask us, for he was like unto us.' When they weary of singing thy praises, they will throw stones and mock at thee and point their fingers at thy sword.

" Thy grave will be their favourite meeting-place. They will stand round it in such numbers that the wise men will not be able to approach thy mouldering bones. But this one thing I say unto thee : Shouldst thou be chosen by the fools, and in spite of this, find the courage in thyself to rise and gather round thee the wise ones, the witnesses to the Truth, the enduring ones, those who are humble in adversity and proud in misfortune—then hast thou stood the test.

" And then wilt thou be such as I would have thee."

Num Eddaula threw himself on to his knees and touched the carpet with his forehead.

" I am a weak man who has been made strong through beholding thee, O King ! I have sinned much in my life, and if I have no scars on my flesh, I have many on my soul. I wish to be forgotten, to be forgotten. And to sleep, to sleep. He who is famous is the slave of others. There is no love powerful enough to bring peace to his

ashes.   Over his grave grows a tree with strangely knotted branches,
and whose leaves murmur ceaselessly of unrest."

No one answered him. . . .

There was silence in the spacious chamber, until suddenly something fell with a clatter on to the brass tray, and the next minute the
King held out a shining coin to the white-bearded fortune-teller,
who, creeping on his knees to the bedside, pressed his face against
the sheet, but refused to take the proffered coin.

" Whether thou livest or whether thou diest," he said, " always
wilt thou be in the midst of strife.   I go to my rest."

Early on the following morning Num Eddaula was executed outside the Sultan's tent.   The certain assurance of oblivion spread a
calm over his last moments.

His servant buried the body in a lonely spot between two cypresses.

When the grave was filled in, he strewed it with maize for the
pigeons that came in hundreds from the trees and groves near by.
Very soon bushes covered with white blossoms grew up out of the
earth.   Tired soldiers and shepherds found there a shady resting-
place.   It was a sacred spot, for there slept a man who was forgotten !

PER HALLSTRÖM
B. 1866

SWEDISH

CARNEOLA

This is the story of how Raymond Lully became the man whose fame spread with paralysing power over the Christian world, and to whom travellers came from afar for the healing of their souls.

They would stand before him spellbound under the death-like calm of his gaze, but nevertheless, in spite of this, and of the awe that filled them when they sought to fathom the mystery of his life, they felt a half-contemptuous pity for his self-imposed poverty.

This is the story as it appeared to Raymond in wakeful visions of the night during the first years of his life as a recluse ; and the story still burned on the funeral-pyre of sorrow, and the colour of it was that of roses that have been caught by the flames, and its scent that of incense and black mould, and the sound was that of weeping and of breathless words—with the steel-blue sky and starlit spaces as a background. It is also the story of a woman.

Her name was Carneola, and her eyes were like fluttering black butterflies ; when she was silent, her lips remained half-open, still quivering as if with an unspoken word, a word that might have turned laughter into tears. She liked to clasp her hands when sitting still, and they showed blue-white and slender against the purple velvet of her gown.

Although it was not longer the fashion to have it so, the under-bodice of her gown fastened closely up round her beautiful throat ; and the gown itself was cut in such a way as to reveal the perfect lines of her waist and hips. It was fastened at her breast with a clasp which held a red stone, that might have been a drop of blood from the Holy Chalice when the light played upon it. Upon her head she wore a black kerchief with a gold border.

Round about her, the happy little kingdom of Majorca glowed and glittered in care-free happiness, gazing idly into the blue atmosphere through the green leaves of the trees, or dozing peacefully within high garden walls, so gleaming warm in the sunlight, that the breeze when it touched them was whirled up and scattered like smoke over their flowering crests.

In the background the round towers of the Castle stretched their

84

watchful, peak-capped heads towards the blue silk of the sea ; otherwise, it was nothing but a mass of ornamented doors and cornices which were the colour of old gold in the noonday light—a palace that a giant child might have built of glittering shells and flints while playing on the sea-shore.

Within its walls life went merrily. Zither music floated like bursting bubbles round the heads of those who whispered and laughed together. The gilded balls of the jugglers, thrown into the air and caught and thrown up again by swift hands, appeared proper time-gauges. If at times the wind waxed strong and pressed its lips against the walls, it was only to warn jestingly, " Remain inside, oh, ye children ; warm yourselves in the warmth of one another's glances ; press one another's hands ; remain where you are for ever."

There were no enemies to fight against on the islands, and no game to hunt. But like every one else, they had falcons, and these they taught to catch the bats, that when driven out of their hiding-places, and blinded by the light, flew wildly about ; or they let out pigeons and amused themselves looking at their pink feet pressed against their bodies, at their soft wings caressing the air, and the blue shadows they cast on the ground when they sought protection near the aviary.

Or one let oneself be caught in love's toils, or become ensnared by fleeting dreams, or absorbed with varied griefs and triumphs ; just as one enjoyed listening to songs that had a note of sorrow in them.

Raymond fell in love with Carneola one evening, when he was tired of the way his latest mistress walked ; for her figure never showed the harmonious lines that embody all the expectant happiness of nature and carve it out against the golden sky beneath the careless folds of a garment.

But Carneola stood leaning against a balustrade ; and from where Raymond sat, a little way from her feet, he could see her cheek with its amber shadows, and the graceful folds of the kerchief on her head, sharply outlined against the orange and green of the sunset sky, and he could not understand how it was he had ever looked at anything else than the dark head-covering where the gold embroidery gleamed dully like the golden border on the velvety wings of a butterfly.

Black butterflies ! Ah, now he understood the expression in her eyes ! Longing ? It was too deep for that ! Sorrow ? She had never complained. Maybe it was only a feeling of loneliness, and the consciousness that, amongst all this crowd of weak-winged creatures around her, there was not one who could follow her soul in its flight over the purple sea of passion. Raymond knew that he could do so. He was made of different stuff from those others with whom he had played for a short while ; and he pressed his clenched hand against the warm earth, and vowed to himself that,

with this woman at his side, he would attain the uttermost limits of
bliss.

She was young, and her husband had been dead several years.
People did not understand why she still wore a widow's veil, for she
could not have loved him so intensely.   Neither could they understand the reserved expression in her eyes, for there where the
laughter was loudest and the play merriest, her voice would always
be heard, but with a break in its tones as if she was listening for an
echo of them with her inward ear.

Some said she was trying to stifle her conscience with silken ribbons—but what could have troubled her conscience ?

At confession the priest's blessing followed as rapidly on the
rustling of her dress when she knelt down as the myrtle lifts itself
after the wind has passed, and no one had ever seen a guilty blush
on her cheek, or the curl of jealousy on her lip.

But Raymond thought he had solved the problem.   It was love
she was waiting for, a great love, like the winged flight of two
spirits through air that grew brighter and more buoyant every
moment—like the drinking of two red mouths side by side, out of
the capacious cup of happiness ! And with his cheek close pressed
against her black veil, he offered her his faith and strength ; what she
sought was not unattainable, it was close at hand.

" Love is the miracle," he said ; " only believe, and it is there in
all its inexplicable greatness, bending over you.   Only believe and
your feet shall tread more lightly even than they do now, for there
are wings already folded up in your little pointed shoes.   Only
believe, and all that you desire in a man will be born in me ; already
I hear the sighing of the palm-trees over our heads."

She lifted her folded hands a little, so that her fingers touched the
clasp on her breast, and shook her head gently.   " But there is
Death," she said.

" Is that quite certain," he replied, " for us, as we are now ? If
we love, death does not exist for us.   It lies, together with sorrow,
deep under our feet, as far away as a vanished dream, in a world
of unrealities."

Then a light came into Carneola's eyes and the red stone at her
breast cast a glow over her hand ; it was as if the mystery had been
revealed to her inner self, as if the darkness had been waveringly
illuminated by lightning.   Then it passed, and she clasped her
hands again desperately, as if in pain.

" I did believe in the miracle," she whispered, " but my eyes were
drawn towards the wounds instead of the glory, and I can only see
that *they* are real."

And Raymond did not dare seize hold of her hand, although, with
a feeling of joy not unmixed with pain, he realised that she was his,
that she believed in him, if she did not believe in love, and that it was

just this made her suffering more intense. He did not grieve, but only sought to follow her thoughts, sought impatiently but with the sure conviction that he would succeed, and it was only when the sun was shining in on to his bed in the morning that sleep came to him, and he slumbered on happily, with an eventful day to look forward to.

One night there was an entertainment at the castle, and they danced the torch-dance. It was dark where the musicians were placed, and it was as if the music had materialised and fluttered bodily towards the swaying light of the torches.

The wavering brightness of the violins and the strong beating of wings of the brass instruments, the stimulating melancholy of the flutes and the stern voice of the drum, all seemed to have hurried to join the dancers, and to be crying: " Fly, fly! At any moment the draught may put out the flame. This is a world of change, of sorrow, and of longing, but we lift the curtain to another world, to that of love. Come, fly with us; fly."

Just before, there had been a blaze of light from a hundred wax candles; now only a flickering red light played on flushed cheeks, and the growing shadows darkened the gleam in shining eyes.

The hands of Raymond and Carneola joined in a firm clasp each time they met in the dance, and they loosened their hold almost fearfully; for their hearts were fuller than ever of happiness, and they felt that this game dispersed all hindering thoughts, and joined them together like two frightened children in the dark, who would be ready to welcome the light afterwards with smiling eyes. Before the music had entirely ceased, and while the lights were being brought in, Carneola whispered a reply to Raymond's question, " Yes, take me! Never to part again! Let us fly from here!"

In the clearer light he saw that her eyes were shining with happiness, her lips trembling with expectation, as if she had been filled with exaltation; yet at the same time it seemed as though despair still chained her feet.

He left her and wandered about the passages and rooms, with his blood keeping time to the music and his mind full of flaming lights. Then his keen hearing recognised her step on the stairs and he caught her up as she reached her room.

A *prie-dieu* was placed before the image of a saint, the red folds of whose draperies were lighted by the rays from a lamp. Otherwise, no light was there but that of the moon shining through the window of stained glass. He laid his head down in Carneola's lap and gave voice to his exultant thoughts—the miracle, the miracle! He pressed her hands against his eyes and clasped her slender form in his arms. " Now all your hesitation is ended and done away with!" he said.

Carneola bent over him until her lips almost touched his hair. " Yes, even if death were near us. Are you sure of your miracle?"

Raymond looked up and shivered at the question, but her love rushed over him with intoxicating power. " Yes," he said firmly ; " love is all ; everything else is but illusion. Love is happiness : the same arm encircles both. Everything else is outside, and can never come inside."

Carneola pressed a burning kiss on his forehead, then disengaged herself from his embrace, and approached the lamp with unsteady steps.

She had thought until she was dizzy. She sang to the accompaniment of the music that still sounded temptingly in the distance. She mumbled incomprehensible words. Then she lifted her trembling hands to her breast and loosened the clasp with the red stone in it.

" I believe in the miracle ; I believe in the miracle ! " she murmured. Her voice was faint like the ring of thin glass. She pushed aside the garments from her neck and breast and looked down as if expecting to see something that would cause her inexpressible and infinite relief. Then, suddenly, her face grew rigid, rigid with the desolation of despair, and her eyes were full of a sorrow that is without hope.

" Look," she said ; " see what I carry about with me."

And Raymond looked and saw something Terrible, and he felt his mind grow as empty as were the depths under his feet ; grief, horror, an immense bitterness and a sickening feeling of disgust all combined to overwhelm him, and he felt near to swoon ; but through it all he heard her voice still speaking :

" I saw it coming several years ago," she said. " I have cradled death in my arms ; I have tried to get rid of him, flee from him ; I have prayed to God for a miracle ; I have tried to forget it out there, laughing and playing with the others. But it only penetrated further and further in ; I felt it and saw it all the time. I loved you, love you still. I thought, I didn't know—I thought a miracle happened just now. God is love, they say, and I thought—do you believe in miracles now, Raymond ? "

Raymond bowed his head ; he was oppressed by a desire to weep, by pity and by something cold as well that terrified him.

" Our God is a God of sorrow, Carneola," he replied.

She spoke in the wailing voice of a frightened child :

" I knew that before, have always known it, and have fled from Him. I have played like others, repeated their words, but it was only a dream, and this is reality. Do they not all bear such wounds, and is it not for that reason that they play like that ? Hark ! there is some one crying at the door."

Raymond did not dare to look up ; she came close up to him and moaned like a starving creature.

" Can you stay with me all the same," she said ; " can you love me ? I have longed for your love, and I shall not die just yet. I am afraid of solitude, and I was so happy a few moments ago. I cannot live without love."

But Raymond was powerless to revive the feeling that now lay trampled underfoot by an inexorable Fate. When, as a child, he had chanced to find a wounded bird, he had felt the same thing, although in a lesser degree, and he had always given it the *coup de grâce* as quickly as possible.

" I can weep with you," he said gently.

His tone brought her to herself with a shock, as of cold steel on her aching brow. She covered up her breast, and went towards the door, signing to him to follow.

" Farewell ! " she said, and it was with something of her former pride that she now gave him her hand to kiss, and the power in her glance held his, while he caught a brief glimpse of regions that were vaster and darker than any he had ever imagined before.

They smiled sadly at each other as the music floated up to them from below, and it was thus, with a sad smile on her trembling lips and her black butterfly eyes drowned in sorrow, that Carneola always appeared to Raymond in after years, whenever he chanced to hear her name mentioned, or whenever the thought of a woman dwelt in his mind.

He never saw her again, or made inquiries regarding her fate. That same night he left the glimmering lights of Majorca behind him, and steered his course towards the steel-blue sea. He understood everything, all the treachery that lies hidden in happiness and beauty ; he had desired to embrace Life, and he had found that it was but a shadow, and his pain was great in consequence.

The voice of pain was Truth's voice. It was a divine voice, and it alone never lied. And was it not only the fright inspired by mythical legends that caused her to be shunned ? Was not all the beauty of the world embodied in her ?

Pain was the drop sprinkled on the breast of Nature in order to wean the children from it, that, thirsty, they should turn to spiritual sources and prepare themselves for the life eternal. It were vain to seek for love or mercy on this earth, to try to turn the cry of a human heart into a divine promise !

When a young bird stretches its downy head out over the edge of the nest, and sees that underneath the blue arch, which was all it had hitherto known, there lies an earth all ablaze with light, it does not know that the hawk that is destined one day to silence its frightened chirp is at that moment breaking out of its shell !

When the youth looks down from the pure heights of his boyish dreams on to the alluring world, then is put in movement the misfortune that will strike his forehead as it had been a stone from a sling. For the chain of events reaches very far back, and the black threads of Sorrow have intertwined themselves with the coloured ones spun by Fate ever since the beginning, and the exact moment when the black threads should intertwine with the coloured ones was also determined from the beginning of all things.

But outside is God, Truth, where all desire and all hope are extinguished as sparks by the water, and the soul knows itself, for its greatness is enclosed in the Universe.

And Raymond retired within the walls of a monastery, and devoted himself to the reading of books, and to the conversation of holy men, for he wanted to discover whether any one else had understood this, but he avoided the churches whose arches reared on high like outstretched arms, and whose songs of praise were full of feverish longings.

And though Raymond spoke little, he was always ready to give help where it was needed ; and if he never prayed, all men knew that God was with him.

THE LION

PER HALLSTRÖM

AN Emir of the island of Gelbes, near Tunis, had presented the people of Florence with a handsome, full-grown lion ; he did this, either in the hope of obtaining some service in return for the gift, or as a mark of sympathy for Pisa's enemy.

When it arrived, large crowds of people streamed out through the San Frediano gate to meet it, and, drawn by white oxen that snorted in a vague terror and hastened their slow steps, the desert king entered the town through rows of people in holiday garb who hailed him with cries of joy and a waving of caps, while the air seemed as if it would bubble over with the clang of the bells.

The animal paced the floor of its cage with nervous steps that revealed the bluish claws, but it held its head proudly still, and looked disdainfully upon the people and upon all that was incomprehensible around it.

The inhabitants of Florence had never seen a lion before, and they were filled with joy and pride over their new possession.

It seemed to all that it was a very conqueror they were bringing in to their town, and all hearts swelled with the same defiance for the envy of their enemies, both those of the nobles in their stone nests which were even now threatened with destruction, and those of the burghers, who were conscious of a strength and desire for liberty that grew stronger day by day.

On the Piazza San Giovanni, behind the octagonal church which, as yet, possessed neither its marble walls nor its Paradise doors, a strong enclosure had been built. Here they put the lion, and after they had gazed their fill at it, the people went back to their homes, leaving it there, with its eyes shining like big, yellow sparks in the darkness.

   .   .   .   .

As a rule it lay immovable on the floor of the cage, with head erect, and calm, wide-open eyes. It appeared unconscious of its surroundings, and seemed to be seeking in dreamland a wider horizon and a more brilliant sun.

The busy life of the Piazza, the cries of admiration, or the impertinent remarks of the curious, only caused the sinews of its paws to twitch, or the muscles of its hind legs to contract as if for a spring, but almost immediately they would relax, without a hair of its bushy mane having moved, or its eyes having quitted for one instant their far-off vision. The food that was brought to it, it would leave untouched for hours at a time without even glancing at it, and then, when it was dark, devour it with a roar that caused children to wake from their sleep in fright, and even horses to break loose in their stables; sometimes, too, it would purr loudly while feeding, as if to deceive itself with an illusion of freedom.

   .   .   .   .

The lion became the idol of the Florentines, and, at the same time, a kind of symbol of future grandeur for their town. They brought it captive wolves, the armorial beasts of their arch-enemy Sienna, and rejoiced when they whined with terror like beaten pups, and took their death-blow without an effort of resistance.

But the lion never touched the dead bodies of the wolves, and after it had killed them would sit as immovable and proudly disdainful as before.

One day the guardian, in a moment of carelessness, left the door of the cage imperfectly closed. Slowly, without a gleam in its yellow eyes changing, the lion arose from its dreaming, and demolishing the remaining obstacles with a stroke of its paw, calmly, as if it could have done so any time but had disdained to, it strode out on to the Piazza, with head erect and far-away gaze, free once more.

Then a terror, worse than any that had gone before, spread with almost supernatural rapidity through the town.

As when a sudden gust of wind swoops down, and, whirling a thousand objects into the air, drives all before it in wild confusion, so did the terror sweep over the Piazza. No one turned to look back, for all, beasts and men alike, felt its awful nearness.

With a tramp of flying feet and clatter of hoofs the Piazza was swept clear ; the neighbouring streets were filled as with a human flood, and every man sought his own dwelling and only felt secure when within its walls. Voices that hardly dared make themselves heard wailed at doors, hands knocked on wooden panels until the blood came, windows and doors were shut, bolts were pushed, and indoors there was a terrified counting to see if any of the members of the family were missing.

In ever-widening circles the noise spread over the town, but in the centre, just where it began, there reigned a horrible, strained silence, as if the Piazza had been suddenly turned into a desert. Farther and farther it went, this silence, doubly fearsome after the noise, and through it, still dreaming as if amid the quiet of desert sands, walked the lion. As usual, his gaze glided past all that was strange and unknown, to seek something that was far away.

People peeped from the top window of their houses in doubtful timidity, having weapons in their hands, but being most of them uncertain as to their right to use them against the pride of the town ; others threw their javelins, but the lion did not turn its head ; it just walked on past where the steel rattled harmlessly against the paving stones. . . .

There was no church at Orto San Michele in those days, only a bit of green meadow with a few bushes, a little chapel to the Virgin Mary, and a statue of the Archangel Michael. During the various revolutions it had been used as a place of execution for the stiff-necked Florentine nobles ; now it was the children's playground.

They had not noticed the noise made by the flying people. On the outskirts of the " Orto " a few of the little ones had been swept along with the crowd in a state of dumb terror, but in the centre of the open space a little knot of them still romped in blissful ignorance.

When the lion caught sight of the green grass and bushes, it stopped and its look changed. Perhaps it thought it was nearing home, as the strange streets had come to an end, and the ground was once more soft beneath its feet ! Its big eyes left off gazing at a far-away vision, and fixed themselves upon the surrounding world.

Suddenly, one of the children spied it ; there was a scream and a wild stampede as of frightened chickens. The lion made a spring ; the little ones fled in all directions, but one of their number, a little boy, was knocked down in the confusion, and was left on the ground. The animal placed its heavy paw on the child, and lay down beside it to rest.

This little boy had a special history. His name was Orlando, and he was the son of a wool-dyer named Gherardo, who, during one of the numerous riots, had been killed by a dagger-thrust from his

enemy, the smith Pela.   His wife Sobilia was then with child, their
first, and it was when she was being told about the murder of her
husband, when despair and hatred had transformed her world into
one of darkness and confusion, that she first felt the child move
within her.   She was of a violent and excitable nature, but at this
sign she stifled her screams and did not shed a single tear, for she
took it as a promise of vengeance, and felt certain that she would
give birth to a son.

When the babe was born, not a sound of complaint passed her lips.
She lay the whole time with flushed cheeks and shining eyes, and
sometimes she would sing wild songs that had been sung 'mid the
clash of arms, and by angry, excited crowds.

The child grew to be her all-in-all.

She held herself erect in spite of her poverty, and each time she
met Pela the smith there was such a strange gleam in her eyes that
he felt constrained to turn away his own in confusion.   He sur-
mised the nature of her thoughts, but would have been ashamed to
feel any fear, even if the child had been a man, for he had many sons
and numerous male relations, and was, in any case, quite able to
defend himself.

Orlanduccio grew, and was strong and vigorous as befitted his
years.

At the time of the lion's escape Sobilia was seated at her spinning-
wheel.   Hearing the noise outside, she sprang up and rushed out,
but the people only gave her a word of warning in reply to her
questions, as they dashed past her into their houses, shutting the
doors hastily after them.   Her one thought was of her son, and she
hurried off in the wake of the fast thinning stream of people, straight
on towards the threatened danger.

" Bilia," the people cried, " Bilia, the lion has got out !   Turn
back ! " but she shook her head and hurried on a little faster than
before.

" Not that way, not that way," they called after her ; " he is in
the Orto San Michele."

As she passed Pela's house, she glanced up at the windows, as
was her custom.   There he stood, the hated one, surrounded by his
healthy, red-cheeked children, the door of his comfortable home shut
tight, and a smile of conscious security on his face.   It seemed to
Sobilia that they were all laughing at her, and she felt once again the
same anguish of heart as on the day when they brought her the news
of her husband's death ; but then, consolation was near at hand,
while now ! now !—she felt as if she could have fallen down, overcome by the powerlessness of her hatred.

At this moment, while the blood throbbed in her temples and she
gasped for breath, the thoughts which had been momentarily paralysed by anguish began to take shape in her brain, and her lips moved

rapidly. She heard herself speaking, in a strangely hoarse and horrible voice, that broke off sharply when it would have risen to a shriek.

" Maybe now, at this very minute, the beast is smashing his skull, as it did those of the wolves. If only I had been there, I could have stopped it with a shriek, I would have found breath enough for that, or scared it by a look, or waved my arms at it like this ! I have but the one—he over there has many—they stand and laugh at me. Heaven and Hell ! what will become of my revenge ? "

She was at the place now. Some one lay there, Orlanduccio of course—who else could it be ? Was he already dead or did he still live ?

In the midst of her terror she felt instinctively that she must show calmness ; otherwise she would achieve nothing ! Therefore she controlled her feelings and slackened her steps, though her hands were trembling and the blood beating in her veins with a noise as of muffled drums, while her eyes smarted with the strain of her agonised effort to see if her son still lived.

Although the child lay motionless, there trickled no red stream from under him, and the small, rounded limbs were not set in the rigidity of death. Maybe he was unhurt after all !

Now, for the first time, she caught sight of the lion, and her eyes sought those of the animal. He lay as usual, with head erect, and his gaze directed towards some far-off vision.

Was he dreaming as usual, or only thinking ? Had he looked around, and seen how all the grey nests shut him in on every side ? Had he realised how vain it was to seek a way out from among them, that the world was a different one, no longer one in which he could breathe freely—no longer *his* world, in fact ! Was it sorrow in the big, yellow eyes, or a longing for a great, golden space that ended in an illimitable blue line that glowed and sparkled, or deepened into purple or the hue of burnished copper—a world which perhaps did not possess more reality for his clouded memory than those visions of the night from which he was awakened by the cold ? Or was it pride, and pride alone ?—that kind of pride that lets everything go, and only dreams on, without even troubling to give shape to its dreams ?

The animal had not even looked at the prey that lay beneath its paw. It did not move its head at Sobilia's approach, but only gazed at her with eyes the pupils of which appeared to grow imperceptibly larger.

Sobilia began to speak to the lion :

" Give him to me," she said ; " give him to me. You don't know what he is to me, nor how much I need him ! Others have so much. They have money, husbands, and many children ; also horses and mules decked with bells and red ribbons ; they go to bed satisfied and contented ; they strut about in their fine clothes, and the people murmur enviously when they pass."

The lion's gaze had wandered back to the far-off vision of its dreams, and its attitude was one of proud disdain and aloofness.

Sobilia went on talking, getting more and more excited as she talked, and stopping every now and then to make her meaning clearer by means of gestures.

" Things were very different with me once," she said. " I was merry and gay, and I had a strong, brave husband. And he was murdered by a scoundrel ! Since then I have thought of nothing but revenge. I have worked at my spinning from morn till night ; my fingers have grown as hard and smooth as wood. The wheel goes round and round, and each time I say to myself, if the thread holds, I shall get my revenge ! . . ."

The lion's gaze remained wonderfully calm and remote, but it seemed to Sobilia that it had become less unapproachable, and she hastened to avail herself of the opportunity :

" You see, it is Orlanduccio there, who is to revenge his father's death ! He is the only one I have, and that is why you must give him back to me."

She was close to the animal now, and ready to bend down and take her child from it, for she thought that it *must* understand by now !

But the lion did not remove its paw, and did not move at all, only gazed at her, and beyond her to far-distant scenes.

Then Sobilia got angry and shook her head threateningly at him.

" Are you one of those cowards that delight in trampling on the fallen ? Are you a dog ? Must I drive you away with blows ? You might have taken Pela the murderer's children ! He has a whole lot of them, plump, rosy, hateful creatures ! But that you dared not do ! You only think you are going to rob me of my all, of my revenge too ! "

She raised her hand to strike. The lion turned its eyes towards her, and she saw them, big and yellow, and filled with dancing sparks. She began to tremble, and could hardly keep back her tears of terror, but she succeeded in doing so, for she knew that if she gave way, all would be lost. She kept her eyes fixed on the lion's, though they were again turned towards some far-distant scene.

" No, no, dear friend," she went on, " I see that you are not one of those. Let me take him now. Don't show your claws ; take care you don't scratch him, he has such a tender skin. Now I am going to bend down, and trust in you that you will not hurt me—lift your paw a little when I draw him from underneath, so that you do not scratch him—that's right ; now I have him ! You have not hurt him at all ; I thank you from the bottom of my heart."

And kneeling down, Sobilia began to draw the child towards her, very slowly and gently, so as not to jerk the animal's paw. She was so near that she felt its hot breath in her hair. But it never moved, neither did it appear to notice either mother or child. Then she crept backwards a few steps, holding the child on her out-stretched hands, and at last could stand erect and clasp him to her bosom.

And just then she realised in a flash the extent of the danger. Up till this moment she had only been playing with it. In truth it was a wonderful game, but now her knees knocked together, and everything turned black before her eyes. She was filled with the dread of her new-born joy being, even now, reft from her.

The lion lay so still, it might have been a bronze statue, paying no attention to her as she retreated slowly, holding her treasure with trembling arms, while her eyes still gazed as if fascinated into the animal's glittering yellow ones.

.   .   .   .

At last, behind some bushes, she dared to look at her child. He was quite unhurt, and had not even fainted. Although not aware of the greatness of his danger, he had wisely kept perfectly still so as not to irritate the animal. Sobilia threw him up in the air and caught him as he fell, in an ecstasy of joy. And now her tears gushed forth in an irresistible flood, infinitely sweet and pleas-ant. Her eyes met those of her son, which were darker even than was their wont, and they reminded her of those others, closed long since in Death, and the remembrance of all she had thought and of all she had said, in the confusion of her mind, came back to her. No weeping now ! She had not wept on that day, long ago, either ! No tears now, only joy, and a triumphant hope that was now more certain to be realised than ever before. She gazed down into the boy's eyes, and they seemed to grow deeper and larger and wiser under her gaze, and here were gleams of light in their depths.

" You heard what I said to him, Orlanduccio," she said ; " did you understand that it was for that he gave you back to me ? "

The child understood, and his eyes grew hard like those of his mother.

With a firm, proud step, Sobilia strode out into the street, smiling disdainfully as she went.

" Bilia, Bilia," they called from the windows, " where have you been ? Did you see the lion ? "

" It had taken my chlid, and I took him from it," she answered. " It is still lying over there. Why do you creep into your homes so timidly, when I, a woman, have dared to approach it ? "

And she walked along the empty street, an object of wonder to all, feeling herself greater than a queen. When she came to Pela's house, she glanced up at the windows again. They were still stand-ing there, and they looked at her. But they smiled no longer, when she drew her son's attention to them with the words: " See, Orlanduccio, there they are ! "

They hardly knew what had happened, but were conscious of approaching misfortune.

Sobilia went on her way homewards, and the men began to be ashamed of their fears, and assembled together to take counsel as to the steps to be taken in the matter.

It was discovered that all the gates leading into the Orto San Michele could be closed ; the terror that had paralysed them was at an end, and they were able to act once more.

The lion let them do as they pleased ; he lay as before, immovable, indifferent to everything around him, his eyes appearing only to see that which did not really exist, that which he had dreamed of in the night-time, when all that was strange and perplexing had been swallowed up in the darkness. He inhaled the air slowly and inquiringly, but it brought him no message from familiar things. His open, yellow gaze sought no longer, but remained fixed on one spot ; perhaps he felt there was nothing here worth seeking for, nothing worth wishing for. And at last, when the night fell, and they brought his old cage with some food in it, he sprang into it, as if his one desire were to get away from all that he could not understand, back to rest, and, maybe, his dreams once again.

Great was then the joy of the Florentines, and Orlanduccio and his mother, whose wonderful experiences had been noised abroad through the town, were borne in triumph through its streets. They called the boy Orlanduccio of the Lion ever after. One might expect great things of such a lad, and no man would have liked to stand in Pela's shoes !

.   .   .   .

Time passed, and Orlanduccio grew from boyhood to manhood. He was very fond of going alone to the Square of San Giovanni to look at the lion. He felt that there was a special link between himself and the animal, and this conviction increased his courage and filled his soul with ambition. Sobilia was no longer poor ; she obtained good payment for her labour, and her position was a respectable one. Her greatest joy was to pass the house of her enemy, Pela ! Times had changed with him. He guessed what all those around him were thinking of and waiting for, and now that the strength and courage of his youth were slowly but surely disappearing, the crime committed so long ago stood out ever clearer and more distinct.

Even if he had wished to commit another crime in order to ensure his safety, a crime to the baseness of which he might have succeeded in reconciling himself, it would not have remained unpunished long, for Orlanduccio del Leone was, in a way, the adopted child of the town ! Pela's strong, healthy children fell victims to strange accidents ; some were drowned in the Arno, another went mad from injuries received in a fire, his wife died, and his friends dropped away from him.   Now, he trembled when he met Sobilia's gaze, and was ever conscious at such times of the approach of some new disaster.

Times had changed, too, with the lion !

It had sickened with a chill, brought on by the unaccustomed damp and cold of two winters !   It coughed, and its strong limbs grew weak, while a great restlessness, stronger than ever before, seemed to have taken possession of it, as if memories from out the past had grown clearer and more real, now that Death was gnawing at its vitals !   It seemed, too, as if it longed all the more passionately for freedom, now that it felt the near approach of an incomprehensible and binding force !

Now and then it would shake the bars of its cage with such roars that half the town would be wakened from its sleep.   Otherwise, the animal appeared quieter than before sickness overtook it ; its big yellow eyes looked upon the people outside with an expression of weary thoughtfulness, and no evilly glittering sparks in their depths.   It seemed to Orlanduccio that the lion's gaze was especially kind and friendly when it met his own, and he felt as if it were drawing him away towards grief and longing, and vague visions, of which he did not understand the meaning.

He was standing before the cage on the day the lion died.   It lay on its side, with flabby, powerless limbs, and its breast heaving so that it seemed as if its ribs must crack and break !   The big yellow eyes were closed, except during the paroxysms of coughing, when the eyelids were drawn up mechanically.   At such times one saw that the eyes were dull and expressionless, waiting for the final extinction of their light by death !

Orlanduccio refused to leave the spot until he had received one last glance from the lion's dying eyes.   At supper-time he was still standing there, and Sobilia, who had waited for him to come in, but in vain, came to the Piazza to fetch him.

The animal lay motionless on the floor of its cage when she came.

" It is dead," she said, but Orlando lifted a finger to enjoin silence, and then they heard a muffled rattling in the lion's breast.   They saw how the sinews in the once powerful limbs twitched and trembled, how the muscles alternately expanded and contracted, as if, in the dream he was then dreaming, he were preparing to spring towards some unknown object.

" He *must* look at me," said Orlando ; " wait, soon he will, look, now ! "

With a sudden movement, as rapid as a flash of lightning, the lion stood once more erect, with his head held proudly as of yore !

His eyes were big and shining, with a wonderfully calm and proud expression in their depths. They seemed to see farther than they had ever seen before, past the grey houses with the sunlight gilding their tiled roofs, past the Arno too, whose waters were probably dancing just then, without the walls, in the golden light ; beyond the silver-grey hills, beyond the distant blue mountains, farther and farther still ! What was it he saw ? Was he dreaming again ?

Ah, no ! there was no need to dream any longer now !

For now he knew, with no shadow of doubt, that his fleeting dream-visions had once been realities, that there *was* really a land, the glowing soil of which his feet had trod, that he had been created for such a land as this, and not for the cage and its torments ! Yes, it was around him now, he saw it now as a glorious reality, and not as a vague dream-picture.

The low hill upon which he stood sloped downwards towards the peace of the mighty desert in gentle undulations, that were blue and purple in the shade. The sky stretched in an unbroken line of flaming blue overhead ; straight in front of him, the sun poured down its rain of fire. The air quivered and vibrated with the heat, and there appeared to be a cloud of vapour rising from the burning sand. How is it possible to express, in human language, what it feels like for a lion to stand as king over such a land, with its waves of golden sand !

Sobilia seized her son's hand violently, filled with a sudden terror. " Come away now," she cried. But Orlando took away his hand from hers, and said, " He is beautiful, I want to look at him."

Roused by the sound of their voices, the animal looked at them in surprise.

" Where was he ? Where was the wonderful land ? And what was it that was burning and tearing inside him ? "

For one brief moment his gaze rested on Orlando ; it was wonderfully sad and hopeless, yet at the same time commanding, and it filled the boy's soul with dark foreboding.

Then it was withdrawn, and the lion looked once again on distant scenes, but not the same as before ! He saw much further now.

Gigantic and menacing, vague, but deep as life itself, thus did realisation come to the dying animal. His mighty form trembled, blood spurted from his nostrils, and very soon he lay there before them, stiff and stark.

" You see that he is dead," said Sobilia ; " mind you remember the reason why he gave you back to me that time."

Orlando shook himself impatiently.

" Yes, of course, it was an understood thing. That first, and then all the other great ones afterwards ! " But he was very thoughtful, and continually saw before him the lion's dying eyes, the expression of which he was unable to fathom.

. . . .

Time passed, and Orlanduccio of the Lion grew to be a strong and self-reliant young man, as became the bearer of such a name as his.

Sobilia rejoiced in secret over the play of his muscles and the energy displayed in his movements.

" It will soon be time," she thought, and Orlando thought the same, and looked forward in proud certainty of triumph.

The circle drawn by the hand of sorrow round Pela the Smith had narrowed. His fear had taken shape now—he saw it as a shadowy lion, watching and waiting, each time the darkness fell, crouching as if for a spring. He used to ask himself in the morning what would happen before the sun set.

" Maybe just now, even at this moment, it will spring," he would say to himself. One by one, his remaining children were taken from him. Each time he met Sobilia, he guessed by the gleam in her eyes that she was counting inwardly : " Four left, three more than I ; three left, still two too many."

He was afraid of her, but found, to his surprise, that he felt no hatred towards her. He had lost the power to hate !

Pela had lived his life without care, with a light laugh, drinking deeply when occasion arose, but keeping ever a sharp eye and ready hand. He had been violent in his desires and violent in his anger. But Time and Sorrow, the great transformers, had done their work on him. Each time Fate had struck down one of his nearest and dearest, he had suffered as only a violent man can suffer. He had a strange sensation of having lived in a shady wood, the trees of which were now being cut down, and that through the clearing thus made a new light streamed in on to him. It was a dreary light, a terrible light, but one could really see by it.

His thoughts wandered back to the past, and came upon things that had been half-forgotten, and that Time hitherto had kept covered up under his veil, like ruins under creepers, golden sunlight and blue skies !

Each day, too, his thoughts gathered more closely round the murder of Orlando's father. At the time he had been conscious only of satisfied hate and desire for revenge ! Now everything had gradually taken on a different aspect.

He had no feelings of remorse or despair, for such emotions were not to be found in his firmly moulded character. That which had happened *had* happened, and that was the end of it !

He felt a strange pity for the dead man, and for himself for killing him, for every one who suffered, for Sobilia even ! When his last remaining child died, he felt as if his sorrow had become too great to allow of its taking one special object into its vast embrace. His heart had been turned into a stone, but a stone which, like that of the legend, vibrates with sounds that cannot be perceived by the ear of an ordinary mortal. He knew that it would be his turn next ; he knew, too, how the blow would fall, but he felt no fear. He was conscious instead of a longing for the end. Only from a sense of duty did he take a few simple precautions.

When Sobilia heard of his latest bereavement, she was filled with joy, but also with anxiety.

Time pressed. The slowly ripened fruit might fall to the ground before its time had come !

" Thy father's dagger hangs upon the wall. There is yet time. Maybe soon it will be too late," she said to her son, in tones the wild power of which pierced his innermost soul.

He took down the weapon and fastened it in his belt, smiling indifferently as he did so.

This seemed such a small, insignificant thing compared to the deeds he dreamt of performing ; and as he meditated on it, his love for his mother cooled somewhat.

Day by day Sobilia waited for the fatal hour to strike, and Pela waited too.

One evening he found himself outside the walls, on his way home from a walk ; he had neglected his usual precautionary measures, and had taken no one with him. The sun was setting, and behind the poplar trees that lined the road the waters of the Arno glittered in golden light. His eyes were blinded by the glare for a moment, then, just as their sight was returning, from out the midst of blackening flames, he fancied he saw the shadow-lion, crouched ready to spring. He had not seen it for some time, and he wondered, in bitterness of heart, what it could want with him now ! It had taken all he possessed already ! And then he remembered that still one thing remained—his own life !

Coming along the road from the city gates, clearly and sharply defined in the mellow light, Pela saw a slight figure approaching ; it was that of Orlanduccio of the Lion !

And he understood, but nevertheless continued to walk with a firm step. He had a dagger, but felt no desire to use it, not even in self-defence ! He felt very old and tired, and his eyes followed vaguely the lines of his shadow that preceded him.

Orlando's step was buoyant as he came along with the golden sunlight on his face. He looked at the old man with cold disdain, and then his gaze wandered away to the blue hills and the glittering waters, and to that which the future hid.

Then they began to fight, without a word having been said on either side. Pela only parried the thrusts of Orlando's dagger in a lame fashion, and very soon he lay prone on the grass by the side of the road.

The young man shivered as he felt the blood on his hand. He bent down to see if his enemy had had enough—if the act of retribution was fully accomplished. The sunlight gleamed and glittered so that he could hardly see, and at the same time he felt a desire to recall some half-forgotten memory, lighted by the rays of the setting sun too, as now.

He turned his head, and saw that Pela had had enough. But Orlanduccio's attention was specially drawn to the eyes of the dying man. There was no hate in their depths, only an infinite sadness, a proud and silent resignation, and a certain knowledge, and Orlanduccio felt a sudden chill at his heart as he looked at them. Where had he seen that look before ? Why, the lion—the lion's eyes were like that when he died, of course ! That was it !

Orlanduccio longed and yet feared to meet his enemy's gaze. " Orlanduccio," the dying man said, " I am sorry for you. I did you an injury, you have avenged it. From year to year, the heavy burden made lighter, one link the less in the endless chain, but will it never come to an end ? "

He said no more, but turned his eyes away towards some distant and mysterious vision. And it overwhelmed him ; his life went to pieces like a bubble that has risen to a lighter and colder atmosphere.

Orlanduccio felt bitterly cold, and was filled with sadness and regret as he stood there with the setting sun gilding his eyelashes ; he was conscious of a dark foreboding that mingled with dreams and memories, and overwhelmed him. He wended his way homewards, silent and thoughtful, after having washed the blood from his hands in the Arno, whose waters now flowed by grey and cold, for the sunlight had left them.

Sobilia looked out of the shadowy room with eyes full of expectancy.

Orlanduccio answered her unspoken question shortly. " It is done," he said, and threw the dagger on to the floor. She would have taken him in her arms and kissed him and rejoiced over him, but, with a gesture, he restrained her, and with the tones of his voice he raised up a barrier between them.

" I have come to say farewell," he said, " but first of all, to return you *that*."

" Yes, of course," she answered, " you must go away for a short time ; that will be easy to arrange."

But his next words put an end to hope.

" For a short time or a long time, it matters nought, for I shall never return here again. You have obtained your wish, let that suffice you. I have much to find, much to think about ! Do you remember the lion, and how he died ?   Now I have seen another death, and I am going, I know not whither ! "

He went.

Sobilia sat still in the darkness, and played with the dagger, listening absently to the noise of its falling on the tiled floor, while she tried to think, to understand, fumbling blindly between cold triumph and bitter weeping.

The expected story of the life of Orlanduccio of the Lion remained unwritten, and his name never figured in Florentine history.

It may be that he lived and worked elsewhere under another name, or it may be, too, that he had enough to do to find himself in the labyrinth of Existence !

HANS CHRISTIAN ANDERSEN

DANISH

1805–1875

IB AND LITTLE CHRISTINA

NOT far from the clear stream Gudenau, in North Jutland, in the forest which extends by its banks and far into the country, a great ridge of land rises and stretches along like a wall through the wood. By this ridge, westward, stands a farmhouse, surrounded by poor land ; the sandy soil is seen through the spare rye and wheat-ears that grow upon it. Some years have elapsed since the time of which we speak. The people who lived here cultivated the fields, and moreover kept three sheep, a pig, and two oxen ; in fact, they supported themselves quite comfortably, for they had enough to live on if they took things as they came. Indeed, they could have managed to save enough to keep two horses ; but, like the other peasants of the neighbourhood, they said, " The horse eats itself up "—that is to say, it eats as much as it earns. Jeppe-Jäns cultivated his field in summer. In the winter he made wooden shoes, and then he had an assistant, a journeyman, who understood as well as he himself did how to make the wooden shoes strong, and light, and graceful. They carved shoes and spoons, and that brought in money. It would have been wronging the Jeppe-Jänses to call them poor people.

Little Ib, a boy seven years old, the only child of the family, would sit by, looking at the workmen, cutting at a stick, and occasionally cutting his finger. But one day Ib succeeded so well with two pieces of wood that they really looked like little wooden shoes ; and these he wanted to give to little Christina. And who was little Christina ? She was the boatman's daughter, and was graceful and delicate as a gentleman's child : had she been differently dressed, no one would have imagined that she came out of the hut on the neighbouring heath. There lived her father, who was a widower, and supported himself by carrying firewood in his great boat out of the forest to the estate of Silkeborg, with its great eel-pond and eel-weir, and sometimes even to the distant little town of Randers. He had no one who could take care of little Christina, and therefore the child was almost always with him in his boat, or in the forest among the heath plants and barberry bushes. Sometimes, when he had to go as far as the town, he would bring little Christina, who was a year younger than Ib, to stay with the Jeppe-Jänses.

Ib and Christina agreed very well in every particular : they divided their bread and berries when they were hungry, they dug in the ground together for treasures, and they ran, and crept, and played about everywhere. And one day they ventured together up the high ridge, and a long way into the forest ; once they found a few snipe's eggs there, and that was a great event for them.

Ib had never been on the heath where Christina's father lived, nor had he ever been on the river. But even this was to happen ; for Christina's father once invited him to go with them, and on the evening before the excursion he followed the boatman over the heath to the house of the latter.

Next morning early, the two children were sitting high up on the pile of firewood in the boat, eating bread and whortleberries. Christina's father and his assistant propelled the boat with staves. They had the current with them, and swiftly they glided down the stream, through the lakes it forms in its course, and which sometimes seemed shut in by reeds and water-plants, though there was always room for them to pass, and though the old trees bent quite forward over the water, and the old oaks bent down their bare branches, as if they had turned up their sleeves, and wanted to show their knotty naked arms. Old elder trees, which the stream had washed away from the bank, clung with their fibrous roots to the bottom of the stream, and looked like little wooded islands. The water-lilies rocked themselves on the river. It was a splendid excursion ; and at last they came to the great eel-weir, where the water rushed through the flood-gates ; and Ib and Christina thought this was beautiful to behold.

In those days there was no manufactory there, nor was there any town : only the old great farmyard, with its scanty fields, with few servants and a few head of cattle, could be seen there ; and the rushing of the water through the weir and the cry of the wild ducks were the only signs of life in Silkeborg. After the firewood had been unloaded, the father of Christina bought a whole bundle of eels and a slaughtered sucking-pig, and all was put into a basket and placed in the stern of the boat. Then they went back again up the stream ; but the wind was favourable, and when the sails were hoisted it was as good as if two horses had been harnessed to the boat.

When they had arrived at a point in the stream where the assistant-boatman dwelt, a little way from the bank, the boat was moored and the two men landed, after exhorting the children to sit still. But the children did not do that, or at least they obeyed only for a very short time. They must be peeping into the basket in which the eels and the sucking-pig had been placed, and they must needs pull the sucking-pig out, and take it in their hands, and feel and touch it all over ; and as both wanted to hold it at the same time, it came to pass that they let it fall into the water, and the sucking-pig drifted away with the stream—and here was a terrible event !

Ib jumped ashore, and ran a little distance along the bank, and Christina sprang after him.

" Take me with you ! " she cried.

And in a few minutes they were deep in the thicket, and could no longer see either the boat or the bank. They ran on a little farther, and then Christina fell down on the ground and began to cry ; but Ib picked her up.

" Follow me ! " he cried. " Yonder lies the house."

But the house was not yonder. They wandered on and on, over the dry, rustling, last year's leaves, and over fallen branches that crackled beneath their feet. Soon they heard a loud piercing scream. They stood still and listened, and presently the scream of an eagle sounded through the wood. It was an ugly scream, and they were frightened at it ; but before them, in the thick wood, the most beautiful blueberries grew in wonderful profusion. They were so inviting that the children could not do otherwise than stop ; and they lingered for some time, eating the blueberries till they had quite blue mouths and blue cheeks. Now again they heard the cry they had heard before.

" We shall get into trouble about the pig," said Christina.

" Come, let us go to our house," said Ib : " it is here in the wood."

And they went forward. They presently came to a wood, but it did not lead them home ; and darkness came on, and they were afraid. The wonderful stillness that reigned around was interrupted now and then by the shrill cries of the great horrid owl, and of birds that were strange to them. At last they both lost themselves in a thicket. Christina cried, and Ib cried too ; and after they had bemoaned themselves for a time, they threw themselves down on the dry leaves, and went fast asleep.

The sun was high in the heavens when the two children awoke. They were cold ; but in the neighbourhood of this resting-place, on the hill, the sun shone through the trees, and there they thought they would warm themselves ; and from there Ib fancied they would be able to see his parents' house. But they were far away from the house in question, in quite another part of the forest. They clambered to the top of the rising ground, and found themselves on the summit of a slope running down to the margin of a transparent lake. They could see fish in great numbers in the pure water illuminated by the sun's rays. This spectacle was quite a sudden surprise for them ; but close beside them grew a nut bush covered with the finest nuts ; and now they picked the nuts, and cracked them, and ate the delicate young kernels, which had only just become perfect. But there was another surprise and another fright in store for them. Out of the thicket stepped a tall old woman : her face was quite brown, and her hair was deep black and shining. The whites of her eyes gleamed like a negro's ; on her back she carried a bundle, in her hand she bore a knotted stick. She was a gipsy. The children did not at once understand what she said. She brought three nuts out of her pocket, and told them that in these nuts the most beautiful, the loveliest things were hidden, for they were wishing-nuts.

Ib looked at her, and she seemed so friendly that he plucked up courage and asked her if she would give him the nuts ; and the woman gave them to him, and gathered some more for herself, a whole pocketful, from the nut bush.

And Ib and Christina looked at the wishing-nuts with great eyes.

" Is there a carriage with a pair of horses in this nut ? " he asked.

" Yes, there's a golden carriage with two horses," answered the woman.

" Then give me the nut," said little Christina.

And Ib gave it to her, and the strange woman tied it in her pocket-handkerchief for her.

" Is there in this nut a pretty little neckerchief, like the one Christina wears round her neck ? " inquired Ib.

" There are ten neckerchiefs in it," answered the woman. " There are beautiful dresses in it, and stockings, and a hat with a veil."

" Then I will have that one, too," cried little Christina.

And Ib gave her the second nut also. The third was a little black thing.

" That one you can keep," said Christina ; " and it is a pretty one too."

" What is in it ? " inquired Ib.

" The best of all things for you," replied the gipsy woman.

And Ib held the nut very tight. The woman promised to lead the children into the right path, so that they might find their way home ; and now they went forward, certainly in quite a different direction from the path they should have followed. But that is no reason why we should suspect the gipsy woman of wanting to steal the children. In the wild wood-path they met the forest bailiff, who knew Ib ; and by his help, Ib and Christina both arrived at home, where their friends had been very anxious about them. They were pardoned and forgiven, although they had indeed both deserved " to get into trouble " ; firstly, because they had let the sucking-pig fall into the water, and secondly, because they had run away.

Christina was taken back to her father on the heath, and Ib remained in the farmhouse on the margin of the wood by the great ridge.   The first thing he did in the evening was to bring forth out of his pocket the little black nut, in which " the best thing of all " was said to be enclosed.   He placed it carefully in the crack of the door, and then shut the door so as to break the nut ; but there was not much kernel in it.   The nut looked as if it were filled with tobacco or black rich earth ; it was what we call hollow or worm-eaten.

" Yes, that's exactly what I thought," said Ib.   " How could the very best thing be contained in this little nut ?   And Christina will get just as little out of her two nuts, and will have neither fine clothes nor the golden carriage."

.   .   .   .

And winter came on, and the new year began ; indeed, several years went by.

Ib was at last to be confirmed ; and for this reason he went during a whole winter to the clergyman, far away in the nearest village, to prepare.   About this time the boatman one day visited Ib's parents, and told them that Christina was now going into service, and that she had been really fortunate in getting a remarkably good place, and falling into worthy hands.

" Only think ! " he said ;   " she is going to the rich innkeeper's, in the inn at Herning, far towards the west, many miles from here. She is to assist the hostess in keeping the house ; and afterwards, if she takes to it well, and stays to be confirmed there, the people are going to adopt her as their own daughter."

And Ib and Christina took leave of one another.   People called them " the betrothed " ;   and at parting, the girl showed Ib that she had still the two nuts which he had given her long ago, during their wanderings in the forest ;   and she told him, moreover, that in a drawer she had carefully kept the little wooden shoes which he had carved as a present for her in their childish days.   And thereupon they parted.

Ib was confirmed.   But he remained in his mother's house, for he had become a clever maker of wooden shoes, and in summer he looked after the field.   He did it all alone, for his mother kept no farm-servant, and his father had died long ago.

Only seldom he got news of Christina from some passing postilion or eel-fisher.   But she was well off at the rich innkeeper's ; and after she had been confirmed, she wrote a letter to her father, and sent a kind message to Ib and his mother ;   and in the letter there was mention made of certain linen garments and a fine new gown, which Christina had received as a present from her employers. This was certainly good news.

Next spring, there was a knock one day at the door of our Ib's old mother, and behold, the boatman and Christina stepped into the room.   She had come on a visit to spend the day : a carriage had to come from the Herning inn to the next village, and she had taken the opportunity to see her friends once again. She looked as handsome as a real lady, and she had a pretty gown on, which had been well sewn and made expressly for her.   There she stood, in grand array, and Ib was in his working clothes.   He could not utter a word : he certainly seized her hand, and held it fast in his own, and was heartily glad ; but he could not get his tongue to obey him.   Christina was not embarrassed, however, for she went on talking and talking, and moreover, kissed Ib on his mouth in the heartiest manner.

" Did you know me again directly, Ib ? " she asked ; but even afterwards, when they were left quite by themselves, and he stood there still holding her hand in his, he could only say :

" You look quite like a real lady, and I am so uncouth.   How often I have thought of you, Christina, and of the old times ! "

And arm in arm they sauntered up the great ridge, and looked across the stream towards the heath, towards the great hills overgrown with bloom.   It was perfectly silent ; but by the time they parted it had grown quite clear to him that Christina must be his wife.   Had they not, even in their childhood, been called the betrothed pair ?   To him they seemed to be really engaged to each other, though neither of them had spoken a word on the subject. Only for a few more hours could they remain together, for Christina was obliged to go back into the next village, whence the carriage was to start early next morning for Herning.   Her father and Ib escorted her as far as the village.   It was a fair moonlight evening, and when they reached their destination, and Ib still held Christina's hand in his own, he could not make up his mind to let her go.   His eyes brightened, but still the words came halting over his lips.   Yet they came from the depths of his heart, when he said :

" If you have not become too grand, Christina, and if you can make up your mind to live with me in my mother's house as my wife, we must become a wedded pair some day ; but we can wait awhile yet."

" Yes, let us wait for a time, Ib," she replied ; and he kissed her lips.   " I confide in you, Ib," said Christina ; " and I think that I love you—but I will sleep upon it."

And with that they parted.   And on the way home Ib told the boatman that he and Christina were as good as betrothed ; and the boatman declared he had always expected it would turn out so ; and he went home with Ib, and remained that night in the young man's house ; but nothing further was said of the betrothal.

A year passed by, in the course of which two letters were exchanged between Ib and Christina.   The signature was prefaced by the words, " Faithful till death ! "   One day the boatman came in to Ib, and brought him a greeting from Christina.   What he had further to say was brought out in somewhat hesitating fashion, but it was to the effect that Christina was almost more than prosperous, for she was a

pretty girl, courted and loved.   The son of the host had been home
on a visit : he was employed in the office of some great institution in
Copenhagen ; and he was very much pleased with Christina, and she
had taken a fancy to him : his parents were ready to give their
consent ; but Christina was very anxious to retain Ib's good opinion ;
" and so she had thought of refusing this great piece of good fortune," said the boatman.

At first Ib said not a word, but he became as white as the wall,
and slightly shook his head.   Then he said slowly :

" Christina must not refuse this advantageous offer."

" Then do you write a few words to her," said the boatman.

And Ib sat down to write ; but he could not manage it well : the
words would not come as he wished them ; and first he altered and
then he tore up the page ; but the next morning a letter lay ready
to be sent to Christina, and it contained the following words :

I have read the letter you have sent to your father, and gather
from it that you are prospering in all things, and that there is a
prospect of higher fortune for you.   Ask your heart, Christina, and
ponder well the fate that awaits you, if you take me for your
husband ; what I possess is but little.   Do not think of me, or my
position, but think of your own welfare.   You are bound to me by
no promise, and if in your heart you have given me one, I release
you from it.   May all treasures of happiness be poured out upon you,
Christina.   Heaven will console me in its own good time.

Ever your sincere friend,

IB.

And the letter was despatched, and Christina duly received it.

In the course of that November her banns were published in the
church on the heath, and in Copenhagen, where her bridegroom lived ;
and to Copenhagen she proceeded, under the protection of her future
mother-in-law, because the bridegroom could not undertake the
journey into Jutland on account of his various occupations.   On
the journey, Christina met her father in a certain village, and here
the two took leave of one another.   A few words were mentioned
concerning this fact, but Ib made no remark upon it : his mother
said he had grown very silent of late ; indeed, he had become very
pensive, and thus the three nuts came into his mind which the gipsy
woman had given him long ago, and of which he had given two to
Christina.   Yes, it seemed right—they were wishing-nuts, and in one
of them lay a golden carriage with two horses, and in the other very
elegant clothes ; all those luxuries would now be Christina's in the
capital.   Her part had thus come true.   And to him, Ib, the nut
had offered only black earth.   The gipsy woman had said this was
" the best of all for him."   Yes, it was right—that also was coming

true. The black earth was the best for him. Now he understood clearly what had been the woman's meaning. In the black earth, in the dark grave, would be the best happiness for him.

. . . .

And once again years passed by, not very many, but they seemed long years to Ib. The old innkeeper and his wife died, and the whole of their property, many hundreds of pounds, came to the son. Yes, now Christina could have the golden carriage and plenty of fine clothes.

During the two long years that followed no letter came from Christina ; and when her father at length received one from her, it was not written in prosperity, by any means. Poor Christina ! neither she nor her husband had understood how to keep the money together, and there seemed to be no blessing with it, because they had not sought it.

And again the summer bloomed and faded. The winter had swept for many years across the heath, and over the ridge beneath which Ib dwelt, sheltered from the rough winds. The spring sun shone bright, and Ib guided the plough across his field, when one day it glided over what appeared to be a fire-stone. Something like a great black ship came out of the ground, and when Ib took it up it proved to be a piece of metal ; and the place from which the plough had cut the stone gleamed brightly with ore. It was a great golden armlet of ancient workmanship that he had found. He had disturbed a " Hun's Grave," and discovered the costly treasure buried in it. Ib showed what he had found to the clergyman, who explained its value to him, and then he betook himself to the local judges, who reported the discovery to the keeper of the museum, and recommended Ib to deliver up the treasure in person.

" You have found in the earth the best thing you could find," said the judge.

" The best thing ! " thought Ib. " The very best thing for me, and found in the earth ! Well, if that is the best, the gipsy woman was correct in what she prophesied to me."

So Ib travelled with the ferry-boat from Aarhus to Copenhagen. To him, who had but once or twice passed beyond the river that rolled by his home, this seemed like a voyage across the ocean. And he arrived in Copenhagen.

The value of the gold he had found was paid over to him ; it was a large sum—one hundred and twenty pounds. And Ib of the heath wandered about in the great capital.

On the day on which he had settled to go back with the captain, Ib lost his way in the streets, and took quite a different direction from the one he intended to follow. He had wandered into the suburb of Christianshaven, into a poor little street. Not a human being was to be seen. At last a very little girl came out of one of the wretched houses. Ib inquired of the little one the way to the street which he wanted ; but she looked shyly at him, and began to cry bitterly. He asked her what ailed her, but could not understand what she said in reply. But as they went along the street together, they passed beneath the light of a lamp ; and when the light fell on the girl's face, he felt a strange and sharp emotion, for Christina stood bodily before him, just as he remembered her from the days of his childhood.

And he went with the little maiden into the wretched house, and ascended the narrow crazy staircase, which led to a little attic chamber in the roof. The air in this chamber was heavy and almost suffocating : no light was burning ; but there was a heavy sighing and moaning in one corner. Ib struck a light with the help of a match. It was the mother of the child who lay sighing on the miserable bed.

" Can I be of any service to you ? " asked Ib. " This little girl has brought me up here, but I am a stranger in this city. Are there no neighbours or friends whom I could call to you ? " And he raised the sick woman's head and smoothed her pillow.

It was Christina of the heath !

For years her name had not been mentioned yonder, for the mention of her would have disturbed Ib's peace of mind, and rumour had told nothing good of her. The wealth which her husband had inherited from his parents had made him proud and arrogant. He had given up his certain appointment, had travelled for half a year in foreign lands, and on his return had incurred debts, and yet lived in an expensive fashion. His carriage had bent over more and more, so to speak, until at last it turned over completely. The many merry companions and table friends he had entertained declared it served him right, for he had kept house like a madman ; and one morning his corpse was found in the canal.

The icy hand of death was already on Christina. Her youngest child, only a few weeks old, expected in prosperity and born in misery, was already in its grave, and it had come to this with Christina herself, that she lay sick to death and forsaken in a miserable room, amid a poverty that she might well have borne in her childish days, but which now oppressed her painfully, since she had been accustomed to better things. It was her eldest child, also a little Christina, who here suffered hunger and poverty with her, and whom Ib had now brought home.

" I am unhappy at the thought of dying and leaving the poor child here alone," she said. " Ah, what is to become of the poor thing ? " And not a word more could she utter.

And Ib brought out another match, and lighted up a piece of candle he found in the room, and the flame illumined the wretched dwelling. And Ib looked at the little girl, and thought how Christina had looked when she was young ; and he felt that for her sake he would be fond of this child, who was as yet a stranger to him. The dying woman gazed at him, and her eyes opened wider and wider—did she recognise him ? He never knew, for no further word passed over her lips.

And it was in the forest by the river Gudenau, in the region of the heath. The air was thick and dark, and there were no blossoms on the heath plant ; but the autumn tempests whirled the yellow leaves from the wood into the stream, and out over the heath towards the hut of the boatman, in which strangers now dwelt ; but below the ridge, safe beneath the protection of the high trees, stood the little farm, trimly whitewashed and painted, and within it the turf blazed up cheerily in the chimney ; for within was sunlight, the beaming sunlight of a child's two eyes ; and the tones of the spring birds sounded in the words that came from the child's rosy lips : she sat on Ib's knee, and Ib was to her both father and mother, for her own parents were dead, and had vanished from her as a dream vanishes alike from children and grown men. Ib sat in the pretty neat house, for he was a prosperous man, while the mother of the little girl rested in the churchyard at Copenhagen, where she had died in poverty.

Ib had money, and was said to have provided for the future. He had won gold out of the black earth, and he had a Christina for his own, after all.

THE NIGHTINGALE

Hans Christian Andersen

In China, you must know, the Emperor is a Chinaman, and all whom he has about him are Chinamen too. It happened a good many years ago, but that's just why it's worth while to hear the story, before it is forgotten. The Emperor's palace was the most splendid in the world ; it was made entirely of porcelain, very costly, but so delicate and brittle that one had to take care how one touched it. In the garden were to be seen the most wonderful flowers, and to the costliest of them silver bells were tied, which sounded, so that nobody should pass by without noticing the flowers. Yes, everything in the Emperor's garden was admirably arranged. And it extended so far, that the gardener himself did not know where the end was. If a man went on and on, he came into a glorious forest with high trees and deep lakes. The wood extended straight down to the sea, which was blue and deep ; great ships could sail too beneath the branches of the trees ; and in the trees lived a Nightingale, which sang so splendidly that even the poor fisherman, who had many other things to do, stopped still and listened, when he had gone out at night to throw out his nets, and heard the Nightingale.

" How beautiful that is ! " he said ; but he was obliged to attend to his property, and thus forgot the bird. But when in the next night the bird sang again, and the fisherman heard it, he exclaimed again, " How beautiful that is ! "

From all the countries of the world travellers came to the city of the Emperor, and admired it, and the palace and the garden, but when they heard the Nightingale, they said, " That is the best of all ! "

And the travellers told of it when they came home ; and the learned men wrote many books about the town, the palace, and the garden. But they did not forget the Nightingale : that was placed highest of all ; and those who were poets wrote most magnificent poems about the Nightingale in the wood by the deep lake.

The books went through all the world, and a few of them once came to the Emperor. He sat in his golden chair, and read, and read : every moment he nodded his head, for it pleased him to peruse the masterly descriptions of the city, the palace, and the garden. " But the Nightingale is the best of all," it stood written there.

" What's that ? " exclaimed the Emperor. " I don't know the Nightingale at all ! Is there such a bird in my empire, and even in my garden ? I've never heard of that. To think that I should have to learn such a thing for the first time from books ! "

And hereupon he called his cavalier. This cavalier was so grand that if any one lower in rank than himself dared to speak to him, or to ask him any question, he answered nothing but " P ! "—and that meant nothing.

" There is said to be a wonderful bird here called a Nightingale," said the Emperor. " They say it is the best thing in all my great empire. Why have I never heard anything about it ? "

" I have never heard him named," replied the cavalier. " He has never been introduced at Court."

" I command that he shall appear this evening, and sing before me," said the Emperor. " All the world knows what I possess, and I do not know it myself ! "

" I have never heard him mentioned," said the cavalier. " I will seek for him. I will find him."

But where was he to be found ? The cavalier ran up and down all the staircases, through halls and passages, but no one among all those whom he met had heard talk of the Nightingale. And the cavalier ran back to the Emperor, and said that it must be a fable invented by the writers of books.

" Your Imperial Majesty cannot believe how much is written that is fiction, besides something that they call the black art."

" But the book in which I read this," said the Emperor, " was sent to me by the high and mighty Emperor of Japan, and therefore it cannot be a falsehood. I *will* hear the Nightingale! It must be here this evening! It has my Imperial favour ; and if it does not come, all the Court shall be trampled upon after the Court has supped ! "

" Tsing-pe ! " said the cavalier ; and again he ran up and down all the staircases, and through all the halls and corridors ; and half the Court ran with him, for the courtiers did not like being trampled upon.

Then there was a great inquiry after the wonderful Nightingale, which all the world knew excepting the people at Court.

At last they met with a poor little girl in the kitchen, who said :

" The Nightingale ? I know it well ; yes, it can sing gloriously. Every evening I get leave to carry my poor sick mother the scraps from the table. She lives down by the strand ; and when I get back and am tired, and rest in the wood, then I hear the Nightingale sing. And then the water comes into my eyes, and it is just as if my mother kissed me."

" Little kitchen girl," said the cavalier, " I will get you a place in the kitchen, with permission to see the Emperor dine, if you will but lead us to the Nightingale, for it is announced for this evening."

So they all went out into the wood where the Nightingale was accustomed to sing ; half the Court went forth. When they were in the midst of their journey a cow began to low.

" Oh ! " cried the Court pages, " now we have it ! That shows a wonderful power in so small a creature ! I have certainly heard it before."

" No, those are cows lowing," said the little kitchen girl. " We are a long way from the place yet."

Now the frogs began to croak in the marsh.

" Glorious ! " said the Chinese Court preacher. " Now I hear it —it sounds just like little church bells."

" No, those are frogs," said the little kitchenmaid. " But now I think we shall soon hear it."

And then the Nightingale began to sing.

" That is it ! " exclaimed the little girl. " Listen, listen ! and yonder it sits."

And she pointed to a little grey bird up in the boughs.

" Is it possible ? " cried the cavalier. " I should never have thought it looked like that ! How simple it looks ! It must certainly have lost its colour at seeing such grand people around."

" Little Nightingale ! " called the little kitchenmaid, quite loudly, " our gracious Emperor wishes you to sing before him."

" With the greatest pleasure ! " replied the Nightingale, and began to sing most delightfully.

" It sounds just like glass bells ! " said the cavalier.   " And look at its little throat, how it's working !   It's wonderful that we should never have heard it before.   That bird will be a great success at Court."

" Shall I sing once more before the Emperor ? " inquired the Nightingale, for it thought the Emperor was present.

" My excellent little Nightingale," said the cavalier, " I have great pleasure in inviting you to a Court festival this evening, when you shall charm his Imperial Majesty with your beautiful singing."

" My song sounds best in the green wood," replied the Nightingale ; still it came willingly when it heard what the Emperor wished.

The palace was festively adorned.   The walls and the flooring, which were of porcelain, gleamed in the rays of thousands of golden lamps.   The most glorious flowers, which could ring clearly, had been placed in the passages.   There was running to and fro, and a thorough draught, and all the bells rang so loudly that one could not hear oneself speak.

In the midst of the great hall, where the Emperor sat, a golden perch had been placed, on which the Nightingale was to sit.   The whole Court was there, and the little cook-maid had got leave to stand behind the door, as she had now received the title of a real Court cook.   All were in full dress, and all looked at the little grey bird, to which the Emperor nodded.

And the Nightingale sang so gloriously that the tears came into the Emperor's eyes, and the tears ran down over his cheeks ; then the Nightingale sang still more sweetly, in a way that went straight to the heart.   The Emperor was so much pleased that he said the Nightingale should have his golden slipper to wear round its neck. But the Nightingale declined this with thanks, saying it had already received a sufficient reward.

" I have seen tears in the Emperor's eyes—that is the real treasure to me.   An Emperor's tears have a peculiar power.   I am rewarded enough ! "   And then it sang again with a sweet, glorious voice.

" That's the most amiable coquetry I ever saw ! " said the ladies who stood round about, and then they took water in their mouths to gurgle when any one spoke to them.   They thought they should be nightingales too.   And the lackeys and chambermaids reported that they were satisfied also ; and that was saying a good deal, for they are the most difficult to please.   In short, the Nightingale achieved a real success.

It was now to remain at Court, to have its own cage, with liberty to go out twice every day and once at night. Twelve servants were appointed when the Nightingale went out, each of whom had a silken string fastened to the bird's legs, which they held very tight. There was really no pleasure in an excursion of that kind.

The whole city spoke of the wonderful bird, and whenever two people met, one said nothing but " Nightin," and the other said " gale " ; and then they both sighed, and understood one another. Eleven pedlars' children were named after the bird, but not one of them could sing a note.

One day the Emperor received a large parcel, on which was written " The Nightingale."

" There we have a new book about this celebrated bird," said the Emperor.

But it was not a book, but a little work of art, contained in a box, an artificial nightingale, which was to sing like a natural one, and was brilliantly ornamented with diamonds, sapphires, and rubies. So soon as the artificial bird was wound up, he could sing one of the pieces that he really sang, and then his tail moved up and down, and shone with silver and gold. Round his neck hung a little ribbon, and on that was written, " The Emperor of China's nightingale is poor compared to that of the Emperor of Japan."

" That is capital ! " said they all, and he who had brought the artificial bird immediately received the title, Imperial Head-Nightingale-Bringer.

" Now they must sing together ; what a duet that will be ! " cried the courtiers.

And so they had to sing together ; but it did not sound very well, for the real Nightingale sang in its own way, and the artificial bird sang waltzes.

" That's not his fault," said the playmaster ; " he's quite perfect, and very much in my style."

Now the artificial bird was to sing alone. It had just as much success as the real one, and was much handsomer to look at—it shone like bracelets and breast-pins.

Three and thirty times over did it sing the same piece, and yet was not tired. The people would gladly have heard it again, but the Emperor said that the living Nightingale ought to sing something now. But where was it ? No one had noticed that it had flown away out of the open window, back to the green wood.

" But what has become of it ? " asked the Emperor.

And all the courtiers abused the Nightingale, and declared that it was a very ungrateful creature.

" We have the best bird after all," said they.

And so the artificial bird had to sing again, and that was the thirty-fourth time that they listened to the same piece. For all that they did not know it quite by heart, for it was so very difficult.

And the playmaster praised the bird particularly ; yes, he declared that it was better than a nightingale, not only with regard to its plumage and the many beautiful diamonds, but inside as well.

" For you see, ladies and gentlemen, and above all, your Imperial Majesty, with a real nightingale one can never calculate what is coming, but in this artificial bird everything is settled. One can explain it ; one can open it and make people understand where the waltzes come from, how they go, and how one follows up another."

" Those are quite our own ideas," they all said.

And the speaker received permission to show the bird to the people on the next Sunday. The people were to hear it sing too, the Emperor commanded ; and they did hear it, and were as much pleased as if they had all got tipsy upon tea, for that's quite the Chinese fashion, and they all said, " Oh ! " and held up their fore-fingers and nodded. But the poor fisherman, who had heard the real Nightingale, said :

" It sounds pretty enough, and the melodies resemble each other, but there's something wanting, though I know not what ! "

The real Nightingale was banished from the country and empire. The artificial bird had its place on a silken cushion close to the Emperor's bed ; all the presents it had received, gold and precious stones, were ranged about it ; in title it had advanced to be the High Imperial After-Dinner-Singer, and in rank to Number One on the left hand ; for the Emperor considered that side the most important on which the heart is placed, and even in an Emperor the heart is on the left side ; and the playmaster wrote a work of five and twenty volumes about the artificial bird : it was very learned and very long, full of the most difficult Chinese words ; but yet all the people declared that they had read it and understood it, for fear of being considered stupid, and having their bodies trampled on.

So a whole year went by. The Emperor, the Court, and all the other Chinese knew every little twitter in the artificial bird's song by heart. But just for that reason it pleased them best—they could sing with it themselves, and they did so. The street boys sang, " Tsi-tsi-tsi-glug-glug ! " and the Emperor himself sang it too. Yes, that was certainly famous.

But one evening when the artificial bird was singing its best, and the Emperor lay in bed listening to it, something inside the bird said, " Whizz ! " Something cracked. " Whir-r-r ! " All the wheels ran round, and then the music stopped.

The Emperor immediately sprang out of bed, and caused his body physician to be called ; but what could *he* do ? Then they sent for a watchmaker, and after a good deal of talking and investigation, the bird was put into something like order, but the watchmaker said that the bird must be carefully treated, for the barrels were worn, and it would be impossible to put new ones in in such a manner that the music would go. There was a great lamentation ; only once in the year was it permitted to let the bird sing, and that was almost too much. But then the playmaster made a little speech, full of heavy words, and said this was just as good as before—and so of course it was as good as before.

Now five years had gone by, and a real grief came upon the whole nation. The Chinese were really fond of their Emperor, and now he was ill, and could not, it was said, live much longer. Already a new Emperor had been chosen, and the people stood out in the street and asked the cavalier how the Emperor did.

" P ! " said he, and shook his head.

Cold and pale lay the Emperor in his great gorgeous bed ; the whole Court thought him dead, and each one ran to pay homage to the new ruler. The chamberlains ran out to talk it over, and the ladies'-maids had a great coffee party. All about, in all the halls and passages, cloth had been laid down so that no footstep could be heard, and therefore it was quiet there, quite quiet. But the Emperor was not dead yet : stiff and pale he lay on the gorgeous bed with the long velvet curtains and the heavy gold tassels ; high up, a window stood open, and the moon shone in upon the Emperor and the artificial bird.

The poor Emperor could scarcely breathe ; it was just as if something lay upon his chest ; he opened his eyes, and then he saw that it was Death who sat upon his chest, and had put on his golden crown, and held in one hand the Emperor's sword, in the other his beautiful banner. And all around, from among the folds of the splendid velvet curtains, strange heads peered forth ; a few very ugly, the rest quite lovely and mild. These were all the Emperor's bad and good deeds, that stood before him now that Death sat upon his heart.

" Do you remember this ? " whispered one to the other. " Do you remember that ? " and then they told him so much that the perspiration ran from his forehead.

" I did not know that ! " said the Emperor. " Music ! music ! the great Chinese drum ! " he cried, " so that I need not hear all they say ! "

And they continued speaking, and Death nodded like a Chinaman to all they said.

" Music ! music ! " cried the Emperor. " You little precious golden bird, sing, sing ! I have given you gold and costly presents ; I have even hung my golden slipper around your neck—sing now, sing ! "

But the bird stood still ; no one was there to wind him up, and he could not sing without that ; but Death continued to stare at the Emperor with his great hollow eyes, and it was quiet, fearfully quiet.

Then there sounded from the window, suddenly, the most lovely song. It was the little live Nightingale, that sat outside on a spray. It had heard of the Emperor's sad plight, and had come to sing to him of comfort and hope. As it sang the spectres grew paler and paler ; the blood ran quicker and more quickly through the Emperor's weak limbs ; and even Death listened, and said :

" Go on, little Nightingale, go on ! "

" But will you give me that splendid golden sword ? Will you give me that rich banner ? Will you give me the Emperor's crown ? "

And Death gave up each of these treasures for a song. And the Nightingale sang on and on ; and it sang of the quiet churchyard where the white roses grow, where the elder blossoms smell sweet, and where the fresh grass is moistened by the tears of survivors. Then Death felt a longing to see his garden, and floated out at the window in the form of a cold white mist.

" Thanks ! thanks ! " said the Emperor. " You heavenly little bird ! I know you well. I banished you from my country and empire, and yet you have charmed away the evil faces from my couch, and banished Death from my heart ! How can I reward you ? "

" You have rewarded me ! " replied the Nightingale. " I have drawn tears from your eyes, when I sang the first time—I shall never forget that. Those are the jewels that rejoice a singer's heart. But now sleep, and grow fresh and strong again. I will sing you something."

And it sang, and the Emperor fell into a sweet slumber. Ah ! how mild and refreshing that sleep was ! The sun shone upon him through the windows, when he awoke refreshed and restored : not one of his servants had yet returned, for they all thought he was dead ; only the Nightingale still sat beside him and sang.

" You must always stay with me," said the Emperor. " You shall sing as you please ; and I'll break the artificial bird into a thousand pieces."

" Not so," replied the Nightingale. " It did well as long as it could : keep it as you have done till now. I cannot build my nest in the palace to dwell in it, but let me come when I feel the wish ; then I will sit in the evening on the spray yonder by the window, and sing you something, so that you may be glad and thoughtful at once. I will sing of those who are happy and of those who suffer. I will sing of good and of evil that remains hidden round about you. The little singing bird flies far around, to the poor fisherman, to the peasant's roof, to every one who dwells far away from you and from your Court. I love your heart more than your crown, and yet the crown has an air of sanctity about it. I will come and sing to you— but one thing you must promise me."

"Everything!" said the Emperor; and he stood there in his Imperial robes, which he had put on himself, and pressed the sword which was heavy with gold to his heart.

"One thing I beg of you : tell no one that you have a little bird who tells you everything. Then it will go all the better."

And the Nightingale flew away.

The servants came in to look at their dead Emperor, and—yes, there he stood, and the Emperor said " Good morning ! "

THE FIR TREE

HANS CHRISTIAN ANDERSEN

OUT in the forest stood a pretty little Fir Tree. It had a good place ; it could have sunlight, air there was in plenty, and all around grew many larger comrades—pines as well as firs. But the little Fir Tree wished ardently to become greater. It did not care for the warm sun and the fresh air ; it took no notice of the peasant children, who went about talking together, when they had come out to look for strawberries and raspberries. Often they came with a whole pot-full, or had strung berries on a straw ; then they would sit down by the little Fir Tree and say, " How pretty and small that one is ! " and the Fir Tree did not like to hear that at all.

Next year he had grown a great joint, and the following year he was longer still, for in fir trees one can always tell by the number of rings they have how many years they have been growing.

" Oh, if I were only as great a tree as the other ! " sighed the little Fir, " then I would spread my branches far around, and look out from my crown into the wide world. The birds would then build nests in my boughs, and when the wind blew I could nod just as grandly as the others yonder."

It took no pleasure in the sunshine, in the birds, and in the red clouds that went sailing over him morning and evening.

When it was winter, and the snow lay all around, white and sparkling, a hare would often come jumping along, and spring right over the little Fir Tree. Oh! this made him so angry. But two winters went by, and when the third came the little Tree had grown so tall that the hare was obliged to run round it.

" Oh! to grow, to grow, and become old ; that's the only fine thing in the world," thought the Tree.

In the autumn woodcutters always came and felled a few of the largest trees ; that was done this year too, and the little Fir Tree, that was now quite well grown, shuddered with fear, for the great stately trees fell to the ground with a crash, and their branches were cut off, so that the trees looked quite naked, long, and slender—they could hardly be recognised. But then they were laid upon wagons, and horses dragged them away out of the wood. Where were they going? What destiny awaited them?

In the spring, when the Swallows and the Stork came, the Tree asked them, " Do you know where they were taken? Did you not meet them?"

The Swallows knew nothing about it, but the Stork looked thoughtful, nodded his head, and said :

" Yes, I think so. I met many new ships when I flew out of Egypt ; on the ships were stately masts ; I fancy these were the trees. They smelt like fir. I can assure you they're stately—very stately."

" Oh that I were only big enough to go over the sea! What kind of thing is this sea, and how does it look? "

" It would take too long to explain all that," said the Stork, and he went away.

" Rejoice in thy youth," said the Sunbeams ; " rejoice in thy fresh growth, and in the young life that is within thee."

And the wind kissed the Tree, and the dew wept tears upon it ; but the Fir Tree did not understand that.

When Christmas-time approached, quite young trees were felled, sometimes trees which were neither so old nor so large as this Fir Tree, that never rested, but always wanted to go away. These young trees, which were almost the most beautiful, kept all their branches ; they were put upon wagons, and horses dragged them away out of the wood.

" Where are they all going? " asked the Fir Tree. " They are not greater than I—indeed, one of them was much smaller. Why do they keep all their branches? Whither are they taken? "

" We know that! We know that! " chirped the Sparrows. " Yonder in the town we looked in at the windows. We know where they go. Oh! they are dressed up in the greatest pomp and splendour that can be imagined. We have looked in at the windows, and have seen that they are planted in the middle of the warm room, and adorned with the most beautiful things—gilt apples, honey-cakes, playthings, and many hundreds of candles."

" And then? " asked the Fir Tree, and trembled through all its branches. " And then? What happens then? "

" Why, we have not seen anything more. But it was incomparable."

" Perhaps I may be destined to tread this glorious path one day! " cried the Fir Tree rejoicingly. " That is even better than travelling across the sea. How painfully I long for it! If it were only

Christmas now! Now I am great and grown up, like the rest who
were led away last year. Oh, if I were only on the carriage! If I
were only in the warm room, among all the pomp and splendour!
And then? Yes, then something even better will come, something
far more charming, or else why should they adorn me so? There
must be something grander, something greater still to come; but
what? Oh! I'm suffering, I'm longing! I don't know myself
what is the matter with me!"

"Rejoice in us," said Air and Sunshine. "Rejoice in thy fresh
youth here in the woodland."

But the Fir Tree did not rejoice at all, but it grew and grew;
winter and summer it stood there, green, dark green. The people
who saw it said, "That's a handsome tree!" and at Christmas-time
it was felled before any one of the others. The axe cut deep into its
marrow and the tree fell to the ground with a sigh: it felt a pain, a
sensation of faintness, and could not think at all of happiness, for
it was sad at parting from its home, from the place where it had
grown up: it knew that it should never again see the dear old companions, the little bushes and flowers all around—perhaps not even
the birds. The parting was not at all agreeable.

The Tree only came to itself when it was unloaded in a yard, with
other trees, and heard a man say:

"This one is famous; we only want this one!"

Now two servants came in gay liveries, and carried the Fir Tree
into a large beautiful saloon. All around the walls hung pictures,
and by the great stove stood large Chinese vases with lions on the
covers; there were rocking-chairs, silken sofas, great tables covered
with picture-books, and toys worth a hundred times a hundred
crowns, at least the children said so. And the Fir Tree was put into
a great tub filled with sand; but no one could see that it was a tub,
for it was hung round with green cloth, and stood on a large many-
coloured carpet. Oh, how the Tree trembled! What was to happen
now? The servants, and the young ladies also, decked it out. On
one branch they hung little nets, cut out of coloured paper; every
net was filled with sweetmeats; golden apples and walnuts hung
down as if they grew there, and more than a hundred little candles,
red, white, and blue, were fastened to the different boughs. Dolls
that looked exactly like real people—the Tree had never seen such
before—swung among the foliage, and high on the summit of the
Tree was fixed a star. It was splendid, particularly splendid.

"This evening," said all, "this evening it will shine."

"Oh," thought the Tree, "that it were evening already! Oh
that the lights may be soon lit up! When may that be done? I
wonder if trees will come out of the forest to look at me? Will the
sparrows fly against the panes? Shall I grow fast here, and stand
adorned in summer and winter?"

Yes, he did not guess badly. But he had a complete backache from mere longing, and the backache is just as bad for a Tree as the headache for a person.

At last the candles were lighted. What a brilliance, what splendour! The Tree trembled so in all its branches that one of the candles set fire to a green twig, and it was scorched.

"Heaven preserve us!" cried the young ladies; and they hastily put the fire out.

Now the Tree might not even tremble. Oh, that was terrible! It was so afraid of setting fire to some of its ornaments, and it was quite bewildered with all the brilliance. And now the folding-doors were thrown open, and a number of children rushed in as if they would have overturned the whole Tree: the older people followed more deliberately. The little ones stood quite silent, but only for a minute; then they shouted till the room rang: they danced gleefully round the Tree, and one present after another was plucked from it.

"What are they about?" thought the Tree. "What's going to be done?"

And the candles burned down to the twigs, and as they burned down they were extinguished, and then the children received permission to plunder the Tree. Oh! they rushed in upon it, so that every branch cracked again: if it had not been fastened by the top and by the golden star to the ceiling, it would have fallen down.

The children danced about with their pretty toys. No one looked at the Tree except one old man, who came up and peeped among the branches, but only to see if a fig or an apple had not been forgotten.

"A story! a story!" shouted the children; and they drew a little fat man towards the Tree; and he sat down just beneath it, "for then we shall be in the green wood," said he, "and the tree may have the advantage of listening to my tale. But I can only tell one. Will you hear the story of Ivede-Avede, or of Klumpey-Dumpey, who fell downstairs, and still was raised up to honour and married the Princess?"

"Ivede-Avede!" cried some; "Klumpey-Dumpey!" cried others, and there was a great crying and shouting. Only the Fir Tree was quite silent, and thought, "Shall I not be in it? shall I have nothing to do in it?" But he had been in the evening's amusement, and had done what was required of him.

And the fat man told about Klumpey-Dumpey who fell downstairs, and yet was raised to honour and married the Princess. And the children clapped their hands, and cried, "Tell another! tell another!" for they wanted to hear about Ivede-Avede; but they only got the story of Klumpey-Dumpey. The Fir Tree stood quite silent and thoughtful; never had the birds in the wood told such a story as that. Klumpey-Dumpey fell downstairs, and yet came to honour and married the Princess!

"Yes, so it happens in the world!" thought the Fir Tree, and believed it must be true, because that was such a nice man who told it. "Well, who can know? Perhaps I shall fall downstairs too, and marry a Princess!" And it looked forward with pleasure to being adorned again, the next evening, with candles and toys, gold and fruit. "To-morrow I shall not tremble," it thought. "I will rejoice in all my splendour. To-morrow I shall hear the story of Klumpey-Dumpey again, and perhaps that of Ivede-Avede too."

And the Tree stood all night quiet and thoughtful.

In the morning the servants and the chambermaid came in.

"Now my splendour will begin afresh," thought the Tree. But they dragged him out of the room, and upstairs to the garret, and here they put him in a dark corner where no daylight shone.

"What's the meaning of this?" thought the Tree. "What am I to do here? What is to happen?"

And he leaned against the wall, and thought, and thought. And he had time enough, for days and nights went by, and nobody came up; and when at length some one came, it was only to put some great boxes in a corner. Now the Tree stood quite hidden away, and the supposition is that it was quite forgotten.

"Now it's winter outside," thought the Tree. "The earth is hard and covered with snow, and people cannot plant me; therefore I suppose I'm to be sheltered here until spring comes. How considerate that is! How good people are! If it were only not so dark here, and so terribly solitary!—not even a little hare! That was pretty out there in the wood, when the snow lay thick and the hare sprang past; yes, even when he jumped over me; but then I did not like it. It is terribly lonely up here!"

"Piep! piep!" said a little Mouse, and crept forward, and then came another little one. They smelt at the Fir Tree, and then slipped among the branches.

"It's horribly cold," said the two little Mice, "or else it would be comfortable here. Don't you think so, you old Fir Tree?"

"I'm not old at all," said the Fir Tree. "There are many much older than I."

"Where do you come from?" asked the Mice. "And what do you know?" They were dreadfully inquisitive. "Tell us about the most beautiful spot on earth. Have you been there? Have you been in the store-room, where cheeses lie on the shelves, and hams hang from the ceiling, where one dances on tallow candles, and goes in thin and comes out fat?"

"I don't know that," replied the Tree; "but I know the wood, where the sun shines and the birds sing."

And then it told all about its youth.

And the little Mice had never heard anything of the kind; and they listened and said :

" What a number of things you have seen ! How happy you must have been ! "

" I ? " replied the Fir Tree ; and it thought about what it had told. " Yes, those were really quite happy times." But then he told of the Christmas Eve, when he had been hung with sweetmeats and candles.

" Oh ! " said the little Mice, " how happy you have been, you old Fir Tree ! "

" I'm not old at all," said the Tree. " I only came out of the wood this winter. I'm only rather backward in my growth."

" What splendid stories you can tell ! " said the little Mice.

And next night they came with four other little Mice, to hear what the Tree had to relate ; and the more it said, the more clearly did it remember everything, and thought, " Those were quite merry days ! But they may come again. Klumpey-Dumpey fell downstairs, and yet he married the Princess. Perhaps I may marry a Princess too ! " And then the Fir Tree thought of a pretty little birch tree that grew out in the forest : for the Fir Tree, that birch was a real Princess.

" Who's Klumpey-Dumpey ? " asked the little Mice.

And then the Fir Tree told the whole story. It could remember every single word ; and the little Mice were ready to leap to the very top of the tree with pleasure. Next night a great many more Mice came, and on Sunday two Rats even appeared ; but these thought the story was not pretty, and the little Mice were sorry for that, for now they also did not like it so much as before.

" Do you only know one story ? " asked the Rats.

" Only that one," replied the Tree. " I heard that on the happiest evening of my life ; I did not think then how happy I was."

" That's a very miserable story. Don't you know any about bacon and tallow candles—a store-room story ? "

" No," said the Tree.

" Then we'd rather not hear you," said the Rats.

And they went back to their own people. The little Mice at last stayed away also ; and then the Tree sighed and said :

" It was very nice when they sat round me, the merry little Mice, and listened when I spoke to them. Now that's past too. But I shall remember to be pleased when they take me out."

But when did that happen ? Why, it was one morning that people came and rummaged in the garret : the boxes were put away, and the Tree brought out ; they certainly threw him rather roughly on the floor, but a servant dragged him away at once to the stairs, where the daylight shone.

" Now life is beginning again ! " thought the Tree.

It felt the fresh air and the first sunbeams, and now it was out in the courtyard. Everything passed so quickly that the Tree quite forgot to look at itself, there was so much to look at all round. The courtyard was close to a garden, and here everything was blooming ; the roses hung fresh and fragrant over the little paling, the linden trees were in blossom, and the swallows cried, " Quinze-wit ! quinze-wit ! my husband's come ! " But it was not the Fir Tree that they meant.

" Now I shall live ! " said the Tree rejoicingly, and spread its branches far out ; but, alas ! they were all withered and yellow ; and it lay in the corner among nettles and weeds. The tinsel star was still upon it, and shone in the bright sunshine.

In the courtyard a couple of the merry children were playing, who had danced round the tree at Christmas-time, and had rejoiced over it. One of the youngest ran up and tore off the golden star.

" Look what is sticking to the ugly old fir tree," said the child, and he trod upon the branches till they cracked again under his boots.

And the Tree looked at all the blooming flowers and the splendour of the garden, and then looked at itself, and wished it had remained in the dark corner of the garret ; it thought of its fresh youth in the wood, of the merry Christmas Eve, and of the little Mice which had listened so pleasantly to the story of Klumpey-Dumpey.

" Past ! past ! " said the old Tree. " Had I but rejoiced when I could have done so ! Past ! past ! "

And the servant came and chopped the Tree into little pieces ; a whole bundle lay there ; it blazed brightly under the great brewing copper, and it sighed deeply, and each sigh was like a little shot ; and the children who were at play there ran up and seated themselves at the fire, looked into it, and cried " Puff ! puff ! " But at each explosion, which was a deep sigh, the Tree thought of a summer day in the woods, or of a winter night there, when the stars beamed ; he thought of Christmas Eve and of Klumpey-Dumpey, the only story he had ever heard or knew how to tell ; and then the Tree was burned.

The boys played in the garden, and the youngest had on his breast a golden star, which the Tree had worn on its happiest evening. Now that was past, and the Tree's life was past, and the story is past too : past ! past !—and that's the way with all stories.

THE STORY OF A MOTHER

HANS CHRISTIAN ANDERSEN

A MOTHER sat by her little child: she was very sorrowful, and feared that it would die. Its little face was pale, and its eyes were closed. The child drew its breath with difficulty, and sometimes so deeply as if it were sighing; and then the mother looked more sorrowfully than before on the little creature.

Then there was a knock at the door, and a poor old man came in wrapped up in something that looked like a great horse-cloth, for that keeps warm; and he required it, for it was cold winter. Without, everything was covered with ice and snow, and the wind blew so sharply that it cut one's face.

And as the old man trembled with cold, and the child was quiet for a moment, the mother went and put some beer on the stove in a little pot, to warm it for him. The old man sat down and rocked the cradle, and the mother seated herself on an old chair by him, looked at her sick child that drew its breath so painfully, and seized the little hand.

"You think I shall keep it, do you not?" she asked. "The good God will not take it from me!"

And the old man—he was *Death*—nodded in such a strange way, that it might just as well mean *yes* as *no*. And the mother cast down her eyes, and tears rolled down her cheeks. Her head became heavy: for three days and three nights she had not closed her eyes; and now she slept, but only for a minute; then she started up and shivered with cold.

"What is that?" she asked, and looked round on all sides; but the old man was gone, and her little child was gone; he had taken it with him. And there in the corner the old clock was humming and whirring; the heavy leaden weight ran down to the floor—plump!—and the clock stopped.

But the poor mother rushed out of the house crying for her child.

Out in the snow sat a woman in long black garments, and she said, "Death has been with you in your room; I saw him hasten away with your child: he strides faster than the wind, and never brings back what he has taken away."

"Only tell me which way he has gone," said the mother. "Tell me the way, and I will find him."

"I know him," said the woman in the black garments; "but before I tell you, you must sing me all the songs that you have sung to your child. I love those songs; I have heard them before. I am Night, and I saw your tears when you sang them."

"I will sing them all, all!" said the mother. "But do not detain me, that I may overtake him, and find my child."

But Night sat dumb and still. Then the mother wrung her hands, and sang and wept. And there were many songs, but yet more tears, and then Night said, "Go to the right into the dark fir wood; for I saw Death take that path with your little child."

Deep in the forest there was a cross road, and she did not know which way to take. There stood a Blackthorn Bush, with not a leaf or a blossom upon it; for it was in the cold winter-time, and icicles hung from the twigs.

"Have you not seen Death go by, with my little child?"

"Yes," replied the Bush; "but I shall not tell you which way he went unless you warm me on your bosom. I'm freezing to death here, I'm turning to ice."

And she pressed the Blackthorn Bush to her bosom, quite close, that it might be well warmed. And the thorns pierced into her flesh, and her blood oozed out in great drops. But the Blackthorn shot out fresh green leaves, and blossomed in the dark winter night: so warm is the heart of a sorrowing mother! And the Blackthorn Bush told her the way that she should go.

Then she came to a great Lake, on which there was neither ship nor boat. The Lake was not frozen enough to carry her, nor sufficiently open to allow her to wade through, and yet she must cross it if she was to find her child. Then she laid herself down to drink the Lake; and that was impossible for anyone to do. But the sorrowing mother thought that perhaps a miracle might be wrought.

"No, that can never succeed," said the Lake. "Let us rather see how we can agree. I'm fond of collecting pearls, and your eyes are the two clearest I have ever seen: if you will weep them out into me I will carry you over into the great greenhouse, where Death lives and cultivates flowers and trees; each of these is a human life."

"Oh, what would I not give to get my child!" said the afflicted mother; and she wept yet more, and her eyes fell into the depths of the Lake, and became two costly pearls. But the Lake lifted her up, as if she sat in a swing, and she was wafted to the opposite shore, where stood a wonderful house, miles in length. One could not tell if it was a mountain containing forests and caves, or a place that had been built. But the poor mother could not see it, for she had wept her eyes out.

"Where shall I find Death, who went away with my little child?" she asked.

" He has not arrived here yet," said an old grey-haired woman, who was going about and watching the hot-house of Death. " How have you found your way here, and who helped you ? "

" The good God has helped me," she replied. " He is merciful, and you will be merciful too. Where—where shall I find my little child ? "

" I do not know it," said the old woman, " and you cannot see. Many flowers and trees have faded this night, and Death will soon come and transplant them. You know very well that every human being has his tree of life, or his flower of life, just as each is arranged. They look like other plants, but their hearts beat. Children's hearts can beat too. Think of this. Perhaps you may recognise the beating of your child's heart. But what will you give me if I tell you what more you must do ? "

" I have nothing more to give," said the afflicted mother. " But I will go for you to the ends of the earth."

" I have nothing for you to do there," said the old woman, " but you can give me your long black hair. You must know yourself that it is beautiful, and it pleases me. You can take my white hair for it, and that is always something."

" Do you ask for nothing more ? " asked she. " I will give you that gladly." And she gave her beautiful hair, and received in exchange the old woman's white hair.

And then they went into the great hot-house of Death, where flowers and trees were growing marvellously intertwined. There stood the fine hyacinths under glass bells, some quite fresh, others somewhat sickly ; water-snakes were twining about them, and black crabs clung tightly to the stalks. There stood gallant palm trees, oaks, and plantains, and parsley and blooming thyme. Each tree and flower had its name ; each was a human life : the people were still alive, one in China, another in Greenland, scattered about in the world. There were great trees thrust into little pots, so that they stood quite crowded, and were nearly bursting the pots ; there was also many a little weakly flower in rich earth, with moss round about it, cared for and tended. But the sorrowful mother bent down over all the smallest plants, and heard the human heart beating in each, and out of millions she recognised that of her child.

" That is it ! " she cried, and stretched out her hands over a little crocus flower, which hung down quite sick and pale.

" Do not touch the flower," said the old dame ; " but place yourself here ; and when Death comes—I expect him every minute— then don't let him pull up the plant, but threaten him that you will do the same to the other plants ; then he'll be frightened. He has to account for them all ; not one may be pulled up till he receives commission from Heaven."

And all at once there was an icy cold rush through the hall, and the blind mother felt that Death was arriving.

" How did you find your way hither ? " said he. " How have you been able to come quicker than I ? "

" I am a mother," she answered.

And Death stretched out his long hands towards the little delicate flower ; but she kept her hands tight about it, and held it fast ; and yet she was full of anxious care lest he should touch one of the leaves. Then Death breathed upon her hands, and she felt that his breath was colder than the icy wind ; and her hands sank down powerless.

" You can do nothing against me," said Death.

" But the merciful God can," she replied.

" I only do what He commands," said Death. " I am His gardener. I take all His trees and flowers, and transplant them into the great Paradise gardens, in the unknown land. But how they will flourish there, and how it is there, I may not tell you."

" Give me back my child," said the mother ; and she implored and wept. All at once she grasped two pretty flowers with her two hands, and called to Death, " I'll tear off all your flowers, for I am in despair."

" Do not touch them," said Death. " You say you are so unhappy, and now you would make another mother just as unhappy ! "

" Another mother ? " said the poor woman ; and she let the flowers go.

" There are your eyes for you," said Death. " I have fished them out of the lake ; they gleamed up quite brightly. I did not know that they were yours. Take them back—they are clearer now than before—and then look down into the deep well close by. I will tell you the names of the two flowers you wanted to pull up, and you will see what you were about to frustrate and destroy."

And she looked down into the well, and it was a happiness to see how one of them became a blessing to the world, how much joy and gladness she diffused around her. And the woman looked at the life of the other, and it was made up of care and poverty, misery and woe.

" Both are the will of God." said Death.

" Which of them is the flower of misfortune, and which the blessed one ? " she asked.

" That I may not tell you," answered Death, " but this much you shall hear, that one of these two flowers is that of your child. It was the fate of your child that you were—the future of your own child."

Then the mother screamed aloud for terror.

" Which of them belongs to my child ? Tell me that ! Release the innocent child! Let my child free from all that misery! Rather carry it away! Carry it into God's kingdom! Forget my tears, forget my entreaties, and all that I have done!"

"I do not understand you," said Death. "Will you have your child back, or shall I carry it to that place that you know not?"

Then the mother wrung her hands, and fell on her knees, and prayed to the good God.

"Hear me not when I pray against Thy will, which is at all times the best! Hear me not! hear me not!" And she let her head sink down on her bosom.

And Death went away with her child into the unknown land.

THE LITTLE MATCH-GIRL

HANS CHRISTIAN ANDERSEN

IT was terribly cold; it snowed and was already almost dark, and evening came on, the last evening of the year. In the cold and gloom a poor little girl, bareheaded and barefoot was walking through the streets. When she left her own house she certainly had had slippers on; but of what use were they? They were very big slippers, and her mother had used them till then, so big were they. The little maid lost them as she slipped across the road, where two carriages were rattling by terribly fast. One slipper was not to be found again, and a boy had seized the other, and run away with it. He thought he could use it very well as a cradle, some day when he had children of his own. So now the little girl went with her little naked feet, which were quite red and blue with the cold. In an old apron she carried a number of matches, and a bundle of them in her hand. No one had bought anything of her all day, and no one had given her a farthing.

Shivering with cold and hunger, she crept along, a picture of misery, poor little girl! Snow-flakes covered her long fair hair, which fell in pretty curls over her neck; but she did not think of that now. In all the windows lights were shining, and there was a glorious smell of roast goose, for it was New Year's Eve. Yes, she thought of that!

In a corner formed by two houses, one of which projected beyond the other, she sat down, cowering. She had drawn up her little feet, but she was still colder, and she did not dare to go home, for she had sold no matches, and did not bring a farthing of money. From her father she would certainly receive a beating, and besides, it was cold at home, for they had nothing over them but a roof through which the wind whistled.

Her little hands were almost benumbed with the cold ! Ah ! a match might do her good, if she could only draw one from the bundle, and rub it against the wall, and warm her hands at it. She drew one out. R-r-atch ! how it sputtered and burned ! It was a warm bright flame, like a little candle, when she held her hands over it ; it was a wonderful little light ! It really seemed to the little girl as if she sat before a great polished stove, with bright brass feet and a brass cover. How the fire burned ! How comfortable it was ! But the little flame went out, and the stove vanished, and she had only the remains of the burned match in her hand.

A second was rubbed against the wall. It burned up, and when the light fell upon the wall it became transparent like a thin veil, and she could see through it into the room. On the table a snow-white cloth was spread ; upon it stood a shining dinner service ; the roast goose smoked gloriously, stuffed with apples and dried plums. And what was still more splendid to behold, the goose hopped down from the dish, and waddled along the floor, with a knife and fork in its breast, to the little girl. Then the match went out, and only the thick, damp, cold wall was before her. She lighted another match. Then she was sitting under a beautiful Christmas tree : it was greater and more ornamental than the one she had seen through the glass door at the rich merchant's. Thousands of candles burned upon the green branches, and coloured pictures like those in the print-shops looked down upon them. The little girl stretched forth her hand towards them ; then the match went out. The Christmas lights mounted higher. She saw them now as stars in the sky : one of them fell down, forming a long line of fire.

" Now some one is dying," thought the little girl, for her old grandmother, the only person who had loved her, and who was now dead, had told her that when a star fell down a soul mounted up to God. She rubbed another match against the wall ; it became bright again, and in the brightness the old grandmother stood clear and shining, mild and lovely.

" Grandmother ! " cried the child, " take me with you ! I know you will go when the match is burned out. You will vanish like the warm fire, the warm food, and the great glorious Christmas tree ! "

And she hastily rubbed the whole bundle of matches, for she wished to hold her grandmother fast. And the matches burned with such a glow that it became brighter than in the middle of the day : grandmother had never been so large or so beautiful. She took the little girl in her arms, and both flew in brightness and joy above the earth, very, very high, and up there was neither cold, nor hunger, nor care—they were with God !

But in the corner, leaning against the wall, sat the poor girl with red cheeks and smiling mouth, frozen to death on the last evening of the Old Year.   The New Year's sun rose upon a little corpse ! The child sat there, stiff and cold, with the matches, of which one bundle was burned.   " She wanted to warm herself," the people said.   No one knew what a beautiful thing she had seen, and in what glory she had gone in with her grandmother to the New Year's Day.

DANISH   MEYER ARON
GOLDSCHMIDT
1819–1887

THE FLYING MAIL

I

FRITZ BAGGER had just been admitted to the bar. He had come home and entered his room, seeking rest. All his mental faculties were now relaxed after their recent exertion, and a long-restrained power was awakened. He had reached a crisis in life : the future lay before him,—the future, the future ! What was it to be ? He was twenty-four years old, and could turn himself whichever way he pleased, let fancy run to any line of the compass. Out upon the horizon, he saw little rose-coloured clouds, and nothing therein but a certain undefined bliss. He put his hands over his eyes, and sought to bring this uncertainty into clear vision ; and after a long time had elapsed, he said : " Yes, and so one marries."

" Yes, one marries," he continued, after a pause ; " but whom ? "

The truth was, he didn't know anybody to whom he could give his heart, but longed, with a certain twenty-four-year power, for her to whom he could offer it,—her who was worthy to receive his whole self-made being, and in exchange give him all that queer imagined bliss, which is or ought to be in the world, as every one so firmly believes.

" Oh, I am a fool ! " he said, as he suddenly became conscious that he was merely dreaming and wishing.

He leaned upon the window-seat—it was in an attic—and let the wind cool his forehead. But while the wind refreshed, the street itself gave his mind new nourishment. Down there it moved, to him unknown, and veiled and hidden as at a masquerade. What a treasure might not that easy virgin foot carry ! What a fancy might there not be moving in the head under that little bonnet, and what a heart might there not be beating under the folds of that shawl ! But, too, all this treasure might belong to another.

" Oh ! life is a lottery, a cruel lottery ; for to everybody there is but one drawing, and the whole man is at stake. Woe to the loser ! "

For the second time he stroked his forehead, shook these thoughts from him, seeking more practical ones, and for the second time it terminated in going to the window and gazing out.

A whirlwind filled the street, slamming gates and doors, shaking windows and carrying dust with it up to his attic chamber.   He was in the act of drawing back, when he saw a little piece of paper whirled in the dust cloud coming closely near him.   He shut his eyes to keep out the dust, grasping at random for the paper, which he caught.   At the same moment the whirlwind ceased, and the sky was again clear. This appeared to him ominous ; the scrap of paper had certainly a meaning to him, a meaning for him ; the unknown whom he had not really spoken to, yet had been so exceedingly busy with, could not quite accidentally have thus conveyed this to his hands, and with throbbing heart he retired from the window to read the message.

One side of the paper was blank ; in the left-hand corner of the other side was written " beloved," and a little below it seemed as if there had been a signature, but now there was nothing left excepting the letters " geb."

" ' Geb,' what does that mean ? " asked Fritz Bagger, with dark humour.   " If it had been gek, I could have understood it, although it were incorrectly written.   Geb, Gebrer, Algebra, Gebrüderbuh,— I am a big fool."

" But it is no matter, she shall have an answer," he shouted after a while, and seated himself to write a long, glowing love-letter. When it was finished and read, he tore it in pieces.

" No," said he, " if destiny has intended the least thing by acting to me as mail-carrier through the window, let me act reasonably." He wrote on a little piece of paper :

" As the old Norwegians, when they went to Iceland threw their high-seat pillars into the sea with the resolution to settle where they should go ashore, so I send this out.   My faith follows after ; and it is my conviction that where this alights, I shall one day come, and salute you as my chosen, as my——"   " Yes, now what more shall I add ? " he asked himself.   " Ay, as my—' geb '— ! " he added, with an outburst of merry humour, that just completed the whole sentimental outburst.   He went to the window and threw the paper out ; it alighted with a slow quivering.   He was already afraid that it would go directly down into the ditch ; but then a breeze came lifting it almost up to himself again, then a new current carried it away, lifting it higher and higher, whirling it, till at last it disappeared from his sight in continual ascent.

" After all, I have become engaged to-day," he said to himself, with a certain quiet humour, and yet impressed by a feeling that he had really given himself to the unknown.

II

Six years had passed, and Fritz Bagger had made his mark, although not as a lover. He had become Counsellor, and was particularly distinguished for the skill and energy with which he brought criminals to confession. It is thus that a man of fine and poetic feelings can satisfy himself in such a business, for a time at least : with the half of his soul he can lead a life which to himself and others seems entire only because it is busy, because it keeps him at work, and fills him with a consciousness of accomplishing something practical and good.

Be it because his professional duties gave him no time or opportunity for courtship, or for some other reason, Fritz Bagger remained a bachelor ; and a bachelor with the income of his profession is looked upon as a rich man. Counsellor Bagger would, when business allowed, enter into social life, treating it in that elegant, independent, almost poetic manner, which in most cases is denied to married men, and which is one reason why they press the hand of a bachelor with a sigh, a mixture of envy, admiration, and compassion. If we add here that a bachelor with such a professional income is the possible stepping-stone to an advantageous marriage, it is easily seen that Fritz Bagger was much sought for in company. He went into society, too, as often as his legal duties allowed, hastening in the black " swallow-tail " to a dinner or soirée, and often amusing himself where others were weary. For conversation about anything whatever with the cultivated was to him a refreshment, and he brought with him a good appetite and good humour, resting upon conscientious work. He could show interest in trifles, because in their nothingness (quite contrary to the trifles in which half an hour previous, with painful interest, he had ferreted out crime) they appeared to him as belonging to an innocent, childish world ; and if conversation approached more earnest things, he spoke freely, and evidently gave himself quite up to the subject, letting the whole surface of his soul flow out. And thus he procured friendship and reputation.

In this way, then, six years had slipped by, when Counsellor Bagger, or rather Fritz Bagger as we will call him, in remembrance of his examination-day, and his notes by the flying mail, was invited to a wedding-party on the shooting-ground. The company was not very large—only thirty couples—but very select. Bagger was a friend in the families of both bride and bridegroom, and consequently being well known to nearly all present he felt himself as among friends gathered by a mutual joy, and was more than usually animated. A superb wine, which the bride's father had himself brought, crowned their spirits with the last perfect wreath. Although the toast to the bridal pair had been officially proposed,

Bagger took occasion to offer his congratulations in a second encomium of love and matrimony ; which gave a solid, prosaic man opportunity for the witty remark and hearty wish that so distinguished a practical office-holder as Counsellor Bagger would carry his fine theories upon matrimony into practice.   The toast was drunk with enthusiasm, and just at that moment a strong wind shook the windows, and burst open one of the doors, blowing so far into the hall as to cause the lights to flicker much.

Bagger became, through the influence of the wine, the company, and the sight of the happy bridal pair, six years younger.   His soul was carried away from criminal and police courts, and found itself on high, as in the attic chamber, with a vision of the small tinted clouds and the angel-heads.   The sudden gust of wind carried him quite back to the moment when he sent out his note as the Norwegian heroes their high-seat pillars : the spirit of his twenty-fourth year came wholly over him, queerly mixed with the half-regretful reflection of the thirtieth year, with fun, and inclination to talk and to breathe.   He exclaimed, as he rose to acknowledge the toast :

" I am engaged."

" Ay ! ay ! Congratulations ! congratulations ! " sounded from all sides.

" This gust of wind, which nearly extinguished the lights, brought me a message from my betrothed ! "

" What ? "   " What is it ? " asked the company, their heads at that moment not in the least condition for guessing charades.

" Counsellor Bagger, have you, like the Doge of Venice, betrothed yourself to the sea or storm ? " asked the bridegroom.

" Yes," exclaimed Bagger, " just like the Doge of Venice, but not as aristocratic !   From my attic chamber, where I sat on my examination-day, guided by Cupid, in a manner which it would take too long to narrate, I gave to the whirlwind a love-letter, and at any moment *She* can step forward with my letter, my promise, and demand me soul and body."

" Who is it, then ? " asked bridegroom and bride, with the most earnest interest.

" Yes, how can I tell that ?   Do I know the whirlwind's roads ? "

" Was the letter signed with your name ? "

" No ; but don't you think I will acknowledge my handwriting ? " replied Bagger, quite earnestly.

This earnestness with reference to an obligation which no one understood became comical ; and Bagger felt at the moment that he was on the brink of the ridiculous.   Trying to collect himself, he said :

" Is it not an obligation we all have ?   Do not both bride and bridegroom acknowledge that long before they knew each other the obligation was present ? "

" Yes, yes ! " exclaimed the bridegroom.

" And the whirlwind, accident, the unknown power, brought them together so that the obligation was redeemed ? "

" Yes, yes ! "

" Let us, then," continued Bagger, " drink a toast to the wind, the accident, the moving power, unknown and yet controlling. To those of us who, as yet, are unprovided for and under forty, it will at some time undoubtedly bring a bride ; to those who are already provided for will come the expected in another form. So a toast to the wind that came in here and flickered the lights ; to the unknown, that brings us the wished for ; and to ourselves, that we may be prepared to receive it when announced."

" Bravo ! " exclaimed the bridgroom, looking upon his bride.

" Puh-h-h ! " thought Bagger, seating himself with intense relief, " I have come out of it somewhat decently after all. The deuce take me before I again express a sentimentality."

How Counsellor Bagger that night could have fallen asleep, between memory, or longing and discontent, is difficult to tell, had he not on his arrival home found a package of papers, an interesting theft case. He sat down instantly to read, and day dawned ere they were finished. His last thought, before his eyelids closed, was—Two years in the House of Correction.

III

A month later, toward the close of September, two ladies, twenty or twenty-two years of age, were walking in a garden about ten miles from Copenhagen. One of the ladies apparently was at home there : this was evident partly from her dress, which, although elegant, was domestic, and partly by her taking the lead and paying honour, by drawing boughs and branches aside, holding them until her companion, who was more showily dressed, had slipped past. This companion, a handsome, cultivated girl of the well-to-do middle class, had certainly a soul, but yet was far less busy with the world in her own heart than with the world of fashion. It was about the world, the world of Copenhagen, that Miss Brandt at this moment was telling Miss Hjelm, and although Miss Hjelm was not, nun-like, indifferent either to fashions or incidents in high life, the earnest manner in which Miss Brandt spoke of these things caused her to go politely in front.

" But you have heard about Emmy Ibsen's marriage ? " asked Miss Brandt.

" Yes, it was about a month ago, I think."

" Yes, I was bridesmaid."

" Indeed ! " said Miss Hjelm, in a voice which atoned for her brevity.

" The party was at the shooting-ground."

" So ! " said Miss Hjelm again, with as correct an intonation as
if she had substituted it for " I don't care." " Take care, Miss
Brandt," she added, stooping to avoid an apple-branch.

" Take care ?—oh, for that branch ! " said Miss Brandt, and
avoided it as charmingly and coquettishly as if it had been living.

" It was very gay," she added, " even more so than wedding-
parties commonly are ; but this was caused a good deal by Counsellor Bagger."

" So ! "

" Yes, he was very gay. . . .   I was his companion at table."

" Ah ! "

" Oh, only to think ! he stood up at the table declaring that he
was engaged."

" Was his lady present ? "

" No, that she was not, I think.   Do you know who it was ? "

" No.   How should I know that, Miss Brandt ? "

" The whirlwind ! "

" The whirlwind ? "

" Yes.   He said that he, as a young man, in a solemn moment
had sent his love-letter or his promise out with the wind, and he was
continually waiting for an answer : he had given his promise, was
betrothed !—Ou ! "

" What is it ? " asked Hiss Hjelm sympathetically.   The truth
was, the young hostess at this moment had relaxed her polite care,
and a limb of a gooseberry bush had struck against Miss Brandt's
ankle.

The pain was soon over ; and the two ladies, who now had reached
the termination of the walk, turned toward the house side by side,
each protecting herself, unconscious that any change had occurred.

" But I hardly believe it," continued Miss Brandt ; " he said it
perhaps only to make himself conspicuous, for certain gentlemen are
just as coquettish as . . . as they accuse us of being."

Miss Hjelm uttered a doubting " Um ! "

" Yes, that they really are !   Have you ever seen any lady as
coquettish as an actor ? "

" I don't know any of them, but I should suppose an actress
might be."

" No : no actress I have ever met of the better sort was really
coquettish.   I don't know how it is with them, but I believe they
have overcome coquettishness."

" But you think, then, Counsellor Bang is coquettish ? "

" Not Bang—Bagger.   Yes ; for although he said he had this
romantic love for a fairy, he often does court to modest earthly ladies.
He is certainly something of a flirt ! "

" How unbecoming in an old man ! "

" Yes ; but he is not old."

"Oh!" said Miss Hjelm, laughing: "I have only known one war counsellor, and he was old; so I thought of all war counsellors as old."

"Yes; but Counsellor Bagger is not war counsellor, but a real Superior Court Counsellor."

"Oh, how earnest that is! And so he is in love with a fairy?"

"Yes: it is ridiculous!" said Miss Brandt, laughing. During this conversation they had reached the house, and Miss Brandt complained that something was yet pricking her ankle. They went into Miss Hjelm's room, and here a thorn was discovered and taken out.

"How pretty and cosy this room really is!" said Miss Brandt, looking around. "In a situation like this, one can surely live in the country summer and winter. Out with us at Taarback it blows in through the windows, doors, and very walls."

"That must be bad in a whirlwind."

"Yes—yes: still, it might be quite amusing when the whirlwind carried such billets: not that one would care for them; yet they might be interesting for a while."

"Oh, yes! perhaps."

"Yes: how do you think a young girl would like it, when there came from Heaven a billet in which one pledged himself to her for time and eternity?"

"That isn't easy to say; but I don't believe the occurrence quite so uncommon. A friend of mine once had such a billet blown to her, and she presented me with it."

"Does one give such things away? Have you the billet?"

"I will look for it," answered Miss Hjelm; and surely enough, after longer search in the sewing-table, in drawers and small boxes, than was really necessary, she found it. Miss Brandt read it, taking care not to remark that it very much appeared to her as if it resembled the one the counsellor had mentioned.

"And one gives such a billet away!" she said, after a pause.

"Yes: will you have it?" asked Miss Hjelm, as though after a sudden resolution.

Miss Brandt's first impulse was an eager acceptance; but she checked herself almost as quickly, and answered:

"Oh, yes, thank you, as a curiosity." Then slowly put it between her glove and hand.

When Miss Brandt and her company rode away, Miss Hjelm's cousin, a handsome, middle-aged widow, said to her:

"How is it, Ingeborg? It appears to me you laugh with one eye and weep with the other."

"Yes: a soap-bubble has burst for me, and glitters, maybe, for another."

" You know I seldom understand the sentimental enigmas : can you not interpret your words ? "

" Yes : to-day an illusion has vanished, that had lasted for six years."

" For six years ? " said her cousin, with an inquiring or sympathising look.   " So it began when you were hardly sixteen years."

" Now do you believe that when I was in my sixteenth year I saw an ideal of a man, and was enamoured of him, and to-day I hear that he is married ? "

" No, I don't know that I believe all that," answered the cousin, dropping her eyes ; " but I suppose that then you had a pretty vision, and have carried it along with you in silence—and with faith."

" But it was something more than a vision ; it was a letter—a love-letter."

The cousin looked upon Ingeborg so inquiringly, so anxiously, that words were unnecessary. Beside this the cousin knew that when Ingeborg was inclined to talk she did so without being asked, and if she wished to be silent she was silent.

Ingeborg continued : " One day I drove to town with my dear father. Father was to go on further than to Noerrebro, and I had an errand at Vestervold. So I stepped out and went through the Love-path. As I came to the corner of the path and the Ladegaardsway the wind blew so violently against me that I could hardly breathe, and something blew against my veil, fluttering with wings like a humming-bird. I tried to drive it away, for it blinded one of my eyes ; but it blew back again. So I caught it and was going to let it fly away over my head, but that moment I saw it was written upon, and read it. It was a love-letter ! A man wrote that he sent this as in old times the Norwegian emigrants let their high-seat pillars be carried by the sea, and where it came he would one time come, and bring his faith to his destined ' Geb.' "

" ' Geb ' ? What is that ? " asked the cousin.

" That is Ingeborg," answered Miss Hjelm, with a plain simplicity, showing how deeply she had believed in the earnestness of the message.

" It was really remarkable ! " said the cousin, and added with a smile which perhaps was somewhat ironical : " And did you then resolve to remain unmarried, until the unknown letter-writer should come and redeem his vow ? "

" I will not say that," answered Ingeborg, who quickly became more guarded ; " but the letter perhaps contained some stronger requirements than under the circumstances could be fulfilled."

" So ! and now ? "

" Now I have presented the letter to Miss Brandt."

" You gave it away ? Why ? "

" Because I learned that the man, who perhaps or probably wrote it in his youth, has spoken about it publicly, and is Counsellor in one of the courts."

" Oh, I understand," said the cousin, half audibly : " when the ideal is found out to be a counsellor, then——"

" Then it is not an ideal any longer ? No. The whole had been spoiled by being talked about in public. I wanted to get away from the temptation to think of him. Pay court to him, announce myself to him as the happy finder—I could not."

" That I understand very well," said the cousin, putting her arm affectionately around Ingeborg's waist ; " but why did you just give Miss Brandt the letter ? "

" Because she is acquainted with the counsellor, and indeed, as far as I could understand, feels somewhat for him. They two can get each other ; and what a wonderful consecration it will be, when she on the marriage-day gives him the letter ! "

IV

Good fortune seldom comes singly. One morning Criminal and Court Counsellor Bagger got, at his residence at Noerre Street, official intelligence that from the first of next month he was transferred to the King's Court, and in grace was promoted to be veritable Counsellor of Justice there ; rank, fourth-class, number three. As, gratified by this friendly smile from above, he went out to repair to the court-house, he met in the porch a postman, who delivered him a letter. With thoughts yet busy with new title and court, Counsellor Bagger broke the letter, but remained as if fixed to the ground. In it he read :

" The high-seat pillars have come on shore.   —' GEB.'—"

One says well that a man's love or season of courtship lasts till his thirtieth year, and after that time he is ambitious ; but it is not always so, and with Counsellor Bagger it was in all respects the contrary. His ambition was already, if not fully reached, yet in some degree satisfied. The faculty of love had not been at all employed, and the letter came like a spark in a powder-cask ; it ran glowing through every nerve. The youthful half of his soul, which had slept within him, wakened with such sudden revolutionary strength that the other half soul, which until now had borne rule, became completely subject ; yes, so wholly, that Counsellor Bagger went past the court-house and came down in Court-house Street without noticing it. Suddenly he missed the big building with the pillars and inscription : " With law shall Lands be built " ; looked around confused, and turned back.

So much was he still at this moment Criminal Examiner, that among the first thoughts or feelings which the mysterious letter excited in him was this : It can be a trick, a foolery.   But in the next moment it occurred to him that never to any living soul had he mentioned his bold figure of the high-seat pillars, and still less revealed the mysterious, to him so valued, syllable—geb—.   No doubt could exist : the fine, perfumed paper, the delicate lady hand-writing, and the few significant words testified that the billet which once in youthful, sanguine longing he had entrusted to the winds of heaven had come to a lady, and that in one way or another she had found him out.   He remembered very well that on a single occasion, five or six weeks before, he had in a numerous company mentioned that incident, and he did not doubt that the story had extended itself as ripples do when one throws a stone into the water ; but where in the whole town, or indeed the land, had the ripple hit the exact point ?   He looked again at the envelope.   It bore the stamp of the Copenhagen city mail : that was all.   But that showed with some probability that the writer lived in Copenhagen, and maybe at this moment she looked down upon him from its many windows.   There was something in the paper, the handwriting, that made her seem young, spirited, beautiful, piquant.   There was something fairy-like, exalted, intoxicating, in the feeling that the object of the longing and hope of his youth had been under the protection of a good spirit, and that the great unknown had taken care of and prepared for him a companion, a wife, just at the moment when he had become Counsellor of Justice of the Superior Court.   But who was she ?   This was the only thing painful in the affair ; but this intriguing annoyance was not to be avoided, if the lady was to remain within her sphere, surrounded by respect and esteem.

"What would I have thought of a lady, a woman, who came straight forward and handed out the billet, saying : ' Here I am ' ? " he asked himself, at the moment when at last he had found the court-house stairs and was ascending.

How it fared that day with the examinations is recorded in criminal and police-court documents; but a veil is thrown over it in considera-tion of the fact that a man only once in his life is made Counsellor of Justice in the King's Court.   The day following it went better ; although it is pretty sure that a horse thief went free from further reproof, because the counsellor was busy rolling this stone up the mountain : Where shall I seek her if she does not write again ?   Will she write again ?   If she would do that, why did she not write a little more at first ?

A couple of weeks after the receipt of the letter, one evening about seven o'clock, the counsellor sat at home, not as before by his writing-table busy with acts, but on a corner of the sofa, with drooping arms, deeply absorbed in a mixture of anxious doubts and dreaming expectations. One of his fancies was that his lady summoned him—he would not even in thought use the expression : gave him an interview—to a masquerade. It was consequently no common masquerade, but a grand, elegant masked ball, to which a true lady could repair. The clock was at eleven, the appointed hour : he waited anxiously the pressing five minutes ; then she came and extended him the fine hand in the finest straw-coloured glove—

" Letter to the Counsellor of Justice," said Jens, with strong Funen accent, and short, soldierly pronunciation.

It is rarely that what one longs for comes just at the moment of most earnest desire ; but notwithstanding the letter was from her, the Counsellor of Justice knew the superscription, would have known it among a hundred thousand. The letter read thus :

" I ought to be open towards you ; and, as we shall never meet, I can be so."

Here the Counsellor of Justice stopped a moment and caught for breath. A good many of our twenty-year-old beaux, who have never been admitted to the bar, far less have been Court Counsellors, would under similar circumstances have said to themselves : " She writes that she will be open ; that is to say, now she will fool me : we shall never meet ; that is to say, now I shall soon see her." But Counsellor Bagger believed every word as gospel, and his knees trembled. He read further :

" I am ashamed of the few words I last wrote you ; but my apology is, that it is only two days since I learned that you are married. I have been mistaken, but more in what may be imputed to me than in what I have thought. My only comfort is, that I shall never be known by you or anybody, and that I shall be forgotten, as I shall forget."

" Never ! But who can have spread the infamous slander ! What dreadful treachery of some wretch or gossiping wench who knows nothing about me ! And how can she believe it ! How in such a town as Copenhagen can it be a matter of doubt for five minutes, if a Superior Court Counsellor is married or not ! Or maybe there is some other Counsellor Bagger married—a Town Councillor or the like ? Or maybe she lives at a distance, in a quiet world, so that the truth of it does not easily reach her ?

" If she should sometime meet me, and know that I was, am, and have been unmarried, that meanwhile we have both become old and grey—can one think of anything more sad ? But suppose, too, that to-morrow she finds out that she has been deceived : she has once written, ' I was mistaken,' and cannot, as a true woman, write it again, unless she first heard from me, and learned how I longed—and so I am cut off from her, as if I lived in the moon."

A thought came suddenly, like a meteor in the dark : advertise. What family in Copenhagen did not the *Address Paper* reach ? He would put in an advertisement—but how ? " Fritz Bagger is not married."—No : that was too plain. " F.B. is not married."—No : that was not plain enough. As he could find no successful use for his own name, it flashed into his mind to use hers—" geb "—; and although it was painful to him to publish this, to him, almost sacred syllable for profane eyes to gaze upon, yet it comforted him that only one, she herself, would understand it. Yet he hesitated. But one cannot make an omelet without breaking eggs ; and although the heart's finest fibres ache at the thought of sending a message to a fairy through the *Address Paper*, yet one yields to this rather than lose the fairy.

At last, after numerous efforts he stopped at this : " —geb—! It is a mistake : he waits only for—geb." It appeared to him to contain the approach to a happy result, and tired out by emotion he fell asleep on his sofa.

Some days after came a new letter with the dear handwriting : its contents were :

" Well ! appear eight days from to-day at Mrs. Canuteson's, to congratulate her upon her birthday."

This was sunshine after thunder ; this was hope's rainbow which arched itself up to heaven from the earth, yet wet with tears.

" And so she belongs to good society," said the Counsellor of Justice, without noticing how by these words he discovered to himself that a doubt or suspicion had lain until now behind his ecstasy. " But," he added, " consequently, it is my own friends who have spread the rumour of my marriage. Friends indeed ! A wife is a man's only friend. It is hard, suicidal, to remain a bachelor."

On the appointed day he went too early. Mrs. Canuteson was yet alone. She was surprised at his congratulatory visit ; but, however, as it was a courtesy, the surprise was mingled with delight, for Bagger was not the man whose visit a lady would not receive with pleasure. With that ingenuity of wit one can sometimes have, just when the heart is full and taken possession of, he did wonders, and entertained the lady in so lively a manner that she did not perceive how long a time he was passing with her. As the door at length opened, the lady exclaimed :

" Oh, this is charming ! How welcome you are ! How is your mother ? This dear young lady's acquaintance I made last summer when we were in the country, and at last she is so good as to keep her promise and visit me. Counsellor Bagger—Miss Hjelm."

The Counsellor wasn't sure that it was She, but he was convinced that it ought to be. Not to speak of Ingeborg Hjelm's being really amiable and *distinguée*, his heart was now prepared, as a photographer's glass which has received collodion, and took the first girl picture that met it.

He approached and spoke to Miss Hjelm with deep emotion. She was friendly and open, for the name Counsellor Bagger did not occur to her ; and the idea she had formed of him did not at all compare with the young, elegant, handsome man before her. True enough, his manner was somewhat peculiarly gallant, which a lady cannot easily mistake ; but this gallantry was united with such an unmistakable respect, or more properly awe, that he gave her the impression of a poetical, chivalrous nature.

By and by there came more ladies, both married and unmarried, but Bagger had almost forgotten what errand they could have with him. At last Miss Brandt came also, accompanied by her sister. As she opened the door, and saw Bagger by the side of Miss Hjelm, she gave a little, a very little, cry, or, more properly, gasped aloud for breath, and made a movement, as if something kept her back.

" Oh ! my dress caught," she said, and having arranged it a little, she approached Mrs. Canuteson, with smiling face, to offer her congratulation.

Bagger looked at the watch : he had been there two hours ! Then lingering to exchange a few polite words with Miss Brandt, he took his leave.

v

Within eight days from Mrs. Canuteson's birthday Counsellor Bagger had not only learned where Miss Hjelm lived, but had established himself at an inn close by the farm, and obtained admittance to the house, which last was not so difficult, since Mrs. Hjelm was a friendly, hospitable lady, and since neither her daughter nor niece thought they ought to prejudice her against him.

In this manner four or five days passed away, which, to judge from Bagger's appearance, were very pleasant. He wrote to his colleagues in the Superior Court, that one could only value an autumn in Nature's lap after so laborious and health-destroying work as his life for many years had been. Then one day he received a letter from the unknown, reading thus :

" Be more successful than last time, at Mrs. Emmy Lund's on Tuesday, two o'clock. Please notice, two o'clock precisely."

" Does she mean this ? Is she really coquettish ? Yet I think I have been successful so far," said Bagger to himself, and waited for

the Tuesday with comparative ease ; in truth he did not at all understand why he should be troubled to go to town.

Early on Tuesday morning he went over to the farm, and was
somewhat surprised that there was to be seen no preparation for a
town journey.   Ingeborg, in her usual morning dress, was seated at
the sewing-table.   He waited until near twelve o'clock, calculating
that two hours was the least she needed in which to dress and drive
to town.   The long hand threatened to touch the short hand at the
number twelve without any appearance of Ingeborg's noticing it.
She only now and then cast a stealthy look at him, for it had not
escaped her, nor the others, that he was in expectancy and excitement.   When the clock struck twelve—he was alone with her—he
asked suddenly, in a quick, trembling voice :

" Miss Hjelm, you know I am Superior Court Counsellor ? "

" No ; that I did not know," she said almost with dread, and
arose.   " No ; that I have never known ! "

" But allow me, dear lady ; so you know it now," he said,
surprised that the title or profession produced so strong an
effect.

" Yes, now I know it," she said, and held her hand upon
her heart.   " Why do you tell me that ?   What does that
signify ? "

" Nothing else, Miss Hjelm, than that you may understand that
I don't believe in witchcraft."

" But, Mr. Counsellor, is there then anybody who has accused you
of believing in witchcraft ? "

" No, dear madam ; but for all that I can assure you, that at the
moment the clock struck twelve I thought that you, by two o'clock,
must fly away in the form of a bird."

" As the clock struck twelve now, at noon ?—not at midnight ?
Can you satisfy my curiosity, and tell me why ? "

" Because under ordinary circumstances it appears to me impossible for a lady to make her toilette and drive ten miles in less than
two hours."

" That is quite true, Mr. Counsellor ; but neither do I intend to
drive ten miles to-day."

" It was for that reason that I said, fly."

" No, nor fly.   And to convince you and quite certainly rid you of
the idea of witchcraft, you can stay here, if you please, until—what
time was it ? "

" Two o'clock."

" That is two long hours ; but the Counsellor can, if he please,
lay that offering upon the altar of education."

" Oh ! I know another altar upon which I would rather offer the
two only all too short hours——"

" Let it now be upon that of education.   You promised my cousin and me that you would read to us about popular science of nature and interesting facts in the life of animals."

"Yes, dear madam; but *I* cannot fly: my carriage stands waiting at the inn."

"Oh, I beg pardon! an agreeable journey, Mr. Counsellor."

"Yes; but I don't understand why I shall drive the ten miles."

"Every one knows his own concerns best."

"Oh, yes! that is true. But I at least don't know mine."

Miss Hjelm made no answer to this, and there was a little pause.

"I would," continued the Counsellor, somewhat puzzled, "take the liberty to propose that you should ride with me."

"I have already told the Counsellor that I did not intend to go to town to-day," answered Miss Hjelm coldly.

"Yes," continued Bagger, following his own ideas, "and so I thought, also, that we could as well stay here."

At this moment Bagger was so earnest and impassioned that Ingeborg, in hearing words so very wide of what she regarded as reasonable, began to suspect his mind of being a little disordered, and with an inquiring anxiousness looked at him.

Meeting the look from these eyes, Bagger could no longer continue the inquisition which he had carried on for the sake of involving Miss Hjelm in self-contradiction and bringing her to confession. He himself came to confession, and exclaimed:

"Miss Ingeborg, I ask you for Heaven's sake have pity on me, and tell me if you expect me at two o'clock to-day at Mrs. Lund's!"

"I expect you at Mrs. Lund's!" exclaimed Miss Hjelm.

"Is it not you, then, who have written me that——"

"I have never written to you!" cried Ingeborg, and almost tore away the hand which Bagger tried to hold.

"For God's sake, don't go, Miss——! My dear madam, you must forgive me: you shall know all!"

And now he began to tell his tale, not according to rules of rhetoric and logic, but on the contrary in a way which certainly showed how little even our abler lawyers are educated to extemporise.

But, however, there was in his words a certain almost wild eloquence; and, beside, Miss Hjelm had some foreknowledge, that helped her to understand and fill up what was wanting under the Counsellor's restless eloquence.

"Yes; but what then?" at last asked Ingeborg, with a soft smile and not withdrawing the hand that Bagger had seized. "The correct meaning of what you have told me is that your troth is plighted to another, unknown lady."

"No: that isn't the correct meaning——"

"But yet it is a fact. At the moment when you stand at the altar with one, another can step forward and claim you."

"Oh, that kind of a claim! A piece of paper without signature, sent away in the air! In law it has no validity at all, and morally it has no power, when I love another as I love you, Ingeborg!"

"That I am not sure of. It appears to me there is something painful in not being faithful to one's youth and its promises, and in the consciousness of having deceived another."

As Ingeborg knew so much about it, she could not regard the matter as earnestly as her words denoted. Quite another reason had suddenly made her feel serious. It would not do to have a husband with so much fancy as Bagger, always having something unknown, fairy-like, lying out upon the horizon, holding claim upon him from his youth; and on the other hand it was against her principles, notwithstanding her confidence in his silence, to convey to him the knowledge that it was Miss Brandt who played fairy.

She said to him: "You must have your letter, your obligation, your marriage promise back."

"Yes," he answered with a sigh of discouragement. "It is true enough I ought; but where shall I turn? That is just the immeasurable difficulty."

"Let the whirlwind, that brought the first letter to its destination, also take care of this, in which you demand your word back."

"Oh, you don't mean that! I have not courage to write anything, for fear it should come to others instead of you."

"So I see that, after all, I may act as witch to-day. Write, and I will take care of the letter: do you hesitate!"

"No: I obey you blindly; but what shall I write?"

"Write: 'Dear fairy—Since I woo Miss Hjelm's hand and heart——'"

"Oh, you acknowledge it! O Ingeborg, the Lord's blessing upon you!" said Bagger, and would rise.

"'I ask you to send me my billet back.'—Have you that?"

"Yes, Ingeborg, my Ingeborg, my unspeakably loved Ingeborg! How poor language is, when the heart is so full!"

"Now, name, date, and address. Have you that? 'Postscriptum. I give you my word of honour, that I neither know who you are, or how this letter shall reach you.'—Have you that?"

"That I can truly give. I am as blind as . . .'"

"Let me add the witch-formulae."

"O Ingeborg, you will write upon the same paper with me, in a letter where I have written your name!"

"Hand me the pen. We must have the letter sent to the mail before two o'clock."

"Two o'clock. How queer! That last letter reads: 'Please notice two o'clock precisely.'"

"That we will," said Ingeborg.

She wrote : " Dear Miss Brandt, I, too, ask you to send the Counsellor his billet, and I pray you to write upon it : ' Given me by Miss Hjelm.' It is best for all parties that the fun does not come out in gossip. You shall, by return of mail, receive back your letters."

VI

It is allowed to charitable minds to remain in doubt about what had really been Miss Brandt's design. Perhaps she only wished to make roguish psychological experiments, to convince herself of the number of congratulatory visits a Counsellor of Justice of the Superior Court could be brought to pay. The emotion she almost exposed, when at Mrs. Canuteson's she saw Bagger by Miss Hjelm's side, may have been pure surprise at the working of the affair. Every one of the rest of us who have been conversant with the whirlwind, the letter, and Ingeborg's relinquishment of the same, would also have been surprised at seeing her and the letter-writer brought together notwithstanding, and would not, perhaps, have been able with as much ease and success to hide our surprise. The letter to Bagger, in which Miss Brandt, contrary to her better knowledge, spoke of him as married, may have been a sincere attempt to end the whole in a way which repentance and anxiety quickly seized upon to put an insurmountable hindrance before herself ; but it may surely enough have had also the aim to see how far Bagger had gone and how much spirit and fancy he had to carry the intrigue out. The more one thinks upon it, the less one feels able to give either of the two interpretations absolute prefer- ence. Yet one will have remarked that Ingeborg herself in her little note mentioned the matter as " fun." On the other side, if it was earnestness, if she had felt " somewhat " for Counsellor Bagger, then let us take comfort in the fact that Miss Brandt was a well-cultivated girl, and that her intellect held dominion over her heart. Next day the letter came in an envelope directed to the counsellor.

As Bagger in the presence of Ingeborg opened the letter and again saw the long-lost epistle of his early days, he trembled like a man before whom the spirit-world apparently passes. But as he perceived the added words, he exclaimed in utter perplexity : " Am I awake ? Do I dream ? How is this possible ? "

" Why should it not be possible ? " asked Ingeborg. " To whom else should the letter originally have come, than to—geb— ? "

" —Geb— ?—geb ? Yes, who is—geb— ? " asked Bagger with bewildered look.

" Who other than Ingeborg ? is it not the third, fourth, and fifth letters of my name ? "

" Oh ! " exclaimed Bagger, pressing his hand upon his forehead ;

and, as he at the next moment seized Ingeborg's hand, added with an eye which had become dim with joy, " Truly, I have had more fortune than sense."

Ingeborg answered, smiling :

" That ought he to expect who entrusts his fate to the wind's flying mail."

DANISH   HOLGER DRACHMANN
1846–1908

BJÖRN SIVERTSEN'S
WEDDING TRIP

THE "strong Björn" was about to be married. The usual signs of such an occurrence had come to pass, even to the most important of them all ; he had become engaged.

Exactly how this happened, however, history does not state. After the death of the head fisher-master he had inherited the house and had paid off his brother Niels for his share with a good sum of money, so that the latter could build his own home farther off in the village. There sat Björn then with his house and his sail-maker's outfit, very lonely in all his new glory.

He got into the habit of sauntering more frequently than usual down to the inn, to get his short pipe filled, to drink a glass and spin a yarn. The jolly innkeeper had been married about a year, and was as busy as could be, running in at the door of the inner room every few minutes " to look after something."

" What is the matter there ? " asked Björn. " Can't you let the women attend to the child ? "

The innkeeper explained it was the " teeth " that he was so interested in.

" Teeth ? "

" Yes, Björn. When the teeth come the crying stops."

" Is that so ? Say, tell me, could I see the child ? "

The father escorted him proudly into the nursery where the young wife sat at a window with the child on her lap. She was bending over it, and was also looking for " the teeth."

Björn saluted and came slowly nearer.

" Come and look at him," she said, smiling.

The giant bent his head, but the child became frightened at the heavy hair and beard and screamed. Björn drew back in alarm, but during his retreat he turned several times and looked back at the window.

When he and the innkeeper were alone in the latter's private room Björn stood a while in thought, scratching with his thick finger in his mane.

"Say, innkeeper, what a wonderful thing such a little fellow is ! He had real nails on his fingers, and he looked at me."

The young father grew knock-kneed with pleasure, and, rubbing his hands, answered : " You ought to have just such a one yourself. You have a house and money."

"Yes. But it is not so easy to find a wife, friend."

Björn sat down, lost in thought, and when the innkeeper touched his glass with his own, he looked up absently. " Do you know what I am thinking of, innkeeper ? "

" No. Let us hear it."

" I was wondering if at any time I could really have been as small as that."

" I hope, for your mother's sake," said the innkeeper, laughing, " that when you were born you were a good deal smaller than my baby is now."

Then there was no more talk on that subject.

Several days later Björn set out in his good old boat with a load of potatoes for the nearest town.

The boat was known as *The Pail*.

Heaven knows where it got the name ; probably from some nickname given in mockery—people are so wicked. But, as it often happens, the nickname had become a pet name, and the boat was always called *The Pail*. Red Anders, a relative, went along with him, and after having sold their potatoes—and sold them well at that—they were now lying alongside the wharf waiting for a little more wind. Then it happened that an old skipper of the town, who had retired, but could not altogether keep away from the water, came sauntering down to the dock, his hands in his pockets and his little twinkling eyes on the look-out for something of interest. He stopped on the dock, blinking still more, and seemed to be taking the measure of *The Pail*.

" Heh, boys, where are you from ? "

Björn looked up, surprised at this question about anything so well known.

" From Fiskebäk, of course."

" Are you the owner ? "

Björn looked up at the skipper, with his hand behind his ear.

" I am a little deaf ; but if you are speaking of the boat, it is *The Pail*, and I am the owner."

" Why do you call her *The Pail* ? "

" That is her name."

" Has she any faults ? "

" We all have faults ourselves, and so do boats."

" She is not very new ? "

Björn began to get somewhat impatient.

"See here, my man, how old are you yourself?"

The skipper laughed and took his hands from his pockets.

"Will you sell your boat?"

Björn looked at Red Anders, and Red Anders looked at Björn. Then they both looked up at the questioner, and at last they looked around at the boat.

"What do you say, Anders?" asked Björn.

Björn was in good humour. The potato transaction had gone off famously, and the buyer had, over and above, treated them well. Finally he slapped his leg and said, with a broad grin:

"My soul! Why shouldn't I sell her?"

"Yes, why not? Then you can buy a new one."

"That's so," said Björn, and nodded to the skipper.

"How much do you want for her?" asked the latter.

"Forty pounds as she swims now."

"Thirty-five," was bidden.

Björn did not answer, but prepared to let go the mooring.

"Who made her sails?" was asked.

"The man with the rudder," answered Björn, and cut the after-ropes loose.

"All right. Tie up again and let me come aboard."

Then came a turning upside down and a ransacking of everything inside *The Pail*. The bulkheads, the flooring, the combing, the seats, nails, cleats, and painting, masts and oars were examined, and about an hour later Björn and Anders stood outside the tavern, where the bargain had been sealed with a drink. The summer sun shone down on their burning faces and beaming eyes, but when Björn looked toward the harbour and saw *The Pail* being taken away from its place his expression changed, and, turning to Anders, he asked: "What do you think they will say when we come home without *The Pail*?"

Anders put on a thoughtful mien. "I don't know. But, anyway, it was your boat, and the skipper promised to be good to her, and keep her scraped and tarred and painted when she needed it."

"You are right," said Björn. "But are we to *walk* home?"

It was very hot and the sun burned. It was a good twelve miles to the fishing village, and the road was for the most part flat, sandy, and open.

"Do you want to ride?" asked Anders. "I am afraid most of the wagons have gone home, unless you want to hire one."

Björn stood a moment without answering. It was perhaps not such a bad idea to postpone the homecoming and the explanations for a little.

"I propose we go to the capital."

"Do you treat?" asked Anders cautiously.

" Certainly," answered Björn, and slapped his pocket where the money lay. They went through the town to the railway station, where a train was just about to start. The two were like two big children. They had been to the capital already, but neither of them had ever ridden on the railroad.

Some one showed them the way to the ticket-office. Björn planted himself in front of the opening, with his pocket-book in his hands.

" Can I get a cabin for two men to the capital ? " he asked, in a tone which he took for a whisper, but which could be heard throughout the hall. " Return ? " was asked.

" What's that he says ? " asked Björn of his comrade.

" Second or third ? " came again from the office, in rather an angry tone.

" Take what you can get," whispered Anders, who, as his expenses were paid for him, saw no reason for being economical.

" All right, give me the whole thing," said Björn, and pushed a bill in at the impatient voice.

" Two excursions, second. You can come back on the evening train, do you hear ? " said the voice.

Björn received a number of silver coins for his bill. He took it all but one piece. " We can afford to tip to-day," he said to his cousin, in the same loud voice.

The ticket-seller put his head out of the opening. " Take your money ! " he called angrily.

" All right," said Björn, crestfallen. He put the coin in his pocket, and as they walked through the waiting-rooms to the platform he muttered : " That villain of an innkeeper at home told me that if you want to ride comfortably on the railroad you must tip the conductors. But it doesn't seem to go here."

They entered the compartment, where sat a stout man, with close-cropped hair, white neckband, and long black coat. His face was red and good-natured.

" Whew, it's warm here," said Björn, and opened a window. The stout man coughed. The engine whistled, and the train began to move.

" There she goes, d—— me," said Anders.

" Some speed in her," answered Björn with a similar oath as the car began to lurch.

" Open the other porthole," cried Björn, after a while. " I'll suffocate in this box. This is a new sort of sailing on dry land." The stout man coughed still more.

" Does it trouble you, sir ? " asked Bjôrn politely.

" Yes."

Björn gave orders for Anders to close the porthole. The stout gentleman eyed him sharply.

They came to a sharp curve in the road, the car swung round, and Björn nearly fell off his seat.

"Well, I'll be blasted eternally," he cried, half surprised and half in sly cunning. "Do you think they'll send us to hell in this hurry, Anders?"

"Do you always swear like this, my man?" asked the stout gentleman. Björn looked at him with a wink.

"That's as it happens, my good sir, but I generally do when on shore. Meat goes with bread, as the baker's dog said when he stole the steak."

"I do not think it is quite necessary," said the stout gentleman. "I know, for I am a clergyman."

"A clergyman?" repeated Björn, looking at him. "Beg pardon, but will you swear to that?"

The stout gentleman looked severely at him at first. But the big child was in such a good-humour that day that he was quite irresistible, with his half-simple, half-roguish smile, and his good-nature, from which all severity ran off like water from a duck's back.

In five minutes they were the best of friends. Björn told, in his own style, his story of *The Pail*, and the jolly priest laughed until his asthma nearly choked him, and before they reached the capital he had Björn's promise to visit him next day in his little village rectory near the city.

Anders went home that night on his excursion ticket, and Björn set out alone next day for the country. Then it happened that after that day Björn undertook several excursions to Copenhagen with corresponding journeyings to the rectory, until, according to his own version, he was "caught by a petticoat."

But this was all he would say about it. He went around wearing a broad, shining gold ring, which pinched his fat finger. How the ring was ever squeezed on that finger in the beginning was a mystery, but there it sat, and there sat Björn.

All winter long he pondered over his thoughts of marriage. The innkeeper and his wife teased him, at which he grew angry in jest and then in earnest. And then, when his anger had passed, he showed them first the photograph of a girl with a very dark face and two bright pink hat ribbons. The picture appeared to need much polishing of Björn's coat sleeve, to give it, as he said, "the proper point of view." He did not at all like any sport being made of this picture, but was honest enough to acknowledge that it looked more like "the portrait of a nigger than of a respectable country girl."

During the winter he bought himself a new boat. With all necessary ceremonies this boat was christened *The Flying Fish*. But during the christening feast there was a considerable row. The otherwise good-natured Björn fired up about some chance teasing words, some mocking nickname given the boat. Without knowing just why the matter excited him so, he became first sarcastic, and then rude and threatening. Next day, however, he was much dissatisfied with himself, and went to consult with his friend the innkeeper, accusing himself of having forgotten his duties as host. But the innkeeper comforted him, and told him that was all the fault of his approaching marriage. A man in that condition can't keep the right balance, and is liable to slop over either way on the slightest provocation. That was always so. The thing to do was to close the matter as soon as possible.

Björn did not answer. He muttered something about spring, and sheets and linen, etc., and then went for a sail in his new boat. She was a flyer and no mistake, he could prove that to the scoffers on shore any day !

Then spring came at last, and now " this nonsense should have an end." He had a good new boat ; all he wanted was a wife, so Björn swore to himself.

Thus the marriage came about.

The ceremony, naturally, was to be held in the little country church. A relative of Stine—Stine was the bride—had suggested that as Stine's parents were both dead, and he himself was an innkeeper in Copenhagen, he should give the wedding feast in his house. Björn protested vigorously against this. He and his brother were to sail to the city, and lay up the boat at Kroyer's Wharf. Niels would take care of the boat, and he himself would " play monkey just long enough for the splice " ; then back to the city, and on board the boat to take his wife home.

Stine and her party protested against this arrangement with equal energy, if not with equal warmth of expression. A wedding without a feast was an impossibility, and there would always be time enough for the sail, thought Stine to herself. So she clung to her decision, supported by her cousin of The Gilded Tarpot, and for the first time in his life, even before the " splice," Björn learned what unlooked-for obstacles can be put in our way by the so-called weaker sex. At least, so the old poets call it.

Björn grumbled, but was clever enough to hold his peace. In all secrecy he laid a counter-mine, telling his brother to take *The Flying Fish* out as far as the custom-house and lay her up in the ferry harbour, with all ropes clear for sailing, and when that was done to come himself to The Gilded Tarpot, which was a favourite place of refreshment for country people, soldiers, and petty officials.

In this way each party felt sure of the eventual victory, and the marriage could come off. The minister tied the knot in his little country church and gave them a glass of sherry and a silver soup-ladle in the rectory. Björn put both " inside his vest," and then the innkeeper drove them into town. The village people gave them a

hurrah, and finally the merry company sat down in The Gilded Tarpot's basement rooms to a board laden with roasts of lamb and pork,
ham and vegetables, and all manner of other good things.   Sweet
cordials were there for the ladies, and French wines, while for the
men there was brandy and punch.

Through the basement window one could see a high brick wall,
gleaming in the strong sunlight, and if one laid oneself over the
table, with one's head in the neighbour's lap, 'way high up one could
see a tiny piece of blue sky as large as a handkerchief perhaps, with
feathery clouds driving over it.

Some of Stine's female relatives were there, and the innkeeper's
family and best friends.   Among the family was a ship's-joiner, who
proved his sympathetic comprehension of the importance of the
occasion by getting drunk at once and making pathetic speeches.
And among the good friends was a " former officer of justice," as he
called himself, a man with a decoration in his buttonhole ; also a
drunken-looking gaoler, who wore a stiff collar and his service medal
to remind the world that he had once been a non-commissioned
officer.   He looked as if he had his serious doubts about the company, and expected the one or the other of them to make away with
the spoons.   Probably because of this doubt therefore he kept a
distance between himself and the rest of the company, and poured
out an endless series of small whiskies for himself, " on the top of the
glass," as he expressed it, without any appreciable effect.   He
laughed a sudden and ferocious-sounding laugh, drank half his glass,
cleared his throat, poked his elbows in the host's ribs, and said :
" Old comrade, here's to the good old times."   This for him was the
height of sociability.

He called Björn " Captain," but after a few repetitions of the
word the bridegroom laid down his fork, with a large slice of beet on
it, and remarked :

" Port your helm, friend, and let up on that ' Captain,' if you
don't want to make me angry."

After this admonition he compromised on " Boatsman."

Björn was decidedly out of sorts.   He had the impression of being
left out in the cold, which was probably due to his deafness.   He
certainly filled his place in the literal sense, but Niels did not come,
and Stine, the bride—well, Stine sat there at his side in a black
merino gown, with wreath and veil, her red hands in her lap, as
straight up and down in her chair as if she had swallowed a yardstick.

That was probably the correct thing to do, for a northern bride
should not be too vivacious.   But there seemed to be in her nature
a certain dignity, which would be a good thing in a home no doubt,
but which seemed out of place here between roast and cordial.

" One certainly could not call her too affectionate," Björn said
afterward, when describing the occasion.

He sat alone and she sat alone. She ate very little; he ate enough for two. The ship's-joiner made one speech after another, the sun shone down on the brick wall, and Björn leaned over on Stine and looked up out of the window.

Stine pulled her veil aside, smoothed her dress, and asked: " What are you looking at ? "

" Fine opportunity that," said Björn. Her eyes followed his.

" You mean that fourth story to let up there ? Yes, I would rather like to live there. Then one would not have to be on the water so much."

" A fine opportunity to sail home, I mean," explained Björn. " The wind is strong from the south."

Stine glanced at him uneasily, and then at the innkeeper.

" A stiff south breeze," continued Björn. " It has been a north wind for some time, and will be to-night again. We don't have a chance like this every day."

At a glance from Stine the innkeeper proposed a " good, old-time Danish cheer " for Björn, in the attempt to change the train of his thoughts, and the ship's-joiner made his fifth speech.

Then mine host proposed a song, in which all joined, even the gaoler, who held second voice and tooted like a clarionet.

After that, in spite of some objection, the ship's-joiner rose, and, supporting himself by his neighbour's shoulders, began, with tears in his eyes :

" Good friends and hearers, we are all that, I think——"

" Yes, yes," they answered.

" We will now—something must be said to them before they leave father and mother—I mean before they leave the circle of these kind friends——"

" They don't go until to-morrow," said mine host.

" No," said Björn, banging the table with his fist.

" He's right," said Niels, coming in just then. " The wind is fresh from the south, Björn."

" I know," said Björn, getting up.

" Hush ! " whispered the innkeeper. " Let the joiner finish his speech."

" Listen, dear friends," continued the joiner, reeling from side to side. " We are all mortal, and we all love our native country. I do not say fatherland ; I say native country. We do not know where our fathers came from, but we know where we were born our- selves——"

" What nonsense is this ? " whispered Niels, who grasped the situation and was ready to fight.

" Who is that man ? " asked the joiner, trying to fix his bleary gaze on Niels and holding fast to his neighbour's shoulder. " Is that a man who will not drink to his native country ? If he is, then I say, ' Fie, for shame,' say I."

Niels looked meaningly at Björn.

" Shall we clear the place and take Stine with us ? "

Björn motioned to him. But one of the guests who supported the joiner heard what Niels said. He drew away his shoulder, the joiner fell to the floor, and in a minute the place was in an uproar. Every one spoke or screamed at once. Niels had already collared the gaoler. Then, at this highly critical moment, the sense of duty of the women of the old days awoke in Stine. She placed herself by the side of her chosen lord and master and announced that " she would sail to Jutland with him rather than have a fight on her wedding day." That settled the matter. The joiner was carried into the next room and put to bed, the guests shook hands cordially and drank one another's health. Niels and Björn became most amiable at once, and Niels ordered more punch. The innkeeper made the best of a bad business, and peace settled down on the spirits of the company.

Then the party broke up.

In his delight at his victory Björn invited the entire party, even the gaoler, to take a sail on *The Flying Fish*. He would put them ashore at the limekilns when they had had enough, he said.

The invitation was accepted, probably in the desire not to disturb the nearly sealed peace. But when they all came up out of The Gilded Tarpot, the fresh air and the sunshine, or the joy of his own victory, or the feelings of a bridegroom, or all of them at once, so overcame Björn that he took Stine round the waist and swore he would dance a waltz with her then and there. Which he did, in spite of her obstinate protest, to the great delight of the passers-by. Then he dropped Stine, and, seizing the gaoler, danced a polka with him. He next insisted upon carrying off a sentry-box to try the sentry's gun on the Amalienplads. But this last was too much for the military feelings of the gaoler. He declared it " scandalous " and walked away as red in the face as a lobster, and took the innkeeper with him. At the next corner was a flaring menagerie poster, with pictures of elephants, monkeys, and bears. These last caught Björn's attention ; he declared that he must go and see his cousins perform, and the wedding guests had difficulty in getting him away safely. By this time quite a crowd had collected, which listened with interest to the lively remarks made by the big fisherman, and when at last, to the immense delight of the crowd, he gave a plastic imitation of a dancing bear, the rest of the invited guests fled, and an assemblage of those not invited followed Björn, Niels, and Stine down to the harbour.

" Come now, Björn, keep quiet," said Niels soothingly, as a policeman appeared interested in their movements.

" Shouldn't I be merry on my wedding day ? " queried Björn, looking around beamingly.

Stine was ready to cry, but held out heroically. She had chosen her lot in life, and was ready to take whatever came.

" It will be better later," was her consoling thought.

They got down to the harbour somehow and into the boat.

" You'll have to reef," said the ferry-keeper.

" Full sail ! " called Björn. " This is my wedding trip."

" All right," said the ferry-keeper. But he whispered aside to Niels : " Can he sail a boat ? "

" Well, rather," laughed Niels.

" All ready, Niels ? " asked Björn.

" Yes."

" Stine stowed away safely ? "

" Yes."

" All off, then ; let go ! "

" Hurrah ! " called the ferrymen, but shook their heads nevertheless.

" That will be a wet wedding trip if he doesn't take in some of that sail," they commented.

And it certainly was wet.

Stine will never forget it, and Björn tells the story himself in this wise :

" We just skipped through the water. I must say *The Flying Fish* did fly that day. As we went past the ferry-boats and the pilot-boats they called out to us, but I waved my hat and asked if they could see the colour of her bottom.

" ' I hope she will stand it,' said Niels.

" ' She'll have to,' I answered.

" Stine lay in the bottom of the boat and gave up all the good dinner they served us in the inn. It was a good thing she had not eaten more.

" I tried to cheer her up, but I don't think she heard me.

" Niels and I were dripping wet, the sails were dripping wet, and so was Stine. I haven't sailed like that before or since.

" I didn't dare sail all the way home with her like that, so put up at the dock of the town.

" The old skipper who bought *The Pail* came down to the water. ' What sort of weather is that for full sail ? ' he asked. ' Have you a cargo ? '

" ' A wedding cargo,' I answered, ' but it's more dead than alive, I guess. Come, help us get the old woman ashore, or she will give up the ghost right here.' We handed Stine up. She couldn't stand on her legs at all, and we had to leave her at the house of a good friend in the town. She stayed there three days and nights, and I had to go round with a dry mouth, couldn't get even so much as a kiss.

"It was all right afterward, but she was angry at me for some time because I had 'made a fool of her in that way.' What can one expect from such land-lubbers, who have never seen more water than a pool in a village street in all their lives?

"Whenever I speak of that day Stine gets cross, but I rub my nose with the back of my hand and say: 'Well, anyway, that was the most wonderful wedding trip I ever heard of.'

"And that is why I haven't made any more like it."

JENS PETER JACOBSEN   DANISH
1847–1885

THE PLAGUE AT BERGAMO

OLD BERGAMO lay up there at the top of a squatty mountain encircled by walls and towers. New Bergamo lay below at the foot of the mountain, exposed to every wind that blows.

In the new town the plague broke out and wrought havoc indescribable. Many died, and the rest fled across the plains to every point of the compass. The men of Old Bergamo set fire to the deserted town, to disinfect the air. In vain. Men began to die on the mountain also; at first one a day, then five, then ten, then a dozen.

There were many who sought to escape, but they could not flee as those in the new town had done ; they lived like hunted beasts, hiding in tombs, under bridges, behind hedges, and in the tall grass of the green fields. For the peasants stoned all strangers from their hearths, or beat them as they would mad dogs, cruelly, pitilessly—in self-protection, as they thought, for the first fugitives had brought with them the pestilence into their houses.

So the people of Old Bergamo were as prisoners in their own town. Day by day the sun blazed hotter, and day by day the terrible infection carried off more victims.

In the very beginning, when the plague came among them, they bound themselves together in unity and peace, and had taken care decently to bury the dead, and had kindled great fires in the markets and open places, so that the purging fumes might be blown through the streets. Juniper and vinegar had been given to the poor. Above all they had gone to church, early and late, singly and in processions ; each day they lifted their voices in prayer. As the sun sank behind the mountains the church bells tolled their dirge from a hundred hanging mouths. Days were set aside for fasting, and the relics were placed upon the altars.

At last, in their extremity, amid the blare of trumpets and tubas, they proclaimed the Holy Virgin for evermore Podesta of the city.

All this was of no help. And when the people saw that nothing could aid them, that Heaven either would not or could not send them relief, they did not fold their hands together and say, " God's will be done." It was as if sin, growing by a secret, stealthy sickness, had flared into an evil, open, raging pestilence, stalking hand in hand with the body's disease, the one to kill their souls, even as the other defiled their flesh—so incredible were their deeds, so monstrous their cruelty.

"Let us eat to-day, for to-morrow we die!" It was as if this theme, set to music, were played in an endless, devilish symphony on instruments without number. The most unnatural vices flourished among them. Even such rare arts as necromancy, sorcery, and devil-worship became familiar to them; for there were many who sought from the powers of hell that protection which Providence had not been willing to accord them. Everything that suggested charity and sympathy had vanished; each thought only of himself. If a beggar, faint with the first delirium of the plague, fell in the street, he was driven from door to door with sharp weapons and with stones.

From the dead that lay rotting in the houses, and from the bodies hastily buried in the earth, arose a sickening stench that mingled with the heavy air of the streets, and drew ravens and crows hither in swarms and in clouds, so that the walls and housetops were black with them. And about the town walls great strange birds perched here and there—birds that came from afar, with rapacious beaks and talons expectantly curved; and they sat and stared with their quiet, hungry eyes as if awaiting the moment when the doomed town would be reduced to a heap of carrion.

Eleven weeks had passed since the plague had first broken out. Then the tower watchman and others who chanced to be on high ground perceived a singular procession winding from the plains into the narrow streets of the new town, between the smoke-blackened stone walls and the charred frames of houses. A great throng! Assuredly six hundred or more, men and women, young and old. Some among them bore large, black crosses, and some held above their heads broad banners, red as blood and fire. They sang as they marched, and strange, despairingly plaintive melodies rose in the still, oppressively hot air.

Brown, grey, black, were the colours these people wore. Yet all had a red sign on their breasts. As they came nearer and nearer this was seen to be the sign of the cross. They crowded up the steep, stone-girt space that led to the old town. Their faces were as waves of white sea; they bore scourges in their hands; a rain of fire was painted on their banners. And in the surging mass the black crosses swung from side to side. Face after face plunged into the gloom of the tower gate and emerged into the light on the other side with blinking eyes.

Then the chant was taken up anew—a *miserere*. They grasped their scourges and marched even more sturdily than if their chant

had been a battle-song.   Their aspect was that of a people who had
come from a starving town.   Their cheeks were sunken ;   their
cheek-bones protruded ;   their lips were bloodless, and dark rings
encircled their eyes.   All the scourges were stained with blood.

With astonishment and uneasiness all Bergamo flocked together
to gaze upon them.   Red, bloated faces stood out against those that
were pale ;   heavy, lust-weary eyes were lowered before the keen,
flashing glances of the pilgrims ;   grinning, blasphemous mouths were
struck dumb by these chants.   The townspeople were spellbound.

But it was not long before the pall was shaken off.   Some recognised among the cross-bearers a half-crazed cobbler of Brescia, and
in a moment the procession became a butt of ridicule.   Moreover,
this was something new, a diversion from the monotony of everyday
life, and as the strangers marched on to the cathedral, they were
followed as a band of jugglers might be or as a tame bear is followed.

But soon anger seized the jostling crowd.   It was clear that these
cobblers and tailors had come to convert them, to pray, and to
speak words that none wished to hear.   Two gaunt, grizzled
philosophers who had formulated blasphemy into a system incited
the populace out of sheer wickedness of heart, so that the mob grew
more threatening as the procession marched to the church, and more
fiercely enraged.   Bergamo was about to lay hands on these singular
scourge-bearing tailors.   Not a hundred paces from the portal of
the church a tavern opened its doors and a whole band of roisterers
poured out, one on the shoulders of another.   And they took their
places at the head of the procession, singing and howling, assuming
a mock-religious mien—all save one, who jerked his thumbs con-
temptuously toward the grass-grown steps of the church.   Rough
laughter then arose, and pilgrims and blasphemers entered the
sanctuary in peace.

Meanwhile the tavern roisterers played their pranks on the main
altar itself.   A tall, strong young butcher removed his white apron
and wound it about his neck so that it hung at his back like a cloak.
Thus arrayed, he celebrated mass, with the wildest and most shocking words of sacrilege.   A small, elderly, round-bellied fellow, lively
and agile in spite of his fat, with the face of a peeled pumpkin,
played sexton and responded with ribald songs ;   he made his genuflexions and turned his back upon the altar, and rang his bell like
a clown ;   and the other tipplers, as they made their genuflexions,
threw themselves flat on the ground and roared with laughter,
hiccuping drunkenly.

All within the church laughed, hooted, and jeered at the strangers,
and bade them notice how God was esteemed in Old Bergamo.
Yet they wished not so much to mock God as to rack the souls of
these penitents with their impiety.

In the centre of the nave the pilgrims halted and groaned, such

was their anguish.   Their blood boiled with hate, and they thirsted
for vengeance.   They prayed to God, with hands and eyes uplifted,
that He might smite His blasphemers for the mockery offered Him in
His house.   Gladly would they perish with the presumptuous
infidels, if He would but show His might ; blissfully would they be
crushed beneath His feet, if He would but triumph, and if these
godless throats might be made to shriek in agony and despair.

They lifted up their voices in a *miserere*, each note of which rang
like a prayer for that rain of fire that once swept over Sodom, for
the strength that was Samson's when he grasped the pillars of the
Philistine temple.   They prayed with words and with song ; they
bared their shoulders and prayed with their scourges.   Kneeling,
row on row, stripped to the waist, they whirled stinging, knotted
cords over their backs.

Frantically they scourged, until the blood spurted under their
hissing lashes.   Each stroke was an offering to God.   Stroke on
stroke came down, until arms sank or were cramped into knots.
Thus they lay, row on row, with frenzied look and foaming mouth,
blood dripping from their bodies.

And those that saw this of a sudden felt their hearts beat, felt the
blood mount to their temples, their breathing grow hard.   Their
knees shook.   To be the slave of a powerful, stern divinity, to fling
oneself at the feet of the Lord, to be His own, not in mute devotion,
not in the mild inefficacy of prayer, but in a fury of passion, in the
intoxication of self-humiliation, in blood and lamentation, and
smitten with the moist, glistening tongues of scourges—this they
could understand.   Even the butcher held his peace ; and the
toothless philosophers bowed their grizzled heads.

Silence reigned in the church ; only a gentle breathing passed
through the multitude.

Then one of the strangers, a young friar, rose and spoke.   His was
the pallor of bloodless flesh ; his black eyes glowed ; and the sad
lines of his mouth were as if cut with a knife in wood, and not mere
furrows in a human face.

He lifted up his thin, suffering hands in prayer to Heaven, and the
black sleeves of his gown slipped back from his lean arms.

Then he spoke—of hell, of its eternity, of the eternity of Heaven,
of the solitary world of pain which each of the damned must suffer
and must fill with his cries of agony.   In that world were seas of
sulphur, meadows of wasps, flames to be wrapped about them like a
cloak, and hard flames that would pierce them like a probe twisting
in a wound.

Breathlessly all listened to his words ; for he spoke as if he had
seen these things with his own eyes.   And they asked themselves :
" Is this man not one of the damned, sent to us from the mouth of
hell, to testify ? "

Then he preached long of the commandments and their rigour, of the need of obeying them to the very letter, and of the dire punishment that awaited him who sinned against them. " ' But Christ died for our sins,' ye say. ' We are no longer bound by the Word.' But I say that hell will not be cheated of one of you, and not one of the iron teeth of hell's wheel will your flesh escape. Ye build upon Calvary's cross? Come! Come and see it! I will lead you to its foot. It was on a Friday, as ye know, when they cast Him from their gates and laid the heavier end of a cross upon His shoulders and suffered Him to bear it to a barren and naked hill without the city ; and they walked beside Him and stirred up the dust with their feet, so that it rested over them like a red cloud. And they tore His garments from Him, even as the lords of justice strip a criminal before all eyes, that all might see His body. And they threw Him down upon His cross, and stretched Him upon it, and drove an iron nail through each of His unresistant hands and a nail through His crossed feet. And they raised the cross in a hole dug in the earth ; but it would stand neither firm nor upright. So they shook it and drove wedges and blocks around it. And those that did this turned down the brims of their hats so that the blood of His hands might not drip into their eyes.

" And He from on high looked down upon the soldiers casting dice for His seamless coat, and down upon all the howling mob for whose salvation He suffered. Not one tearful eye was there in all the multitude. And those who were below looked up at Him, hanging from the cross, suffering and faint. They read the inscription above His head, ' King of the Jews,' and they mocked Him and called up to Him : ' Thou that destroyest the temple, and buildest it in three days, save Thyself. If Thou be the Son of God, come down from the cross.'

" Then God's noble Son waxed wroth and saw that these were unworthy of salvation, this mob that swarmed over the earth ; and He wrenched His feet from the nail, and He clenched His fingers and tore His hands away, so that the arms of the cross bent as a bow. And He leaped to the earth and caught up His garment, so that the dice rolled over the precipice of Golgotha, and threw it about His person with the righteous wrath of a king, and ascended into heaven. And the cross stood bare ; and the great work of atonement remained unfulfilled. No mediator stands between us and God. No Jesus died for us on the cross ! No Jesus died for us on the cross ! "

He ceased.

As he uttered the last words he bent toward the multitude and with his lips and hands flung his words, as it were, upon their heads. A groan of fear ran through the church. Sobs could be heard.

Then the butcher with uplifted, threatening hands, pallid as a corpse, stepped forward and commanded :

" Monk, nail Him to the cross again, nail Him—— ! "

And from all lips, pleadingly, threateningly, a storm of voices rolled to the vault above : " Crucify Him ! "

But the monk looked down upon these fluttering, uplifted hands, upon these distorted faces with the dark openings of their screaming mouths, from which the teeth flashed like those of tormented beasts of prey ; and in the ecstasy of the moment he extended his arms toward Heaven, and laughed. Then he descended ; and his people raised the banners of the fiery rain and their plain, black crosses and pushed out of the church. Once more they marched, singing, across the market-place, and once more they passed through the mouth of the tower gate.

And the people of Old Bergamo stared after them, as they proceeded down the mountain. The steep, wall-girt road was obscured in the uncertain light of the setting sun, and the procession could be only half seen in the glare. Their huge crosses, swaying in the crowd from side to side, cast sharp, black shadows on the glowing walls of the town.

In the distance a chant could be heard. A banner or two gleamed red from the charred site of the new town, and the pilgrims vanished into the bright plain.

HERMANN BANG   DANISH
1857–1912

IRENE HOLM

I

ONE Sunday morning, after service, the bailiff's son announced to the gathering at the meeting-stone outside the church that Miss Irene Holm, dancer from the Royal Theatre in Copenhagen, would open a course for dancing and deportment, for children, ladies, and gentlemen, if a sufficient number of subscribers could be found. The lessons would begin the first of November, in the inn, and the price would be five crowns for each child, with a discount for several in the same family.

Seven names were signed. Jens Larsens put up his three on the discount.

Miss Irene Holm considered the number sufficient. She arrived toward the end of October, and stopped at the inn with her only baggage, an old champagne basket tied up with a cord. She was little and wearily meagre in form, had a childish face with the lines of forty years in it, under her fur cap, and she wore old handkerchiefs wrapped about her wrists, because of the gout. She pronounced all the consonants most carefully, and said, " Oh, thank you, I can do it myself," for everything, looking very helpless the while. She wanted nothing but a cup of tea, and then crept into her bed in the tiny room, trembling in fear of ghosts.

Next morning she appeared with a head full of curls, her figure encased in a tight-fitting, fur-trimmed coat, much the worse for wear. She was going to call upon the parents of her pupils. She inquired the way timidly. Madame Henriksen came out to the door with her, and pointed over the fields. At every step Miss Holm bowed once in her gratitude. " Such a good-looking creature ! " thought Madame Henriksen, and stood in the doorway looking out after her. Miss Holm walked toward Jens Larsens', choosing the dike path to save her shoes. Miss Holm was wearing leather shoes and fancy knit stockings.

When she had visited all the parents—Jens Larsens gave nine crowns for his three children—Miss Holm looked about for a place to live. She hired a tiny whitewashed room at the smith's, the window looking out over the level fields. The entire furnishing consisted of a bed, a bureau, and a chair. The champagne basket was placed between the bureau and the window.

Miss Holm moved into her new quarters. Her mornings were given up to busy handling of curling tongs and pins, and much drinking of cold tea. When her hair was dressed she tidied up her room, and then she knitted all the afternoon. She sat on her basket in the corner, trying to catch the last rays of light. The smith's wife would drop in, sit down on the chair and talk, Miss Holm listening with a pleasant smile and a graceful nod of her curly head.

The hostess spun out her stories until it was time for supper. But Miss Holm seldom knew what she had been talking about. With the exception of dance, and positions, and the calculation for one's daily bread—a tiresome, never-ending calculation—the things of this world seldom filtered into Miss Holm's brain. When left alone she sat silent on her basket, her hands in her lap, gazing at the narrow strip of light that came in under the door.

She never went out. The level, dreary fields made her homesick, and she was afraid of wild horses.

When evening came, she cooked her simple supper, and then busied herself with her curl papers. When she had divested herself of her skirts she practised her " pas " beside the bedpost, stretching her legs energetically. The smith and his wife clung to the keyhole during this proceeding. They could just see the high kicks from behind, and the curl papers standing up on the dancer's head like quills on a porcupine. She danced so eagerly that she began to hum gently as she hopped up and down in the little room, the whole family outside hugging the keyhole closely.

When Miss Holm had practised her accustomed time, she crept into bed. While she practised, her thoughts would wander back to the time " when she was at dancing school." And she would suddenly laugh, a gentle, girlish laugh, as she lay still in the darkness. She fell asleep thinking of that time—that happy, merry time—the rehearsals, when they pricked each other in the calves with pins— and screamed so merrily. And then the evenings in the dressing-rooms, with the whirr and tumult of voices, and the silence as the stage-manager's bell shrilled out. Miss Holm would wake up in a fright, dreaming that she had missed her entrance.

II

" Now, then—one—two "—Miss Irene Holm raised her skirt and put out her foot—" feet out—one—two—three."

The seven pupils toed in, and hopped about with their fingers in their mouths.

" Here, little Jens—toes out—one, two, three—bow—one, two, three—now once more."

Jens bowed, his tongue hanging out of his mouth.

" Now, Maren, left—one, two, three ; Maren turns to the right— once more—one, two, three."

Miss Holm sprang about like a kid, so that one could see long stretches of fancy stockings.

The dancing lessons were in full swing, and were held three times a week in the hall of the inn, under the two old lamps that hung from the beams. The long-undisturbed dust in the cold room whirled up under their feet. The seven pupils flew about wildly like a flock of magpies, Miss Holm straightening their backs and bending their arms. " One, two, three—*battement*—one, two, three—*battement*." The seven bobbed at " battement " and stepped out energetically.

The dust gathered in Miss Holm's throat as she called out her orders. Now the pupils were to dance a round dance in couples. They held their partners at arm's length, stiff-armed and em- barrassed, and turned in sleepy circles. Miss Holm swung them around, with encouraging words. " Good—now around—four, five—turn again—good." She took hold of Jens Larsens' second and little Jette, and turned them as one would turn a top.

Jette's mother had come to look on. The peasant women would drop in for the lessons, their cap-bands tied in stiff bows, and sit motionless as wooden figures against the wall, without speaking a word even to each other. Miss Holm addressed them as " Madame," and smiled at them as she skipped about.

Now it was the turn of the lancers. " Ladies to the right—good —now three steps to the left, Jette—good." The lancers was more like a general skirmish than a dance.

Miss Holm groaned from her exertions. She leaned against the wall, her temples beating with hammer-strokes. " Good—this way, Jette." The dust hurt her eyes as the seven hopped about in the dusk.

When Miss Holm came home after her dancing lessons, she wrapped her head up in a handkerchief. But in spite of this, she suffered from an everlasting cold, and sat, most of her leisure hours, with her head over a bowl of hot water.

Finally, they had music for their lessons—Mr. Broderson's violin. Two new pupils, a couple of half-grown young people, joined the class. They all hopped about to the tune of tailor Broderson's fiddle, as the dust flew up in clouds, and the old stove seemed to dance on its rough carved feet.

They had spectators, too, and once the young people from the rectory, the pastor's daughter and the curate, came to look on. Miss Holm danced out more energetically under the two dim lamps, threw out her chest, and arched her feet. " Throw out your feet like this,

children—throw out your feet." She threw out her feet proudly
and raised the hem of her skirt—now she had an audience !

* * * * * * * *

Every week Miss Holm sent a package of knitting to Copenhagen.
The teacher took charge of the package. Each time it was clumsily
wrapped or addressed wrong, and he had to put it to rights himself.
She stood watching him with her girlish nod and the smile of faded
sixteen. The newspapers that had come by the mail lay ready for
distribution on one of the school-tables. One day Miss Holm asked
timidly if she might look at the *Berlinske*. She had gazed longingly
at the bundle for a week before she could pluck up courage enough to
proffer her request. After that she came every day, in the noon
pause. The school teacher soon came to recognise her timid knock.
" Come in, little lady, the door is open," he would call.

She tripped across the schoolroom and took her chosen paper from
the bundle. She read the theatrical advertisements, the repertoire,
and the criticisms, of which she understood but little. But it was
about " those over there." She needed a lengthy time to go the
length of a column, following the words with one gracefully pointed
finger. When she had finished reading she crossed the hall and
knocked once more at the other door. " Well ? " said the teacher.
" Anything new happened in the city ? "

" It's only about—those over there—the old friends," she would
answer.

The school teacher looked after her as she wandered home to her
knitting. " Poor little creature ! " he sighed. " She's really quite
excited about her dancing master." It was the news of a new
ballet, by a lately promoted master of the ballet, that had so excited
her. Miss Holm knew the list of names by heart, and knew the
names of every solo dance. " We went to school together," she
would say.

And on the evening when the ballet was performed for the first
time she fevered with excitement, as if she were to dance in it herself.
She lit the two candles, grey with age and dust, that stood one on
each side of a plaster cast of Thorwaldsen's Christ on the bureau,
and sat down on her champagne basket, staring into the light. But
she couldn't bear to be alone that evening. All the old unrest of
theatrical life came over her. She went into the room where the
smith and his wife were, and sat down beside the tall clock. She
talked more during the next hour than she had talked for a whole
year. She talked about the theatre and about first nights ; she
talked about the big " solos " and the famous " pas." She
hummed and she swayed in her chair while she talked.

The novelty of it all so excited the smith that he began to sing an
old cavalry song, and finally called out : " Mother, shan't we have a
punch to-night ? "

The punch was brewed, the two candles brought out from the little room, and they sat there and chatted merrily. But in the midst of all the gaiety, Miss Holm grew suddenly silent, and sat still, great tears welling up in her eyes. Then she rose quietly and went to her room. In there she sat down on her basket and wept quietly and bitterly before she undressed and went to bed. She did not practise her steps that evening. She could think of but one thing : he had gone to school with her.

She lay sobbing gently in the darkness. Her head moved uneasily on the pillow as the remembered voice of the old dancing master of the school rang in her ears, cross and excited : " Holm has no *élan*—Holm has no *élan*." He cried it out for all the hall to hear. How plainly she could hear it now—how plainly she could see the great bare hall—the long rows of *figurantes* practising their steps—she herself leaning for a moment against the wall with the feeling as if her tired limbs had been cut off from her body altogether—and then the voice of the dancing master : " Haven't you any ambition, Holm ? "

Then she saw her little home, her mother shrunken down into the great armchair, her sister bending over the rattling sewing-machine. And she heard her mother ask, in her asthmatic voice : " Didn't Anna Stein dance a solo ? "   " Yes, mother."   " Did they give her ' la grande Napolitaine ' ? "   " Yes, mother."   " You both entered the school at the same time ? " she asked, looking over at her from behind the lamp.   " Yes, mother."   And she saw Anna Stein in her gay-coloured skirts, with the fluttering ribbons on her tambourine, so happy and smiling in the glare of the footlights as she danced her solo.

And suddenly the little woman in the darkness buried her head in her pillow and sobbed convulsive, heart-breaking, unchecked sobs of impotent and despairing grief. It was dawn before she fell asleep.

The new ballet was a success. Miss Holm read the notices, and two little, old woman's tears fell softly down upon the printed page as she read.

Letters came now and then from her sisters, letters about pawn-tickets and dire need. The days such letters came Miss Holm would forget her knitting and sit with her hands pressed to her temples, the open letter lying before her. Finally, one day, she made the round of the homes of her pupils, and begged shyly, with painful blushes, for the advance of half her money. This she sent home to her family.

. . . .

So the days passed. Miss Irene Holm went back and forth to her dancing lessons. More pupils came to her, a half-score young peasants formed an evening class that met three times a week in

Peter Madsen's big room on the edge of the woods. Miss Holm walked the half-mile in the darkness, timid as a hare, pursued by all the old ghost stories of the ballet school. At one place she had to pass a pond deeply fringed with willows. She would stare up at the trees that stretched their great arms weirdly in the blackness, her heart hanging dead as a stone in her breast.

They danced three hours each evening. Miss Holm called out, commanded, skipped here and there, and danced with the gentlemen pupils until two deep red spots appeared on her withered cheeks. Then it was time to go home. A boy would open the gate for her, and hold up a lantern to start her on the way. She heard his " Goodnight " behind her and then the locking of the gate as it rasped over the rough stone pavement. Along the first stretch of the path was a hedge of bushes that bent over at her and nodded their heads.

It was nearly spring when Miss Holm's course of lessons came to an end. The company at Peter Madsen's decided to finish off with a ball at the inn.

III

It was quite an affair, this ball, with a transparency, " Welcome," over the door, and a cold supper at two crowns a plate, with the pastor's daughter and the curate to grace the table.

Miss Holm wore a barege gown much betrimmed, and Roman bands around her head. Her fingers were full of keepsake rings from her ballet-school friends. Between the dances she sprinkled lavender water about the floor, and threatened the " ladies " with the bottle. Miss Holm never felt so young again on any such festive occasion. The ball began with a quadrille. The parents of the pupils and other older people stood around the walls, each looking after his own young ones with secret pride. The young dancers walked through the quadrille with faces set as masks, placing their feet as carefully as if they were walking on peas. Miss Holm was all encouraging smiles and nods as she murmured her French commands. The music was furnished by Mr. Broderson and his son, the latter maltreating the piano kindly lent for the occasion by the pastor.

Then the round dances began, and the tone grew more free and easy. The elder men discovered the punch bowl in the next room and the gentlemen pupils danced in turn with Miss Holm. She danced with her head on one side, raising herself on her toes, and smiling with her faded grace of sixteen years. After a while the other couples stopped dancing to watch Miss Holm and her partner. The men came out of the other room, stood in the doorway, and murmured admiration as Miss Holm passed, raising her feet a little higher under her skirt, and rocking gracefully in the hips. The pastor's daughter was so amused that she pinched the curate's arm

repeatedly. After the mazurka, the school teacher cried out
" Bravo ! " and they all clapped hands. Miss Holm gave the
elegant ballet bow, laying two fingers on her heart.

When supper-time came, she arranged a polonaise and made them
all join in. The women giggled and nudged each other in their
embarrassment, and the men said : " Well—let's get in line." One
couple began a march song, beating time with their feet.

Miss Holm sat next the school teacher, in the place of honour
under the bust of his Majesty the King. They all grew solemn again
at the table, and Miss Holm was almost the only one who conversed.
She spoke in the high-pitched tone of the actors in the modern
society dramas of Scribe. After a while the company became more
jovial, the men began to laugh and drink toasts, touching glasses
across the table. Things were very lively at the end of the table
where the young people sat, and it was not easy to obtain quiet for
the schoolmaster, who rose to make a speech. He spoke at some
length, mentioning Miss Holm and the nine Muses, and ending up
with a toast to " The Priestess of Art, Miss Irene Holm ! " All
joined in the cheers, and everybody came up to touch glasses with
Miss Holm.

Miss Holm had understood very little of the long speech, but she
felt greatly flattered. She rose and bowed to the company, her
glass held high in her curved arm. Her face-powder, put on for
the festive occasion, had quite disappeared in the heat and exertion,
and two deep red spots shone on her cheeks.

The fun waxed fast and furious. The young people began to sing,
the old men drank a glass or two extra on the sly, and stood up from
their places to hit each other on the shoulder, amid shouts of
laughter. The women threw anxious glances at the sinners, fearing
they might indulge too deeply. Amid all the noise Miss Holm's
laugh rang out, a girlish laugh, bright and merry as thirty years
before in the ballet school.

Then the schoolmaster said that Miss Holm ought to dance. " But
I have danced." Yes, but she should dance for them—a solo—that
would be fine.

Miss Holm understood at once—and a great desire grew up in her
heart—she was to dance—a solo ! But she pretended to laugh, and
smiling up at Peter Madsen's wife, she said, " The gentleman
says I ought to dance," as if it were the most absurd thing in the
world.

Several heard it, and they all called out in answer, " Yes, yes, do
dance."

Miss Holm blushed to the roots of her hair, and said that she
thought the fun was getting just a little too outspoken. " And,
besides, there was no music ; and one couldn't dance in long skirts."
A man somewhere in the background called out : " You can lift

them up, can't you ? " The guests all laughed at this, and began to renew their entreaties.

" Well, yes, if the young lady from the rectory will play for me ? —a tarantella." They surrounded the pastor's daughter, and she consented to lend her services. The schoolmaster rose and beat on his glass. " Ladies and gentlemen," he announced, " Miss Holm will do us the honour to perform a solo dance for us." The guests cheered, and the last diners arose from the table. The curate's arm was black and blue where the young lady from the rectory had pinched him.

Miss Holm and the pastor's daughter went to the piano to try the music. Miss Holm was feverish with excitement, and tripped back and forth, trying the muscles of her feet. She pointed to the humps and bumps in the floor : " I'm not quite used to dancing in a circus." Then again : " Well, the fun can begin now " ; her voice was hoarse with emotion. " I'll come in after the first ten bars," she said to the pianist ; " I'll give you a sign when to begin." Then she went out into a little neighbouring room and waited there. The audience filed in and stood around in a circle, whispering and very curious. The schoolmaster brought the lights from the table, and stood them up in the windows. It was quite an illumination. Then there came a light knock at the door of the little room.

The rector's daughter began to play, and the guests looked eagerly at the closed door. At the tenth bar of the music it opened, and they all clapped loudly. Miss Holm danced out, her skirt caught up with a Roman scarf. It was to be " la grande Napolitaine." She danced on toe-tips, she twisted and turned. The audience gazed, dumbfounded, in admiration at the little feet that moved up and down as rapidly as a couple of drumsticks. They cheered and clapped wildly as she stood on one leg for a moment.

She called out " Quicker," and began to sway again. She smiled and nodded and waved her arms. There was more and more motion of the body from the waist up, more gestures with the arms ; the dance became more and more mimic. She could no longer see the faces of her audience ; she opened her mouth, smiling so that all her teeth, a few very bad teeth, could be seen ; she began to act in pantomime ; she felt and knew only that she was dancing a solo—at last a solo, the solo for which she had waited so long. It was no longer the " grande Napolitaine." It was Fenella who knelt, Fenella who implored, Fenella who suffered, the beautiful, tragic Fenella.

She hardly knew how she had risen from the floor, or how she had come from the room. She heard only the sudden ceasing of the music, and the laughter—the terrible laughter, the laughter she heard and the laughter she saw on all these faces, to which she had suddenly become alive again.

She had risen from her knees, raised her arms mechanically, from force of habit, and bowed amid shouting. In there, in the little room, she stood, supporting herself on the edge of the table. It was all so dark around and in her—so empty. She loosened the scarf from her gown with strangely stiff hands, smoothed her skirts, and went back again to the room where the audience were now clapping politely. She bowed her thanks, standing by the piano, but she did not raise her eyes. The others began to dance again, eager to resume the fun. Miss Holm went about among them, saying farewell. Her pupils pressed the paper packages containing their money into her hands. Peter Madsen's wife helped her into her cloak, and at the door she was met by the pastor's daughter and the curate, ready to accompany her home.

They walked along in silence. The young lady from the rectory was very unhappy about the evening's occurrence, and wanted to excuse it somehow, but didn't know what to say. The little dancer walked along at her side, pale and quiet.

Finally, the curate, embarrassed at the silence, remarked hesitatingly : " You see, miss—these people—they don't understand tragic art." Miss Holm did not answer. When they came to her door she bowed and gave them her hand in silence. The rector's daughter caught her in her arms and kissed her. " Good night, good night," she said, her voice trembling. Then she waited outside with the curate until they saw a light in the little dancer's room.

．　　　．　　　．　　　．　　　．

Miss Holm took off her barege gown and folded it carefully. She unwrapped the money from the paper parcels, counted it, and sewed it into a little pocket in her bodice. She handled the needle awkwardly, sitting bowed over the tiny light.

The next morning her champagne basket was lifted on to a wagon of the country post. It rained, and Miss Holm huddled down under a broken umbrella. She drew her legs up under her, and sat on her basket like a Turk. When it was time to leave, the driver ran alongside. The young lady from the rectory came running up bareheaded. She had a white basket in her hands, and said she had brought " just a little food for the journey."

She bent down under the umbrella, caught Miss Holm's head in her hands, and kissed her twice. The old dancer broke into sobs, and grasping the young girl's hand, she kissed it violently.

The rector's daughter stood and looked for a long time after the old umbrella swaying on top of the little cart.

Miss Irene Holm had announced a " spring course in modern society dances " in a little town near by. Six pupils were promised. It was thither she was going now—to continue the thing we call Life.

NORWEGIAN   HENRIK STEFFENS

1773–1845

THE MYSTERIOUS WEDDING

ON the north-west of the Isle of Zealand stretches a small peninsular district, fertile and studded with hamlets, and connected with the mainland by a narrow strip of sandy waste. Beyond the only town which this little peninsula possesses the land runs into the restless waves of the Cattegat, and presents a wild and sterile appearance. The living sands have here obliterated every trace of vegetation ; and the storms which blow from all points of the wild ocean are constantly operating a change on the fluctuating surface of the desert, whose hills of sand rise and disappear with constant alternation, restless as the waves which roar around them. In travelling through this country, I here spent upwards of an hour, and never shall I forget the impression which the scene made upon my mind.

While riding alone through the desolate region, a thunderstorm rose over the ocean towards the north. The waves roared—the clouds were driven along before the wind—the sky grew every instant more gloomy, " menacing earth and sea "—the sand began to move in increasing masses under my horse's feet—a whirlwind arose and filled the atmosphere with dust—the traces of the path became invisible—my horse floundered deeper and deeper in the sand—while sky, earth, and ocean seemed mingled and blended together, every object being involved in a cloud of dust and vapour. I could not discern the slightest trace of life or vegetation. The storm howled above me—the waves of the sea lashed mournfully against the shore—the thunder rolled in the distance—and scarcely could the lurid lightning-flash pierce the heavy cloud of sand which whirled around me ; my danger was evident and extreme, when a sudden shower of rain laid the sand, and enabled me to push my way to the little town. The storm I had just encountered was a horrid mingling of all elements.

An earthquake has been described as the sigh which troubled Nature heaves from the depth of her bosom : perhaps not more fancifully this chaotic tempest might have typified the confusion of a wildly distracted mind, to which pleasure and even hope itself

have been long strangers—the cheerless desert of the past revealing
only remorse and grief—the voice of conscience threatening like the
thunder, while awful anticipations shed their lurid light over the
dark spirit—till at last the long dried-up sources of tears open a
way to their powerful floods, and bury the anguish of the soul
beneath their waves.

In this desolate country lay, in former times, a village called
Roerwig, about a mile distant from the shore. The moving sands
have buried the village, and the inhabitants—mostly shepherds and
fishermen—have removed their cottages close to the shore. A
single solitary building, the village church, which is situated upon
a hill, yet rears its head above the cheerless shifting desert. This
church was the scene of the following mysterious transaction.

.   .   .   .

In an early part of the eighteenth century the venerable curé of
Roerwig was one night seated in his study, absorbed in pious medita-
tions. It was near midnight. The house lay at the extremity of the
village, and the simple manners of the inhabitants were so little
tinged with distrust that bolts and locks were unknown among them,
and every door remained open and unguarded.

The night-lamp burned gloomily, the sullen silence of that dark
hour was only interrupted by the rushing noise of the sea, on whose
waves the pale moon was reflected, when the curé heard the door
below open, and, soon after, the sound of men's steps upon the
stair. He was just anticipating a call to administer the last holy
offices of religion to some one of his parishioners on the point of
death, when two foreigners, wrapped in white cloaks, stepped hastily
into the room. One of them approached him with politeness :

" Sir," said he, " you will have the goodness to follow us instantly. You must perform a marriage ceremony ; the bride and
bridegroom are already waiting your arrival at the church. This
sum," continued the stranger, exhibiting to the old man a purse
full of gold, " will sufficiently recompense you for the trouble and
alarm our sudden demand has given you."

The curé stared in mute terror upon the strangers, who seemed
to have something fearful, almost ghastly in their looks. The
demand was repeated in an earnest and authoritative tone. When
the old man had recovered from his first surprise, he began mildly
to represent that his duty did not allow him to perform so solemn
an action without some knowledge of the parties, and the inter-
vention of those formalities required by law. The other stranger
hereupon stepped forward in a menacing attitude :

" Sir," said he, " you have your choice : follow us ; take the sum
we offer now ; or remain, and this bullet goes through your head."

He levelled his pistol at the forehead of the venerable man, and
waited his answer ; whereupon the latter rose, dressed himself,

and informed his visitants, who had hitherto spoken Danish, but with a foreign accent, that he was ready to accompany them.

The mysterious strangers now proceeded silently through the village, followed by the clergyman.   It was a dark autumn night, the moon having already set ; but when they emerged from the village, the old man perceived with terror and astonishment that the distant church was all illuminated.   Meanwhile his companions, wrapped in their white cloaks, stepped hastily on before him across the barren sandy plain.   On reaching the church they bound up his eyes ; a side-door opened with a creaking noise, and he felt himself violently pushed into a crowd of people ; all around him he heard a murmuring of voices, and near to him a conversation carried on in a language quite unknown to him, but which he thought was Russian.

As he stood helpless, blindfolded, pressed upon from every side, and in the utmost confusion, he felt himself seized upon by a man's hand and violently drawn through the crowd.   At last it seemed to him as if the people fell back, the bandage was loosed, and he found himself standing with one of the two strangers before the altar.   A row of large lighted tapers, in magnificent silver candlesticks, adorned the altar, and the church itself was splendidly illuminated by a profusion of candles.   If before, while standing blindfolded, the murmur of the surrounding crowd had filled his soul with consternation, not less amazed was he now at the unbroken silence which reigned throughout the church.   The side passages and all the seats were crowded to excess, but the middle passage was quite clear, and he perceived in it a newly opened grave, and the stone which had covered it leaning against a bench ; around him he only saw male figures, but on one of the distant benches he thought he indistinctly perceived a female form.   The silence lasted for some minutes, during which not a motion could be detected in that vast multitude.   Thus, when a spirit is bent on deeds of darkness, a silent gloomy brooding of soul often precedes the horrid action.

At last a man, whose magnificent dress distinguished him from all the rest and bespoke his elevated rank, rose and walked hastily up the empty passage ; as he passed along, his steps resounded through the building, and every eye was turned upon him ; he appeared to be of middle stature, with broad shoulders and strong limbs ; his gait was commanding, his complexion of a yellowish brown, and his hair raven black ; his features were severe, and his lips compressed as if in wrath ; a bold aquiline nose heightened the haughty appearance of his countenance ; and dark shaggy brows lowered over his fiery eyes.   He wore a green coat, with large golden braids, and a glittering star.

The bride, who now kneeled beside him, was magnificently dressed.

A sky-blue roquelaure, richly trimmed with silver, enveloped her slender limbs, and floated in large folds over her graceful form ; a diadem sparkling with diamonds adorned her fair hair.   The utmost loveliness and beauty might be traced in her features, although despair now expressed itself in them ; her cheeks were pale as those of a corpse, her features unanimated, her lips were blanched, her eyes dimmed, and her powerless arms hung motionless beside her almost lifeless form.   As she knelt before the altar, the picture of death itself, terror seemed to have wrapped her consciousness as well as her vital powers in a fortunate slumber.

The curé now discovered near him an old ugly hag, in a particoloured dress, her head covered with a blood-red turban, who stood gazing with an expression of fury and mockery on the kneeling bride ;   and behind the bridegroom he noticed a man of gigantic size and gloomy appearance, whose eyes were fixed upon the ground.

Horror-struck, the priest stood mute for some time, till a thrilling look from the bridegroom reminded him of the ceremony he had come thither to perform.   But the uncertainty whether the couple he was now about to marry understood his language afforded him a fresh source of uneasiness.   He ventured, however, to ask the bridegroom for his name and that of his bride.

" Neander and Feodora," was the answer given in a rough voice.

The priest now began to read the ritual in faltering accents, frequently mistaking and stopping to repeat the words, without, however, either the bride or bridegroom appearing to observe his confusion, which confirmed him in the conjecture that his language was almost unknown to either of them.   On putting the question, " Neander, wilt thou have this woman for thy wedded wife ? " he doubted whether he should receive any answer ; but, to his astonishment, the bridegroom answered in the affirmative with a loud and almost screaming voice, which rung throughout the whole church, while deep sighs from the whole spectators accompanied the awful " yes " ;   and a silent quivering, like the reflection of a flash of distant lightning, threw a transitory motion over the death-pale features of the bride.

The priest turned to her, speaking louder to rouse her :

" Feodora, wilt thou have this man for thy wedded husband ? "

The lifeless form before him at this question seemed to awake, a deep convulsive throb of terror trembled on her cheeks, her pale lips quivered, a passing gleam of fire shone in her eyes, her breast heaved, a violent gush of tears flooded the brilliance of her eyes, and the " yes " was heard pronounced like the scream of anguish uttered by a dying person, and seemed to find a deep echo in the sounds of grief which burst from the surrounding multitude.

The bride sank into the arms of the horrid old hag ; some minutes passed in awful silence ; the pale corpse-like female then kneeled again, as if in a deep trance, and the ceremony was finished. The bridegroom now rose and led the trembling bride to her former place, followed by the tall man and the old woman ; the two strangers then appeared again, and having bound the priest's eyes, drew him with violence through the crowd, and pushed him out at the door, which they then bolted within.

For some minutes he stood endeavouring to recollect himself, and uncertain whether the horrid scene, with all its ghastly attendant circumstances, might not have been a dream ; but when he had torn the bandage from his eyes, and saw the illuminated church before him, and heard the murmuring of the crowd, he was forced to believe its reality. To learn the issue, he hid himself in a corner of the building, and while listening here he heard the murmuring within grow louder and louder. Then it seemed as if a fierce altercation arose, in which he thought he could recognise the rough voice of the bridegroom commanding silence. A long pause followed—a shot fell—the shriek of a female voice was heard, which was succeeded by another pause—then followed a sound of labour, which lasted about a quarter of an hour—the candles were extinguished—the murmuring arose again—the door was flung open, and a multitude of persons rushed out of the church and ran towards the sea.

The old priest now arose from his hiding-place and hastened back to the village, where he awoke his neighbours and friends, and related to them his incredible and marvellous adventure ; but everything which had hitherto fallen out amongst these simple people had been so calm and tranquil, so much measured by the laws of daily routine, that they were seized with a very different terror, they believed that some unfortunate accident had deranged the intellect of their beloved pastor, and it was not without difficulty that he prevailed on some of them to follow him to the church, provided with picks and spades.

Meanwhile the morning had dawned. The sun arose, and when the priest and his companions ascended the hill towards the church, they saw a man-of-war standing off from the shore under full sail towards the north. So surprising a sight in this remote district made his companions already hesitate to reject his story as improbable, and still more were they inclined to listen to him when they saw that the side-door of the church had been violently burst open. They entered full of expectation, and the priest showed them the grave which he had seen opened in the night-time ; it was easily perceived that the stone had been lifted up and replaced again. They put their implements in motion, and soon came to a new richly adorned coffin ; the old man descended with almost youthful impatience into the grave, and others followed him, the cover was taken off, and the priest found all his awful forebodings confirmed.

In the coffin lay the murdered bride—a bullet had pierced her breast right to the heart. The magnificent diadem she had worn had disappeared ; but the distracted expression of deep grief had vanished from her countenance, and a heavenly calm seemed spread over her features as she lay there like an angel. The old man threw himself down on his knees near the coffin, and wept and prayed aloud for the soul of the murdered, while mute astonishment and horror seized his companions.

The clergyman found himself obliged to make this event instantly known, with all its circumstances, to his superior, the Bishop of Zealand. Meanwhile, until he got further instructions from Copenhagen, he bound all his friends to secrecy by an oath. Shortly afterwards a person of high rank suddenly arrived from the capital ; he inquired into all the circumstances, visited the grave, commended the silence which had been hitherto observed, and stated that the whole event must remain for ever a secret, threatening at the same time with a severe punishment any person who should dare to speak of it.

After the death of the priest a writing was found in the parochial register narrating this event. Some believed that it might have some secret connection with the violent political changes which occurred in Russia after the death of Catherine and Peter I. ; but to resolve the deep riddle of this mysterious affair will ever be a difficult, if not impossible, task.

NORWEGIAN   BJÖRNSTJERNE
                             BJÖRNSON
                             1832–1910

THE RAILWAY AND THE
CHURCHYARD

I

KNUT AAKRE belonged to an ancient family of the parish, where it
had always been distinguished for its intelligence and care for the
public good.   His father through self-exertion had attained to the
ministry, but had died early, and his widow being by birth a
peasant, the children were brought up as farmers.   Consequently,
Knut's education was only of the kind afforded by the elementary
school ; but his father's library had early inspired him with a desire
for knowledge, which was increased by association with his friend
Henrik Wergeland, who often visited him or sent him books, seeds
for his farm, and much good counsel.   Agreeably to his advice,
Knut early got up a club, for practice in debating and study of the
constitution, which finally became a practical agricultural society,
for this and the surrounding parishes.   He also established a parish
library, giving his father's books as its first endowment, and organ-
ised in his own house a Sunday-school for persons wishing to learn
penmanship, arithmetic, and history.   In this way the attention of
the public was fixed upon him, and he was chosen a member of the
board of parish commissioners, of which he soon became chairman.
Here he continued his endeavours to advance the school interests,
which he succeeded in placing in an admirable condition.

Knut Aakre was a short-built, active man, with small sharp eyes
and disorderly hair.   He had large lips, which seemed constantly
working, and a row of excellent teeth that had the same appearance,
for they shone when he spoke his clear sharp words, which came out
with a snap, as when sparks are emitted from a great fire.

Among the many he had helped to an education, his neighbour
Lars Hogstad stood foremost.   Lars was not much younger than
Knut, but had developed more slowly.   Being in the habit of talking
much of what he read and thought, Knut found in Lars, who bore a

quiet, earnest manner, a good listener, and step by step a sensible judge. The result was that he went reluctantly to the meetings of the board, unless first furnished with Lars Hogstad's advice concerning whatever matter of importance was before it, which matter was thus most likely to result in practical improvement. Knut's influence, therefore, brought his neighbour in as a member of the board, and finally into everything with which he himself was connected. They always rode together to the meetings, at which Lars never spoke, and only on the road to and from them could Knut learn his opinion. The two were looked upon as inseparable.

One fine autumn day the parish commissioners were convened for the purpose of considering, among other matters, a proposal made by the Foged to sell the public grain-magazine, and with the proceeds establish a savings-bank. Knut Aakre, the chairman, would certainly have approved this, had he been guided by his better judgment ; but, in the first place, the motion was made by the Foged, whom Wergeland did not like, consequently, neither did Knut ; secondly, the grain-magazine had been erected by his powerful paternal grandfather, by whom it was presented to the parish. To him the proposal was not free from an appearance of personal offence ; therefore he had not spoken of it to anyone, not even to Lars, who never himself introduced a subject.

As chairman, Knut read the proposal without comment, but, according to his habit, looked over to Lars, who sat as usual a little to one side, holding a straw beneath his teeth ; this he always did when entering upon a subject, using it as he would a toothpick, letting it hang loosely in one corner of his mouth, or turning it more quickly or slowly, according to the humour he was in. Knut now saw, with surprise, that the straw moved very fast. He asked quickly, " Do you think we ought to agree to this ? "

Lars answered dryly, " Yes, I do."

The whole assembly, feeling that Knut was of quite a different opinion, seemed struck, and looked at Lars, who said nothing further, nor was further questioned. Knut turned to another subject, as if nothing had happened, and did not again resume the question till towards the close of the meeting, when he asked, with an air of indifference, if they should send it back to the Foged for closer consideration, as it certainly was contrary to the mind of the people of the parish, by whom the grain-magazine was highly valued ; also, if he should put upon the record, " Proposal deemed inexpedient."

" Against one vote," said Lars.

" Against two," said another instantly.

" Against three," said a third, and before the chairman had recovered from his surprise, a majority had declared in favour of the proposal.

He wrote ; then read in a low tone, " Referred for acceptance, and the meeting adjourned." Knut, rising and closing the " Records," blushed deeply, but resolved to have this vote defeated at the parish meeting. In the yard he hitched his horse to the wagon, and Lars came and seated himself by his side. On the way home they spoke upon various subjects, but not upon this.

On the following day Knut's wife started for Lars' house, to inquire of his wife if anything had happened between their husbands ; Knut had appeared so queerly when he returned home the evening previous. A little beyond the house she met Lars' wife, who came to make the same inquiry on account of a similar peculiar behaviour in her husband. Lars' wife was a quiet, timid thing, easily frightened, not by hard words, but by silence ; for Lars never spoke to her unless she had done wrong, or he feared she would do so. On the contrary, Knut Aakre's wife spoke much with her husband, and particularly about the commissioners' meetings, for lately they had taken his thoughts, work, and love from her and the children. She was jealous of it as of a woman, she wept at night about it, and quarrelled with her husband concerning it in the day. But now she could say nothing ; for once he had returned home unhappy ; she immediately became much more so than he, and for the life of her she must know what was the matter. So as Lars' wife could tell her nothing, she had to go for information out in the parish, where she obtained it, and of course was instantly of her husband's opinion, thinking Lars incomprehensible, not to say bad. But when she let her husband perceive this, she felt that, notwithstanding what had occurred, no friendship was broken between them ; on the contrary, that he liked Lars very much.

The day for the parish meeting came. In the morning, Lars Hogstad drove over for Knut Aakre, who came out and took a seat beside him. They saluted each other as usual, spoke a little less than they were wont on the way, but not at all of the proposal. The meeting was full ; some, too, had come in as spectators, which Knut did not like, for he perceived by this a little excitement in the parish. Lars had his straw, and stood by the stove, warming himself, for the autumn had begun to be cold. The chairman read the proposal in a subdued and careful manner, adding that it came from the Foged, who was not habitually fortunate. The building was a gift, and such things it was not customary to part with, least of all when there was no necessity for it.

Lars, who never before had spoken in the meetings, to the surprise of all, took the floor. His voice trembled ; whether this was caused by regard for Knut, or anxiety for the success of the bill, we cannot say ; but his arguments were clear, good, and of such a comprehensive and compact character as had hardly before been heard in these meetings. In concluding, he said :

" Of what importance is it that the proposal is from the Foged ?
None.   Or who it was that erected the house, or in what way it
became the public property ? "

Knut, who blushed easily, turned very red, and moved nervously
as usual when he was impatient ; but notwithstanding, he answered,
in a low, careful tone, that there were savings-banks enough in the
country, he thought, quite near, and almost too near.   But, if one
was to be instituted, there were other ways of attaining this end than
by trampling upon the gifts of the dead and the love of the living.
His voice was a little unsteady when he said this, but recovered its
composure when he began to speak of the grain-magazine as such,
and reason concerning its utility.

Lars answered him ably on this last, adding : " Besides, for many
reasons I would be led to doubt whether the affairs of this parish are
to be conducted for the best interests of the living, or for the memory
of the dead ; or further, whether it is the love and hate of a single
family which rules, rather than the welfare of the whole."

Knut answered quickly : " I don't know whether the last speaker
has been the one least benefited not only by the dead of this
family, but also by its still living representative."

In this remark he aimed first at the fact that his powerful grandfather had, in his day, managed the farm for Lars' grandfather,
when the latter, on his own account, was on a little visit to the
penitentiary.

The straw, which had been moving quickly for a long time, was
now still :

" I am not in the habit of speaking everywhere of myself and
family," said Lars, treating the matter with calm superiority ; then
he reviewed the whole matter in question, aiming throughout at a
particular point.

Knut was forced to acknowledge to himself that he had never
looked upon it from that standpoint, or heard such reasoning ; involuntarily he had to turn his eye upon Lars.   There he stood tall
and portly, with clearness marked upon the strongly-built forehead
and in the deep eyes.   His mouth was compressed, the straw still
hung playing in its corner, but great strength lay around.   He kept
his hands behind him, standing erect, while his low deep intonations
seemed as if from the ground in which he was rooted.   Knut saw
him for the first time in his life, and from his inmost soul felt a dread
of him ; for unmistakably this man had always been his superior !
He had taken all Knut himself knew or could impart, but retained
only what had nourished this strong hidden growth.

He had loved and cherished Lars, but now that he had become a
giant, he hated him deeply, fearfully ; he could not explain to himself why he thought so, but he felt it instinctively, while gazing upon
him ; and in this, forgetting all else, he exclaimed :

" But Lars ! Lars ! what in the Lord's name ails you ? "

He lost all self-control—" you, whom I have "—" you, who have"
—he couldn't get out another word, and seated himself, only to
struggle against the excitement which he was unwilling to have
Lars see ; he drew himself up, struck the table with his fist, and his
eyes snapped from below the stiff disorderly hair which always
shaded them. Lars appeared as if he had not been interrupted,
only turning his head to the assembly, asking if this should be considered the decisive blow in the matter, for in such a case nothing
more need be said.

Knut could not endure this calmness.

" What is it that has come among us ? " he cried. " Us, who to
this day have never debated but in love and upright zeal ? We are
infuriated at each other as if incited by an evil spirit " ; and he
looked with fiery eyes upon Lars, who answered :

" You yourself surely bring in this spirit, Knut, for I have spoken
only of the case. But you will look upon it only through your own
self-will ; now we shall see if your love and upright zeal will endure,
when once it is decided agreeably to our wish."

" Have I not, then, taken good care of the interests of the
parish ? "

No reply. This grieved Knut, and he continued :

" Really, I did not think otherwise than that I had accomplished
something—something for the good of the parish—but maybe I
have deceived myself."

He became excited again, for it was a fiery spirit within him,
which was broken in many ways, and the parting with Lars
grieved him, so that he could hardly control himself. Lars
answered :

" Yes, I know you give yourself the credit for all that is done here,
and, should one judge by much speaking in the meetings, then surely
you have accomplished the most."

" Oh, is it this ! " shouted Knut, looking sharply upon Lars :
" it is you who have the honour of it ! "

" Since we necessarily talk of ourselves," replied Lars, " I will say
that all matters have been carefully considered by us before they
were introduced here."

Here little Knut Aakre resumed his quick way of speaking :

" In God's name take the honour, I am content to live without it ;
there are other things harder to lose ! "

Involuntarily Lars turned his eye from Knut, but said, the straw
moving very quickly : " If I were to speak my mind, I should say
there is not much to take honour for ; of course ministers and
teachers may be satisfied with what has been done ; but, certainly,
the common men say only that up to this time the taxes have become
heavier and heavier."

A murmur arose in the assembly, which now became restless. Lars continued :

" Finally, to-day, a proposal is made which, if carried, would recompense the parish for all it has laid out ; perhaps, for this reason, it meets such opposition. It is the affair of the parish, for the benefit of all its inhabitants, and ought to be rescued from being a family matter."

The audience exchanged glances, and spoke half audibly, when one threw out a remark, as he rose to go to his dinner-pail, that these were " the truest words he had heard in the meetings for many years." Now all arose, and the conversation became general. Knut Aakre felt as he sat there that the case was lost, fearfully lost ; and tried no more to save it. He had somewhat of the character attributed to Frenchmen, in that he was good for first, second, and third attacks, but poor for self-defence—his sensibilities overpowering his thoughts.

He could not comprehend it, nor could he sit quietly any longer ; so, yielding his place to the vice-chairman, he left—and the audience smiled.

He had come to the meeting accompanied by Lars, but returned home alone, though the road was long. It was a cold autumn day ; the way looked jagged and bare, the meadow grey and yellow ; while frost had begun to appear here and there on the roadside. Disappointment is a dreadful companion. He felt himself so small and desolate, walking there ; but Lars was everywhere before him, like a giant, his head towering, in the dusk of evening, to the sky. It was his own fault that this had been the decisive battle, and the thought grieved him sorely : he had staked too much upon a single little affair. But surprise, pain, anger, had mastered him ; his heart still burned, shrieked, and moaned within him. He heard the rattling of a wagon behind ; it was Lars, who came driving his superb horse past him at a brisk trot, so that the hard road gave a sound of thunder. Knut gazed after him, as he sat there so broad-shouldered in the wagon, while the horse, impatient for home, hurried on unurged by Lars, who only gave loose rein. It was a picture of his power ; this man drove toward the mark ! He, Knut, felt as if thrown out of his wagon to stagger along there in the autumn cold.

Knut's wife was waiting for him at home. She knew there would be a battle ; she had never in her life believed in Lars, and lately had felt a dread of him. It had been no comfort to her that they had ridden away together, nor would it have comforted her if they had returned in the same way. But darkness had fallen, and they had not yet come. She stood in the doorway, went down the road and home again ; but no wagon appeared.

At last she hears a rattling on the road, her heart beats as violently as the wheels revolve ; she clings to the doorpost, looking out ; the wagon is coming ; only one sits there ; she recognises Lars, who sees and recognises her, but is driving past without stopping. Now she is thoroughly alarmed ! Her limbs fail her ; she staggers in, sinking on the bench by the window.

The children, alarmed, gather around, the youngest asking for papa, for the mother never spoke with them but of him. She loved him because he had such a good heart, and now this good heart was not with them ; but, on the contrary, away on all kinds of business, which brought him only unhappiness ; consequently, they were unhappy too.

" Oh, that no harm had come to him to-day ! Knut was so excitable ! Why did Lars come home alone ? Why didn't he stop ? "

Should she run after him, or, in the opposite direction, toward her husband ? She felt faint, and the children pressed around her, asking what was the matter ; but this could not be told to them, so she said they must take supper alone, and, rising, arranged it and helped them. She was constantly glancing out upon the road. He did not come. She undressed and put them to bed, and the youngest repeated the evening prayer, while she bowed over him, praying so fervently in the words which the tiny mouth first uttered that she did not perceive the steps outside.

Knut stood in the doorway, gazing upon his little congregation at prayer. She rose ; all the children shouted " Papa ! " but he seated himself, and said gently :

" Oh ! let him repeat it."

The mother turned again to the bedside, that meantime he might not see her face ; otherwise, it would have been like intermeddling with his grief before he felt a necessity of revealing it. The child folded his hands, the rest following the example, and said :

> I am now a little lad,
> But soon shall grow up tall,
> And make papa and mamma glad,
> I'll be so good to all !
> When in Thy true and holy ways,
> Thou dear, dear God wilt help me keep ;—
> Remember now Thy name to praise,
> And so we'll try to go to sleep !

What a peace now fell ! Not a minute more had passed ere the children all slept in it as in the lap of God ; but the mother went quietly to work arranging supper for the father, who as yet could not eat. But after he had gone to bed, he said :

" Now, after this, I shall be at home."

The mother lay there trembling with joy, not daring to speak, lest she should reveal it ; and she thanked God for all that had happened, for, whatever it was, it had resulted in good.

II

In the course of a year, Lars was chosen head Justice of the Peace, chairman of the board of commissioners, president of the savings-bank, and, in short, was placed in every office of parish trust to which his election was possible. In the county legislature, during the first year, he remained silent, but afterward made himself as conspicuous as in the parish council ; for here, too, stepping up to the contest with him who had always borne sway, he was victorious over the whole line, and afterward himself manager. From this he was elected to the Congress, where his fame had preceded him, and he found no lack of challenge. But here, although steady and independent, he was always retiring, never venturing beyond his depth, lest his post as leader at home should be endangered by a possible defeat abroad.

It was pleasant to him now in his own town. When he stood by the church-wall on Sundays, and the community glided past, saluting and glancing sideways at him—now and then one stepping up for the honour of exchanging a couple of words with him—it could almost be said that, standing there, he controlled the whole parish with a straw, which, of course, hung in the corner of his mouth.

He deserved his popularity ; for he had opened a new road which led to the church ; all this and much more resulted from the savings-bank, which he had instituted and now managed ; and the parish, in its self-management and good order, was held up as an example to all others.

Knut, of his own accord, quite withdrew—not entirely at first, for he had promised himself not thus to yield to pride. In the first proposal he made before the parish board, he became entangled by Lars, who would have it represented in all its details ; and, somewhat hurt, he replied : " When Columbus discovered America he did not have it divided into counties and towns—this came by degrees afterward " ; upon which Lars compared Knut's suggestion (relating to stable improvements) to the discovery of America, and afterward by the commissioners he was called by no other name than " Discovery of America." Knut thought, since his influence had ceased there, so, also, had his duty to work ; and afterwards declined re-election.

But he was industrious, and, in order still to do something for the public good, he enlarged his Sunday-school, and put it, by means of small contributions from the pupils, in connection with the mission cause, of which he soon became the centre and leader in his own and surrounding counties. At this, Lars remarked that if Knut ever wished to collect money for any purpose, he must first know that its benefit was only to be realised some thousands of miles away.

There was no strife between them now. True, they associated with each other no longer, but saluted and exchanged a few words whenever they met. Knut always felt a little pain in remembering Lars, but struggled to overcome it, by saying to himself that it must have been so. Many years afterward, at a large wedding-party, where both were present and a litle gay, Knut stepped upon a chair and proposed a toast to the chairman of the parish council and the county's first congressman. He spoke until he manifested emotion, and, as usual, in an exceedingly handsome way. It was honourably done, and Lars came to him, saying, with an unsteady eye, that for much of what he knew and was he had to thank him.

At the next election Knut was again elected chairman.

But if Lars Hogstad had foreseen what was to follow, he would not have influenced this. It is a saying that " all events happen in their time," and just as Knut appeared again in the council, the ablest men in the parish were threatened with bankruptcy, the result of a speculative fever which had been raging long, but now first began to react. They said that Lars Hogstad had caused this great epidemic, for it was he who had brought the spirit of speculation into the parish. This penny malady had originated in the parish board ; for this body itself had acted as leading speculator. Down to the youth of twenty years, all were endeavouring by sharp bargains to make the one shilling ten ; extreme parsimony, in order to lay up in the beginning, was followed by an exceeding lavishness in the end : and as the thoughts of all were directed to money only, a disposition to selfishness, suspicion, and disunion had developed itself, which at last turned to prosecutions and hatred. It was said that the parish board had set the example in this also ; for one of the first acts performed by Lars as chairman was a prosecution against the minister, concerning doubtful prerogatives. The venerable pastor had lost, but had also immediately resigned.

At the time some had praised, others denounced, this act of Lars ; but it had proved a bad example. Now came the effects of his management in the form of loss to all the leading men of the parish ; and consequently, public opinion quickly changed. The opposite party immediately found a champion ; for Knut Aakre had come into the parish board, introduced there by Lars himself.

The struggle at once began. All those youths who, in their time, had been under Knut Aakre's instruction, were now grown-up men, the best educated, conversant with all the business and public transactions in the parish ; Lars had now to contend against these and others like them, who had disliked him from their childhood. One evening, after a stormy debate, as he stood on the platform outside his door, looking over the parish, a sound of distant threatening thunder came toward him from the large farms, lying in the storm. He knew that that day their owners had become insolvent, that he himself and the savings-bank were going the same way ; and his whole long work would culminate in condemnation against him.

In these days of struggle and despair, a company of surveyors came one evening to Hogstad, which was the first farm at the entrance of the parish, to mark out the line of a new railway. In the course of conversation, Lars perceived it was still a question with them whether the road should run through this valley or another parallel one.

Like a flash of lightning it darted through his mind that, if he could manage to get it through here, all real estate would rise in value, and not only he himself be saved, but his popularity handed down to future generations. He could not sleep that night, for his eyes were dazzled with visions ; sometimes he seemed to hear the noise of an engine. The next day he accompanied the surveyors in their examination of the locality ; his horses carried them, and to his farm they returned. The following day they drove through the other valley, he still with them, and again carrying them back home. The whole house was illuminated, the first men of the parish having been invited to a party made for the surveyors, which terminated in a carouse that lasted until morning. But to no avail ; for the nearer they came to the decision, the clearer it was to be seen that the road could not be built through here without great extra expense. The entrance to the valley was narrow, through a rocky chasm, and the moment it swung into the parish the river made a curve in its way, so that the railway would either have to make the same—crossing the river twice—or go straight forward through the old, now unused, churchyard. Yet it was not long since the last burials there, for the church had been but recently moved.

Did it only depend upon a strip of an old churchyard, thought Lars, whether the parish should have this great blessing or not ?— then he would use his name and energy for the removal of the obstacle. So immediately he made a visit to minister and bishop, from them to county legislature and Department of the Interior ; he reasoned and negotiated ; for he had possessed himself of all possible information concerning the vast profits that would accrue on the one side, and the feelings of the parish on the other, and had really succeeded in gaining over all parties. It was promised him that, by the reinternment of some bodies in the new churchyard, the only objection to this line might be considered as removed, and the king's approbation guaranteed. It was told him that he need only make the motion in the county meeting.

The parish had become as excited on the question as himself. The spirit of speculation, which had been prevalent so many years, now became jubilant. No one spoke or thought of anything but Lars' journey and its probable result. Consequently, when he returned with the most splendid promises, they made much ado

about him; songs were sung to his praise; yes, if at that time one
after another of the largest farms had toppled over, not a soul
would have given it any attention; the former speculation fever
had been succeeded by the new one of the railway.

The county board met; a humble petition that the old churchyard might be used for the railway was drawn up to be presented
to the king.   This was unanimously voted; yes, there was even talk
of voting thanks to Lars, and a gift of a coffee-pot, in the model
of a locomotive.   But finally, it was thought best to wait until
everything was accomplished.   The petition from the parish to the
county board was sent back, with a requirement of a list of the names
of all bodies which must necessarily be removed.   The minister
made out this, but instead of sending it directly to the county board,
had his reasons for communicating it first to the parish.   One of the
members brought it to the next meeting.   Here Lars opened the
envelope, and as chairman read the names.

Now it happened that the first body to be removed was that of
Lars' own grandfather.   A little shudder passed through the
assembly; Lars himself was taken by surprise; but continued.
Secondly came the name of Knut Aakre's grandfather; for the
two had died at nearly the same time.   Knut Aakre sprang from his
seat; Lars stopped; all looked up with dread, for the name of the
elder Knut Aakre had been the one most beloved in the parish for
generations.   There was a pause of some minutes.   At last Lars
hemmed, and continued.   But the matter became worse, for the
further he proceeded, the nearer it approached their own day, and
the dearer the dead became.   When he ceased, Knut Aakre asked
quietly if others did not think as he, that spirits were around them.
It had begun to grow dusk in the room, and although they were
mature men sitting in company, they almost felt themselves
frightened.   Lars took a bundle of matches from his pocket and lit
a candle, somewhat dryly remarking that this was no more than
they had known beforehand.

"No," replied Knut, pacing the floor, "this is more than I knew
beforehand.   Now I begin to think that even railways can be bought
too dearly."

This electrified the audience, and Knut continued that the whole
affair must be reconsidered, and made a motion to that effect.   In
the excitement which had prevailed, he said it was also true that the
benefit to be derived from the railway had been considerably over-
rated; for if it did not pass through the parish, there would have to
be a station at each extremity; true, it would be a little more trouble
to drive there than to a station within; yet not so great that for this
reason they should dishonour the rest of the dead.

Knut was one of those who, when his thoughts were excited, could
extemporise and present most sound reasons; he had not a moment

previously thought of what he now said ; but the truth of it struck all. Lars, seeing the danger of his position, thought it best to be careful, and so apparently acquiesced in Knut's proposition to reconsider ; for such emotions, thought he, are always strongest in the beginning ; one must temporise with them.

But here he had miscalculated. In constantly increasing waves the dread of touching their dead overswept the parish ; what no one had thought of as long as the matter existed only in talk became a serious question when it came to touch themselves. The women particularly were excited, and at the parish house, on the day of the next meeting, the road was black with the gathered multitude. It was a warm summer day, the windows were taken out, and as many stood without as within. All felt that that day would witness a great battle.

Lars came, driving his handsome horse, saluted by all ; he looked quietly and confidently around, not seeming surprised at the throng. He seated himself, straw in mouth, near the window, and not without a smile saw Knut rise to speak, as he thought, for all the dead lying over there in the old churchyard.

But Knut Aakre did not begin with the churchyard. He made a stricter investigation into the profits likely to accrue from carrying the railway through the parish, showing that in all this excitement they had been over-estimated. He had calculated the distance of each farm from the nearest station, should the road be taken through the neighbouring valley, and finally asked :

" Why has such a fuss been made about this railway, when it would not be for the good of the parish after all ? "

This he could explain ; there were those who had brought about such a previous disturbance, that a greater was necessary in order that the first might be forgotten. Then, too, there were those who, while the thing was new, could sell their farms and lands to strangers foolish enough to buy ; it was a shameful speculation, which not the living only but the dead also must be made to promote !

The effect produced by his address was very considerable. But Lars had firmly resolved, come what would, to keep cool, and smilingly replied that he supposed Knut Aakre himself had been anxious for the railway, and surely no one would accuse him of understanding speculation. (A little laugh ensued.) Knut had had no objection to the removal of bodies of common people for the sake of the railway, but when it came to that of his own grandfather, the question became suddenly of vital importance to the whole parish. He said no more, but looked smilingly at Knut, as did also several others. Meanwhile, Knut Aakre surprised both him and them by replying :

" I confess it ; I did not realise what was at stake until it touched my own dead ; possibly this is a shame, but really it would have been a greater one not even then to have realised it, as is the case with Lars! Never, I think, could Lars' raillery have been more out of place: for folks with common feelings the thing is really revolting."

" This feeling has come up quite recently," answered Lars, " and so we will hope for its speedy disappearance also. It may be well to think upon what minister, bishop, county officers, engineers, and Department will say, if we first unanimously set the ball in motion and then come asking to have it stopped; if we first are jubilant and sing songs, then weep and chant requiems. If they do not say that we have run mad here in the parish, at least they may say that we have grown a little queer lately."

" Yes, God knows, they can say so," answered Knut; " we have been acting strangely enough during the last few days—it is time for us to retract. It has really gone far when we can dig up, each his own grandfather to make way for a railway; when, in order that our loads may be carried more easily forward, we can violate the resting-place of the dead. For is not overhauling our churchyard the same as making it yield us food? What has been buried there in Jesus' name, shall we take up in the name of Mammon? It is but little better than eating our progenitors' bones."

" That is according to the order of nature," said Lars dryly.

" Yes, the nature of plants and animals," replied Knut.

" Are we not then animals?" asked Lars.

" Yes, but also the children of the living God, who have buried our dead in faith upon Him; it is He who shall raise them, and not we."

" Oh, you prate! Are not the graves dug over at certain fixed periods anyway? What evil is there in that it happens some years earlier?" asked Lars.

" I will tell you! What was born of them yet lives; what they built yet remains; what they loved, taught, and suffered for is all around us and within us; and shall we not, then, let their bodies rest in peace?"

" I see by your warmth that you are thinking of your grandfather again," replied Lars; " and will say it is high time you ceased to bother the parish about him, for he monopolised space enough in his lifetime; it isn't worth while to have him lie in the way now he is dead. Should his corpse prevent a blessing to the parish that would reach to a hundred generations, we surely would have reason to say that, of all born here, he has done us most harm."

Knut Aakre tossed back his disorderly hair, his eyes darted fire, his whole frame appeared like a drawn bow.

" What sort of a blessing this is that you speak of, I have already proved. It is of the same character as all the others which you have brought to the parish, namely, a doubtful one. True enough, you

have provided us with a new church ; but, too, you have filled it
with a new spirit—and not that of love.   True, you have made us
new roads—but also new roads to destruction, as is now plainly
evident in the misfortunes of many.   True, you have lessened our
taxes to the public ; but, too, you have increased those to ourselves ;
prosecutions, protests, and failures are no blessing to a community.
And you dare not scoff at the man in his grave whom the whole
parish blesses !   You dare say he lies in our way—yes, very likely
he lies in your way.   This is plainly to be seen ; but over this grave
you shall fall !   The spirit which has reigned over you, and at the
same time until now over us, was not born to rule, only to serve.
The churchyard shall surely remain undisturbed ; but to-day it
numbers one more grave, namely, that of your popularity, which
shall now be interred in it."

Lars Hogstad rose, white as a sheet ; he opened his mouth, but
was unable to speak a word, and the straw fell.   After three or
four vain attempts to recover it and to find utterance, he belched
forth like a volcano :

" Are these the thanks I get for all my toils and struggles ?   Shall
such a woman-preacher be able to direct ?   Ah, then, the devil be
your chairman if ever more I set my foot here !   I have kept your
petty business in order until to-day ; and after me it will fall into a
thousand pieces ; but let it go now.   Here are the ' Records ' ! (and
he flung them across the table).   Out on such a company of wenches
and brats ! (striking the table with his fist).   Out on the whole
parish, that it can see a man recompensed as I now am ! "

He brought down his fist once more with such force that the leaf
of the great table sprang upward, and the inkstand with all its contents downward upon the floor, marking for coming generations the
spot where Lars Hogstad, in spite of all his prudence, lost his
patience and his rule.

He sprang for the door, and soon after was away from the house.
The whole audience stood fixed—for the power of his voice and his
wrath had frightened them—until Knut Aakre, remembering the
taunt he had received at the time of his fall, with beaming countenance, and assuming Lars' voice, exclaimed :

" Is this the decisive blow in the matter ? "

The assembly burst into uproarious merriment.   The grave meeting closed amid laughter, talk, and high glee ; only few left the
place, those remaining called for drink, and made a night of thunder
succeed a day of lightning.   They felt happy and independent as in
old days, before the time in which the commanding spirit of Lars
had cowed their souls into silent obedience.   They drank toasts to
their liberty, they sang, yes, finally they danced, Knut Aakre with
the vice-chairman taking lead, and all the members of the council
following, and boys and girls too, while the young ones outside

shouted " Hurrah ! " for such a spectacle they had never before witnessed.

III

Lars moved around in the large rooms at Hogstad without uttering a word. His wife, who loved him, but always with fear and trembling, dared not so much as show herself in his presence. The management of the farm and house had to go on as it would, while a multitude of letters were passing to and fro between Hogstad and the parish, Hogstad and the capital ; for he had charges against the county board which were not acknowledged, and a prosecution ensued ; against the savings-bank, which were also unacknowledged, and so came another prosecution. He took offence at articles in the *Christiania Correspondence*, and prosecuted again, first the chairman of the county board, and then the directors of the savings-bank. At the same time there were bitter articles in the papers, which according to report were by him, and were the cause of great strife in the parish, setting neighbour against neighbour. Sometimes he was absent whole weeks at once, nobody knowing where, and after returning lived secluded as before. At church he was not seen after the grand scene in the representatives' meeting.

Then, one Saturday night, the post brought news that the railway was to go through the parish after all, and through the old churchyard. It struck like lightning into every home. The unanimous veto of the county board had been in vain ; Lars Hogstad's influence had proved stronger. This was what his absence meant, this was his work ! It was involuntary on the part of the people that admiration of the man and his dogged persistency should lessen dissatisfaction at their own defeat ; and the more they talked of the matter the more reconciled they seemed to become : for whatever has once been settled beyond all change develops in itself, little by little, reasons why it is so, which we are accordingly brought to acknowledge.

In going to church next day, as they encountered each other they could not help laughing ; and before the service, just as nearly all were convened outside—young and old, men and women, yes, even children—talking about Lars Hogstad, his talents, his strong will, and his great influence, he himself with his household came driving up in four carriages. Two years had passed since he was last there. He alighted and walked through the crowd, when involuntarily all lifted their hats to him like one man ; but he looked neither to the right nor the left, nor returned a single salutation. His little wife, pale as death, walked behind him. In the building, the surprise became so great that one after another, noticing him, stopped singing and stared. Knut Aakre, who sat in his pew in front of Lars', turned around and saw Lars sitting bowed over his hymn-book, looking for the place.

He had not seen him until now since the day of the representatives' meeting, and such a change in a man he never could have imagined. This was no victor.   His head was becoming bald, his face was lean and contracted, his eyes hollow and bloodshot, and the giant neck presented wrinkles and cords.   At a glance he perceived what this man had endured, and was as suddenly seized with a feeling of strong pity, yes, even with a touch of the old love.   In his heart he prayed for him, and promised himself surely to seek him after service ; but, ere he had opportunity, Lars had gone.   Knut resolved he would call upon him at his home that night, but his wife kept him back.

" Lars is one of the kind," said she, " who cannot endure a debt of gratitude : keep away from him until possibly he can in some way do you a favour, and then perhaps he will come to you."

However, he did not come.   He appeared now and then at church, but nowhere else, and associated with no one.   On the contrary, he devoted himself to his farm and other business with an earnestness which showed a determination to make up in one year for the neglect of many ; and, too, there were those who said it was necessary.

Railway operations in the valley began very soon.   As the line was to go directly past his house, Lars remodelled the side facing it, connecting with it an elegant verandah, for of course his residence must attract attention.   They were just engaged in this work when the rails were laid for the conveyance of gravel and timber, and a small locomotive was brought up.   It was a fine autumn evening when the first gravel train was to come down.   Lars stood on the platform of his house to hear the first signal, and see the first column of smoke ; all the hands on the farm were gathered around him. He looked out over the parish, lying in the setting sun, and felt that he was to be remembered so long as a train should roar through the fruitful valley.   A feeling of forgiveness crept into his soul.   He looked toward the churchyard, of which a part remained, with crosses bowing toward the earth, but a part had become railway. He was trying to define his feelings, when, whistle went the first signal, and a while after the train came slowly along, puffing out smoke mingled with sparks, for wood was used instead of coal ; the wind blew toward the house, and standing there they soon found themselves enveloped in a dense smoke ; but by and by, as it cleared away, Lars saw the train working through the valley like a strong will.

He was satisfied, and entered the house as after a long day's work. The image of his grandfather stood before him at this moment. This grandfather had raised the family from poverty to comfortable circumstances ; true, a part of his citizen-honour had been lost, but forward he had pushed, nevertheless.   His faults were those of his time ; they were to be found on the uncertain borders of the moral conceptions of that period, and are of no consideration now. Honour to him in his grave, for he suffered and worked ; peace to his ashes. It is good to rest at last. But he could get no rest because of his grandson's great ambition. He was thrown up with stone and gravel. Pshaw ! very likely he would only smile that his grandson's work passed above his head.

With such thoughts he had undressed and gone to bed. Again his grandfather's image glided forth. What did he wish ? Surely he ought to be satisfied now, with the family's honour sounding forth above his grave ; who else had such a monument ?

But yet, what mean these two great eyes of fire ? This hissing, roaring, is no longer the locomotive, for see ! it comes from the churchyard directly toward the house : an immense procession ! The eyes of fire are his grandfather's, and the train behind are all the dead. It advances continually toward the house, roaring, crackling, flashing. The windows burn in the reflection of dead men's eyes. . . . He made a mighty effort to collect himself, " For it was a dream, of course, only a dream ; but let me waken ! . . . See : now I am awake ; come, ghosts ! "

And behold : they really come from the churchyard, overthrowing track, rails, locomotive and train with such violence that they sink in the ground ; and then all is still there, covered with sod and crosses as before. But like giants the spirits advance, and the hymn, " Let the dead have rest ! " goes before them. He knows it ; for daily in all these years it has sounded through his soul, and now it becomes his own requiem ; for this was death and its visions.

The perspiration started out over his whole body, for nearer and nearer—and see there, on the window-pane ! there, there they were now ; and he heard his name. Overpowered with dread he struggled to shout, for he was strangling ; a dead, cold hand already clenched his throat, when he regained his voice in a shrieking " Help me ! " and awoke.

At that moment the window was burst in with such force that the pieces flew on to his bed. He sprang up ; a man stood in the opening, around him smoke and tongues of fire.

" The house is burning, Lars, we'll help you out ! "

It was Knut Aakre.

When again he recovered consciousness, he was lying out in a piercing wind that chilled his limbs. No one was by him ; on the left he saw his burning house ; around him grazed, bellowed, bleated, and neighed his stock ; the sheep huddled together in a terrified flock ; the furniture recklessly scattered : but, on looking around more carefully, he discovered somebody sitting on a knoll near him, weeping. It was his wife. He called her name. She started.

" The Lord Jesus be thanked that you live," she exclaimed, com-

ing forward and seating herself, or rather falling down before him.
" O God ! O God ! now we have enough of that railway ! "

" The railway ? " he asked ; but ere he spoke, it had flashed
through his mind how it was ; for, of course, the cause of the fire
was the falling of sparks from the locomotive among the shavings
by the new side-wall.   He remained sitting, silent and thoughtful ;
his wife dared say no more, but was trying to find clothes for him,
the things with which she had covered him, as he lay unconscious,
having fallen off.   He received her attentions in silence, but as she
crouched down to cover his feet, he laid a hand upon her head.   She
hid her face in his lap, and wept aloud.   At last he had noticed her.
Lars understood, and said :

" You are the only friend I have."

Although to hear these words had cost the house, no matter, they
made her happy ; she gathered courage and said, rising and looking
submissively at him :

" That is because no one else understands you."

Now again they talked of all that had transpired, or rather he
remained silent, while she told about it.   Knut Aakre had been first
to perceive the fire, had awakened his people, sent the girls out
through the parish, while he himself hastened with men and horses
to the spot where all were sleeping.   He had taken charge of extin-
guishing the fire and saving the property ; Lars himself he had
dragged from the burning room and brought him here on the left,
to the windward—here, out on the churchyard.

While they were talking of all this, someone came driving rapidly
up the road and turned off toward them ; soon he alighted.   It was
Knut who had been home after his church wagon ; the one in which
so many times they had ridden together to and from the parish
meetings.   Now Lars must get in and ride home with him.   They
took each other by the hand, one sitting, the other standing.

" You must come with me now," said Knut.   Without reply Lars
rose ; they walked side by side to the wagon.   Lars was helped in ;
Knut seated himself by his side.   What they talked about as they
rode, or afterward in the little chamber at Aakre, in which they
remained until morning, has never been known ; but from that day
they were again inseparable.

As soon as disaster befalls a man, all seem to understand his worth.
So the parish took upon themselves to rebuild Lars Hogstad's houses
larger and handsomer than any others in the valley.   Again he
became chairman, but with Knut Aakre at his side, and from that
day all went well.

A DANGEROUS WOOING

Björnstjerne Björnson

When Aslaug had become a grown-up girl, there was no longer any peace to be had at Huseby; in fact the handsomest youths in the parish quarrelled and fought there night after night. It was worst of all on Saturday nights; then old Knut Huseby never went to bed without keeping his leather breeches on, nor without having a birch stick by his bedside.

" If I have a pretty daughter, I must look after her," he said.

Thore Naeset was only a cottager's son; nevertheless there were those who said that he was the one who came oftenest to see old Knut's daughter at Huseby. Old Knut did not like this, and declared also that it was not true, " for he had never seen him there." But people smiled slyly among themselves, and thought that, had he searched in the hayloft, where Aslaug had many an errand, instead of fighting with all those who were making a noise and uproar outside, he would have found Thore.

Spring came and Aslaug went to the mountain chalet with the cattle. Then, when the day was warm down in the valley, and the mountain rose cool above the haze, when the cow-bells tinkled, the shepherd dog barked, and Aslaug sang and blew the cow-horn on the mountain side, then the hearts of all the young fellows who were at work down on the meadow would ache. And on the first Saturday night they all started up the mountain, each one faster than the other. But still more rapidly did they come down again, for behind the door at the chalet there stood a man on guard who gave each one as he came up such a warm reception that he forever afterward remembered the threat that followed it :

" Come again another time and you shall have some more."

According to what these young fellows knew, there was only one in the parish who could use his fists in this way, and that was Thore Naeset. And these rich farmers' sons thought it was a shame that this cottager's son should cut them all out.

So thought, also, old Knut, when the matter reached his ears, and he said, moreover, that if there was nobody else who could tackle Thore, then he and his sons would try it. Knut, it is true, was growing old, but although he was nearly sixty he would at times enjoy a wrestling match with his eldest son, when it was too dull for him at some party or other.

Up to the chalet there was but one road, and that led straight through the farmhouse yard. The next Saturday evening, as Thore was going to the chalet, and was stealing on his tiptoes across the yard, a man rushed right at his breast as he came near the barn.

"What do you want of me?" said Thore, and knocked his assailant flat on the ground.

"That you shall soon find out," said another fellow from behind, giving Thore a blow on the back of the head. This was the brother of the first assailant.

"Here comes the third," said old Knut, rushing forward to join in the fray.

The danger made Thore stronger. He was as lithe as a willow and his blows left their marks. He dodged from one side to the other. Where the blows fell he was not, and where his opponents least expected blows from him, they got them. He was, however, at last completely beaten; but old Knut frequently said afterwards that a stouter fellow he had scarcely ever tackled. The fight was continued until blood flowed, and then Huseby cried:

"Stop!" and added, "If you can manage to get by the Huseby wolf and his cubs next Saturday night, the girl shall be yours."

Thore dragged himself homewards as best he could; and as soon as he got home he went to bed.

At Huseby there was much talk about the fight; but everybody said:

"What did he want there?"

There was one, however, who did not say so, and that was Aslaug. She had expected Thore that Saturday night, and when she heard what had taken place between him and her father, she sat down and had a good cry, saying to herself:

"If I cannot have Thore, there will never be another happy day for me in this world."

Thore had to keep his bed all day Sunday; on Monday, too, he felt that he must do the same. Tuesday came, and it was such a beautiful day. It had rained during the night. The mountain was wet and green. The fragrance of the leaves was wafted in through the open widow, down the mountain sides came the sound of the cow-bells, and some one was heard singing up in the glen. Had it not been for his mother, who was sitting in the room, Thore would have wept from vexation.

Wednesday came and still Thore was in bed; but on Thursday he began to wonder whether he could not get well by Saturday, and on Friday he rose. He remembered well the words Aslaug's father had spoken: "If you can manage to get by the Huseby wolf and his cubs next Saturday, the girl shall be yours." He looked over towards the chalet again and again. " I cannot live through another thrashing," thought Thore.

Up to the Huseby chalet there was but one road, as before stated, but a clever fellow might manage to get there, even if he did not take the beaten track. If he rowed out on the fjord below, and past the little tongue of land yonder, and thus reached the other side of the mountain, he might contrive to climb it, though it was so steep that a goat could scarcely venture there—and a goat is not very apt to be timid in climbing the mountains, you know.

Saturday came, and Thore stayed out of doors all day long. The sunlight played upon the foliage, and every now and then an alluring song was heard from the mountain. As evening drew near, and the mist was stealing up the slope, he was still sitting outside the door. He looked up toward the chalet, and all was still. He looked over toward the Huseby farmhouse. Then he pushed out his boat and rowed round the point of land.

Up at the chalet sat Aslaug, her day's work done. She was thinking that Thore would not come this evening, but that there would come all the more in his stead. Presently she let loose the dog, but told no one whither she was going. She seated herself where she could look down into the valley ; but a dense mist was rising, and, moreover, she felt little disposed to look down that way, for everything reminded her of what had occurred. So she moved, and without thinking what she was doing, she happened to go over to the other side of the summit, and there she sat down and gazed out over the sea. There was so much peace in this far-reaching view !

Then she felt like singing. She chose a song with long notes, and the music sounded far into the still night. She felt gladdened by it, and so she sang another verse. But then it seemed to her as if some one answered her from the glen far below. " Dear me, what can that be ? " thought Aslaug. She went forward to the brink of the precipice, and threw her arms around a slender birch, which hung trembling over the steep. She looked down but saw nothing. The fjord lay silent and calm. Not even a bird ruffled its smooth surface. Aslaug sat down and began singing again. Then she was sure that some one responded with the same tune and nearer than the first time. " It must be somebody, after all." Aslaug sprang up and bent out over the brink, and there, down at the foot of a rocky wall, she saw a boat moored, and it was so far down that it appeared like a tiny shell. She looked a little farther up, and her eyes fell on a red cap, and under the cap she saw a young man, who was working his way up the almost perpendicular side of the mountain. " Dear me, who can that be ? " asked Aslaug, as she let go of the birch and sprang far back.

She dared not answer her own question, for she knew very well who it was. She threw herself down on the greensward and took hold of the grass with both hands, as though it were *she* who must not let go her hold. But the grass came up by the roots.

She cried aloud and prayed to God to help Thore. But then it struck her that this conduct of Thore's was really tempting God, and therefore no help could be expected.

" Just this once ! " she implored.

And she threw her arms around the dog, as if it were Thore she were keeping from losing his hold. She rolled over the grass with him and the moments seemed years. But then the dog tore himself away. " Bow-wow," he barked over the brink of the steep and wagged his tail. " Bow-wow," he barked at Aslaug, and threw his forepaws up on her. " Bow-wow," over the precipice again ; and a red cap appeared over the brow of the mountain and Thore lay in her arms.

Now when old Knut Huseby heard of this, he made a very sensible remark, for he said :

" That boy is worth having ; the girl shall be his."

THE FATHER

BJÖRNTSJERNE BJÖRNSON

THE man whose story is here to be told was the wealthiest and most influential person in his parish ; his name was Thord Overaas. He appeared in the priest's study one day, tall and earnest.

" I have got a son," said he, " and I wish to present him for baptism."

" What shall his name be ? "

" Finn—after my father."

" And the sponsors ? "

They were mentioned, and proved to be the best men and women of Thord's relations in the parish.

" Is there anything else ? " inquired the priest, and looked up.

The man hesitated a little.

" I should like very much to have him baptised by himself," said he finally.

" That is to say on a week-day ? "

" Next Saturday, at twelve o'clock noon."

" Is there anything else ? " inquired the priest.

" There is nothing else " ; and the man twirled his cap, as though he were about to go.

Then the priest rose. " There is yet this, however," said he, and walking toward Thord, he took him by the hand and looked gravely into his eyes : " God grant that the child may become a blessing to you ! "

One day sixteen years later, Thord stood once more in the priest's study.

" Really, you carry your age astonishingly well, Thord," said the priest ; for he saw no change whatever in the man.

" That is because I have no troubles," replied Thord.

To this the priest said nothing, but after a while he asked: " What is your pleasure this evening ? "

" I have come this evening about that son of mine who is to be confirmed to-morrow."

" He is a bright boy."

" I did not wish to pay the priest until I heard what number the boy would have when he takes his place in church to-morrow."

" He will stand number one."

" So I have heard ; and here is the money for the priest."

" Is there anything else I can do for you ? " inquired the priest, fixing his eyes on Thord.

" There is nothing else."

Thord went out.

Eight years more rolled by, and then one day a noise was heard outside of the priest's study, for many men were approaching, and at their head was Thord, who entered first.

The priest looked up and recognised him.

" You come well attended this evening, Thord," said he.

" I am here to request that the banns may be published for my son ; he is about to marry Karen Storliden, daughter of Gudmund, who stands here beside me."

" Why, that is the richest girl in the parish."

" So they say," replied the peasant, stroking back his hair with one hand.

The priest sat a while as if in deep thought, then entered the names in his book, without making any comments, and the men wrote their signatures underneath. Thord laid three notes on the table.

" One is all I am to have," said the priest.

" I know that very well ; but he is my only child, I want to do it handsomely."

The priest took the money.

" This is now the third time, Thord, that you have come here on your son's account."

" But now I am through with him," said Thord, and folding up his pocket-book he said farewell and walked away.

The men slowly followed him.

A fortnight later, the father and son were rowing across the lake, one calm, still day, to Storliden to make arrangements for the wedding.

" This thwart is not secure," said the son, and stood up to straighten the seat on which he was sitting.

At the same moment the board he was standing on slipped from under him ; he threw out his arms, uttered a shriek, and fell overboard.

" Take hold of the oar ! " shouted the father, springing to his feet and holding out the oar.

But when his son had made a couple of efforts he grew stiff.

" Wait a moment ! " cried the father, and began to row toward his son.

Then the son rolled over on his back, gave his father one long look, and sank.

Thord could scarcely believe it ; he held the boat still, and stared at the spot where his son had gone down, as though he must surely come to the surface again.   There rose some bubbles, then some more, and finally a large one that burst ; and the lake lay there as smooth and bright as a mirror again.

For three days and three nights people saw the father rowing round and round the spot, without taking either food or sleep ; he was dragging the lake for the body of his son.   And toward morning of the third day he found it, and carried it in his arms up over the hills to his farm.

It might have been about a year from that day, when the priest, late one autumn evening, heard some one in the passage outside of the door, carefully trying to find the latch.   The priest opened the door, and in walked a tall, thin man, with bowed form and white hair. The priest looked long at him before he recognised him.   It was Thord.

" Are you out walking so late ? " said the priest, and stood still in front of him.

" Ah, yes ! it is late," said Thord, and took a seat.

The priest sat down also, as though waiting.   A long, long silence followed.   At last Thord said :

" I have something with me that I should like to give to the poor ; I want it to be invested as a legacy in my son's name."

He rose, laid some money on the table, and sat down again.   The priest counted it.

" It is a great deal of money," said he.

" It is half the price of my farm.   I sold it to-day."

The priest sat long in silence.   At last he asked, but gently :

" What do you propose to do now, Thord ? "

" Something better."

They sat there for a while, Thord with downcast eyes, the priest with his eyes fixed on Thord.   Presently the priest said, slowly and softly :

" I think your son has at last brought you a true blessing."

" Yes, I think so myself," said Thord, looking up, while two big tears coursed slowly down his cheeks.

NORWEGIAN

JONAS LIE
1833–1908

PEASANT AND PRIMA

FAR away in the Finland forests, on the shore of Lake Vermund, dwelt a lonely peasant who came down to the village in winter and earned a few pennies by sweeping chimneys. His only companion was his daughter Evina.

Their hut lay miles away from all inhabited places except a little farm on the other side of the lake where lived an aged couple and their son, who bore also the name Vermund. Father and son had by degrees cleared the slope with axe and fire and had built the cottage from which the chimney-sweep and his child could see the smoke arise and the light shine forth across the water. The lake abounded in pickerel and many other kinds of fish, while the forest furnished a generous supply of game, and thus there was seldom any lack of food, but unless some forester or hunter or traveller from afar passed, never a soul did they see except on their semi-annual churchgoing, or when, perchance, they went to sell game or fish in the village.

From her earliest girlhood, Evina, as she fished from her boat, had always found pleasure in song. She knew many places where there was a clear and beautiful echo, and when she lingered until late in the evening, the sounds would soar far, far away toward the other shore and over the sunlit tree-tops.

Her powers of song were rare and manifold. She would take a note as clear as the clearest willow flute and suddenly break into a warble pure and resonant like that of the lark, when, after rising toward the clouds, it again darts earthward. She would take another note lower than that of the wood grouse as it drones its love-song in the pine tree. There was not a bird in the forest that she could not imitate and put to shame by the melody and power of her voice.

When her voice called across the lake, Vermund knew that she wished him to go fishing, or follow her upon the heather, or gather berries, and he dropped his axe and stopped work to do her bidding. He supposed that all girls could sing like Evina, for he knew no others.

As the two grew up and these rambles became less frequent,

Vermund began to think that those days were long and tedious when he could not see or speak to her. He longed and yearned for her company and often went forth to listen idly in the hope of hearing her call. More and more the idea impressed itself upon him that it would be lovely indeed if he could have her always with him in his home instead of waiting for the summons now so rare. Moreover, the lake was broad and its waters were easily ruffled by the winds. When the ice came in the autumn and when it thawed in the spring, it even became impassable for weeks at a time.

Thus Vermund began to carry fish and game to the village and to bring back cakes and gingerbread, candy and sweet wine.

In his boat he always brought sweetmeats or pretty things for her, and when he stayed too long away she would now again call him as of old. In his journeys to the village, Vermund had observed that young couples like himself and Evina usually married after a brief courtship, and it dawned upon him that they might do the same. All that was needed was to go to the village store with game and fish until he had enough money and then visit the preacher and order the banns.

And so it was agreed. Morn and even Evina now called and sang across the lake to him during those late autumn days. The foliage around Lake Vermund was beginning to assume its hues of red and yellow, and shone back from the shimmering water with a silvery brightness. Only three Sundays remained before they were to enter the church arm in arm.

Evina hummed and sang from morning till night during that happy time. The atmosphere was so clear and the woods were so silent that the sound of her voice was carried afar and wafted back in harmonious cadence from the sylvan glades. Never before had she succeeded in producing notes so clear and beautiful and never before had she felt so bewildering a joy. Only three weeks and she would move across the lake to him! "To him! To him!" she sang, and the song resounded trembling in the air and re-echoed from the hills and passed in strong full tones out over Lake Vermund.

One day when she had been singing to her heart's content, some fine gentlemen, hunting with their hounds and wearing horns slung over their shoulders, came upon her in the woods and spoke to her. They had been listening with rapture to her little songs, and each declared that he had never before heard such a voice in any land.

To Evina this did not seem improbable, for she had always felt that in the whole Finland forest none other could sing as could she. So she consented to tell them where she lived and led them through the trees to her father's hut. He was the chimney-sweep of the village, she told them, and if they had any chimneys to be swept he would charge eight pennies and board for each one.

Among themselves they spoke a language that she could not understand, and they looked at her and nodded to one another and talked with lively interest.

When they reached the hut, the chimney-sweep was cutting and binding twigs for those long brooms which he used in his trade. He had seen fine folks before and understood at once that they did not come to engage him to sweep chimneys. He therefore told his daughter to hold her tongue so that he might hear what they had to say, but he was thoroughly startled when the gentleman who carried the bright brass horn laid a £20 note on the rough broom and asked that Evina should go at once with them to the city to sing. He said that she would there be furnished with fine dresses and jewels, and that before the year was over she would have enough money to buy a farm.

Evina had never hoped that the day would come when she might go to the city. Neither did she know where it lay in the far country beyond the village, but she would gladly go there and sing. She only begged that she might marry Vermund before she left.

The gentlemen laughed and told her that it was out of the question, but that when she became rich she could return to her home and marry whomsoever she pleased. For the present she must go with them, that very evening. And so they were taken across the lake by the chimney-sweep, and, as they rowed along, she sang and called to Vermund to say farewell—and so expressively that it made them all weep to hear. The fine gentlemen were lost in wonder and listened rapturously, only nodding to one another from time to time. The one whom she thought the leader, the one with the bright brass horn who had put down the £20 note, took out his handkerchief now and then as if to dry his tears, and indeed he was shedding tears although he knew nothing of Vermund.

Her father accompanied them as a guide until, after an hour or two, they reached the highway. There they found two fine carriages, and on the front seats sat liveried coachmen with long whips. Then they started for the city.

Evina had never rested as she did that night on her soft and downy bed, nor had she ever imagined the existence of such spacious halls and wonderful things as met her eyes in this place, yet she felt caged and wished she might get out into the free and open air. In the middle of the night the feeling became so strong that she stole from her room, determined to go to her home; but every door was closed and locked. Then she returned to her bed and wept until morning, when sugared coffee and a great pile of wheat biscuits were brought to her room. After she had breakfasted and dressed, kind and considerate people came and instructed her as to how she was to act when she should sing before an audience.

They gave her beautiful gowns and finery and trained her in a large hall with lights at the ceiling, evening after evening—how to walk when on the stage, how to bow to an audience, to sing and bow again, how to leave the stage, and when the gentleman of the bright brass horn clapped his hands, to come out again and bow as often as he clapped and shouted.

Then came the evening when the public was to hear her. There was a multitude of musicians playing when she appeared and the people were sitting with their heads so close together that she was at once reminded of the tree-tops of her native forest and of Vermund. She began with those silvery, harmonious notes, and she warbled and sang on and on up into the air, like the little birds at home. Then she became more and more jubilant, filling the hall with melody pure and powerful that would easily have carried across Lake Vermund.

When she had finished, there was a deep silence over the whole human forest. No one applauded or acted as the man of the bright brass horn had led her to expect, so she did as she had been taught and retired, keeping her face toward the audience. Then the applause came! They shouted, "Evina! Evina!" and clapped their hands and stormed like wild men.

She sang again and again, and each time they clapped their hands and shouted until she could do nothing but pick up the finest flowers and bow as she stepped backwards towards the exit.

On the following morning a dark-browed man came with a greeting from the man of the bright brass horn and placed before her on the table a money box with the key to it. The box was full of notes and shining coins wrapped in little cylinders, and when he told her that it was all hers, she wished to take the box and go home to Vermund.

Then the dark-browed man laughed and told her that this was only a very, very small beginning. If she would learn to sing still better and would journey with him to strange lands, there would be many boxes like this one to take back to Vermund so that he could buy the largest farm in the Finland forest.

Evina hesitated. It was a delight to sing and make the people under the chandeliers shout her name until they were frantic with enthusiasm. Perhaps it would be better to continue until she could carry home a greater pile of money.

A master came who taught her to read her songs from little dots printed on paper. Another taught her how to walk and stand and strike the appropriate pose. After these lessons were over, the dressmakers and the milliners came and tried on beautiful gowns and more beautiful hats. Then came the jewellers with costly gems and precious ornaments.

Then she sang and studied and travelled from land to land with the dark-browed man. She learned to speak foreign tongues, to drink champagne, and to like many dainty things that she had never known before. And at last they wished her to go to the place where it was greatest and most glorious to sing—to the opera. This too she did.

Ere long she became so famous that everybody talked of her, and the more she sang and the farther she travelled, the louder they shouted. They clapped their hands wildly, frantically, and cried, " Brava ! " and called for Signora Evina.

Heavier and heavier became the heaps of flowers each evening, as did also the money pile the next morning. Kings and emperors gave her bracelets and ornaments of pearls and diamonds. After the auditors had shouted themselves hoarse in calling for Evina, they harnessed themselves to her carriage and drew her home in triumph to her hotel. They showered so many presents upon her that she hardly remembered to express her appreciation of the homage. Thus she sang and travelled about the world, treading upon a path of flowers. Money came and money went. She scarcely knew or cared how much she had.

She sent one letter home with money for her father. Letters were not easy for her to write. Then she received a letter from the parish priest to say that her father was dead.

She went to her villa in the Pyrenees for the summer. Servants, travelling expenses, and entertaining cost large sums which she always paid by cheque on the bank, and thus she lived for many years until she scarcely remembered that she had been a poor girl on the shores of Lake Vermund.

One evening she sang to a house that was filled from the floor to the highest gallery up next the ceiling. In the box with the crown over it sat the emperor and the empress, the princes and princesses and all the most distinguished members of the Court. As she reached the romanza, the most beautiful part of her song, she raised her eyes and saw in the upper gallery a face bending forward and staring at her. The blood rushed at once to her heart and she thought of Vermund, her betrothed of former days. Perhaps it was but a fancy, some one who resembled him, but she looked again and again, and during the whole evening her eyes were oftenest fixed upon that face. That he could have come thither seemed to her as impossible as that Lake Vermund itself should come, but the more she looked, the more it seemed like her lover. She thought that she recognised the peculiar pose of his head, the wave of his hair as he sat listening, and even the contraction of his lips when some impassioned passage appealed to him.

Then she took the notes with such a tearful, trembling voice as had not issued from her throat since she had left her home on Lake Vermund.

When he took from his pocket a blue-checked bandanna hand-kerchief and wiped first one eye and then the other, finally folding it again and replacing it in his pocket, she came very near breaking down in her part. She knew now that it was Vermund, and was so overcome with ecstatic joy that she ran out to the footlights and sang in her native tongue as of old, " Vermund, Vermund, come over, come over ! "

Then the emperor arose and applauded, while the whole house thundered and trembled with bravas, thinking that this wonderful new feature had been introduced especially for the great diva.   Then, after the closing aria, flowers and costly gems were thrown in showers upon the stage.

Seven times she was called before the curtain, and while they were shouting and calling for her the eighth time, and a vast number had rushed forth to unharness her horses and draw her home, she had disappeared.

Evina had ordered the carriage to wait on the other side of the street and had sent word to Vermund that she was waiting for him. He came and told her of his waiting and yearning, of the longing that had finally drawn him from the old home to seek her.   In the village, people had read the newspapers and had talked of the chimney-sweep's Evina who was making her fortune by singing as a prima donna out in the great world, but when he had spoken of her at the village store and had intimated that he believed she would come back to her Finland forests, the shopkeeper had only laughed and winked. This had brought him to a decision, and so he had set out on the journey.   He had worked his way from town to town and had earned his passage across the water until finally he had arrived here and learned that she was to sing that night.

Questions came from her lips like a waterfall, now that she could speak to some one who understood the native tongue, inquiries about all those things that she had not been able to mention to her friends during these years of exile, some of them things to which she herself had not given a thought.

They passed rapidly from one subject to another. They talked of the hut and the clearing, the old dog that had accompanied them on their rambles. They talked of Lake Vermund and the old boat, the grouse, the trout, and the woodcock, and of the new bucket that had been given her as a present and which had been left hanging in the well when she had gone away. They talked of the goats and the horses he intended to buy when he went home and of a hundred other things until the carriage drew up at the hotel, and then he entered with her to continue the conversation. At intervals gentlemen scaled the stairs to pay their compliments to the diva, to Signora Evina. They thanked her and gesticulated, telling her that never had she sung so magnificently as on this night.   From the emperor came a shining bracelet for which she had to thank him and grant a lengthy interview, and thus was her peace invaded, but Vermund promised to come again in the morning as soon as he could get the time.

During the whole night sleep would not come to Evina because of the memories of home that filled her throbbing heart. She could only think of Vermund and long for daylight, when she could show him all the wonderful things she possessed and tell him of the life that she now led.

Then she imagined that she was lying in the chimney-sweep's hut and would have to arise at sunlight to go out fishing in the old boat. She remembered every knot in the fish-line ! She rowed and rowed, but could make no progress on account of the rushes which kept catching the line and tearing off the bait.

When Vermund came again in the morning, they talked and laughed and chatted away harder than ever. There was no end to all the new and old subjects of interest at home, where the two huts used to send up their smoke from opposite sides of Lake Vermund. She was moved then to repeat the old call, " Vermund, Vermund, come over ! " and had already put her hand to her mouth, but suddenly restrained herself—and he understood, alas ! that he could not hope for marriage now.

She wished him to drive with her in the carriage to see the points of interest in the city, and the lions, tigers, serpents, and other wild beasts in the zoological garden, so they set out with the liveried coachman on the box, and hats were raised to them wherever they went. Through the whole day they went about sight-seeing, and the time was only too short. When they stood before the lion's cage, they spoke of the wolf that had again appeared in the forest at home, and when they looked at the ostriches, they spoke of the herons that used to frequent the little promontory in Lake Vermund. Nothing but the affairs of their old home ever entered their minds.

When they returned to the hotel, the table was set in a private dining-room decked with flowers and shining silver and crystal vases that fairly dazzled the eyes. The servants came and went with course after course, but there they sat and talked about the ginger-bread and the cakes and the candy that they had shared between them in the boat on the lake, so that they lacked appetite for all else. The next summer, she declared, she would go home to Lake Vermund in preference to her villa in the Pyrenees. She became quite enthusiastic over the idea, and made him take enough money to restore the hut of her father, the chimney-sweep. She was going to live there and have it exactly as it had been in the olden days, she said.

Finally he bade her farewell and departed, but when he had returned to his native woods and told the village storekeeper that Evina had promised to return, the worthy merchant only winked and smiled. Nevertheless she did come and Vermund was happy.

For a whole week she wandered about and sang and called through the forest and out over the lake from all those places where in her girlhood she had found the echo the clearest and most beautiful. She went out with Vermund in the boat and again tried her hand at fishing with a line in all the old pools.

Nothing so good as the pickerel and trout she caught herself, or the berries she gathered on the heather, had passed her lips since the days when she had lived there as a girl, or so it seemed, at least. The air was so fresh and pure and warm that she wondered why she had stayed so long away.

One morning, however, when she awoke, a dreary fog was hanging over the tree-tops and a heavy rain had soaked the ground. The next day it was no better, and frequent showers fell upon lake and forest. It was sad and depressing to sit there the whole day while the wind blew and the rain pattered against the window-pane. Then she suddenly departed from the humble hut and was met at the village by a closed carriage and pair of horses that carried her swiftly away through the country and into the city beyond.

There she found again the dark-browed impresario waiting for her and together they returned into the world, to the old round of triumph in the brilliant capitals of civilisation.

Year after year passed in rapid succession. Money came and money went. In the summer-time she no longer went to her villa in the Pyrenees, but to sanatoriums where her throat might recover from its constant toil.

Little by little the newspapers began to hint that her highest notes were no longer so full and pure, while the impresario constantly begged her to take the greatest care of her voice. Greater and greater became the number of those who called upon her for money, and farther and farther must she travel for the engagements that furnished it. More and more protracted became her sojourn in the sanatoriums.

High soprano voices like hers never lasted for many years, the doctors said. Hers should have been sparingly used and carefully protected from the first, instead of being so wantonly wasted.

A few more years passed. To see and hear a world-famed singer always interested and attracted a multitude, but the applause, the bravas, and the flowers became rarer, and the income became less and less.

Finally the time came when the newspapers, vexed and fatigued, spoke out plainly and called her an organ with cracked pipes. The diamonds and ornaments had been pawned long ago, and the villa in the Pyrenees had passed into the hands of her creditors. At last she even went to the villa as a supernumerary and mingled among the very people before whom she had shone as a star of the first magnitude, but they avoided or ignored her.

It was then that Lake Vermund rose in her memory, and it stood out wonderfully clear and blue. There she could still sing and call out over the gilded tree-tops. There no newspapers blamed and no impresarios lamented. No creditors would trouble themselves about the chimney-sweep's old hut.

One summer day, Vermund, looking across the lake, saw smoke arising from the other side. He thought that some stranger had installed himself there, but so long had he cared for the old place while waiting for Evina to come, that he felt it his duty to cross and investigate. There by the hearth sat Evina herself, and she told him that she had arrived by boat the evening before, bringing back but little more than she had taken away in her girlhood.

To Vermund this was more than enough. The less she had, the more surely would she remain. He would earn all they needed there, he said. So he came across on his boat each day. He stuffed moss into the crack under the window-sill and the openings in the wall. He hewed wood and made repairs and brought her fish and game. Once more they shared the sugar and coffee that he brought from the village, and together they rowed about the lake to haul in the nets, but when the cold weather came and the ice grew thicker it was not so easy to cross.

One day she stood on the shore and beckoned to him. He understood that she was calling, but her voice did not carry so far. Then with difficulty he made his way through the drifting ice, and arriving found the hut empty of provisions.

Bashful and hesitating, Vermund intimated that she might better come home with him in the boat, that it was unwise for her to live thus alone, able only to beckon and call when distress or want was pressing.

Snow fell and covered the forest, and the winter passed.

In the little village the people were moved to wonder that she who had once been so famous in the great world was now once more the chimney-sweep's Evina, the wife of Vermund by the lake. In the little cabin, however, they made a cosy home. They gathered brush and wood and lived and laboured on in peace.

In the evening, Evina sat in the chimney-corner and stirred the pot, humming the while arias and fragments of melody from the operas as they rose in her mind, much like a song-bird that is hoarse and only occasionally can bring its voice into tune.

More and more did the two panoramas blend in her confused memory ; the brilliant halls filled with moving heads and resounding with applause, and the sunlit tree-tops of Lake Vermund.

FINN BLOOD

JONAS LIE

IN Svartfjord, north of Senje, dwelt a lad called Eilert. His neighbours were seafaring Finns, and among their children was a pale little girl, remarkable for her long black hair and her large eyes. They dwelt behind the crag on the other side of the promontory, and fished for a livelihood, as also did Eilert's parents ; wherefore there was no particular goodwill between the families, for the nearest fishing ground was but a small one, and each would have liked to have rowed there alone.

Nevertheless, though his parents didn't like it at all, and even forbade it, Eilert used to sneak regularly down to the Finns. There they had always strange tales to tell, and he heard wondrous things about the recesses of the mountains, where the original home of the Finns was, and where, in the olden time, dwelt the Finn kings, who were masters among the magicians. There, too, he heard tell of all that was beneath the sea, where the Mermen and the Draugs hold sway. The latter are gloomy evil powers and many a time his blood stood still in his veins as he sat and listened. They told him that the Draug usually showed himself on the strand in the moonlight on those spots which were covered with sea-wrack ; that he had a bunch of seaweed instead of a head, but shaped so peculiarly that whoever came across him absolutely couldn't help gazing into his pale and horrible face. They themselves had seen him many a time, and once they had driven him, thwart by thwart, out of the boat where he had sat one morning, and turned the oars upside down. When Eilert hastened homewards in the darkness round the headland along the strand, over heaps of seaweed, he dared scarcely look around him, and many a time the sweat absolutely streamed from his forehead.

In proportion as hostility increased among the old people they had a good deal of fault to find with one another, and Eilert heard no end of evil things spoken about the Finns at home. Now it was this, and now it was that. They didn't even row like honest folk, for, after the Finnish fashion, they took high and swift strokes, as if they were womenkind, and they all talked together, and made a noise while they rowed, instead of being " silent in the boat." But what impressed Eilert most of all was the fact that, in the Finn-

woman's family, they practised sorcery and idolatry, or so folks
said. He also heard tell of something beyond all question, and that
was the shame of having Finn blood in one's veins, which also was
the reason why the Finns were not as good as other honest folk,
so that the magistrates gave them their own distinct burial-
ground in the churchyard, and their own separate " Finn-pens "
in church. Eilert had seen this with his own eyes in the church at
Berg.

All this made him very angry, for he could not help liking the Finn
folks down yonder, and especially little Zilla. They two were always
together : she knew such a lot about the Mermen. Henceforth his
conscience always plagued him when he played with her ; and whenever she stared at him with her large black eyes while she told him
tales, he used to begin to feel a little bit afraid, for at such times he
reflected that she and her people belonged to the Damned, and that
was why they knew so much about such things. But, on the other
hand, the thought of it made him so bitterly angry, especially
on her account. She too was frequently taken aback by his odd
behaviour towards her, which she couldn't understand at all ;
and then, as was her wont, she would begin laughing at and
teasing him by making him run after her, while she went and hid
herself.

One day he found her sitting on a boulder by the sea-shore. She
had in her lap an eider duck which had been shot, and could only
have died quite recently, for it was still warm, and she wept bitterly
over it. It was, she sobbed, the same bird which made its nest
every year beneath the shelter of their outhouse—she knew it quite
well—and she showed him a red-coloured feather in its white breast.
It had been struck dead by a single shot, and only a single red
drop had come out of it ; it had tried to reach its nest, but had
died on its way on the strand. She wept as if her heart would
break, and dried her face with her hair in impetuous Finnish
fashion. Eilert laughed at her as boys will, but he overdid it,
and was very pale the whole time. He dared not tell her that
that very day he had taken a random shot with his father's gun
from behind the headland at a bird a long way off which was
swimming ashore.

One autumn Eilert's father was downright desperate. Day after
day on the fishing grounds his lines caught next to nothing, while
he was forced to look on and see the Finn pull up one rich catch after
another. He was sure, too, that he had noticed malicious gestures
over in the Finn's boat. After that his whole house nourished a
double bitterness against them ; and when they talked it over in the
evening, it was agreed, as a thing beyond all question, that Finnish
sorcery had something to do with it. Against this there was only
one remedy, and that was to rub corpse-mould on the lines ; but one

must beware of doing so, lest one should thereby offend the dead, and expose oneself to their vengeance, while the sea-folk would gain power over one at the same time.

Eilert bothered his head a good deal over all this; it almost seemed to him as if he had had a share in the deed, because he was on such a good footing with the Finn folks.

On the following Sunday both he and the Finn folks were at Berg church, and he secretly abstracted a handful of mould from one of the Finn graves, and put it in his pocket. The same evening, when they came home, he strewed the mould over his father's lines unobserved. And, oddly enough, the very next time his father cast his lines, as many fish were caught as in the good old times. But after this Eilert's anxiety became indescribable. He was especially cautious while they were working of an evening round the fireside and it was dark in the distant corners of the room. He sat there with a piece of steel in his pocket. To beg " forgiveness " of the dead is the only helpful means against the consequences of such deeds as his, otherwise one will be dragged off at night, by an invisible hand to the churchyard, though one were lashed fast to the bed by a ship's hawser.

When Eilert, on the following " Preaching Sunday," went to church, he took very good care to go to the grave and beg forgiveness of the dead.

As Eilert grew older, he got to understand that the Finn folks must, after all, be pretty much the same sort of people as his own folks at home ; but, on the other hand, another thought was now uppermost in his mind, the thought, namely, that the Finns must be of an inferior stock, with a taint of disgrace about them. Nevertheless, he could not very well do without Zilla's society, and they were very much together as before, especially at the time of their confirmation.

But when Eilert became a man, and mixed more with the people of the parish, he began to fancy that this old companionship lowered him somewhat in the eyes of his neighbours. There was nobody who did not believe as a matter of course that there was something shameful about Finn blood, and he therefore always tried to avoid her in company.

The girl understood it all well enough, for latterly she took care to keep out of his way. Nevertheless, one day she came, as had been her wont from childhood, down to their house, and begged for leave to go in their boat when they rowed to church next day. There were lots of strangers present from the village, and so Eilert, lest folks should think that he and she were engaged, answered mockingly so that every one could hear him, " that church-cleansing was perhaps a very good thing for Finnish sorcery," but she must find some one else to ferry her across.

After that she never spoke to him at all, but Eilert was anything but happy in consequence.

Now it happened one winter that Eilert was out all alone fishing for Greenland shark. A shark suddenly bit. The boat was small, and the fish was very big ; but Eilert would not give in, and the end of the business was that his boat capsized.

All night long he lay on the top of it in the mist and a cruel sea. As now he sat there almost fainting for drowsiness, and dimly conscious that the end was not far off, and the sooner it came the better, he suddenly saw a man in seaman's clothes sitting astride the other end of the boat's bottom, and glaring savagely at him with a pair of dull reddish eyes. He was so heavy that the boat's bottom began to sink slowly down at the end where he sat. Then he suddenly vanished, but it seemed to Eilert as if the sea-fog lifted a bit ; the sea had all at once grown quite calm (at least, there was now only a gentle swell) ; and right in front of him lay a little low grey island, towards which the boat was slowly drifting.

The skerry was wet, as if the sea had only recently been flowing over it, and on it he saw a pale girl with such lovely eyes. She wore a green kirtle, and round her body a broad silver girdle with figures upon it, such as the Finns use. Her bodice was of tar-brown skin, and beneath her stay-lace, which seemed to be of green sea-grass, was a foam-white chemise, like the feathery breast of a sea-bird.

When the boat came drifting on to the island, she came down to him and said, as if she knew him quite well, " So you're come at last, Eilert ; I've been waiting for you so long ! "

It seemed to Eilert as if an icy cold shudder ran through his body when he took the hand which helped him ashore ; but it was only for the moment, and he forgot it instantly.

In the midst of the island there was an opening with a brazen flight of steps leading down to a splendid cabin. Whilst he stood there thinking things over a bit, he saw two heavy dog-fish swimming close by—they were at least twelve to fourteen ells long.

As they descended, the dog-fish sank down too, each on one side of the brazen steps. Oddly enough, it looked as if the island was transparent. When the girl perceived that he was frightened, she told him that they were only two of her father's bodyguard, and shortly afterwards they disappeared. She then said that she wanted to take him to her father, who was waiting for them. She added that, if he didn't find the old gentleman precisely as handsome as he might expect, he had nevertheless no need to be frightened, nor was he to be astonished too much at what he saw.

He now perceived that he was under water, but, for all that, there was no sign of moisture. He was on a white sandy bottom, covered with chalk-white, red, blue, and silvery-bright shells. He saw meadows of sea-green, mountains thick with woods of bushy seaweed and sea-wrack, and the fishes darted about on every side just as the birds swarm about the rocks that sea-fowl haunt.

As they two were thus walking along together she explained many things to him. High up he saw something which looked like a black cloud with a white lining, and beneath it moved backwards and forwards a shape resembling one of the dog-fish.

"What you see there is a vessel," said she; "there's nasty weather up there now, and beneath the boat goes he who was sitting along with you on the bottom of the boat just now. If it is wrecked, it will belong to us, and then you will not be able to speak to father to-day." As she said this there was a wild rapacious gleam in her eyes, but it was gone again immediately.

And, in point of fact, it was no easy matter to make out the meaning of her eyes. As a rule, they were unfathomably dark with the lustre of a night-billow through which the sea-fire sparkles; but occasionally, when she laughed, they took a bright sea-green glitter, as when the sun shines deep down into the sea.

Now and again they passed by a boat or a vessel half buried in the sand, out and in of the cabin doors and windows of which fishes swam to and fro. Close by the wrecks wandered human shapes which seemed to consist of nothing but blue smoke. His conductress explained to him that these were the spirits of drowned men who had not had Christian burial—one must beware of them, for dead ones of this sort are malignant. They always know when one of their own race is about to be wrecked, and at such times they howl the death-warning of the Draug through the wintry nights.

Then they went farther on their way right across a deep dark valley. In the rocky walls above him he saw a row of four-cornered white doors, from which a sort of glimmer, as from the northern lights, shot downwards through the darkness. This valley stretched in a north-eastwardly direction right under Finmark, she said, and inside the white doors dwelt the old Finn Kings who had perished on the sea. Then she went and opened the nearest of these doors— here, down in the salt ocean, was the last of the kings, who had capsized in the very breeze that he himself had conjured forth, but could not afterwards quell. There, on a block of stone, sat a wrinkled yellow Finn with running eyes and a polished dark-red crown. His large head rocked backwards and forwards on his withered neck, as if it were in the swirl of an ocean current. Beside him, on the same block, sat a still more shrivelled and yellow little woman, who also had a crown on, and her garments were covered with all sorts of coloured stones; she was stirring up a brew with a stick. If she only had fire beneath it, the girl told Eilert, she and her husband would very soon have dominion again over the salt sea, for the thing she was stirring about was magic stuff.

In the middle of a plain, which opened right before them at a turn of the road, stood a few houses together like a little town, and, a little farther on, Eilert saw a church turned upside down, looking, with its long pointed tower, as if it were mirrored in the water. The girl explained to him that her father dwelt in these houses, and the church was one of the seven that stood in this realm, which extended all over Helgeland and Finmark. No service was held in them yet, but it would be held when the drowned bishop, who sat outside in a brown study, could only hit upon the name of the Lord that was to be served, and then all the Draugs would go to church. The bishop, she said, had been sitting and pondering the matter over these eight hundred years, so he would no doubt very soon get to the bottom of it. A hundred years ago the bishop had advised them to send up one of the Draugs to Rödö church to find out all about it ; but every time the word he wanted was mentioned he couldn't catch the sound of it. In the mountain " Kunnan " King Olaf had hung a church-bell of pure gold, and it is guarded by the first priest who ever came to Nordland, who stands there in a white chasuble. On the day the priest rings the bell, Kunnan will become a big stone church, to which all Nordland, both above and below the sea, will resort. But time flies, and therefore all who come down here below are asked by the bishop if they can tell him that name.

At this Eilert felt very queer indeed, and he felt queerer still when he began reflecting and found, to his horror, that he also had forgotten that name.

While he stood there in thought, the girl looked at him anxiously. It was almost as if she wanted to help him to find it and couldn't, and with that she all at once grew deadly pale.

The Draug's house, to which they now came, was built of boats' keels and large pieces of wreckage, in the interstices of which grew all sorts of sea-grass and slimy green stuff. Three monstrously heavy green posts, covered with shell-fish, formed the entrance, and the door consisted of planks which had sunk to the bottom and were full of clincher-nails. In the middle of it, like a knocker, was a heavy rusty iron mooring-ring, with the worn-away stump of a ship's hawser hanging to it. When they came up to it, a large black arm stretched out and opened the door.

They were now in a vaulted chamber, with fine shell-sand on the floor. In the corners lay all sorts of ropes, yarn, and boating-gear, and among them casks and barrels and various ships' inventories. On a heap of yarn, covered by an old red-patched sail, Eilert saw the Draug, a broad-shouldered, strongly-built fellow, with a glazed hat shoved back on to the top of his head, with dark-red tangled hair and beard, small tearful dog-fish eyes, and a broad mouth, round which there lay for the moment a good-natured seaman's grin. The shape of his head reminded one somewhat of the big sort of seal which is called Klakkekal—his skin about the neck looked dark and shaggy,

and the tops of his fingers grew together.   He sat there with turned-
down sea-boots on, and his thick grey woollen stockings reached right
up to his thigh.   He wore, besides, plain frieze clothes with bright
glass buttons on his waistcoat.   His spacious skin jacket was open,
and round his neck he had a cheap red woollen scarf.

When Eilert came up, he made as if he would rise, and said good-
naturedly, " Good-day, Eilert—you've certainly had a hard time of
it to-day !   Now you can sit down, if you like, and take a little grub.
You want it, I'm sure " ;   and with that he squirted out a jet of
tobacco juice like the spouting of a whale.   With one foot, which for
that special purpose all at once grew extraordinarily long, he fished
out of a corner, in true Nordland style, the skull of a whale to serve
as a chair for Eilert, and shoved forward with his hand a long ship's
drawer full of first-rate fare.   There was boiled groats with syrup,
cured fish, oatcakes with butter, a large stack of flatcakes, and a
multitude of the best hotel dishes besides.

The Merman bade him fall to and eat his fill, and ordered his
daughter to bring out the last keg of Trondhjem *aqua vitae*.   " Of
that sort the last is always the best," said he.   When she came with
it, Eilert thought he knew it again ;   it was his father's, and he
himself, only a couple of days before, had bought the brandy from
the wholesale dealer at Kvaeford ;   but he didn't say anything about
that now.   The quid of tobacco, too, which the Draug turned somewhat impatiently in his mouth before he drank, also seemed to him
wonderfully like the lead on his own line.   At first it seemed to him
as if he didn't quite know how to manage with the keg—his mouth
was so sore ;   but afterwards things went along smoothly enough.

So they sat for some time pretty silently, and drank glass after
glass, till Eilert began to think that they had had quite enough.   So
when it came to his turn again he said no, he would rather not ;
whereupon the Merman put the keg to his own mouth and drained
it to the very dregs.   Then he stretched his long arm up to the shelf,
and took down another.   He was now in a better humour, and began
to talk of all sorts of things.   But every time he laughed, Eilert felt
queer, for the Draug's mouth gaped ominously wide, and showed a
greenish pointed row of teeth, with a long interval between each
tooth, so that they resembled a row of boat stakes.

The Merman drained keg after keg, and with every keg he grew
more communicative.   With an air as if he were thinking in his own
mind of something very funny, he looked at Eilert for a while and
blinked his eyes.   Eilert didn't like his expression at all, for it seemed
to him to say :   " Now my lad, whom I have fished up so nicely, look,
out for a change ! "   But instead of that he said, " You had a rough
time of it last night, Eilert, my boy, but it wouldn't have gone so hard
with you if you hadn't streaked the lines with corpse-mould, and
refused to take my daughter to church "—here he suddenly broke

off, as if he had said too much, and to prevent himself from completing the sentence he put the brandy-keg to his mouth once more. But the same instant Eilert caught his glance, and it was so full of deadly hatred that it sent a shiver down his back.

When, after a long, long draught, he again took the keg from his mouth, the Merman was again in a good humour, and told tale after tale. He stretched himself more and more heavily out on the sail, and laughed and grinned complacently at his own narrations, the humour of which was always a wreck or a drowning. From time to time Eilert felt the breath of his laughter, and it was like a cold blast. If folks would only give up their boats, he said, he had no very great desire for the crews. It was driftwood and ship-timber that he was after, and he really couldn't get on without them. When his stock ran out, boat or ship he *must* have, and surely nobody could blame him for it either.

With that he put the keg down empty, and became somewhat more gloomy again. He began to talk about what bad times they were for him and her. It was not as it used to be, he said. He stared blankly before him for a time, as if buried in deep thought. Then he stretched himself out backwards at full length, with feet extending right across the floor, and gasped so dreadfully that his upper and lower jaws resembled two boats' keels facing each other. Then he dozed right off and his neck turned towards the sail.

Again the girl stood by Eilert's side, and bade him follow her.

They now went the same way back, and again ascended up to the skerry. Then she confided to him that the reason why her father had been so bitter against him was because he had mocked her with the taunt about church-cleansing when she had wanted to go to church—the name the folks down below wanted to know might, the Merman thought, be treasured up in Eilert's memory ; but during their conversation on their way down to her father, she had perceived that he had also forgotten it. And now he must look to his life.

It would be a good deal later on in the day before the old fellow would begin inquiring about him. Till then he, Eilert, must sleep so as to have sufficient strength for his flight—she would watch over him.

The girl flung her long dark hair about him like a curtain, and it seemed to him that he knew those eyes so well. He felt as if his cheek were resting against the breast of a white sea-bird, it was so warm and sleep-giving—a single reddish feather in the middle of it recalled a dark memory. Gradually he sank off into a doze, and heard her singing a lullaby, which reminded him of the swell of the billows when it ripples up and down along the beach on a fine sunny day. It was all about how they had once been playmates together, and how later on he would have nothing to say to her. Of all

she sang, however, he could only recollect the last words, which
were these :

> " Oh, thousands of times have we played on the shore,
> And caught little fishes—dost mind it no more ?
> We raced with the surf as it rolled at our feet,
> And the lurking old Merman we always did cheat.

> " Yes, much shalt thou think of at my lullaby,
> Whilst the billows do rock and the breezes do sigh.
> Who sits now and weeps o'er thy cheeks ?   It is she
> Who gave thee her soul, and whose soul lived in thee.

> " But once as an eider-duck homeward I came
> Thou didst lie 'neath a rock, with thy rifle didst aim ;
> In my breast thou didst strike me ; the blood thou dost see
> Is the mark that I bear, oh ! beloved one, of thee."

Then it semed to Eilert as if she sat and wept over him, and that,
from time to time, a drop like a splash of sea-water fell upon his
cheek.   He felt now that he loved her so dearly.

The next moment he again became uneasy.   He fancied that right
up to the skerry came a whale, which said that he, Eilert, must now
make haste ; and when he stood on its back he stuck the shaft of an
oar down its nostril, to prevent it from shooting beneath the sea
again.   He perceived that in this way the whale could be steered
accordingly as he turned the oar to the right or left ; and now they
coasted the whole land of Finmark at such a rate that the huge
mountain islands shot by them like little rocks.   Behind him he saw
the Draug in his half-boat, and he was going so swiftly that the foam
stood mid-mast high.   Shortly afterwards he was again lying on the
skerry, and the lass smiled so blithely ; she bent over him and said,
" It is I, Eilert."

With that he awoke, and saw that the sunbeams were running over
the wet skerry, and the Mermaid was still sitting by his side.   But
presently the whole thing changed before his eyes.   It was the sun
shining through the window-panes, on a bed in the Finn's hut, and
by his side sat the Finn girl supporting his back, for they thought he
was about to die.   He had lain there delirious for six weeks, ever
since the Finn had rescued him after capsizing, and this was his
first moment of consciousness.

After that it seemed to him that he had never heard anything so
absurd and presumptuous as the twaddle that would fix a stigma of
shame or contempt on Finn blood, and the same spring he and the
Finn girl Zilla were betrothed, and in the autumn they were married.

There were Finns in the bridal procession, and perhaps many said
a little more about that than they need have done ; but every one
at the wedding agreed that the fiddler, who was also a Finn, was the
best fiddler, in the whole parish, and the bride the prettiest girl.

NORWEGIAN

ALEXANDER KIELLAND
1848–1906

KAREN

THERE was once upon a time in Kraruper Inn a maiden named Karen. She attended to the serving of the guests herself, for the landlady lived among her pots and pans in the kitchen. And many people came to Kraruper Inn—neighbours who collected there when the autumn evenings began to darken, and sat in the warm room and drank unlimited quantities of coffee punch. Travellers and wanderers, too, who came in blue with cold, stamping their feet and calling for something hot, that would enable them to reach the next station.

Karen went about silently, without haste, serving each in his turn. She was small and delicate, only a child, earnest and reserved, and the young fellows did not notice her. But she was very dear to the older customers, to whom a visit to the inn was an event of importance. She prepared their coffee quickly, and served it seven times hot. When she moved about among the guests with her waiter the burly, coarsely dressed men stood aside, and made place for her, and every one looked admiringly after her. Karen had great grey eyes that took in everything, and seemed to look far, far away, and her eyebrows were arched in surprise and wonder. Strangers thought she did not understand their orders; but Karen heard them all, and made never a mistake. She had a way all her own, whether she gazed off into the distance, or listened, or waited, or dreamed.

The west wind blew strong; it threw up long, heavy waves from the west sea. Salt and damp, with froth and foam it threw them on the sands. But when the wind reached Kraruper Inn it had only strength enough left to tear open the stable door, and then that which connected the kitchen with the stable. It burst in, filled the space, swung the lantern that hung from the roof back and forth; tore off the ostler's cap and rolled it out into the darkness; threw the horses' blankets over their heads, and finally blew a white hen from her perch into the water trough. The hen squawked frightfully, the

227

ostler swore, the chickens cackled.   The kitchen was full of smoke ;
the horses grew restless and beat sparks of fire from the stones with
their hoofs.   Even the ducks, which were gathered quacking together
near the manger to be at hand when the oats were scattered, began
to chatter, and through it all the wind roared fearfully.   At last two
men came out of the inn parlour and, putting their broad backs
against the door, pushed it to, while a shower of sparks rained from
their pipes over their dark beards.   Having done all the mischief
possible the wind fled back over the plain, crossed the great pond,
and shook the mail coach that rolled majestically along about half a
mile from the inn.

" What terrible haste he always makes to reach Kraruper Inn,"
muttered the postilion, Anders, cracking his whip over the smoking
horses.   For the twentieth time the conductor had let down the
window to call to him.   At first it had been a friendly invitation
to take a coffee punch with him, then little by little the good-
nature disappeared.   Finally the window went down with a bang,
and remarks far from conciliating were showered on driver and
horses.

The wind swept low on the ground, and long, mysterious sighs
murmured through the heather bushes.   The moon was full, but
thick clouds obscured its light.   Behind Kraruper Inn lay the
gloomy moor, covered by black heaps of peat and deep, treacherous
holes.   And between the heather bushes wound a strip of grass that
looked like a path, but it was no path, for it came to a sudden end at
the brink of a hole deeper than the others, and filled with water.   In
the grass a sleek fox crouched and waited, and a hare hopped softly
over the plain.   The fox could reckon with certainty that the hare
would not make a long circuit so late in the evening.   He stretched
out a cautious nose, and, as he sniffed in the direction of the wind and
sought a secure post of observation, he thought how wise foxes always
were and how stupid the hares.

Yonder in the inn there was an unusual commotion.   A couple of
travellers had ordered roast hare.   The landlord had gone to an
auction at Thisted, and his wife was used only to the responsibilities
of her kitchen.   Now it happened unfortunately that the advocate
wished to speak with the host on business, and because he was not at
home the good woman had to listen to a long speech and take charge
of an important letter, a proceeding that sadly disturbed her composure.   A stranger, who was waiting for a bottle of soda-water,
stood by the stove in greasy sailor clothes.   Two fish pedlars had
three times ordered brandy for their coffee.   The stable boy stood
with an empty lantern and waited for a candle, and a tall, rough
farmer followed Karen with longing eyes—she owed him change for a
crown he had just given her.   Karen came and went without haste,
without error.   One would hardly imagine she could attend to so

many things at once. The great eyes and the high arched brows
were full of wonder and expectation. The fine little head was held
straight and still. If she would make no mistakes she must keep
her thoughts collected. Her blue woollen dress was too small for
her. The tight neckband wrinkled her flesh just under the hair.
" The maiden from Agger has a white skin," said one fish pedlar to
the other. They were young people and spoke of Karen as con-
noisseurs.

Some one stood near the window, and looking at the clock said :
" The post is early to-night." It rattled over the pavement, the
doors were thrown open, and the wind blew the smoke from the
stove. Karen entered from the kitchen just as the conductor
stepped into the door and greeted the company with a hearty
" Good evening ! " He was a tall, handsome man, with dark eyes, a
crisp brown beard framed his face, and curly brown hair covered his
small head. His long heavy mantle of beautiful red royal Danish
cloth was trimmed with black fur, and hung from his shoulders.
The entire light of the two dim paraffin lamps that were suspended
from the wall over the table centred itself on this spot of glorious
crimson, as if it loved it, and left all the black and grey of the room
to grow still greyer and blacker. On the tall figure with the fine,
dark curly head, the long folds of the crimson cloak shone like a very
marvel of splendour and colour.

Karen came in quickly from the kitchen with her waiter. She
bent her head so that no one could see her face, as she hastened from
one guest to the other. She set the roast hare before the fish pedlars,
and brought the commercial traveller, who sat in an adjacent room,
the bottle of soda-water. She gave the anxious farmer a tallow
candle, and, slipping to the stranger by the stove, she thrust the
change from the crown in his hand.

The hostess was in the deepest despair. Everything had gone
wrong in the kitchen. She had lost the advocate's letter, and boundless confusion filled the inn. The traveller pounded the table with
the bell loudly ; the fish pedlars laughed until they were half dead
over the hare spread before them ; the bewildered farmer tapped the
landlady on the shoulder with the candle and puffed himself out like
a turkey cock.

And amid all this maddening confusion Karen had disappeared.
The postilion Anders sat on the driver's seat ; the stable boy stood
ready to open the door ; the travellers in the mail coach were impatient and so were the horses, although they had nothing pleasant
to look forward to, and the wind still rattled and whistled through
the stable. At last the conductor, whom they all awaited, came.
He carried his mantle over his arm as he stepped into the coach, and
excused his delay with a few curt words. He laughed to himself as
he drew his cloak about him and took his seat. The door was closed :

the mail coach rolled on. Anders let the horses trot gently, now there was no more need of haste. From time to time he glanced slyly at the conductor, who still laughed to himself, while the wind ruffled his hair. The postilion laughed too. He suspected something. The wind followed the coach to a turn in the road, then threw itself again over the plain and sighed mysteriously through the heather bushes.

The fox lay at his post. All was ready now, the hare must soon come. Yonder at the inn harmony was restored, the anxious farmer was relieved of his candle and received his change, and the travellers consumed their hare. The hostess complained a little, but she did not blame Karen. No one in all the world had ever scolded Karen. Quietly, unconsciously she hastened from one to the other, and the serene satisfaction that always followed her footsteps spread through the cozy half-dark inn parlour.

The two fish pedlars who had ordered a second cup of cognac and coffee, to follow the first, were especially pleased with her. A soft pink flush rested on her pale cheek, the glimmer of a smile on her lip, and once when she raised her eyes their light was dazzling. When she felt the men's eyes followed her she went into the next room where the travellers sat, pretending that she wanted some teaspoons from the cupboard. "Did you notice the conductor?" asked one of them.

"No; not till he went out. He left very quickly," answered the other with his mouth full of roast hare.

"A devilish handsome fellow. I attended his wedding."

"So, is he married?"

"Yes, indeed; his wife is the daughter of the landlord at Ulstrup, and I got there the night of the wedding. That was a jolly time, I assure you. They have two children, I believe."

Karen dropped the teaspoons and went out. She heard nothing that was called after her from the inn. She went across the court to her room and began mechanically to make her bed. Her eyes stared into the darkness. She pressed her hands to her head, to her breast; she groaned. She could comprehend nothing—nothing! She heard the landlady's complaining voice: "Karen, dear Karen!" it called. She ran out across the court, behind the inn, across the moor.

The winding strip of grass glimmered in the half-light as if it were a path, but it was no path. No one dared to follow it, for it led abruptly to the brink of the great pond. The hare quickened his steps. He heard a rustling. He gave long jumps as if he were mad to escape; not knowing what he feared, he fled over the plain. The fox stretched out his sharp nose and stared in surprise at the hare. He had heard nothing. According to the instincts of his kind he had crouched there in the hollow—he was conscious of no error. He could not understand the action of the hare. He stood long with outstretched head and slinking body. His bushy tail was hid by the heather bushes, and he began to wonder if foxes were getting duller or hares wiser. But when the west wind had run its long course it turned into a north wind, and then into an east wind, and then into the south wind, and at last came back over the sea as the west wind again, threw itself upon the dunes, and long, mysterious sighs moaned through the heather bushes.

But there were wanting in Kraruper Inn two wondering grey eyes, a little blue woollen gown that had grown too small, and the hostess complained more than ever. She could not understand it at all. No one could understand it, save the postilion Anders, and one other !

A MONKEY

ALEXANDER KIELLAND

FOR it was really a monkey that very nearly got me first class honours in my Legal Qualifying Exam. ; as it was, I only got second class, though that was fair enough.

But my friend the lawyer, who every day had to read, with somewhat mixed feelings, the rough copies of my examination papers, conceived therefrom such a high opinion of my manner of handling legal problems, that he feared the same might result in a possible first class for me. And he objected to my being subjected to the torture and inconvenience of a let-down in the oral exam., for he was my friend, and he knew me.

The monkey was in reality nothing but a coffee stain in the margin of page 496 of Schweigaard's *Legal Problems*, which I had borrowed from my friend Cucumis.

It would be difficult to imagine anything more depressing than going up for a Legal Exam. in the slush and darkness of mid-winter. It might possibly be worse in the summer, but as I have never tried it I cannot say.

One struggles through the eleven questions—or is it thirteen ? (surely the most horrible number that could be imagined !) like an unhappy circus performer at his first performance in public.

Off he gallops at full speed, with his life in his hands and a silly circus smile on his lips, and he has to jump through eleven—or is it thirteen ?—of those ugly paper-covered hoops.

The unfortunate candidate in a Legal Exam. finds himself in exactly the same situation as the circus performer, only that he does not gallop to the sound of music or in a brilliantly lighted building. He sits on a hard chair in half-darkness, and his face is turned towards the wall, and the only sound he hears is the creaking of the Superintendent's boots, for no boots in all the wide, wide world creak like those of a Superintendent at a Legal Exam.

And then comes the terrible moment when the black emissary from the Collegium Juridicum arrives with the list of Questions. He places himself in the doorway, and reads them out, coldly, dispassionately, with a cruel scorn for the fearsomeness of the occasion, and the fatal document he holds in his hands is the ugly paper-covered hoop through which all candidates have to jump, or, failing that, dismount and retire on foot.

You settle yourself in the saddle ; some do not succeed in doing this, but sway this way and that way uneasily.

An unhappy one simply gives it up and dismounts. All eyes are upon him as he moves towards the door, and a sigh goes through the remaining candidates. " You to-day, I to-morrow." In the meantime, however, there are sounds to be heard which indicate that the jumping has begun.

Some jump through steadily and gracefully, and alight on the farther side with a certainty of getting first class ; others, who consider jumping straight through the hoop too easy a feat, turn round while in the air and jump through backwards. It is said, however, that their nimbleness does not win the appreciation it would appear to merit from the Umpires.

Then, again, others jump, but miss the hoop ; they jump under it or at the side of it. Some, too, jump high over it, finding the performance apparently very simple, and continuing their wild ride afterwards with careless assurance.

But when one has no desire to ride, and no experience in jumping through hoops, one is really to be pitied, unless one happens to come across a monkey on page 496 !

It was an unhealthy life we led in those days, jumping through hoops in the daytime and studying how to do it at night.

I had just got half way through Schweigaard's *Legal Problems* one night ; it was very late. I put more wood on the fire when I wanted air, and opened the window when I wanted heat, and every little while I tore through the faded pages of the *Legal Problems* like a whirlwind.

But even whirlwinds ultimately calm down, and when this happened in my case, I sat stiffly upright and read for the eleventh time :
" One might therefore certainly conclude, . . . one might therefore
. . . certainly . . . combine the useful with the agreeable . . . and lean back a little in one's chair. . . . I can read just as well . . .

the lamp isn't in the way at all . . . one . . . might . . . therefore. . . ."

But unlegal pictures floated out of the book, encircled the lamp,
and threatened entirely to overshadow the clearness of my legal
vision.

I could still dimly distinguish the white leaves : " one . . might
. . . therefore. . . ." The rest disappeared in a crowd of little
black letters that swarmed over the closely-printed pages ; my eyes
followed them in weary desperation. Then, I saw, at the bottom,
on the right-hand side of the page . . . a face ! It was that of a
monkey drawn by some one in the margin ; it was beautifully done,
especially the brown face !

My interest in this work of art was greater, I am ashamed to say,
than that I felt for Schweigaard ; I roused myself and leaned forward to see better.

After due examination, I discovered that the wonderful brown hue
of the face was due to coffee, and further, that the whole monkey was
nothing more than a coffee stain !

The artist had added the eyes and a little hair, that was all ! The
genius in the case was the one who had spilt the coffee.

I understood then, because I knew Cucumis could not draw a
line ! but he knew his law thoroughly. And then I began to think
of him, of his successful examination when he took first class honours, of his triumphant return home. How he must have worked to
achieve this ! And musing thus, my conscience began to stir uneasily and awake from its slumbers, until suddenly, like a flash, my
own ignorance stood before me in all its horrible nakedness !

I pictured to myself the disgrace it would mean for me, if I had to
" dismount," or, still worse, if I were to be numbered among those
unhappy ones who remain eternally nameless, of whom it is said,
" He got a ' non contemnendus ' " !

And just as it happens that sometimes people go out of their minds
as a result of too much learning, so did I nearly go out of mine when
I realised the extent of my ignorance.

Up I jumped, and plunged my head into the water-basin, then,
hardly allowing myself time for drying, I started reading with such
determination that every word was indelibly printed on my memory :
" One might therefore certainly conclude, etc., etc."

I hurried through the left-hand page, then, with unabated energy,
down the right-hand one, reached the monkey, passed him, turned
over the leaf and read on bravely.

I did not notice that my powers were exhausted. Although I
caught a glimpse of a new chapter, which, in ordinary cases, acts as
a spur, I could not help getting entangled in one of those perfidious
sentences which one reads over and over again with illusive
gravity.

I groped about for some means of salvation, but there were none.

I began to feel giddy : " Where is the monkey ? . . . a coffee stain ; . . . one cannot show genius on both pages . . . everything in life has a right and a wrong side . . . for example, the University clock, . . . but as I can't swim, let me come out. . . . I'm going to the Circus ! . . . I know very well that you are laughing at me, Cucumis ! But I can jump through the hoop, I tell you, . . . and if only the Professor, who has come out of my lamp, had searched properly in the ' corpus juris,' I should not be lying here, . . . in my shirt in the middle of Karl Johans Street . . . but . . ."

At this juncture I fell into the deep dreamless sleep which only comes to whose who suffer from a bad conscience, when they are very young.

I was early in the saddle the following morning.

I do not know whether the Devil had put on boots that day, but, at any rate, his superintendents had *theirs* on, and they creaked past me, where I sat in my misery with my face turned towards the wall.

A Professor walked about the rooms watching the victims. Now and then, when his eyes happened to fall on one of those miserable toadies who attend Lectures, he would give a nod and an encouraging smile ; but when his eyes rested on me, the smile vanished, and his icy glance seemed to write on the wall above my head, " O wretched one, I know you not ! . . ."

One or two of the Superintendents creaked up to the President and fawned upon him ; I could hear them whispering behind my chair, while I ground my teeth in silent rage at the thought that such wretches should be paid, should in fact earn their living by torturing me as well as some of my best friends !

The door opened, and a ray of yellow light shone in on to the pale faces ; it reminded one of " the Victims of the Terror " in the Luxembourg Museum. Then all was dark again, and the black emissary glided through the room like a bat, with the famous white sheet in his claws.

He began to read.

I never in all my life felt so devoid of hope as I did just then ; and yet the very first words made me jump.

" The monkey ! "

I nearly shouted the words out loud ! for there was no doubt about it, it was page 496 in the *Legal Problems*, just where I had found the monkey ! The problem he was reading out was the very one I had studied with such energy the night before. And I started writing.

After a brief introduction, I worked in the melodious phrase : " One might therefore certainly conclude " . . . and hurried down the left-hand page, then with unabated energy over the right-hand one, reached the monkey, passed him, began to grope, . . . and suddenly came to a standstill.

I knew something was lacking, but I knew also that it was no good trying to think out what it was. What one doesn't know, one *doesn't* know, and that's all about it ! So I put a full stop, and left, long before the others were half finished.

My companions in misfortune thought that I had dismounted, or that I had jumped wide of the hoop—for the problem was a difficult one.

" Well, well," said the lawyer, when he read my paper, " this is better than I expected ! Why, it is just undiluted Schweigaard ! You have omitted the last point, but that is of no great importance ; one can see that you are well up in the subject. But why did you dread the exam. so yesterday ? "

" I didn't know anything."

He smiled. " Was it, then, in the night that you mastered the problem ? "

" Yes ! It was."

" Did any one help you ? "

" Yes."

" It must have been a devil of a teacher to get so much law into your head in one night ! May I ask who the magician was ? "

" A monkey ! " I replied.

TWO FRIENDS

ALEXANDER KIELLAND

No one could understand where he got his money from. But the person who marvelled most at the dashing and luxurious life led by Alphonse was his quondam friend and partner.

After they dissolved partnership, most of the custom and the best connection passed by degrees into Charles's hands. This was not because he in any way sought to run counter to his former partner ; on the contrary, it arose simply from the fact that Charles was the more capable man of the two. And as Alphonse had now to work on his own account, it was soon clear to any one who observed him closely, that in spite of his promptitude, his amiability, and his prepossessing appearance, he was not fitted to be at the head of an independent business.

And there was one person who *did* observe him closely. Charles followed him step by step with his sharp eyes ; every blunder, every extravagance, every loss—he knew all to a nicety, and he wondered that Alphonse could keep going so long.

They had as good as grown up together. Their mothers were cousins ; the families had lived near each other in the same street ; and in a city like Paris proximity is as important as relationship in promoting close intercourse. Moreover, the boys went to the same school.

Thenceforth, as they grew up to manhood, they were inseparable. Mutual adaptation overcame the great difference which originally marked their characters, until at last their idiosyncrasies fitted into each other like the artfully carved pieces of wood which compose the picture-puzzles of our childhood.

The relation between them was really a beautiful one, such as does not often arise between two young men ; for they did not understand friendship as binding the one to bear everything at the hands of the other, but seemed rather to vie with each other in mutual consideration.

If, however, Alphonse in his relations to Charles showed any high degree of consideration, he himself was ignorant of it ; and if any one had told him of it he would doubtless have laughed loudly at such a mistaken compliment.

For as life on the whole appeared to him very simple and straightforward; the idea that his friendship should in any way fetter him was the last thing that could enter his head. That Charles was his best friend seemed to him as entirely natural as that he himself danced best, rode best, was the best shot, and that the whole world was ordered entirely to his mind.

Alphonse was in the highest degree a spoilt child of fortune ; he acquired everything without effort ; existence fitted him like an elegant dress, and he wore it with such unconstrained amiability that people forgot to envy him.

And then he was so handsome. He was tall and slim, with brown hair and big open eyes ; his complexion was clear and smooth, and his teeth shone when he laughed. He was quite conscious of his beauty, but, as everybody had petted him from his earliest days, his vanity was of a cheerful, good-natured sort, which, after all, was not so offensive. He was exceedingly fond of his friend. He amused himself and sometimes others by teasing him and making fun of him ; but he knew Charles's face so thoroughly that he saw at once when the jest was going too far. Then he would resume his natural, kindly tone, until he made the serious and somewhat melancholy Charles laugh again.

From his boyhood Charles had admired Alphonse beyond measure. He himself was small and insignificant; quiet and shy. His friend's brilliant qualities cast a lustre over him as well, and gave a certain impetus to his life.

His mother often said : " This friendship between the boys is a real blessing for my poor Charles, for without it he would certainly have been a melancholy creature."

When Alphonse was on all occasions preferred to him, Charles rejoiced ; he was proud of his friend. He wrote his exercises, prompted him at examination, pleaded his cause with the masters, and fought for him with the boys.

At the commercial academy it was the same story. Charles worked for Alphonse, and Alphonse rewarded him with his inexhaustible amiability and unfailing good-humour.

When subsequently, as quite young men, they were placed in the same banker's office, it happened one day that the principal said to Charles : " From the first of May I will raise your salary."

" I thank you," answered Charles, " both on my own and on my friend's behalf."

" Monsieur Alphonse's salary remains unaltered," replied the chief, and went on writing.

Charles never forgot that morning. It was the first time he had been preferred or distinguished before his friend. And it was his commercial capacity, the quality which, as a young man of business, he valued most, that had procured him this preference ; and it was the head of the firm, the great financier, who had himself accorded him such recognition.

The experience was so strange to him that it seemed like an injustice to his friend. He told Alphonse nothing of the occurrence ; on the contrary, he proposed that they should apply for two vacant places in the Crédit Lyonnais.

Alphonse was quite willing, for he loved change, and the splendid new banking establishment on the Boulevard seemed to him far more attractive than the dark offices in the Rue Bergère. So they removed to the Crédit Lyonnais on the first of May. But as they were in the chief's office taking their leave, the old banker said to Charles, when Alphonse had gone out (Alphonse always took precedence of Charles), " Sentiment won't do for a business man."

From that day forward a change went on in Charles. He not only worked as industriously and conscientiously as before, but developed such energy and such an amazing faculty for labour as soon attracted to him the attention of his superiors. That he was far ahead of his friend in business capacity was soon manifest ; but every time he received a new mark of recognition he had a struggle with himself. For a long time, every advancement brought with it a certain qualm of conscience ; and yet he worked on with restless ardour.

One day Alphonse said, in his light, frank way : " You are really a smart fellow, Charlie ! You're getting ahead of everybody, young and old—not to mention me. I'm quite proud of you."

Charles felt ashamed. He had been thinking that Alphonse must feel wounded at being left on one side, and now he learned that his friend not only did not grudge him his advancement, but was even proud of him.   By degrees his conscience was lulled to rest, and his solid worth was more and more appreciated.

But if he was in reality the more capable, how came it that he was so entirely ignored in society, while Alphonse remained everybody's darling ?   The very promotions and marks of appreciation which he had won for himself by hard work were accorded him in a dry, business manner ; while every one, from the directors to the messengers, had a friendly word or a merry greeting for Alphonse.

In the different offices and departments of the bank they intrigued to obtain possession of Monsieur Alphonse ; for a breath of life and freshness followed ever in the wake of his handsome person and joyous nature.   Charles, on the other hand, had often remarked that his colleagues regarded him as a dry person, who thought only of business and of himself.

The truth was that he had a heart of rare sensitiveness, with no faculty for giving it expression.

Charles was one of those small, black Frenchmen whose beard begins right under the eyes ; his complexion was yellowish and his hair stiff and splintery.   His eyes did not dilate when he was pleased and animated, but they flashed around and glittered.   When he laughed the corners of his mouth turned upward, and many a time, when his heart was full of joy and good-will, he had seen people draw back, half frightened by his forbidding exterior.   Alphonse alone knew him so well that he never seemed to see his ugliness ; every one else misunderstood him.   He became suspicious, and retired more and more within himself.

In an insensible crescendo the thought grew in him : Why should he never attain anything of that which he most longed for—intimate and cordial intercourse and friendliness which should answer to the warmth pent up within him ?   Why should every one smile towards Alphonse with outstretched hands, while he must content himself with stiff bows and cold glances ?

Alphonse knew nothing of all this.   He was joyous and healthy, charmed with life and content with his daily work.   He had been placed in the easiest and most interesting branch of the business, and, with his quick brain and his knack of making himself agreeable, he filled his place satisfactorily.

His social circle was very large—every one set store by his acquaintance, and he was at least as popular among women as among men.

For a time Charles accompanied Alphonse into society, until he was seized by a misgiving that he was invited for his friend's sake alone, when he at once drew back.

When Charles proposed that they should set up in business to-

gether Alphonse had answered : " It is too good of you to choose
me. You could easily find a much better partner."

Charles had imagined that their altered relations and closer
association in work would draw Alphonse out of the circles which
Charles could not now endure, and unite them more closely. For he
had conceived a vague dread of losing his friend.

He did not himself know, nor would it have been easy to decide,
whether he was jealous of all the people who flocked around Alphonse
and drew him to them, or whether he envied his friend's popularity.

They began their business prudently and energetically, and got
on well.

It was generally held that each formed an admirable complement
to the other. Charles represented the solid, confidence-inspiring
element, while the handsome and elegant Alphonse imparted to the
firm a certain lustre which was far from being without value.

Every one who came into the counting-house at once remarked
his handsome figure, and thus it seemed quite natural that all should
address themselves to him.

Charles meanwhile bent over his work and let Alphonse be spokes-
man. When Alphonse asked him about anything, he answered
shortly and quietly without looking up.

Thus most people thought that Charles was a confidential clerk,
while Alphonse was the real head of the house.

As Frenchmen, they thought little about marrying, but as young
Parisians they led a life into which erotics entered largely.

Alphonse was never really in his element except when in female
society. Then all his exhilarating amiability came into play, and
when he leaned back at supper and held out his shallow champagne-
glass to be refilled, he was as beautiful as a happy god.

He had a neck of the kind which women long to caress, and his
soft half-curling hair looked as if it were negligently arranged, or
carefully disarranged, by a woman's coquettish hand.

Indeed, many slim white fingers had passed through those locks ;
for Alphonse had not only the gift of being loved by women, but also
the yet rarer gift of being forgiven by them.

When the friends were together at gay supper-parties, Alphonse
paid no particular heed to Charles. He kept no account of his own
love-affairs, far less of those of his friend. So it might easily happen
that a beauty on whom Charles had cast a longing eye fell into the
hands of Alphonse.

Charles was used to seeing his friend preferred in life ; but there
are certain things to which men can scarcely accustom themselves.
He seldom went with Alphonse to his suppers, and it was always long
before the wine and the general exhilaration could bring him into a
convivial humour.

But then, when the champagne and the bright eyes had gone to his head, he would often be the wildest of all ; he would sing loudly with his harsh voice, laugh and gesticulate so that his stiff black hair fell over his forehead ; and then the merry ladies shrank from him, and called him the " chimney-sweep."

As the sentry paces up and down in the beleaguered fortress, he sometimes hears a strange sound in the silent night, as if something were rustling under his feet. It is the enemy, who has undermined the outworks, and to-night or to-morrow night there will be a hollow explosion, and armed men will storm in through the breach.

If Charles had kept close watch over himself he would have heard strange thoughts rustling within him. But he would not hear—he had only a dim foreboding that sometime there must come an explosion.

One day it came.

It was already after business hours ; the clerks had all left the outer office, and only the principals remained behind.

Charles was busily writing a letter which he wished to finish before he left.

Alphonse had drawn on both his gloves and buttoned them. Then he had brushed his hat until it shone, and now he was walking up and down and peeping into Charles's letter every time he passed the desk.

They used to spend an hour every day before dinner in a café on the great Boulevard, and Alphonse was getting impatient for his newspapers.

" Will you never have finished that letter ? " he said, rather irritably.

Charles was silent a second or two, then he sprang up so that his chair fell over : " Perhaps Alphonse imagined that he could do it better ? Did he not know which of them was really the man of business ? " And now the words streamed out with that incredible rapidity of which the French language is capable when it is used in fiery passion.

But it was a turbid stream, carrying with it many ugly expressions, upbraidings, and recriminations ; and through the whole there sounded something like a suppressed sob.

As he strode up and down the room, with clenched hands and dishevelled hair, Charles looked like a little wiry-haired terrier barking at an elegant Italian greyhound. At last he seized his hat and rushed out.

Alphonse had stood looking at him with great wondering eyes. When he was gone, and there was once more silence in the room, it seemed as though the air was still quivering with the hot words. Alphonse recalled them one by one, as he stood motionless beside the desk.

" Did he not know which was the abler of the two ? " Yes, assuredly! he had never denied that Charles was by far his superior.

" He must not think that he would succeed in winning everything to himself with his smooth face." Alphonse was not conscious of ever having deprived his friend of anything.

" I don't care for your *cocottes*," Charles had said.

Could he really have been interested in the little Spanish dancer ? If Alphonse had only had the faintest suspicion of such a thing he would never have looked at her. But that was nothing to get so wild about ; there were plenty of women in Paris.

And at last : " As sure as to-morrow comes, I will dissolve partnership ! "

Alphonse did not understand it at all. He left the counting-house and walked moodily through the streets until he met an acquaintance. That put other thoughts into his head ; but all day he had a feeling as if something gloomy and uncomfortable lay in wait, ready to seize him so soon as he was alone.

When he reached home, late at night, he found a letter from Charles. He opened it hastily ; but it contained, instead of the apology he had expected, only a coldly-worded request to M. Alphonse to attend at the counting-house early the next morning " in order that the contemplated dissolution of partnership might be effected as quickly as possible."

Now, for the first time, did Alphonse begin to understand that the scene in the counting-house had been more than a passing outburst of passion ; but this only made the affair more inexplicable.

And the longer he thought it over, the more clearly did he feel that Charles had been unjust to him. He had never been angry with his friend, nor was he precisely angry even now. But as he repeated to himself all the insults Charles had heaped upon him, his good-natured heart hardened ; and the next morning he took his place in silence, after a cold " Good-morning."

Although he arrived a whole hour earlier than usual, he could see that Charles had been working long and industriously. There they sat, each on his side of the desk ; they spoke only the most indispensable words ; now and then a paper passed from hand to hand, but they never looked each other in the face.

In this way they both worked—each as busily as the other—until twelve o'clock, their usual luncheon-time.

This hour of *déjeuner* was the favourite time of both. Their custom was to have it served in their office, and when the old housekeeper announced that lunch was ready, they would both rise at once, even if they were in the midst of a sentence or of an account.

They used to eat standing by the fireplace, or walking up and down in the warm, comfortable office. Alphonse had always some piquant stories to tell, and Charles laughed at them. These were his pleasantest hours.

But that day, when Madame said her friendly " *Messieurs, on a servi*," they both remained sitting. She opened her eyes wide, and repeated the words as she went out, but neither moved.

At last Alphonse felt hungry, went to the table, poured out a glass of wine and began to eat his cutlet. But as he stood there eating, with his glass in his hand, and looked round the dear old office where they had spent so many pleasant hours, and then thought that they were to lose all this and embitter their lives for a whim, a sudden burst of passion, the whole situation appeared to him so preposterous that he almost burst out laughing.

" Look here, Charles," he said, in the half-earnest, half-joking tone which always used to make Charles laugh, " it will really be too absurd to advertise : ' According to an amicable agreement, from such and such a date the firm of—' "

" I have been thinking," interrupted Charles quietly, " that we will put : ' According to *mutual* agreement.' "

Alphonse laughed no more ; he put down his glass, and the cutlet tasted bitter in his mouth.

He understood that friendship was dead between them, why or wherefore he could not tell ; but he thought that Charles was hard and unjust to him. He was now stiffer and colder than the other.

They worked together until the business of dissolution was finished ; then they parted.

A considerable time passed, and the two quondam friends worked each in his own quarter in the great Paris. They met at the Bourse, but never did business with each other. Charles never worked against Alphonse ; he did not wish to ruin him ; he wished Alphonse to ruin himself.

And Alphonse seemed likely enough to meet his friend's wishes in this respect. It is true that now and then he did a good stroke of business, but the steady industry he had learned from Charles he soon forgot. He began to neglect his office, and lost many good connections.

He had always had a taste for dainty and luxurious living, but his association with the frugal Charles had hitherto held his extravagances in check. Now, on the contrary, his life became more and more dissipated. He made fresh acquaintances on every hand, and was more than ever the brilliant and popular Monsieur Alphonse ; but Charles kept an eye on his growing debts.

He had Alphonse watched as closely as possible, and, as their business was of the same kind, could form a pretty good estimate of the other's earnings. His expenses were even easier to ascertain, and he soon assured himself of the fact that Alphonse was beginning to run into debt in several quarters.

He cultivated some acquaintances about whom he otherwise cared nothing, merely because through them he got an insight into Alphonse's expensive mode of life and rash prodigality. He sought the same cafés and restaurants as Alphonse, but at different times ; he even had his clothes made by the same tailor, because the talkative little man entertained him with complaints that Monsieur Alphonse never paid his bills.

Charles often thought how easy it would be to buy up a part of Alphonse's liabilities and let them fall into the hands of a grasping usurer. But it would be a great injustice to suppose that Charles for a moment contemplated doing such a thing himself. It was only an idea he was fond of dwelling upon ; he was, as it were, in love with Alphonse's debts.

But things went slowly, and Charles became pale and sallow while he watched and waited.

He was longing for the time when people who had always looked down upon him should have their eyes opened, and see how little the brilliant and idolized Alphonse was really fit for. He wanted to see him humbled, abandoned by his friends, lonely and poor ; and then—!

Beyond that he really did not like to speculate ; for at this point feelings stirred within him which he would not acknowledge.

He *would* hate his former friend ; he *would* have revenge for all the coldness and neglect which had been his own lot in life ; and every time the least thought in defence of Alphonse arose in his mind he pushed it aside, and said, like the old banker. " Sentiment won't do for a business man."

One day he went to his tailor's ; he bought more clothes in these days than he absolutely needed.

The nimble little man at once ran to meet him with a roll of cloth : " See, here is the very stuff for you. Monsieur Alphonse has had a whole suit made of it, and Monsieur Alphonse is a gentleman who knows how to dress."

" I did not think that Monsieur Alphonse was one of your favourite customers," said Charles, rather taken by surprise.

" Oh, *mon Dieu !* " exclaimed the little tailor, " you mean because I have once or twice mentioned that Monsieur Alphonse owed me a few thousand francs. It was very stupid of me to speak so. Monsieur Alphonse has not only paid me the trifle he was owing, but I know that he has also satisfied a number of other creditors. I have done *ce cher beau monsieur* great injustice, and I beg you never to give him a hint of my stupidity."

Charles was no longer listening to the chatter of the garrulous tailor. He soon left the shop, and went up the street, quite absorbed in the one thought that Alphonse had paid.

He thought how foolish it really was of him to wait and wait for the other's ruin. How easily might not the adroit and lucky Alphonse come across many a brilliant business opening, and make plenty of money without a word of it reaching Charles's ears. Perhaps, after all, he was getting on well. Perhaps it would end in people saying, " See, at last Monsieur Alphonse shows what he is fit for, now that he is quit of his dull and crabbed partner ! "

Charles went slowly up the street with his head bent. Many people jostled him, but he heeded not. His life seemed to him so meaningless, as if he had lost all that he had ever possessed—or had he himself cast it from him ? Just then some one ran against him with more than usual violence. He looked up. It was an acquaintance from the time when he and Alphonse had been in the Crédit Lyonnais.

" Ah, good-day, Monsieur Charles ! " cried he. " It is long since we met. Odd, too, that I should meet you to-day. I was just thinking of you this morning."

" Why, may I ask ? " said Charles half-absently.

" Well, you see, only to-day I saw up at the bank a paper—a bill for thirty or forty thousand francs—bearing both your name and that of Monsieur Alphonse. It astonished me, for I thought that you two—h'm !—had done with each other."

" No, we have not quite done with each other yet," said Charles slowly.

He struggled with all his might to keep his face calm, and asked, in as natural a tone as he could command, " When does the bill fall due ? I don't quite recollect."

" To-morrow or the day after, I think," answered the other, who was a hard-worked business man, and was already in a hurry to be off. " It was accepted by Monsieur Alphonse."

" I know that," said Charles ; " but could you not manage to let *me* redeem the bill to-morrow ? It is a courtesy—a favour I am anxious to do."

" With pleasure. Tell your messenger to ask for me personally at the bank to-morrow afternoon. I will arrange it ; nothing easier. Excuse me ; I'm in a hurry. Good-bye ! " and with that he ran on.

Next day Charles sat in his counting-house waiting for the messenger who had gone up to the bank to redeem Alphonse's bill.

At last a clerk entered, laid a folded blue paper by his principal's side, and went out again.

Not until the door was closed did Charles seize the draft, look swiftly round the room, and open it. He stared for a second or two at his name, then lay back in his chair and drew a deep breath. It was as he had expected—the signature was a forgery.

He bent over it again. For long he sat, gazing at his own name, and observing how badly it was counterfeited.

While his sharp eyes followed every line in the letters of his name, he scarcely thought. His mind was so disturbed, and his feelings so strangely conflicting, that it was some time before he became conscious how much they betrayed—these bungling strokes on the blue paper.

He felt a strange lump in his throat, his nose began to tickle a little, and, before he was aware of it, a big tear fell on the paper.

He looked hastily around, took out his pocket-handkerchief, and carefully wiped the wet place on the bill. He thought again of the old banker in the Rue Bergère.

What did it matter to him that Alphonse's weak character had at last led him to crime, and what had he lost ? Nothing, for did he not hate his former friend ? No one could say it was his fault that Alphonse was ruined—he had shared with him honestly, and never harmed him.

Then his thoughts turned to Alphonse. He knew him well enough to be sure that when the refined, delicate Alphonse had sunk so low, he must have come to a jutting headland in life, and be prepared to leap out of it rather than let disgrace reach him.

At this thought Charles sprang up. That must not be. Alphonse should not have time to send a bullet through his head and hide his shame in the mixture of compassion and mysterious horror which follows the suicide. Thus Charles would lose his revenge, and it would be all to no purpose that he had gone and nursed his hatred until he himself had become evil through it. Since he had for ever lost his friend, he would at least expose his enemy, so that all should see what a miserable, despicable being was this charming Alphonse.

He looked at his watch ; it was half-past four. Charles knew the café in which he would find Alphonse at this hour ; he pocketed the bill and buttoned his coat.

But on the way he would call at a police-station, and hand over the bill to a detective, who at a sign from Charles should suddenly advance into the middle of the café where Alphonse was always surrounded by his friends and admirers, and say loudly and distinctly so that all should hear it :

" Monsieur Alphonse, you are charged with forgery."

It was raining in Paris. The day had been foggy, raw, and cold ; and well on in the afternoon it had begun to rain. It was not a downpour—the water did not fall from the clouds in regular drops—but the clouds themselves had, as it were, laid themselves down in the streets of Paris and there slowly condensed into water.

No matter how people might seek to shelter themselves, they got wet on all sides. The moisture slid down the back of your neck, laid itself like a wet towel about your knees, penetrated into your boots and far up your trousers.

A few sanguine ladies were standing in the *portes cochères*, with their skirts tucked up, expecting it to clear ; others waited by the hour in the omnibus stations. But most of the stronger sex hurried along under their umbrellas ; only a few had been sensible enough to give up the battle, and had turned up their collars, stuck their umbrellas under their arms, and their hands in their pockets.

Although it was early in the autumn it was already dusk at five o'clock. A few gas-gets were lighted in the narrowest streets, and in a shop here and there strove to shine out in the thick wet air.

People swarmed as usual in the streets, jostled one another off the pavement, and ruined one another's umbrellas. All the cabs were taken up ; they splashed along and bespattered the foot passengers to the best of their ability, while the asphalt glistened in the dim light with a dense coating of mud.

The cafés were crowded to excess ; regular customers went round and scolded, and the waiters ran against each other in their hurry. Ever and anon, amid the confusion, could be heard the sharp little ting of the bell on the buffet : it was *la dame du comptoir* summoning a waiter, while her calm eyes kept a watch upon the whole café.

A lady sat at the buffet of a large restaurant on the Boulevard Sebastopol. She was widely known for her cleverness and her amiable manners.

She had glossy black hair, which, in spite of the fashion, she wore parted in the middle of her forehead in natural curls. Her eyes were almost black and her mouth full, with a little shadow of a moustache.

Her figure was still very pretty, although, if the truth were known, she had probably passed her thirtieth year ; and she had a soft little hand, with which she wrote elegant figures in her cash-book, and now and then a little note. Madame Virginie could converse with the young dandies who were always hanging about the buffet, and parry their witticisms, while she kept account with the waiters and had her eye upon every corner of the great room.

She was really pretty only from five till seven in the afternoon—that being the time at which Alphonse invariably visited the café. Then her eyes never left him ; she got a fresher colour, her mouth was always trembling into a smile, and her movements became somewhat nervous. That was the only time of the day when she was ever known to give a random answer or to make a mistake in the accounts; and the waiters tittered and nudged each other.

For it was generally thought that she had formerly had relations with Alphonse, and some would even have it that she was still his mistress.

She herself best knew how matters stood ; but it was impossible to be angry with Monsieur Alphonse. She was well aware that he cared no more for her than for twenty others; that she had lost him—nay, that he had never really been hers. And yet her eyes besought a friendly look, and when he left the café without sending her a confidential greeting, it seemed as though she suddenly faded, and the waiters said to each other: "Look at madame; she is grey to-night."

Over at the windows it was still light enough to read the papers; a couple of young men were amusing themselves with watching the crowds which streamed past. Seen through the great plate-glass windows, the busy forms gliding past one another in the dense, wet, rainy air looked like fish in an aquarium. Further back in the café, and over the billiard-tables, the gas was lighted. Alphonse was playing with a couple of friends.

He had been to the buffet and greeted Madame Virginie, and she, who had long noticed how Alphonse was growing paler day by day, had—half in jest, half in anxiety—reproached him with his thoughtless life.

Alphonse answered with a poor joke and asked for absinthe.

How she hated those light ladies of the ballet and the opera who enticed Monsieur Alphonse to revel night after night at the gaming-table, or at interminable suppers! How ill he had been looking these last few weeks! He had grown quite thin, and the great gentle eyes had acquired a piercing, restless look. What would she not give to be able to rescue him out of that life that was dragging him down! She glanced in the opposite mirror and thought she had beauty enough left.

Now and then the door opened and a new guest came in, stamped his feet, and shut his wet umbrella. All bowed to Madame Virginie, and almost all said, "What horrible weather!"

When Charles entered, he saluted shortly and took a seat in the corner beside the fireplace.

Alphonse's eyes had indeed become restless. He looked towards the door every time any one came in; and when Charles appeared, a spasm passed over his face and he missed his stroke.

"Monsieur Alphonse is not in the vein to-day," said an onlooker.

Soon after a strange gentleman came in. Charles looked up from his paper and nodded slightly; the stranger raised his eyebrows a little and looked at Alphonse.

He dropped his cue on the floor.

"Excuse me, gentlemen, I'm not in the mood for billiards to-day," said he, "permit me to leave off. Waiter, being me a bottle of seltzer-water and a spoon—I must take my dose of Vichy salts."

"You should not take so much Vichy salts, Monsieur Alphonse, but rather keep to a sensible diet," said the doctor, who sat a little way off playing chess.

Alphonse laughed, and seated himself at the newspaper table. He seized the *Journal Amusant*, and began to make merry remarks upon the illustrations. A little circle quickly gathered round him, and he was inexhaustible in racy stories and whimsicalities.

While he rattled on under cover of the others' laughter, he poured out a glass of seltzer-water and took from his pocket a little box on which was written, in large letters, " Vichy Salts."

He shook the powder out into the glass and stirred it round with a spoon. There was a little cigar-ash on the floor in front of his chair ; he whipped it off with his pocket-handkerchief, and then stretched out his hand for the glass.

At that moment he felt a hand on his arm. Charles had risen and hurried across the room ; he now bent down over Alphonse.

Alphonse turned his head towards him so that none but Charles could see his face. At first he let his eyes travel furtively over his old friend's figure ; then he looked up, and, gazing straight at Charles, he said, half aloud, " Charlie ! "

It was long since Charles had heard that old pet name. He gazed into the well-known face, and now for the first time saw how it had altered of late. It seemed to him as though he were reading a tragic story about himself.

They remained thus for a second or two, and there glided over Alphonse's features that expression of imploring helplessness which Charles knew so well from the old school-days, when Alphonse came bounding in at the last moment and wanted his composition written.

" Have you done with the *Journal Amusant ?* " asked Charles, with a thick utterance.

" Yes, pray take it," answered Alphonse hurriedly. He reached him the paper, and at the same time got hold of Charles's thumb. He pressed it and whispered, " Thanks," then—drained the glass.

Charles went over to the stranger who sat by the door : " Give me the bill."

" You don't need our assistance, then ? "

" No, thanks."

" So much the better," said the stranger, handing Charles a folded blue paper. Then he paid for his coffee and went.

Madame Virginie rose with a little shriek : " Alphonse ! Oh, my God ! Monsieur Alphonse is ill."

He slipped off his chair ; his shoulders went up and his head fell on one side. He remained sitting on the floor, with his back against the chair.

There was a movement among those nearest ; the doctor sprang over and knelt beside him. When he looked in Alphonse's face he started a little. He took his hand as if to feel his pulse, and at the same time bent down over the glass which stood on the edge of the table.

With a movement of the arm he gave it a slight push, so that it fell on the floor and was smashed. Then he laid down the dead man's hand and bound a handkerchief round his chin.

Not till then did the others understand what had happened. "Dead? Is he dead, doctor? Monsieur Alphonse dead?"

"Heart disease," answered the doctor.

One came running with water, another with vinegar. Amid laughter and noise, the balls could be heard cannoning on the inner billiard-table.

"Hush!" some one whispered. "Hush!" was repeated; and the silence spread in wider and wider circles round the corpse, until all was quite still.

"Come and lend a hand," said the doctor.

The dead man was lifted up; they laid him on a sofa in a corner of the room, and the nearest gas-jets were put out.

Madame Virginie was still standing up; her face was chalk-white, and she held her little soft hand pressed against her breast. They carried him right past the buffet. The doctor had seized him under the back, so that his waistcoat slipped up and a piece of his fine white shirt appeared.

She followed with her eyes the slender, supple limbs she knew so well, and continued to stare towards the dark corner.

Most of the guests went away in silence. A couple of young men entered noisily from the street; a waiter ran towards them and said a few words. They glanced towards the corner, buttoned their coats, and plunged out again into the fog.

The half-darkened café was soon empty; only some of Alphonse's nearest friends stood in a group and whispered. The doctor was talking with the proprietor, who had now appeared on the scene.

The waiters stole to and fro, making great circuits to avoid the dark corner. One of them knelt and gathered up the fragments of the glass on a tray. He did his work as quietly as he could; but for all that it made too much noise.

"Let that alone until by and by," said the host softly.

Leaning against the chimney-piece, Charles looked at the dead man. He slowly tore the folded paper to pieces, while he thought of his friend.

JACOB AHRENBERG   FINNISH

B. 1847

JALO THE TROTTER

It was in the afternoon of an August day, but the sun was still pouring its hot slanting rays into Christian's sitting-room. The flies were buzzing merrily around the head of the landlord, who sat by the window, apparently watching the two balsams blooming in broken china pots on the sill. Christian had been there a long time, staring between the leaves and flowers of the plants at the little gate of the fence, as if he was expecting some one.

He had already reached middle life, but looked considerably older. His eyes were sunk deep in their sockets, and wrinkles seamed his face. His wife, who was working busily at the loom, did not seem to have her mind wholly on her task ; for, whenever Christian made the slightest movement, she glanced anxiously toward the door as if she, too, was expecting somebody.

Suddenly Laurikamen, the assessor of the district court, entered, greeted the couple, and shook hands ceremoniously with them. This guest, whose visit seemed to afford neither pleasure nor surprise, sat down at the table, and, after a short silence, lighted his pipe, and finally remarked that it really was far too hot for five o'clock in the afternoon, to which undeniably truthful remark Christian replied that the heat would at least do the oats good. Gradually the conversation grew more fluent ; they discussed the questions of the day, the fall of stocks, the price of grain at home and in Russia, and the sessions of the court. Then the assessor had reached the point at which he was aiming. Rising deliberately, he went to the hearth, knocked the ashes from his pipe, and remarked, as if casually :

" By the way, you are summoned there."

" I ? To the court ? By whom ? "

" By Jegor Timofitsch Ivanov, your neighbour."

" H'm ! What is he after ? Is it about the beating I gave him last spring ? "

" Not at all ; he must put up with that. It's the affair of Jalo, his trotter, you know."

" Well, what's that to me ? "

" I don't know. Come to-morrow, and you'll find out."

The assessor uttered a sigh of relief, rose, took his leave, and went away.

Christian scratched himself behind the ear, and went out thoughtfully. Sighing heavily, he wandered restlessly over the pastures and meadows until late in the evening.

As it was still too warm in the room, he sat down on the steps to enjoy the cool evening air. It was a damp, hot night ; the stars shone dimly through the air, which lay like a thin veil on the horizon. The full moon was rising in majesty above the moor, looming in a large reddish gold disk through the firwood, which grew sparse and stunted upon the moss-covered hill. The last birds were twittering sleepily, and the nightjar flew clumsily, as if drunk, first to the right, and then to the left, sometimes vanishing in the gloom. Country folk hate the nightjar, and this aversion probably made Christian's whole surroundings suddenly seem unspeakably desolate. His mood was transmitted to the scene about him. He could not possibly drive that business of Jalo the trotter out of his head. All the memories of his life were associated with the name. Everything he had dreamed and hoped, everything which had disturbed and alarmed him, had revolved wholly around Jalo. How well he recollected the day Jegor Timofitsch Ivanov opened his shop in the village of Tervola. Everything that previously was brought from the city could now be bought at Jegor Timofitsch's. How humble and cringing the fellow had been then ; how well he understood how to ingratiate himself with everybody.

At that time Jalo was nearly three years old.

Jegor had been everybody's most humble servant. Doubling up like a pocket-knife in his obsequiousness, he had treated his customers to tobacco and sbitin,[1] promised them unlimited credit, and thereby won all hearts. " You haven't any money ? Oh, that makes no difference—we'll charge it ; you can pay another time." It was all so easy and simple, but when a year had gone by, Jegor's account book was full, and all the insignificant entries were found to amount to an enormous sum.

If anybody needed a loan, who but Jegor had the money ? True, he asked twelve per cent., but then there was no bothering with lawyers, judges, assessors, and such people. And who did not need money in these times ? Everybody wanted it, and Christian, perhaps, most of all.

But when four years had passed, Jegor Timofitsch from being everybody's servant had become everybody's master. Now he carried his back as stiff as a ramrod ; now he used a very different tone ; " Lout, do you mean to sow rye ? No, you must sow oats ; I can't sell rye in these times. You want money to buy a cow ? You

[1] A Russian national drink, very popular among the lower classes, made of syrup, thin beer, and water.

have scarcely enough feed for the one you own. No, that won't
do."

He sold the peasants' grain from the fields before it was mowed.
He felled their woods for fuel and lumber, without any further ceremony than to notify them of his intention. And yet how the terrible debt grew ! It was as insatiable as the Moloch of the Philistines.
Everything disappeared in its mighty jaws. It was never settled in
spite of all the sacrifices and payments in the shape of tar, wood,
tallow, sheep, crabs, game-birds, and oats.

If any one had cause to suffer from this neighbour it was Christian.
Their farms adjoined, and he knew better than all the rest what it
means to be a debtor. It seemed as though the flesh was being
gnawed from his body and the marrow sucked out of his bones. He
often felt utterly defenceless against the cruel foe, and thought seriously of going out to beg his way from door to door, if only he could
be a free man once more.

But in the hour of his sorest need help came. And his deliverer
was Jalo, who had reached his sixth year at Michaelmas.

Oh, what an animal this Jalo was ! His black coat shone like silk.
Looking at his side, darker and lighter circles appeared on his back
and thighs. What a tail, and what a mane he had, both so thick
and long ! His hoofs were like steel, his broad breast inhaled the air
like bellows. His eyes were those of a sea-eagle. He not only saw
at a distance, but in the mist, in the whirling snow, and in the dark.
But of even greater worth than his strength and his beauty was his
noble nature. He was proud. A blow from a whip was an insult
that drove him nearly frantic. He was docile with all his strength,
loving with all his spirit. And what a grateful heart he had ! How
he would rub his velvety muzzle on Christian's arm when he offered
him salt and bread, oats, or a bit of sugar. This animal was better
than many a human being, certainly better than his disobedient
daughter and his ungrateful son-in-law. Had anybody ever seen
Jalo shy ? Never—he would not fear Satan himself. Had he ever
stumbled ? Never, no matter how steep might be the descent of the
hill. Everybody was obliged to admit that Jalo was the finest
animal in all Finland. His equal could scarcely be found in Russia.
When Christian's debts weighed heavily upon him, when Moloch
opened his jaws and demanded fresh sacrifices, Christian went to the
stable, curry-combed his Jalo, blackened his hoofs, braided his mane,
and patted his back. And he always felt light-hearted.

When Jegor Timofitsch's demands had gone far beyond Christian's
powers to meet, and he saw no way of shaking off this vampire, he
harnessed Jalo into a light sleigh and set off for Viborg, to consult a
distinguished lawyer. He could not believe that Jegor had written
things down correctly. His poor little purchases, some tobacco and
grain, coffee, and sugar, could never amount to so large a sum.

Something was surely wrong, and there was Jegor's usurious interest into the bargain !

How vividly he remembered that journey. It was a clear, cold day in January. The snow lay on the fields and meadows as smooth and level as the surface of the lake. The shadows of the fences, hayricks, and rollers lay like blue spots upon the white surface. The snow-birds hopped across the road, and the magpies chattered joyously as they ran up and down the fences. Sipi, the bear-dog, with pointed ears and woolly tail, dashed at full gallop before Jalo, who with a dainty movement of his hoofs, as if it were mere play, rushed forward at lightning speed. It was all so cheering that Christian's depression began to pass away. He had almost reached the Papula quarter, when suddenly he heard some one calling and shouting. Taking the pipe from his mouth, he leaned out of the sleigh and looked behind him. A man in a little racing sleigh was following at full gallop, waving his hand in its fur-edged gauntlet glove. Christian stopped, and the traveller, a short, stout man dressed in furs, driving a mouse-coloured horse, soon reached him.

" Good morning, Landlord. That *is* a trotter you have ! " he said eagerly, biting his frozen moustache. " To tell the truth, I've been driving behind you at least a quarter of an hour without being able to overtake you. Where did you get the animal ? What is his pedigree ? How old is he? Just look at that chest and those thighs ! "

The stranger left his sleigh as he spoke to examine Jalo more closely. Christian was pleased and proud, answered to the best of his ability, and praised the horse to the new-comer, who seemed to be perfectly delighted with him.

" Well, of course, you'll come to the trotting races day after to-morrow. As the owner of an animal like yours, it's your duty to do it. I am Captain T., one of the judges. Remember the first prize is a thousand marks."

Christian had already heard of the races and even thought of them ; but in the country people usually learn facts only after they have occurred. But now—why not, since he was already in the city ?

Christian promised to come, and the men clasped hands on the agreement. Jalo, who was already impatient to go on, vanished from the Captain's admiring gaze beyond the next hill like a streak of lightning.

Christian entered his horse for the races. What glorious days, what a season of triumph and honour for Jalo and his master ! There was not a newspaper in the whole country which did not mention Jalo and his owner. Telegrams announcing the horse's wonderful deeds flew from city to city. His victory was extraordinary ; he carried off the first prize, outstripping famous old trotters. Even now, as Christian sat depressed and sorrowful in his entry, a bright smile flitted over his face as he recalled that glorious time. How distinctly everything rose before his mind : the golden sunlight, the blue sky, the light snow-flakes carried by the winter wind, the music and the cheering, the heating drinks, and Jalo, the hero of the day. It had undoubtedly been the brightest and happiest of his life. But as the highest surges sink the lowest, and the tallest pine trees cast the longest shadows, it also happened that the day when Jalo and his master reached the giddy heights of joy was followed by very sad consequences.

Nothing favourable was obtained from the lawyer. Instead of encouraging counsel he informed Christian that Jegor had already obtained the final judgment from the Governor. Christian's debt must be paid, principal and interest. There was no resource except to sell Jalo, and even that would not completely cover the amount. Christian drank till he was completely dazed, wept, sobered up again, and, during all these varying moods, constantly tried to raise the price. At last the bargain had to be closed. Jalo was sold to a Russian merchant, and Christian returned home, deeply saddened and frantic with rage, driving a mare which he detested from the first moment. It was small consolation that his pocket-book was stuffed with hundred-mark notes, the farewell gift Jalo's victory had brought to his master.

Christian was inconsolable, and it seemed downright madness to pay Jegor so much good money. It was just like throwing it into the sea. But at last he was obliged to make up his mind to it, and went to Jegor's shop at an hour when he was sure of finding him alone, paid his debt, and received his note and other papers. Jegor was incautious enough to let some offensive words escape his lips, and nothing more was required to bring Christian's repressed fury to utterance. If the former had never known before what a drubbing means, he understood it when his neighbour left the shop. From that day there was the bitterest enmity between the two men.

Christian was free ; but though he bragged of it in Jegor's hearing, his heart bled. What did he care for liberty without Jalo ? True, he had escaped an impending danger, but in exchange had sacrificed all the happiness of his life. Existence had lost all charm for him ; he had no more debts to trouble him, but also no Jalo to love. The occasional notices of the animal which he read in the newspapers were like salt in an open wound. " The famous trotter Jalo, that won the first prize at Viborg, has again covered himself with glory," or " the well-known trotter Jalo has again carried off a prize at the races at Savastehus." On such days Christian was like a madman. Either he sat sullen and silent like a chaffinch in the rain, or he was angry and irritable, blazing out at the least provocation like juniper in the flames.

Gradually the resolution to get possession of Jalo again at any cost became fixed in his mind. What was the use of saving and gathering to spend his life in joyless longing ? His daughter and son-in-law were waiting impatiently for his death, that they might inherit his property. He had no grandchildren, so, as matters stood, the best thing he could do would be to try to get possession of Jalo once more.

After much difficulty, he found bondsmen, and pledged his land. Now he need only secure the money, and then set off to bargain for the horse. Even in the worst case, it could not be "dearer than gold."[1] His present owner in Viborg had many horses, and would surely be willing to give up Jalo for a satisfactory price. The day of his departure was already fixed when one beautiful morning in July, just as Christian was in the act of removing a few stubbly grey hairs from his chin, he heard a familiar neigh. There was no mistake ; it must be Jalo, that was just the way he always called his master when he went into his stable late in the morning. Christian threw down the razor and rushed out. There behind the corner of his own stable, to which Jegor's pasture extended, stood Jalo with dilated nostrils, tossing his head up and down. In a second he flew over the fence, and stood upon the ground of his former owner. Christian felt as though he was paralysed in every limb. He could only utter a gasp of astonishment. A joyful smile flitted over his face like sunshine over the moorland, while all the tales of witchcraft he had overheard flashed through his excited brain. While he still stood there, rubbing his eyes, to convince himself that he was not dreaming, Jegor, his enemy, entered the yard, bridle and whip in hand. "The horse belongs to me," he said ; "beware of luring him here."

Jegor seized Jalo by the lock of hair on his forehead, put on the bridle, and swearing violently, protested that he would cure him of leaping the fence. Poor Jalo was roughly dragged away to his own barn, and after a time Christian heard the horse snorting and stamping under the blows of Jegor's whip. To beat Jalo, to abuse such an animal—who ever heard of such a thing ?

From that day Christian's life was a hell. To be compelled to do without the horse was torture enough, but to know that it was in the hands of his worst enemy, that he could never own it again, to see it daily without being able to go near it, was far worse. Everything that Jegor could think of to do to the horse in Christian's presence to torment him he conscientiously did. Every blow he had himself received he returned to Jalo. And when, as sometimes happened, the horse came dashing at a gallop to his old master, as if seeking protection, Christian could be certain that thick wales on Jalo's

[1] A Finnish proverb.

sides would show how Jegor Timofitsch rewarded faithful friendship.

Several weeks passed in this way. It was a hot August day when the baked clods of earth cracked with the heat, and the air quivered and shimmered under the burning sunshine. Even the village dogs had stopped barking and fled to the shade under steps and outbuildings. The cows stood knee-deep in the water beneath the shelter of the dark alders. Only the gnats enjoyed the fierce heat of the sun ; the dragon-flies flew through the air in shimmering circles. Christian lay stretched on the wooden bench in his house watching Jalo with burning eyes as he stood opposite to him in Jegor's meadow in the shade of a gnarled old elm. Christian was dreaming of the happy days when Jalo still belonged to him. How insignificant appeared the troubles of those times, and how great their joys. He was just falling into a light slumber when he was roused by three huntsmen from Viborg inquiring eagerly for the landlord. They had been in pursuit of hares when they unexpectedly encountered a lynx engaged in the same chase. For two days they had followed the trail of the wild beast, which became greatly exhausted, when unluckily their dog hurt its paw and had to be left behind. The hunters now asked where they could borrow one to continue the chase. Christian owned such a dog. His Sipi could be used to track sea-fowl, hares, and bears. The gentlemen, accompanied by Christian and Sipi, hurried back to the moor where they had last seen the trail of the lynx. Within fifteen minutes Sipi found it and, amid joyous barking and waving of his bushy tail, ran towards the woods. Soon furious baying announced that the lynx was either caught or had climbed a tree. When the hunters reached the spot, Sipi was executing a wild war-dance around a pine tree, on whose boughs lay the wild beast, gnashing its teeth at its enemy. With ears laid back smoothly against its head, and eyes glittering with rage, it seemed on the point of leaping down on its shaggy foe. But before determining to commence the fray, it fell under the bullet of the first of the approaching hunters. Its paws were bound together, a pole thrust through them, and it was carried in triumph back to Christian's farm. There the weary men ate a country luncheon, and celebrated their luck thoroughly by consuming plenty of brandy and rum. The heating drinks went to their heads, and by twilight Christian and his guests had become very excited and garrulous.

"Listen to me, Christian," said his wife, who was made somewhat anxious by the noisy company ; " I won't have any loaded guns in the house ; go and fire the bullets out of those barrels."

Christian rose slowly, remarking that women were always great cowards ; took the guns from the bench, and went out. Daylight was failing, but darkness had not yet closed in ; the perfume of new-mown clover drifted in on the breeze. From the distance echoed the notes of the cowherds' horns, and the crickets were chirping loudly in the courtyard.

Christian staggered down the steps. Suddenly he stopped. There by the corner of the stable again stood the dream of his nights and the longings of his days. Jalo raised his delicately formed head, shook his floating mane, and uttered a low, mysterious neigh, as if calling his former master.

Christian went to him and patted his neck. The animal put his velvety nozzle over the low fence into Christian's pocket. The latter, deeply moved, threw his arm over the horse's neck. It was so long since he had caressed Jalo, stoked his soft skin, and spoken to him. While thus passing his hand along the beautiful creature's back, he suddenly felt the wales of Jegor's lashes. The blood surged hotly in his veins. " Miserable brute," he muttered, shaking his fist savagely at Jegor's house. " My poor friend, I'll free you for ever from his whip, his cruelty, and tyranny." Almost before he himself was aware what he was doing, he had snatched the gun from his shoulder—one shot, and the noble creature fell moaning ; one sorrowful glance from the glazing eyes, and Jalo lay lifeless behind the fence which separated him from his former owner. Christian fled into the forest like a murderer. Half an hour later he returned to his home perfectly sober. The hunters had gone to look for their dog. He was alone with his wife. Deeply agitated, he told her what he had done.

" Well, what do you mean to do ? " asked Christian's wife when her husband returned late in the evening from Laurikamen's. " There are no witnesses."

" No, there are no witnesses ; but whatever they may do to me, I will tell them at any rate the whole story of Jalo."

JUHANI AHO   FINNISH

B. 1860

WHEN FATHER BROUGHT HOME THE LAMP

WHEN father bought the lamp, or a little before that, he said to mother :

" Hark ye, mother—oughtn't we to buy us a lamp ? "

" A lamp ? What sort of a lamp ? "

" What ! Don't you know that the storekeeper who lives in the market town has brought from St. Petersburg lamps that actually burn better than ten *päreä* ?[1] They've already got a lamp of the sort at the parsonage."

" Oh, yes ! Isn't it one of those things which shines in the middle of the room so that we can see to read in every corner, just as if it was broad daylight ? "

" That's just it.   There's oil that burns in it, and you only have to light it of an evening, and it burns on without going out till the next morning."

" But how can the wet oil burn ? "

" You might as well ask—how can brandy burn ? "

" But it might set the whole place on fire.   When brandy begins to burn you can't put it out, even with water."

" How can the place be set on fire when the oil is shut up in a glass, and the fire as well ? "

" In a glass ? How can fire burn in a glass—won't it burst ? "

" Won't what burst ? "

" The glass."

" Burst ! No, it never bursts.   It might burst, I grant you, if you screwed the fire up too high, but you're not obliged to do that."

" Screw up the fire ? Nay, dear, you're joking—how *can* you screw up fire ? "

" Listen, now ! When you turn the screw to the right, the wick mounts—the lamp, you know, has a wick, like any common candle,

---

[1] A *päre* (pr. *payray*; Swed., *perta*; Ger., *pergei*) is a resinous pine chip, or splinter, used instead of torch or candle to light the poorer houses in Finland.

and a flame too—but if you turn the screw to the left, the flame gets smaller, and then, when you blow it, it goes out."

" It goes out ! Of course ! But I don't understand it a bit yet, however much you may explain—some sort of new-fangled gentle-folk arrangement, I suppose."

" You'll understand it right enough when I've bought one."

" How much does it cost ? "

" Seven and a half marks, and the oil separate at one mark the can."

" Seven and a half marks and the oil as well ! Why, for that you might buy *pärea* for many a long day—that is, of course, if you were inclined to waste money on such things at all, but when Pekka splits them not a penny is lost."

" And you'll lose nothing by the lamp, either ! *Päre* wood costs money too, and you can't find it everywhere on our land now as you used to. You have to get leave to look for such wood, and drag it hither to the bog from the most out-of-the-way places—and it's soon used up, too."

Mother knew well enough that *päre* wood is not so quickly used up as all that, as nothing had been said about it up to now, and that it was only an excuse to go away and buy this lamp. But she wisely held her tongue so as not to vex father, for then the lamp and all would have been unbought and unseen. Or else some one else might manage to get a lamp first for his farm, and then the whole parish would begin talking about the farm that had been the *first*, after the parsonage, to use a lighted lamp. So mother thought the matter over, and then she said to father :

" Buy it, if you like ; it is all the same to me if it is a *päre* that burns, or any other sort of oil, if only I can see to spin. When, pray, do you think of buying it ? "

" I thought of setting off to-morrow—I have some other little business with the storekeeper as well."

It was now the middle of the week, and mother knew very well that the other business could very well wait till Saturday, but she did not say anything now either, but, " the sooner the better," thought she.

And that same evening father brought in from the storehouse the big travelling chest in which grandfather, in his time, had stowed his provisions when he came from Uleaborg, and bade mother fill it with hay and lay a little cotton-wool in the middle of it. We children asked why they put nothing in the box but hay and a little wool in the middle, but she bade us hold our tongues, the whole lot of us. Father was in a better humour, and explained that he was going to bring a lamp from the storekeeper, and that it was of glass, and might be broken to bits if he stumbled or if the sledge bumped too much.

That evening we children lay awake a long time and thought of the new lamp ; but old scullery-Pekka, the man who used to split up all the *päreä*, began to snore as soon as ever the evening *päre* was put out. And he didn't once ask what sort of a thing the lamp was, although we talked about it ever so much.

The journey took father all day, and a very long time it seemed to us all. We didn't even relish our food that day, although we had milk soup for dinner. But scullery-Pekka gobbled and guzzled as much as all of us put together, and spent the day in splitting *päreä* till he had filled the outhouse full. Mother, too, didn't spin much flax that day either, for she kept on going to the window and peeping out, over the ice, after father. She said to Pekka, now and then, that perhaps we shouldn't want all those *päreä* any more, but Pekka couldn't have laid it very much to heart, for he didn't so much as ask the reason why.

It was not till supper-time that we heard the horses' bells in the courtyard.

With the bread crumbs in our mouths, we children rushed out, but father drove us in again and bade scullery-Pekka come and help with the chest. Pekka, who had already been dozing away on the bench by the stove, was so awkward as to knock the chest against the threshold as he was helping father to carry it into the room, and he would most certainly have got a sound drubbing for it from father if only he had been younger, but he was an old fellow now, and father had never in his life struck a man older than himself. Nevertheless, Pekka would have heard a thing or two from father if the lamp *had* gone to pieces, but fortunately no damage had been done.

" Get up on the stove, you lout ! " roared father at Pekka, and up on the stove Pekka crept.

But father had already taken the lamp out of the chest, and now let it hang down from one hand.

" Look ! there it is now ! How do you think it looks ? You pour the oil into this glass, and that stump of ribbon inside is the wick—hold that *päre* a little farther off, will you ! "

" Shall we light it ? " said the mother as she drew back.

" Are you mad ? How can it be lighted when there's no oil in it ? "

" Well, but can't you pour some in, then ? "

" Pour in oil ? A likely tale ! Yes, that's just the way when people don't understand these things ; but the storekeeper warned me again and again never to pour the oil in by firelight, as it might catch fire and burn the whole house down."

" Then when will you pour the oil into it ! "

" In the daytime—daytime, d'ye hear ? Can't you wait till day ? It isn't such a great marvel as all that."

" Have you *seen* it burn, then ? "

" Of course I have. What a question ! I've seen it burn many a time, both at the parsonage and when we tried this one here at the storekeeper's."

" And it burned, did it ? "

" Burned ? Of course it did, and when we put up the shutters of the shop, you could have seen a needle on the floor. Look here, now ! Here's a sort of capsule, and when the fire is burning in this fixed glass here, the light cannot creep up to the top, where it isn't wanted either, but spreads downward, so that you could find a needle on the floor."

Now we should have all very much liked to try if we could find a needle on the floor, but father hung up the lamp to the roof and began to eat his supper.

" This evening we must be content, once more, with a *päre*," said father, as he ate ; " but to-morrow the lamp shall burn in this very house."

" Look, father ! Pekka has been splitting *päreä* all day, and filled the outhouse with them."

" That's all right. We've fuel now, at any rate, to last us all the winter, for we shan't want them for anything else."

" But how about the bathroom and the stable ? " said mother.

" In the bathroom we'll burn the lamp," said father.

That night I slept still less than the night before, and when I woke in the morning I could almost have wept, if I hadn't been ashamed, when I called to mind that the lamp was not to be lit till the evening. I had dreamed that father had poured oil into the lamp at night and that it had burned the whole day long.

Immediately when it began to dawn, father dug up out of that great travelling chest of his a big bottle, and poured something out of it into a smaller bottle. We should have very much liked to ask what was in this bottle, but we daren't, for father looked so solemn about it that it quite frightened us.

But when he drew the lamp a little lower down from the ceiling and began to bustle about it and unscrew it, mother could contain herself no longer, and asked him what he was doing.

" I am pouring oil into the lamp."

" Well, but you're taking it to pieces ! How will you ever get everything you have unscrewed into its proper place again ? "

Neither mother nor we knew what to call the thing which father took out from the glass holder.

Father said nothing, but he bade us keep farther off. Then he filled the glass holder nearly full from the smaller bottle, and we now guessed that there was oil in the larger bottle also.

" Well, won't you light it now ? " asked mother again, when all the unscrewed things had been put back into their places and father hoisted the lamp up to the ceiling again.

"What ! in the daytime ? "

"Yes—surely we might try it, to see how it will burn."

"It'll burn right enough.   Just wait till the evening, and don't bother."

After dinner, scullery-Pekka brought in a large frozen block of wood to split up into *päreä*, and cast it from his shoulders on to the floor with a thud which shook the whole room and set in motion the oil in the lamp.

"Steady ! " cries father ;   "what are you making that row for ? "

"I brought in this *päre*-block to melt it a bit—nothing else will do it—it is regularly frozen."

"You may save yourself the trouble then," said father, and he winked at us.

"Well, but you can't get a blaze out of it at all, otherwise."

"You may save yourself the trouble, I say."

"Are no more *päreä* to be split up, then ? "

"Well, suppose I *did* say that no more *päreä* were to be split up ? "

"Oh ! 'tis all the same to me if master can get on without 'em."

"Don't you see, Pekka, what is hanging down from the rafters there ? "   When father put this question he looked proudly up at the lamp, and then he looked pityingly down upon Pekka.

Pekka put his clod in the corner, and then, but not till then, looked up at the lamp.

"It's a lamp," says father, "and when it burns you don't want any more *päre* light."

"Oh ! " said Pekka, and, without a single word more, he went off to his chopping-block behind the stable, and all day long, just as on other days, he chopped a branch of his own height into little faggots ; but all the rest of us were scarce able to get on with anything. Mother made believe to spin, but her supply of flax had not diminished by one-half when she shoved aside the spindle and went out. Father chipped away at first at the handle of his axe, but the work must have been a little against the grain, for he left it half done. After mother went away, father went out also, but whether he went to town or not I don't know.   At any rate he forbade us to go out too, and promised us a whipping if we so much as touched the lamp with the tips of our fingers.   Why, we should as soon have thought of fingering the priest's gold-embroidered chasuble.   We were only afraid that the cord which held up all this splendour might break and we should get the blame of it.

But time hung heavily in the sitting-room, and as we couldn't hit upon anything else, we resolved to go in a body to the sleighing hill.   The town had a right of way to the river for fetching water therefrom, and this road ended at the foot of a good hill down which the sleigh could run, and then up the other side along the ice rift.

" Here come the Lamphill children," cried the children of the town as soon as they saw us.

We understood well enough what they meant, but for all that we did not ask what Lamphill children they alluded to, for our farm was, of course, never called Lamphill.

" Ah, ah ! We know ! You've gone and bought one of them lamps for your place. We know all about it ! "

" But how came you to know about it already ? "

" Your mother mentioned it to my mother when she went through our place. She said that your father had bought from the storeman one of that sort of lamps that burn so brightly that one can find a needle on the floor—so at least said the justice's maid."

" It is just like the lamp in the parsonage drawing-room, your father told us just now. I heard him say so with my own ears," said the innkeeper's lad.

" Then you really have got a lamp like that, eh ? " inquired all the children of the town.

" Yes, we have ; but it is nothing to look at in the daytime, but in the evening we'll all go there together."

And we went on sleighing down hill and up hill till dusk, and every time we drew our sleighs up to the hill-top, we talked about the lamp with the children of the town.

In this way the time passed quicker than we thought, and when we had sped down the hill for the last time, the whole lot of us sprang off homeward.

Pekka was standing at the chopping-block and didn't turn his head, although we all called to him with one voice to come and see how the lamp was lit. We children plunged headlong into the room in a body.

But at the door we stood stock-still. The lamp was already burning there beneath the rafters so brightly that we couldn't look at it without blinking.

" Shut the door ; it's rare cold," cried father from behind the table.

" They scurry about like fowls in windy weather," grumbled mother from her place by the fireside.

" No wonder the children are dazed by it, when I, old woman as I am, cannot help looking up at it," said the innkeeper's old mother.

" Our maid also will never get over it," said the magistrate's stepdaughter.

It was only when our eyes had got a little used to the light that we saw that the room was half full of neighbours.

" Come nearer, children, that you may see it properly," said father, in a much milder voice than just before.

" Knock that snow off your feet, and come hither to the stove ; it looks quite splendid from here," said mother, in her turn.

Skipping and jumping, we went toward mother, and sat us all down in a row on the bench beside her. It was only when we were under *her* wing that we dared to examine the lamp more critically. We had never once thought that it would burn as it was burning now, but when we came to sift the matter out we arrived at the conclusion that, after all, it was burning just as it ought to burn. And when we had peeped at it a good bit longer, it seemed to us as if we had fancied all along that it would be exactly as it was.

But what we could not make out at all was how the fire was put into that sort of glass. We asked mother, but she said we should see how it was done afterward.

The townsfolk vied with each other in praising the lamp, and one said one thing, and another said another. The innkeeper's old mother maintained that it shone just as calmly and brightly as the stars of heaven. The magistrate, who had bad eyes, thought it excellent because it didn't smoke, and you could burn it right in the middle of the hall without blackening the walls in the least, to which father replied that it was, in fact, meant for the hall, but did capitally for the dwelling-room as well, and one had no need now to dash hither and thither with *päreä*, for all could now see by a single light, let them be never so many.

When mother observed that the lesser chandelier in church scarcely gave a better light, father bade me take my A B C book, and go to the door to see if I could read it there. I went and began to read : " Our Father." But then they all said : " The lad knows that by heart." Mother then stuck a hymn-book in my hand, and I set off with " By the Waters of Babylon."

" Yes ; it is perfectly marvellous ! " was the testimony of the townsfolk.

Then said father : " Now if any one had a needle, you might throw it on the floor and you would see that it would be found at once."

The magistrate's stepdaughter had a needle in her bosom, but when she threw it on the floor, it fell into a crack, and we couldn't find it at all—it was so small.

It was only after the townsfolk had gone that Pekka came in.

He blinked a bit at first at the unusual lamplight, but then calmly proceeded to take off his jacket and rag boots.

" What's that twinkling in the roof there enough to put your eyes out ? " he asked at last, when he had hung his stockings up on the rafters.

" Come now, guess what it is," said father, and he winked at mother and us.

" I can't guess," said Pekka, and he came nearer to the lamp.

" Perhaps it's the church chandelier, eh ? " said father jokingly.

" Perhaps," admitted Pekka ; but he had become really curious, and passed his thumb along the lamp.

" There's no need to finger it," says father ; " look at it, but don't touch it."

" All right, all right ! I don't want to meddle with it ! " said Pekka, a little put out, and he drew back to the bench alongside the wall by the door.

Mother must have thought that it was a sin to treat poor Pekka so, for she began to explain to him that it was not a church chandelier at all, but what people called a lamp, and that it was lit with oil, and that was why people didn't want *päreä* any more.

But Pekka was so little enlightened by the whole explanation that he immediately began to split up the *päre*-wood log which he had dragged into the room the day before. Then father said to him that he had already told him there was no need to split *päreä* any more.

" Oh ! I quite forgot," said Pekka ; " but there it may bide if it isn't wanted any more," and with that Pekka drove his *päre* knife into a rift in the wall.

" There let it rest at leisure," said father.

But Pekka said never a word more. A little while after that he began to patch up his boots, stretched on tiptoe to reach down a *päre* from the rafters, lit it, stuck it in a slit fagot, and sat him down on his little stool by the stove. We children saw this before father, who stood with his back to Pekka planing away at his axe-shaft under the lamp. We said nothing, however, but laughed and whispered among ourselves, " If only father sees that, what will he say, I wonder ? " And when father did catch sight of him, he planted himself arms akimbo in front of Pekka, and asked him, quite spite-fully, what sort of fine work he had there, since he must needs have a separate light all to himself ?

" I am only patching up my shoes," said Pekka to father.

" Oh, indeed ! Patching your shoes, eh ? Then if you can't see to do that by the same light that does for me, you may take yourself off with your *päre* into the bath-house or behind it if you like."

And Pekka went.

He stuck his boots under his arm, took his stool in one hand and his *päre* in the other, and off he went. He crept softly through the door into the hall, and out of the hall into the yard. The *päre* light flamed outside in the blast, and played a little while, glaring red, over outhouses, stalls, and stables. We children saw the light through the window and thought it looked very pretty. But when Pekka bent down to get behind the bath-house door, it was all dark again in the yard, and instead of the *päre* we saw only the lamp mirroring itself in the dark window-panes.

Henceforth we never burned a *päre* in the dwelling-room again.

The lamp shone victoriously from the roof, and on Sunday evenings all the townsfolk often used to come to look upon and admire it. It was known all over the parish that our house was the first, after the parsonage, where the lamp had been used. After we had set the example, the magistrate bought a lamp like ours, but as he had never learned to light it, he was glad to sell it to the innkeeper, and the innkeeper has it still.

The poorer farmfolk, however, have not been able to get themselves lamps, but even now they do their long evening's work by the glare of a *päre*.

But when he had had the lamp a short time, father planed the walls of the dwelling-room all smooth and white, and they never got black again, especially after the old stove, which used to smoke, had to make room for another, which discharged its smoke outside and had a cowl.

Pekka made a new fireplace in the bath-house out of the stones of the old stove, and the crickets flitted thither with the stones—at least their chirping was never heard any more in the dwelling-room. Father didn't care a bit, but we children felt, now and then, during the long winter evenings, a strange sort of yearning after old times, so we very often found our way down to the bath-house to listen to the crickets, and there was Pekka sitting out the long evenings by the light of his *päre*.

LOYAL

Juhani Aho

I

HE had been obliged to pass the summer in town to relieve a well-to-do colleague, who was spending his vacation in the country. He was engaged, but couldn't think of marrying till he had got a fixed income. So he had to push his way.

It was tiresome and trying to be plodding away in Helsingfors during the summer, and it was especially hard immediately after dinner. The forenoon passed away pretty tolerably in official work, but at three o'clock one had to be off to the eating-house, where the sun shone right into the room, where it was hot, where the furniture had unpleasant white coverings, the chandelier was enveloped in a cloth, wretched oil-paintings hung upon the walls, and where one had neither the feeling of home nor the comfort of a tavern. And from thence one had to drag one's self off to one's lodgings in Kronohagen, and go along streets which the architects had made half as small again as they need have been, and past houses with chalked windows.

It was midsummer—afternoon. All his colleagues had been invited to a picnic somewhere on the coast among the islands. But Antti had no acquaintances, and so, after vainly turning over in his mind what he should do with himself, he had returned to his lodgings. After coming home he usually sat with his elbows resting on the table, smoking and looking through the window over to the other side of the street, where a stone house was being built. Then he would remove the pillow from his bed to his sofa, kick his boots under the table and go to sleep for an hour or two, or perhaps a little more. But even after that a good many hours of the evening still remained empty. What was he to do with them, those long monotonous hours? The Concert Room and the restaurants of Brunspark and Hesperia were dear, and besides, it's not quite the thing to be sitting there *every* evening. Yet, if he recollected aright, he had sat there *nearly* every evening, on Saturday evening because it *was* Saturday, on Sunday for a similar reason ; the other days were regular exceptions.

Regarded from the usual place behind the table the world to-day looked more than usually tiresome. The work-place opposite was also empty, the door in the scaffolding was locked, and there was " no admittance except on business."

To be in the country now, far away in Savolax, at home with his beloved ! What rapture ! To lie at his ease in the hammock, row, sail, wander hand in hand, sit in her lap and make her sit in his, to kiss and caress when nobody was looking !

He began thinking what he should set about doing, and resolved to write a letter. He took out pen and paper, placed them in front of him, and jotted down the date in the upper corner, and a little below it " Dearest Mia " ! But as he was not quite clear with what he should begin and how he should go on, he resolved first of all to sleep off a bit of his midday heaviness.

When, after getting up again, he again sat down in front of his writing-paper, where the lately written words were dry and shiny, he didn't feel in the humour for writing even now. He lit a cigarette, but even that did not give him inspiration. There was absolutely nothing to write about. Everybody who, like Antti, has been engaged for three years will know that a subject is often lacking under such circumstances. One ought to give expression to one's love and interpret one's thoughts, but one cannot hit upon fresh words. Antti had already used all the suitable phrases he knew of in the language, besides inventing not a few brand-new ones.

He was obliged to get up and walk up and down the floor ; he drank some water, opened the window and leaned out of it. As far as his eye could reach, all the streets were as empty as his own thoughts. Everybody must certainly have gone to the country. It was seven o'clock. By this time they were all picnicking at Hogholm or Degerö or Föliso.

He rallied all his energies and succeeded in putting down on his writing-paper, " It is now midsummer afternoon, and I am sitting alone in my room and writing to you. If you only knew how I . . ." But here he stopped short, he suddenly felt himself quite used up, he could no more get along with it than when as a schoolboy he had been obliged to write essays on subjects he didn't understand.

While he was staring at his finger-nails, he heard in the street below the rapid steps and jerky talk of people who are in a violent hurry. Two pretty girls were hastening down to the sea-shore. They had presumably got leave to be out for the whole night. They had their best clothes on, white hoods with long fringes, and clothes which fitted closely to their supple and vigorous shapes.

Antti fell a-thinking that for three years he had been faithful to his sweetheart, and vanquished like a man all the temptations which had come in his way. . . . The girls swung rapidly round the corner, and the street was as empty as before. Antti's thoughts were also empty.

" But why can't I go too ? Why can't I share in the popular festivities at Degerö, whither the steamboat goes every half-hour ? Such a splendid evening as it is, too ! I swallow dust all the week through, and when, for once in a way, the opportunity of flying to Nature's bosom presents itself, I lock myself up in my room ! "

He stretched himself, puffed the air out of his lungs and tapped himself in the ribs. He felt quite a stitch in the side from too much sitting down.

There was one impediment, however. It was mail-day, and he would miss the post if he postponed writing his letter now. Mia will certainly walk the whole of the two miles to the post-office, and if she finds nothing there, she will be unhappy and accuse him of cold- ness, and then there will be long explanations and reassurances. But then, at any rate, one would have something to write about after- wards. Besides, when one returns from a little pleasure trip, one can always manage to scrape together news enough to fill a sheet. But it is of no very great consequence. A fellow doesn't always feel in the humour to write love-letters. If she is offended she must get pleased again, that's all !

If Antti had only been able to search his own heart he would have discovered that this very same frame of mind, an almost unconscious impatience, had revealed itself within him once or twice before. That very winter when his sweetheart was in town, and they were constantly together, a sort of inertia, a sort of unwillingness to give

free play to his feelings, had come over him. He could not throw
into his voice the tenderness he wished to show, and it was only now
and then at the *soirées* of the " Finnish Literary Society," when she
had a new dress on, or when he had become a little warmed up by
refreshments, that he could still wax enthusiastic, as he had done
during the earlier days of his engagement, and so make heart and
voice vibrate in unison.

He stuck the letter he had begun into his drawer, hastily dressed
himself, filled his cigarette-case with cigarettes, stuffed a box of
matches into his pocket, and sprang rapidly down the stairs as if he
were afraid of being too late. When one looked at him from behind
as he hurried along, he gave one the idea of a man who was about
to do something which he felt was not quite right.

In a few moments he was standing by the side of a steamboat at
the South Haven, and watching the pleasure-seekers stepping on
board. Carters, whose horse-collars were covered with birch-leaves
in honour of Midsummer Day, drove, one after the other, through
the market-place down to the strand. Groups of men with flowers
in their hats, and women with roses in their breasts, were hastening
down to the steamboat with their wraps across their arms.

The steamboat was bright with flags from stem to stern, and midsummer birch boughs covered the railings of the deck. Antti also
had bought a little bouquet from a flower-girl.

They are all hastening out into the country. They are all hastening on board along the landing-stage. Antti still hesitates. But
just when they are about to unloose the ropes, he skips on board too.

II

But why does he sit so disconsolately there on a stone by the way-
side, a little distance from the pleasure-ground whence the sounds of
music and a merry hum proceed incessantly ? Why does he long to
be away from all this merry-making the very moment he has
got there, and only awaits another steamboat to take him back to
town ?

When a cat has pounced down upon a flock of chickens without
success, she sneaks shamefacedly away with her tail between her legs
and vexation in her heart.

Antti was convinced within himself that he had meant to pounce
upon nothing, but, for all that, he had turned aside hither, sullen
and depressed, and was now prodding about in the sand with
his cane.

The girls from the steamboat had skipped down upon the bridge.
They were unusually free and lightsome in their movements, and
their kirtles rustled all about them. Young men came forward to
them, nonchalantly took them round their waists or under their

arms, and, without more ado, swung them round once or twice
before they let them go. In a long stream, which filled the whole
road, they then hastened towards the pleasure-ground, frisking and
bouncing as they went.

Antti went slowly forward, though there was a slight tickling
sensation in the soles of his feet, and he let those who were in a hurry
pass him by. One petticoat after another whisked past him. The
lasses pretended to fly from the lads who pelted after them. But
they soon allowed themselves to be caught, and, hand in hand, they
reached the pleasure place.

When Antti came up the dancing was in full swing. The musicians
stood in the centre. The sport was fast and furious. The dancers
held tightly to each other all through ; they took big steps and long
hops, their movements were brisk, and they swung rapidly round and
round. Hoods shrunk down upon shoulders, and hats over necks,
and here and there a cigar could be seen stuck nonchalantly in the
corner of a mouth.

There were soldiers there, broad-chested sailors, sturdy peasants
from the islands, artisans, and a few students in broad-brimmed
hats. The women were shop-girls, milliners, tobacconist nymphs,
artisans' daughters, and servant-girls. Antti knew one or two of
them by sight and a few of them by name. But nobody knew him.
For it was a long time since he had seen one of them.

And not a soul there troubles itself about him. For every one
there has her own young man, nay, there are some of the lads who
have a sweetheart under each arm. Antti has nothing but his stick
on which he leans now and then, while he glances from one group to
the other. Mia is, somehow or other, far, far away. The women
here are, in his opinion, quite pretty. Amongst the mob there were
some so young, so smart, and so fresh, that it was delightful to look
at them. There was something so fresh about them, something so
naïve, something of the artless joy of young calves. They are now
celebrating their midsummer fête ; they have the whole night before
them ; their masters and mistresses are all in the country, and they
have resolved, for once in the year, to revel on the island, on the
green meadow, among the rocks and trees.

What on earth were they laughing at ? Whatever could they find
to amuse them in the dull witticisms of their gallants ? Antti
could not for the life of him make it out. But he would very much
have liked to have been just such a belauded hero in their estimation.
He also would have liked to clip them round the neck, whisper some
such tickling jest in their ears, learn all their little ways, and for that
evening, at any rate, appropriate to himself those half-shamefaced
confidences to which girls abandon themselves so readily.

For a time he stood lurking there with stiff, darkened looks,
stolid features, and a load upon his heart.

Suppose now he were to join the group and partake of its pastimes? Nobody there knew him. What harm could it do to anybody? And how was any one the better for the life he was living now? *Living*, indeed! It was not living; it was withering! The cowardly idealism of these latter days is regular nonsense, or, any rate, sheer childishness. Yes, cowardly, and nothing else. People don't dare to live now as Nature bids them. It is an eternal avoiding opportunities and balancing chances. Not one in a hundred is really loyal at heart. Now look at those people there! Their life is something quite different. They know nothing about the silly prejudices of educated people. They all enjoy life in its fulness, the women as well as the men. That is why they are all so fresh, gay, and lively. They know how to celebrate their midsummer fête, and rejoice in the feast of the sun.

Thus spoke his thoughts, and his eyes followed a fresh and lovely girl who is standing there bareheaded, fanning her burning cheeks with her handkerchief. He plucked up courage and drew near to her. He asks how the young lady is, and remarks that it is fine weather. He tries to be free and easy, but his voice strikes him as hollow and affected. The girl replies as if he were a perfect stranger, nay, almost with awe.

When Antti asks her if she will have a dance, she answers, " Yes ! " but discreetly, solemnly, just as if she were a fashionable young lady, and with nothing at all of that frank abandonment with which Antti saw her skip just now towards another cavalier who was coming to her with an invitation. During the dance Antti pulled her towards him, and pressed her hand, but without meeting with any response. He knows that they do not go well together—don't get along at all, somehow. Whenever he tries to put some go into it and swings her round, they get out of step and have to stop and begin all over again. When the dance is over they stand for some time side by side without speaking a word.

" May I offer you some tea ? " asks Antti at last.

" No, thank you ; it is warm enough without that."

" Perhaps you would like a little lemonade, or something of that sort ? "

" Nothing, thank you."

" Are you looking out for any acquaintance, Miss ? "

" Acquaintance ? What do you mean ? "

" Why, because, Miss, you seem to be peeping about so."

" No ; I have no particular acquaintance."

" Then are you quite alone here, Miss ? "

To this Antti got no answer at all.

" Do you intend to stay here long, Miss ? "

" I don't think of leaving just yet."

" Wouldn't you like a little walk ?   It is certainly very pretty in the woods over there."

" One can walk at any time.   I have come here to dance."

" The dance is just over."

The same instant up came a young artisan swell in a white waist-coat, and took the girl to dance.   They treated each other as equals. They whirled now to the right and now to the left, and laughed good-naturedly whenever any one bumped against them.

Antti followed them with his eyes.   He waited for them to separate, but when the music ceased they went off for a walk with their arms round each other's waists.   All the other couples did the same thing, and soon the whole wood was swarming with people. Every hill-slope was alive with them, and there was a laughing, and a whispering, and a giggling at the foot of every tree.

And that is why Antti sits there so downcast and almost devout, prodding about in the sand with his stick, and with more than half a mind to go home.

It seems to him that he is somewhat superfluous here, and he feels that he has not been a success.   The world is such a meaningless blank to him now ; life tastes like mouldy wood which does not taste of anything at all.

He is quite nauseated by the dance-music, which has now begun again, and by the noise in the pleasure-ground also.   When suchlike folks set to dancing, they hop about like so many calves.   It is really after all, a very rough-and-tumble business.

He feels the want of Mia.   A longing after love suddenly over-comes him, and he is seized with an irresistible desire to write to her, right tenderly and affectionately.

Had he been disloyal ?   In thought, perhaps.   But the fact that he is ready to be off with the very first steamboat proves that he is man enough to overcome temptation and has a will of his own.

III

No sooner did he get into his room than he took from the drawer the letter he had already begun :

" DEAREST MIA—It is now Midsummer afternoon, and I am sitting alone in my room and writing to you.   If you only knew how I——" —here begins the continuation, which ran on now quite easily— " love you beyond everything.   You have no idea how I long for you ; how I regard the prospect of one day possessing you as my highest bliss.   Why are you not here that I might say it to you by word of mouth, and whisper it in your ear ?   Why can I not press you to my breast, kiss your forehead, your red cheeks, your rosy lips, caress you, and throw my arms round your neck ?

" Without you I am nothing ! I thought I would amuse myself a little to-day, so I joined a popular pleasure party at Degerö. But I very soon came back again—came back again full of grief and longing. I couldn't get on at all in such society. Perhaps I am a little too aristocratic ; but, anyway, I feel almost a physical repulsion when I think of how it was there and what I saw. Nothing is so unbeautiful, I think, as when a half-fuddled mob of that sort from town is let loose in the country in the midst of lovely scenery. I was glad to withdraw from it as quickly as possible. As soon as ever I had drunk a cup of tea, I took the first boat and came straight to town.

" Yet I don't at all repent that I went there, for on the way back I began to feel so lonely, so disturbed, my thoughts were of you alone, my own Mia. If I were a poet, if I had the pencil of a painter, what a picture would I not draw of my frame of mind, and what a splendid description I would give of the scenery I saw and admired from the deck of the steamboat. In the front of our steamboat, *The Nixey*, the water foamed and frothed as we passed through the eastern rocky channel. The sea was as still as the forest along the shore. The islands and the sound lay so lovely there in the clearness of the mid-summer night. On the shore burned the bonfires, and here and there one could hear songs and music. What a delicious voyage ! But how many hundreds of times more splendid and more beautiful it would have been if you, my own Mia, had been sitting beside me !

" But although you were not actually present, you were nevertheless with me in spirit. I thought of you the whole time. I conjured up our own pretty little house which we will make for ourselves when I get regular employment. We will live simply for each other, we will choose our own society, we will only invite some of our best friends.

" Do you love me, Mia, as you used to do ? Such strange thoughts are borne in upon me sometimes. I wonder whether you love me now as you loved me when we were first engaged. I am sometimes jealous of the whole world, and fancy that nobody cares about me—not even you. You are forgetting me, perhaps, in the country yonder, where there are so many young people. Forgive me these doubts, which I only mention to you because I promised to be candid. I know that it is all imagination, that not even in thought could you be disloyal to me ; but I feel like this because I am so lonely here, so forsaken by everybody. It would make me so happy to hear that I am mistaken. Say that you love me—I know you *do*—but I implore you to tell me so, and repeat it a thousand times.

" Oh, how delightful it really is to know that there is somebody whom one loves and who loves one in return, to whom one can tell all one's sorrows and open one's heart and one's whole soul!

" Farewell, my own dear, beloved Mia! Write me a long letter—
write about everything you think and feel. Every stroke written by
your hand, every word uttered by your lips, is dearer to me than
gold. What is all earthly gold compared with "—Antti paused for
a moment to reflect how he should go on, but the same instant a
happy thought occurred to him, and he added—" our good fortune
in having discovered one another's hearts?

" My love to Aunt and Uncle. A thousand ardent kisses from
your eternally loyal   ANTTI.

" *P.S.*—I haven't said half I want to say yet, but I must carry this
letter to the railway this very night. I will put it in the post-box
at the station, lest it go astray, and you pay a visit to the post-office
in vain. When I come home again and lay me down to sleep, my
last thought before I close my eyes will be—yourself.—Ever thine."

Such a tender, affectionate letter Mia had not received from Antti
for a long time. She who knew of nothing else, who thought of
nothing else but Antti, she who believed that no other man was so
upright, so pure, so noble—for she knew all about his views on all
subjects—she was so glad when she received this fresh proof of her
sweetheart's love that she locked herself in her own room straight-
way, and wrote him this letter:

She began: " Dearest, dearest, dearest Antti!" And then she
said that she was still all of a tremble with rapture at the thought
that he loved her so intensely. She had read through his letter
again and again, and when she went to sleep, she meant to lay it
under her pillow. She had cried when she thought how lonely
Antti must be in that nasty Helsingfors. Alas! if only she could do
something to hasten on the founding of their own little home!
" How *could* you imagine, Antti, that I would ever be disloyal to
you? I think of nothing else, I care for nothing else but you, only
you. I take no part in the pastimes of the young people here, as
you may suppose, except very, very seldom. And if you only wish
it, I will see no society at all, nor go any excursions, nor accept any
invitations, just as you do not dance nor take any pleasure in popular amusements. Often I sit in the garden beneath the birch-tree
in which your name is carved and in whose shadow we spent so many
unforgettable moments last summer. I sit and sew, and hum the
songs you love. Sometimes I put out the boat, and row out upon
the lake. How lovely it is there! But you have indeed become a
poet. Again and again I have read your fine description of the
steamboat journey along the rocky coast. I read it out to papa
and mamma too. You are not angry, are you? They think so much
of you, and always ask me what you write about."

Mia wrote and wrote sheet after sheet. She was " so happy, so happy." She had been wrong in doubting Antti's feelings and thinking that he was growing cold. Her conscience almost reproached her for having been able to think so ill of her own loyal Antti. And she concluded her letter like this : " Oh, oh, how *frightfully* much I love you ! Farewell, dearest, most beloved Antti. I send you thousands and thousands of kisses.—Thy little MIA."

PIONEERS

JUHANI AHO

THEY were both in service at the parsonage, he as stable-boy she as housemaid. He drove the horses, and she was busy about the house. At meal-times, when they sat each at a corner of the table, they joked together sometimes, but usually they were quarrelling. Their master and mistress thought them a singularly ill-assorted couple : in fact, just like cat and dog, people said.

But, what with fishing-parties at night, what with helping each other at hay-making and corn-cutting by day, the thought of starting a home together gradually grew strong within them. Far away out in the wilderness they had fixed upon a plot for their cottage, by the side of a marsh. There was forest-land and to spare ; it only wanted clearing. The vast, alder-grown flat could be turned into arable land, and meadow-land could be made out of the low-lying ground on both sides of the brook. If only the hut could be built ! But wages were low, and one needed a horse and cow at least to start with. Thus circumstances delayed the marriage. But, in the course of the year, the bonds between them were knit still closer, and their prospects for the future grew brighter every day. They spent their leisure hours in totting up what their savings already amounted to, and in estimating how long they must still wait till the indispensably necessary sum had been scraped together. Nobody dreamed that an eager longing after freedom and a burning desire to keep house on their own account were gradually waxing and waxing in this boy and girl. For they had such a nice easy time of it at the parsonage, no cares at all, and food and clothing found. But their hearts were turned towards the wilderness.

Every one was ready with a warning when, one summer, they both refused to continue in service. " Over yonder the frost rules and rages, and you'll only load yourselves with debt. A family soon grows up, and we've quite enough of beggars already." But they had thought and worked the matter out for the last five years, and their minds were made up. The priest had to put up the banns for them, and in the autumn they quitted his house.

The following winter they were still living in lodgings. Ville, however, was busy with the building of his hut and did a day's work at the parsonage at odd times, and Anni helped the priest's wife with sewing and weaving.

The wedding was celebrated at the Whitsuntide following. The cost of it was paid by the parsonage people, and the vicar himself married his former servants in the large room of the parsonage. But when the married couple had taken their leave and the priest, standing at the window, saw them disappearing down the path, he shook his head anxiously, and said : " Let the young people try what they can make of it, but the wilderness is not to be cleared away by the capital of a boy and girl."

Finland's wilderness had, however, been cleared by such capital, and yet the vicar was right, too.

We, the youths of the parish, escorted our dear old friends to their new home. The long summer day passed away as we wandered through the forest bright with vernal green, and we danced away the night in the new hut. The planks of the new dwelling were still quite roughish ; the jagged, unsawn timber ends jutted unevenly out of the knots in the wood, and the brown river appeared to be spreading everywhere over the newly reclaimed field. But on the hill-slope the fresh rye shoots glistened bright and green amidst the sooty tree-stumps, and on the plot of land cleared for corn the trees were lopped gaunt and dry. The young hostess lit a bonfire on the clearing and milked her cow there for the first time. Ville and I sat on a stone and watched her bustling about in the sickly sheen of the evening sun : she still wore her bridal garments.

Ville had no doubt whatever of success.

" If only we keep our health and the frost doesn't come "—and as if anticipating my thoughts, he added : " I know that the swamp down there is a regular nest of frost, but if a fellow always keeps his arms a-going, I'll drive the forest further away and open up a place for the sun, and then . . . It still feels a little chilly here of an evening perhaps, but come here next summer and have a look at us then."

I paid them no visit next summer or the summer after that either. I must confess that I clean forgot them ; but once, when I was at home, I asked how they were getting on.

" They have been obliged to get into debt," was my father's answer.

" And Anni has been ailing," added my mother.

Some years had passed. I was now a student, and had a gun and a retriever, and was passing my autumn vacation in the country.

One dull October day I was wandering about the woods and hit upon a narrow path which seemed familiar to me. It began to drizzle ; the dog was scampering on in front. Suddenly he began to growl and then to bark fiercely We heard in front of us the tramp of a horse. Presently, at a turn of the road, the horse became visible ; it was harnessed between a pair of shafts the ends of which dragged upon the ground. A white cloth hung upon the collar-trees, and right across the shafts lay a fastened-down coffin. Behind the car tramped Ville, like a plougher after his plough. He had quite enough to do to keep his load in equilibrium.

He looked worn out : his cheeks were pale, and his eyes dim faded.

It was only when he heard my name that he recognised me.

" But what sort of a load have you got there ? " said I.

" My dead wife," was the reply.

" Dead ? "

" Yes, she is dead."

By a little questioning I learnt their brief, predicted story : first debt, many children, his wife sick, and at last dead from overwork. Now he had to carry her to the grave, but the roads were so very bad. He only hoped that the coffin would hold out till he reached the church. He tweaked at the reins, for the horse had overstepped the path and was searching for a little grass among the withered leaves. " Wo-ho ! "

It was trying to satisfy its hunger. The beast was in just as wretched a state as the man : it looked like a skeleton.

Ville took leave of me and went on his way without lifting his eyes from his load. The shaft-poles cut two parallel furrows in the sandy path.

I went in the opposite direction and came to a marsh where they had begun to dig a draining ditch but stopped short when the work was only half done. The path, familiar to me since the bridal tour, led to the little hut.

Behind the fence a lean cow was lowing feebly and a pig was grunting in the plot of yard, the wicket-gate of which had been left open. In the middle of the yard stood an empty bed, and the dead woman's bedclothes had been cast upon the fence. The jagged timber-ends still stuck up out of the knots in the wood of which the hut was built. In the frame of the window, the panes of which were dim and dirty, stood a withering balsam in a little birch-wood box.

The man had succeeded, however, in clearing out a little bit of the wilderness. A small strip of cornland of about a couple of acres in width and about half as much land dug up for sowing formed an opening in the forest. But at this point his powers seemed to have broken down. The birch-wood he had felled and the alder-groves he had changed into meadows. But behind them stood the dark pine forest like an insurmountable wall. There he had been obliged to stop short.

I stood for a long time in the yard of the deserted cottage. The wind whined fiercely in the forest, and called forth from the mouth of my gun-barrel, which lay close to my ear, a mournful wailing sound.

.   .   .   .

The first pioneer has fulfilled his task ; the man can do no more good there now. His strength, his energy are gone, the fire of his eye is extinguished and the self-confidence of his marriage morn has forsaken him.

Another will certainly come after him and take over the cottage plot. He perhaps will have better luck. But he will have a lighter task to begin with, for before him no longer stands the savage forest quite untouched by man. He can settle down into a ready-made hut, and sow in the plot of land which another has ploughed up before him. That cottage plot will, no doubt, become a large and wealthy farm, and in course of time a village will grow up around it.

Nobody thinks of those who first dug up the earth with all their capital, the only capital they possessed—their youthful energies. They were merely a simple lad and lass, and both of them came there with empty hands.

But it is just with such people's capital that Finland's wildernesses have been rooted up and converted into broad acres. Had these two only remained at the parsonage, he as a coachman and she as a housemaid, then perhaps the course of their own lives would have been free enough of care. But the wilderness would not have been cultivated, and the foreposts of civilisation would not have been planted in the midst of the forest.

When the rye blooms and the ears of corn ripen in our fields, let us call to mind these first martyrs of colonisation.

We cannot raise monuments upon their graves, for the tale of them is by thousands, and their names we know not.